The Secret Ingredient *for a* Happy Marriage

ALSO BY SHIRLEY JUMP

The Perfect Recipe for Love and Friendship

The Secret Ingredient *for a* Happy Marriage

Shirley Jump

Best wishes

FOREVER

New York Boston

Copyright © 2018 by Shirley Jump
Excerpt from *The Perfect Recipe for Love and Friendship* copyright © 2017 by Shirley Jump
Reading Group Guide copyright © 2018 by Shirley Jump and Hachette Book Group, Inc.

Cover design by Elizabeth Stokes
Cover copyright © 2018 by Hachette Book Group, Inc.

Forever
Hachette Book Group
1290 Avenue of the Americas, New York, NY 10104
forever-romance.com
twitter.com/foreverromance

First edition: May 2018

Forever is an imprint of Grand Central Publishing. The Forever name and logo are trademarks of Hachette Book Group, Inc.

The publisher is not responsible for websites (or their content) that are not owned by the publisher.

The Hachette Speakers Bureau provides a wide range of authors for speaking events. To find out more, go to www.hachettespeakersbureau.com or call (866) 376-6591.

LCCN: 2018930205
ISBNs: 978-1-4555-7202-1 (trade pbk.), 978-1-4555-7203-8 (ebook)

Printed in the United States of America

LSC-C

10 9 8 7 6 5 4 3 2 1

*To Dad and Kathy, who have that secret
ingredient for a happy marriage and whose
warm and loving relationship made me
believe in love again.*

The Secret Ingredient *for a* Happy Marriage

ONE

From the street, Nora O'Bannon Daniels's life looked almost perfect. The quintessential three-bedroom, two-bath house in a decent neighborhood, with a wooden swing set in the backyard and a pink bike leaning against the garage. The pale green Dutch Colonial sat a hundred yards back from the sidewalk on a leaf-covered quarter-acre lot of weedy grass peppered with the detritus of two kids. A trio of pumpkins marched down the stairs, still whole and uncarved. The brick stoop had weathered from the harsh winters, and the black paint on the railing had peeled down to gray metal, but the house had a well-worn and loved air.

If her life had been a TV show, there'd be some quirky, close-knit family on the other side of the front door, a family whose biggest problem was a lost set of keys. Within thirty minutes, the keys would be found, and the family would be sitting down to a dinner where they'd laugh and hug and pass the creamed corn.

But when Nora parked her aging sedan in the driveway, the grumpy engine ticking as it cooled, she could see the truth she'd been avoiding for months. She didn't live in a sitcom, and there wasn't going to be a lifesaving solution in the next half hour, punctuated by commercials for GEICO and Smucker's jam on either end.

No, in Nora's world, life pretty much sucked. She hadn't thought that the bank would actually do it—some unrealistic part of her had been hoping for some last-minute sympathetic, divine intervention—but the threatened end had finally arrived. While she was at work, a bright yellow sheet of paper had been tacked to her front door, its message stamped in black block letters underscored with a paragraph of red warnings.

NOTICE OF AUCTION

On the welcome mat sat a cellophane-wrapped orange chrysanthemum topped with a Mylar balloon. The balloon waved back and forth in the fall breeze, screaming happy birthday in neon green letters.

Happy birthday, Nora O'Bannon. You've lost your house. Your family is now homeless.

Not exactly the way she'd wanted to turn thirty. The irony of it all would have made her cry, if she'd had the energy to work up some tears. For a year, she'd argued and prayed and strategized and negotiated, so sure she could head off this disaster. Her husband, Ben, had done what he always did, buried his head in the sand and left her to handle the incessant phone calls and letters. Nora, who was the one everyone had said could do anything she set her mind to, had failed. The faceless person on the other end of the phone had no interest in letting them skate on the mortgage. No heart for the two children she was going to have to uproot. And no solution that Nora could actually afford.

Nora got out of the car, carrying a takeout pizza in one hand and a bag of fabric in the other. Sarah wanted to be a princess for Halloween, and in a thick cloud of denial, Nora had bought yards of pink tulle and dozens of sparkly rhinestones. She figured she could whip out the old Singer and stitch up something that would pass for a princess, all in time for Sarah to go trick-or-treating on Friday night. Jacob was still wavering between being a pirate and a ninja, so Nora had grabbed a couple yards of black fabric.

Ben pulled in behind her and climbed out of his ten-year-old Toyota. Every time he got out of the sporty little two-door, Nora wondered how he fit inside. Ben towered over her, a lean but fit six-foot-three man with brown eyes that softened when he was tired, dark wavy hair that curled against convention, and a ready smile for everyone he met. She'd fallen in love with that smile at a party one stormy winter night twelve years ago. She'd been a senior in high school, Ben a college freshman, the two of them on Christmas break and crammed into Tommy O'Brien's basement while Aerosmith thudded from the speakers.

She'd been sitting on a fraying blue cloth sofa, clutching a red Solo cup and pretending to sip Budweiser. Her sisters had always been the ones who fit in at parties, especially Magpie, who made friends with everyone she met. Nora always felt like the little old lady at a party—the one who didn't stay late, didn't drink, and didn't sneak into an empty bedroom to have unmemorable sex.

But going to Tommy's had sounded better than staying home with her mother on a Friday night, especially in her senior year when that kind of thing spelled *loser*. After a bit of small talk when she first arrived, Nora had taken up residence on the sofa, invisible to everyone else. She could have been another throw pillow, given how few people talked to her.

Then Ben sat down beside her, tall and lanky and with longer hair that brushed his brows. "Hey," he said.

She gave him a nod. Lifted the cup to her lips but didn't drink.

"You know, I read somewhere that Canada Dry is a gateway drug."

She turned to him, this stranger with nice eyes and a Rolling Stones T-shirt. "Excuse me?"

He nodded toward the cup in her hands. "You start with ginger ale and next thing you know, you're smoking a candy cigarette before you get out of bed in the morning. When you find yourself on the floor, clutching a bag of gumdrops in one hand and an Orange Crush in the other, you know you've hit rock bottom."

Her cheeks heated, and she wanted to crawl into a corner and die. "How did... how did you know this isn't really beer?"

"I saw you, in the kitchen earlier. You dumped the Bud down the drain and replaced it with some Canada Dry. Not much of a drinker, I take it?"

"Oh, I don't…I'm not…" She didn't have the confidence of Magpie, the easy conversational ability of Bridget, or the tough exterior of Abby. Talking to a boy left Nora flustered, nearly mute.

"It's okay," Ben said. "You're not like everyone else here. I like that. And I have to say, I have a fondness for people who like ginger ale. It's a very underrated soda, if you ask me." He'd smiled then, the kind of smile that spread across his face as easy as butter and lifted a rather ordinary face into something bright, unforgettable.

For twelve years, that smile had convinced her that everything was all right. That things would work out. That if she was just patient—*give me a chance, Nora, to make it right*—the sinking ship they were living on would right itself. She'd given him a hundred chances, and time and time again, he'd blown it. The trust she'd once had in Ben had eroded until there was nothing left.

"Hey," Ben said now. But the word didn't have the friendly note from over a decade ago. It was cold, dispassionate, a greeting issued out of expectation. "They finally did it."

"They told us they would." Nora sighed. "I don't know what I'm going to tell the kids."

"Easy. Don't tell them anything." Ben jogged up the stairs, ripped the yellow notice off the door, and stuffed it into his interior jacket pocket.

The exact way Ben always lived his life. If he didn't say it out loud, it wasn't real. "That doesn't make it go away, Ben. We've lost the house. There's no going back, no passing Go again, no deal to work with the banker."

"There's always a deal, Nora. Just give me a chance—"

She wheeled on him. "You are the reason we're in this mess. You're the reason our kids are being evicted. You—"

"I didn't get here on my own, Nora." He waved at the pizza and the bags. "Takeout? Shopping? What happened to 'we've got to buckle down so we can get caught up'?"

He was really going to compare twenty dollars' worth of pizza and fabric to what he had done to them? She was doing the best she could here, working full-time, being a mom, trying to keep them above water. "We are *three hundred thousand dollars* in debt, Ben. I could buckle down until I'm a hundred and ten and still not pay that off."

"I, me." He threw up his hands and cursed. "What about *we*, Nora? Till death do us part?"

"That ended the day you walked into Mohegan Sun and blew your paycheck at a roulette table. And then did it again two weeks later, and a month after that. Chasing a stupid white ball."

Ben shook his head. "You're never going to let that go, are you? Fuck it. I don't need to listen to this." He slid his key into the door and went inside.

Nora grabbed the plant and balloon—a gift from her sister Abby—bumped the door open with her hip before it could close, and then dumped the pizza on a small table and the flowers and bag of fabric on the floor. She charged down the hall after his retreating figure. That was what Ben did—leave when the conversations got tough. Avoid, withdraw, ignore. "Our kids don't have a home, Ben. You don't get to be selfish now."

"Nora, let it go." He took out his phone. "I'll fix this."

She snorted. Fix it? There was nothing he could do now. That yellow paper said it all. "I've heard you say that twelve thousand times, Ben. And all you've ever done is make it worse." Her gaze skipped over the kitchen, half painted, still missing three upper cabinets, a renovation started four years ago. Yet another of Ben's promises that had been broken the second the work got inconvenient. Once upon a time, she'd thought she could create a home here. Now some other family would stand on the front lawn, hold up a hand, and buy the house she loved for pennies on the dollar. Every memory she had, every mark on the wall for the kids, every fingerprint on the glass, would belong to someone else. "I'm going to pack some things and take the kids to my mom's until I find a better solution."

"You're leaving?"

"Yeah, Ben, I'm leaving. And I don't want to argue about it or cry about it. Let's just be adults here and admit we screwed this up. We"—she waved between them—"screwed us up. This whole thing with the house is a sign. We should go our separate ways and start over."

Silence. She'd finally spoken the words both of them had danced around for two years. Ben's gambling had taken a toll on their marriage, damage they'd never recovered from. He'd gone to rehab almost a year ago, thirty days of a desperate attempt to save his family. But the fractures only widened. It wasn't just the money he'd lost. Nora had watched him put a deck of cards or a roulette table ahead of their marriage, as if it were just another thing to gamble. The promises they'd made to each other on their wedding day became nothing more than words, and at some point, Nora simply stopped trying. They'd gone through the motions for the sake of the kids, but the death knell had sounded the night they'd moved into separate bedrooms.

Ben crossed his arms over his chest. "You're not taking my kids from me, Nora."

"You already did that yourself, Ben." She turned on her heel and walked out of the kitchen. If she stayed there for another second, her foolish heart would cave to the haunted look in his eyes, the pain etched in his forehead. How many times had she done that? How many times had she believed things would change?

All staying with him had done was cost her the only home her children had ever known. Cost her the family she'd wanted to build. The future she had dreamed of having. In the back of her bedroom closet, she found a trio of suitcases. She threw them open on the bed—the bed she had stopped sharing with her husband over a year ago—and started stuffing clean laundry inside. Enough for a few days. She'd figure out the rest later.

Ben leaned against the door, watching her for a long time without a word. Finally he said, "Don't go, Nora."

She hesitated at the hitch in his voice. The exposed

wound in those words. *Stay*, some foolish, hopeful part of her whispered. *Stay and work this out*.

Instead she zipped the largest suitcase shut and then started filling the next one. "Why? Because there's something to save here? You and I both know there isn't."

"It's your birthday. We always go to dinner at Giovanni's on your birthday."

Her hands stilled, halfway through folding a Power Rangers T-shirt. "We *used* to go to Giovanni's, Ben. We haven't been in a long time."

"We went last year—"

"Last year, I spent my birthday driving to Foxwoods. You'd sold your car to some guy in the parking lot for five hundred bucks." There was more, but she didn't say it. Some secrets were better left in the past.

"I know I fucked up. A lot. But things have changed, Nora. *I've* changed."

She looked up at him, into the eyes she'd once thought could see inside her soul. At the face of the man she'd imagined growing old with, sitting on the back deck sipping wine as the sun set. "You have. The trouble is, Ben, so have I."

She closed the last suitcase, propped it on the floor, and wheeled it out of the room and down to her car, leaving the rest behind.

In the end, Nora chickened out on taking the kids to her mother's house. Colleen O'Bannon would have questions, and if there was one thing Nora didn't want right now, it was questions. Instead, she told the kids they were do-ing something special for Mommy's birthday, and she took them to a hotel. One night there nearly maxed out her re-maining credit card, which meant…

Talking to her mother today. Procrastination was clearly one of her special talents.

Nora had bought herself a short reprieve from the tough conversation. Maybe a miracle would occur in those hours, or the world would end, or the Publishers Clearing House folks would show up at her door with a giant card-board check.

Until that happened, Nora kept putting off the act of finding a living solution by working. Right now, that meant frosting four layers of vanilla sponge before stacking them for a wedding cake. Her sister Bridget was here, both of them working in the family-owned bakery where they'd spent most of their lives. Abby, her younger sister, would be in tomorrow morning, getting started at the crack of un-godly early to bake all the bread orders. Their mother, who used to be full-time in the shop, came in less and less as she got older, not to mention busier with a social life. In the last few months, Ma had started volunteering at a shelter named Sophie's Home and spending a lot of time with the director, Roger. Planning programs, Ma claimed, but Nora had detected a hint of a blush whenever Ma talked about Roger.

Bridget slipped into place beside Nora. She was leaner than Nora, a body yet unthickened by having children, but she had the same long, dark hair and blue eyes as all the

O'Bannon girls. It had been a year and a half since Bridget's husband, Jim, had died, and in that time, Nora had begun to see her sister blossom and grow as she found herself and a life of her own. She was now dating a great guy named Garrett and wore that happy smile of new love. A part of Nora envied that smile. Once upon a time, she'd smiled like that when she talked about Ben.

"Want some help?" Bridget asked.

Nora shook off the thoughts of the past and glanced at the work order, flipping past the wedding cake they were working on to what was next, so she could plan the hours ahead. "Sure. I need to have this out the door by four."

The directions on the clipboard gave her pause. A Torta del Cielo cake, something they made often in the shop for a quinceañera, but this time, the customer requested a cake pull. The Victorian tradition used silver charms attached to ribbons that were hidden inside the tiers. Guests would pull on the ribbon and be rewarded with some little trinket.

In that instant, she was twenty-two and sitting in the dining room at her mother's house, with all of her sisters and Ben. Ma ducked into the kitchen and emerged with a three-tier torta, the scent of almond meringue dancing in the air. Instead of putting it on the table, Ma handed the cake to Ben. He'd dropped to one knee—in front of her entire family—and held the platter out to her, turning it so one curl of gold ribbon faced her. "I love you, Nora, and I don't want to spend another day without you. At the end of that ribbon is our future, if you want it. Marry me."

She'd been stunned, completely in the dark that this family dinner was an impromptu engagement party. She tugged on the gold string and out slipped a diamond ring— elegant and simple and perfect. In that moment, with the ring and meringue and the joy in the room, Nora had thought her life forward would be as beautiful and amazing as the cake.

But like the dessert, nothing lasted forever. The gold ribbon had long ago been lost, and the sweet moments had soured and spoiled.

"So...you didn't say. How was your birthday? Do anything special?" Bridget lifted one of the rounds for the layer cake onto a turntable and grabbed a frosting knife. "If I know Ben, he did something huge and over the top for you."

Nora hesitated. Ben's extravagance had been a major source of contention between them for years. Which for Ben meant expending huge amounts of cash they didn't have, and when their savings dipped, he'd gone to the dog track or the horse races, in an ever-spiraling quest to "fix everything."

In the end, all his big gifts and grand plans had cost them everything. She should have known it from that first day with the torta. There was no middle ground with Ben, and only rare moments of him facing reality. She'd been the one who worried and fussed and returned the over-priced sweaters he'd bought her. He'd looked at her like she'd let all the helium out of his balloons, and instead of apologizing or taking things down a notch, Ben had ramped up the celebration for the next holiday. She stopped trusting him with the checkbook and then stopped trusting him with their lives. It had been a year since he went to the gambling rehab place in New Hampshire, but Nora still saw shades of the old Ben in his tendency to overdo a simple holiday. Last Christmas, he'd bought the kids a trampoline without talking to Nora first. A trampoline she had had to return the next week, just to pay the electric bill. Which meant she was the bad guy, yet again.

"You know Ben—of course he did, but a little more muted this time because we've both been so busy." Nora pasted on a smile. She'd gotten so used to lying about her life that the words slipped out with barely a hitch in her chest. "Balloons, flowers, a whole big surprise when I got home last night. We took the kids to Giovanni's for dinner, then called the sitter so Ben and I could walk the beach. He had picked up that Italian pinot gris I love, and we had a little picnic under the stars."

The lie sounded so convincing that for a second, even she could believe it. Maybe she'd imagined the auction notice. The fight with Ben. The night in the hotel and the suitcase in the back of her car.

"You know, you really do have the perfect life," Bridget said with a sigh. "I used to be so jealous, and, hell, maybe I still am even though Garrett is awesome. But Ben...boy, he really does it up right."

Nora checked the smoothness of the frosting job, avoiding Bridget's gaze. Pale pink buttercream wrapped around the moist cake in a flat, even pattern. Her life might be out of control, but inside the walls of the bakery, Nora could keep order. Maybe that was why she liked working here so much. The precision of measuring, the dependability of what emerged from the ovens, the straight, neat decorations that turned ordinary into amazing. "Yeah, he's one of a kind."

Bridget turned her cake as she skimmed frosting along the edges, her movements fluid and practiced. "By the way, Ma said that new girl is starting today. The one she met at Roger's place."

"Oh yeah, the intern. I forgot about that." The extra help would be a blessing, especially since Nora had been so distracted lately. The orders had been piling up while Nora's motivation had been dipping lower every day, and even with her sisters here, it had been hard to keep up. She needed to get back on track, to focus on work. Except her mind kept wandering to that yellow notice, to the house that was no longer hers. To the question of what the hell she was going to do. Nora shook her head and cleared her throat. "Ma spends a lot of time over at the shelter."

Sophie's Home was a shelter started for women and children who were down on their luck or escaping dangerous situations. Nora had seen those women, women who looked just like her. Women who had lost everything.

She was one of them now, she realized. Homeless, broke, lost.

"I think she has a crush on Roger," Bridget said. The founder of the shelter had been introduced to their mother at church last year, and they seemed to have hit it off right away. "And he definitely has one on her. He's over here all the time, for some imaginary reason or another. What was it yesterday? He dropped off an umbrella because there was a thirty percent chance of rain. Ma parks right outside the back door. She doesn't need an umbrella to walk ten feet. Still, it's kinda cute to see him do that kind of thing." Bridget finished frosting the top of the first round, and then set it to the side and placed a second cake on the turnstile. "Okay, how am I beating you at this? You're like the decorating Iron Chef. Usually you've got two and a half cakes done to my one."

"I'm just tired. Late night of birthday celebrating." Which sounded a whole lot better than a sleepless night on a too-firm hotel bed. Nora's mind had churned, panic clawing at the edges of every thought.

Bridget nudged Nora. "You and Ben, just as in love as you were when you got married, huh?"

"Yeah, definitely." Nora and Ben had had sex only once in two years. They'd become glorified roommates who shared two kids. In the middle of the night, when the dark crowded into her space in the guest room, Nora wondered what Ben had done for the last two years. When their marriage had been good, they'd had a healthy sex life. She doubted Ben could go more than two weeks without some kind of physical encounter, and given how little he was home nowadays, she had often wondered who he was spending those late nights with. The thought of Ben with someone else pained her, but she'd never asked. She had checked out of their marriage and essentially left him, which meant he was free to do as he pleased. To share that smile with someone else.

Bridget paused. "Hey, you okay?"

Nora dipped the knife into the tub, scooped up too much buttercream, and then scraped the glob off and grabbed another, smaller one. "Sure. Fine."

Bridget stopped frosting, put her back to the counter, and faced Nora. "You sound a little...different. I don't mean to pry, but you haven't seemed like yourself in a while."

"I'm fine. Just...tired." Nora studied the cake as if her life depended on it. When the bell over the shop door rang, she shoved her knife into the tub. "I'll get that."

"I can—"

But Nora was already out of the kitchen and into the front portion of Charmed by Dessert. She'd always loved the public face of their family-owned bakery. Bright white paint lightened the walls, the starkness offset by pink window trim and black wrought-iron café tables. The glass case, full of pretty much every baked good imaginable, dominated one wall of the shop.

And all a stark contrast to the twentysomething girl standing in the center of the bakery. She was tall, thin as a beanpole, as Gramma used to say, with dark purple hair cut in a short spiky style. Nora counted at least four piercings above her neck—ears, brow, nose—and she could see the edge of a floral tattoo sticking out from under the sleeve of the girl's leather jacket.

"Hey, I'm Iris." The girl nodded toward Nora. "You work here?"

"I'm one of the owners." Nora wiped her hand on her apron and stepped forward. "I'm Nora."

The girl had a firm handshake, but her gaze cut away to the floor. Shy? Or shady? "Uh, Roger says I'm supposed to work here," Iris said. "Said I was supposed to talk to Colleen."

"That's my mother. She owns the bakery, along with me and my sisters. She's not here right now, but she told us you'd be coming in today," Nora said. "Do you have any experience working in a bakery?"

And do you have a criminal record? Probably not a good question to ask, Nora decided.

"No, I mean, like, not a real one." Iris toed the floor. "Before...well, before, I used to help my grandma in the kitchen."

Good Lord. Roger had probably sent her some girl who barely knew how to make a grilled cheese sandwich. The "help" was going to end up being more work than it was worth. Still, Nora couldn't turn her away. If Iris was truly terrible, Nora would just put her on dish duty. "Well, let's get you in the back and get you started. We have a couple orders that have to go out today, so you arrived just in time."

The girl looked ready to bolt. "Wait. Like I start now?"

"Do you have somewhere else you need to be?"

"No. Not really." Iris raised her gaze and met Nora's for a second. Dark kohl eyeliner ringed Iris's blue eyes and dominated her features, emphasized the paleness of her skin. She looked tired and sad, and unsure. "But, like, don't

17

you need to interview me or, like, background check me or piss-test me?"

"Are you a felon? A drug addict?"

Iris shook her head. "I got enough of both in my family."

A sadness hung in Iris's voice, a weariness that seemed decades too old for her young, unlined face. Nora tried to think of something comforting to say back but only came up with, "Well, good."

The girl didn't reply. Nora wondered if maybe she should have done an interview, or something like that. She'd just assumed, after all that Ma had said about the women at Sophie's Home, that Roger had vetted whoever he sent to the shop.

Either way, Nora had more than enough on her plate right now. She didn't need to add a sullen twentysomething who looked like she'd hopped off a Slipknot tour bus five minutes ago. She'd hand Iris off to Bridget and bury herself in decorating until it was time to get the kids from school.

Iris lagged behind as Nora pushed on the swinging door and led her into the kitchen. Bridget looked up and gave them a smile. "Hi. I'm Bridget. Nora's better sister."

Nora scoffed. "That's a matter of opinion."

Bridget waved off the words. "Don't listen to her. She's grumpy because she's thirty now. If you want to grab an apron from the hook, I can get you started."

Iris hesitated. "I...I've never worked in a bakery before. Should I just watch for a while?"

"Baking's the kind of thing you have to do hands-on,"

Bridget said. "So wash your hands, put on the apron, and get ready to get a little messy."

Iris did as she was told, looking over her shoulder every few seconds. Bridget gave the girl an encouraging smile. Even though Nora was the unofficial manager of the bakery, she was more than happy to let Bridget take the lead.

Nora's phone began to buzz. She considered ignoring it—Ben had tried to call six times already this morning, and Nora had ignored them all. After the first couple, she hadn't bothered to listen to the voice mails he'd left or read his texts, because they all said the same thing. *Come home. Let's work this out. I can fix it.*

Nora fished her phone out of her pocket, about to turn it off, when she saw St. Gregory's Elementary School pop up on the caller ID. Her heart did a little trip, that mother instinct kicking in, causing her to start worrying even before she answered. Nora signaled to Bridget and stepped out back. "Hello?"

"Mrs. Daniels? This is Sister Esther, the principal at St. Gregory's." The nun paused, and for a second, Nora's heart froze. Her mind pictured a thousand different scenarios, an accident, a bus crash, a field trip gone wrong. "We, uh, have a problem with Sarah. I need you to come in right away."

TWO

Sarah sat on a bench outside the principal's office, swinging her feet back and forth, her toes skimming along the pale green tile. When Nora had dropped her eight-year-old off this morning, Sarah had been wearing clean jeans, a pale pink T-shirt, and a yellow hoodie, with her long dark hair back in a neat braid.

Now the jeans were scuffed and muddy, the hoodie nowhere to be seen, and most of her hair had escaped the braid. There was a smudge on her chin, and tear tracks ran down her cheeks.

Nora bent down in front of her daughter, trying to hide the worry and fear roaring inside her. She scanned Sarah, looking for a cut or a scrape, but saw only dirt. Thank God. "Hey, sweetie, what happened?"

"Nothin'." Sarah kept her gaze on the floor.

"Did you get hurt?"

Sarah shook her head. Nora brushed a lock of hair away from her daughter's face. At eight, she still had some of that baby roundness in her face, although she was growing tall and gangly like her father. If Nora inhaled, she knew she'd catch the strawberry scent of Sarah's shampoo, a fragrance that didn't square with the dirty, grumpy girl before her. "Then what happened?"

The office door opened and Sister Esther stepped into the hall. She was a short woman, wide in the middle, and her habit swung like a bell over her hips. She'd been here for as long as Nora could remember—the same principal when Nora and her sisters had attended St. Gregory's—and managed to recall nearly every student's name.

She had a kind smile and patience that stretched for miles. Nora had always liked her but still felt that guilty twinge, like she'd been caught sneaking out of class, whenever Sister Esther looked at her.

"Mrs. Daniels," Sister Esther said. "So nice to see you, my dear."

"Thank you, Sister." Nora placed a hand on Sarah's shoulder. Her daughter gave an almost imperceptible twitch, shifting away from her mother's touch. Nora glanced down, but Sarah didn't meet her gaze. "What happened? Did Sarah get hurt today?"

"Perhaps it's best if we talk in my office." Sister Esther bent toward the bench. "Sarah, will you be all right out here for a little longer?"

"Yes, Sister."

"Thank you. Why don't you open up your reading book and start on the homework Sister Margaret gave you while your mother and I chat a bit?" Sister Esther turned and led Nora into the small room that housed her office. Nora shut the door behind them and then took a seat in one of the hard wooden chairs. The principal's desk was tidy, papers stacked in baskets, pencils and pens nestled in a dark brown coffee cup. Pictures of students lined the top of the bookshelf, and a single red carnation sat in a vase on the windowsill. Nora could hear children on the playground, their voices swinging up and down in the air.

The nun sat at her desk and steepled her hands. She paused a moment before speaking. "We've had a few problems with Sarah as of late."

No small talk, no wasted words. "Problems?" Nora echoed.

"As I'm sure you're aware, her grades have been dropping."

"Uh, yes, I knew that." Was it a mortal sin to lie to a nun? Was she going straight to hell for forgetting to check Sarah's backpack every day? Nora had gotten so sidetracked by the bills and arguing with the creditors that the kids' grades had fallen off her priority list.

She bit back a sigh. How did Ben expect her to do it all? Work full-time, deal with the bills and debt calls, and do everything for the kids? The partnership she'd entered into when she said "I do" had become a one-sided, shitty deal.

Sister Esther waited a beat, but Nora didn't fill in the blank with an explanation. "Our greater concern right now is her behavior. Sarah has been acting...out of character." The nun's lips pursed. "There has been some misconduct in class and a fight at recess."

"Sarah got into a fight?" Of all the kids in the world Nora would pick for a fighter, her daughter wouldn't even come to mind. Sarah had a sweet temperament, a fondness for rescuing animals, and an overwhelming love for the color pink. That wasn't a kid who got into fights. "If that's so, then I'm sure she had a good reason. Perhaps someone is bullying her?"

"I'm afraid"—Sister Esther's brows knitted, and she paused a beat again—"Sarah is the bully."

Sarah is the bully. The words took their time connecting in Nora's brain. Her sweet third-grader, who drew pictures of butterflies and named every living creature she saw, was a bully?

"You must be mistaken. Sarah is not a bully. Do you have her confused with another student? Or maybe she was defending herself. Have you talked to the other child involved? Kids lie, you know. Especially when they don't want to get in trouble."

Adults lie too, her mind whispered. Especially when their life is out of control.

Sister Esther's face softened. "Ah, Nora, I know how hard it is to hear that one of your children has done something wrong."

No, Nora thought, *no, you don't. You've never had children. You can't possibly know what is going on in my head.*

"But I am a firm believer in accepting and facing our faults so we can fix them. At St. Gregory's, we have a strict no-bullying policy. Sarah has been picking on several of her classmates for a while now. Because she has always been a good student, and because we know you and your family so well, we tried to be lenient. Her teacher and I have talked to her many times. We have given her second chances we don't give to the other children. But today," the nun sighed, "today was not the kind of day we could turn a blind eye to."

A stone mound of dread and worry formed in Nora's stomach. "What happened?"

"Do you know Anna Richardson?"

Anna, Sarah's best friend in kindergarten. They'd joined Brownies together and been at each other's houses so often during summer break that it almost seemed like Nora had two daughters. Nora tried to think of the last time Anna had been at the house and couldn't remember. Had it been April? March? Or last year?

"Anna and Sarah are friends. They sold Girl Scout cookies together last year in front of the Stop and Shop and then we went out for ice cream." As if sharing some Samoas and a couple cones of mint chocolate chip was enough to convince Sister Esther that she was mistaken about the kids involved.

"Well, sadly, sometimes friendships turn. I don't know what happened between Anna and Sarah, but today on the playground, Sarah was..." Sister Esther's face pinched, and the sympathy vanished. "Well, she had Anna up against the wall, and she was threatening to hit her. Anna was very clearly frightened. Anna tried to get away, Sarah grabbed her, and they ended up on the ground. The fight went on for several seconds before one of the teachers broke it up. No one was hurt, but there are consequences, as you know."

The clock on the wall ticked. A bell rang, and a second later, there was a low roar in the halls. Nora couldn't find her voice.

Sarah had beat up another girl? In third grade? A girl who was her friend? Why?

"I realize how hard this is to hear," Sister Esther went on. "And I'm just as surprised as you are, believe me. Because Sarah is such a good student and has not been in this kind of trouble before, I'm going to meet with her teachers before meting out an appropriate discipline. There will be some kind of suspension, I'm sure. Maybe even..." The nun let out a breath. "Well, let's see what the consensus is before we talk about extreme options."

Like expulsion. Nora shook her head. This couldn't be happening. Maybe all of it—the auction notice, the fight with Ben, this meeting—was some kind of bizarre uber-realistic dream. Maybe that was what Ben was doing—ignoring reality and walking around in some fantasy of everything being okay.

"I can't believe Sarah would do such a thing," Nora said. "You can rest assured, Sister Esther, that her father and I will talk to her."

"I'm glad to hear that. It's always a good thing when the parents are involved and on board. However, you need to know that if Sarah can't learn from this lesson and start being nice to the other children, then...we will have to expel her." The nun sighed. "I really don't want to do that.

I have enjoyed having another generation of O'Bannon girls at this school. You four girls were always such a bright part of my days."

The nun went on to mention possibilities for discipline and remediation. Things like meetings with a counselor, some time spent after school doing menial chores and weekly parental check-ins, while Nora's mind whirled around the information that her daughter had been brawling on the playground. Nora thanked Sister Esther, then headed out of the principal's office. She stopped by the receptionist's desk, made up a doctor appointment for Jake, and then signed both kids out for the day. Given the fight Sarah had been in, both she and Sister Esther had agreed it would be best for Sarah to go home and Nora didn't want to come back up here in a few hours to get Jake. Now Nora was lying to the nuns. Maybe all this was God's way of giving her a little warning smack about the Ten Commandments.

She went into the hall to wait for Jake. Sarah was still sitting on the bench, her gaze locked on the tile floor.

Nora bent down in front of her daughter. Tears hung on the ends of Sarah's eyelashes, and her nose was runny. Any anger and shock Nora had felt in the principal's office disappeared. Nora wanted to scoop her up and tell her that it would all be okay, like she had so many times before. Instead, Nora fished a tissue out of her purse and dabbed at her daughter's face. Sarah drew back, again, an almost imperceptible distance. The first time, Nora could write it off as embarrassment or upset, but the second time the cold

front moved in between her and her daughter, there was no
denying Sarah was avoiding Nora's touch. When they were
out of the shadows of St. Gregory's, Nora would see if she
could figure out what was wrong. "Honey, let's go home,
okay? Then we can talk."

"I don't wanna talk."

"That's okay, for now. I signed Jake out so you two can
skip out of school early today," Nora said, trying to make
the whole thing sound like a fun-fun idea. "You guys can
come to the bakery with me, and then tonight, how about
we go to Grandma's house?"

Sarah shook her head. "I wanna go home. I don't
wanna go to Grandma's house."

"Grandma's house is fun," Nora said, still in that peppy,
this-is-awesome voice. "And I bet she'll make you guys
some cookies. We can rent a movie and stay up late."

When Sister Esther had mentioned consequences,
Nora was pretty sure the nun didn't mean cookies, movies,
and delayed bedtimes. Nora knew she should be harsher,
angrier, but she couldn't summon up the energy right now.
In the scheme of things, a playground fight ranked a lot
lower than homelessness.

"I wanna sleep in *my* room," Sarah said. "I wanna read
my Harry Potter books. I wanna see Daddy."

Three things that Nora couldn't give her daughter
right now. Jake came bounding down the hall, his usual af-
fable self, and saved Nora from an answer. "Hi, Mommy,"
Jake said. "Sister Mary said I get to go home early. Do I
gotta go see the doctor?"

Nora ruffled Jake's dark brown hair and smoothed the unruly waves he'd inherited from his father. "Nope, no doctor. Just a fun day at the bakery with me, Aunt Bridget, and Grandma. And then we can go stay at Grandma's house and have a sleepover. Sound good?"

"Yeah! I love going to Grandma's!" Jake, the child who took everything in stride, who rarely complained, danced beside Nora as the three of them walked down the hall and out to the car.

Sarah didn't say a word. When had her eight-year-old gone from bubbly and talkative to silent and sullen? In those hours when Nora had stayed late at the bakery, pouring herself into the job, because that was the only place where she could feel like she had some kind of control? Or on those nights when Nora had paced the kitchen, drowning in a pile of bills and demand letters, trying to balance a budget that was forever uneven? Or in those weeks when Nora had drawn into herself, while her husband was gambling their future away?

Ben should have been there for the kids when Nora couldn't be. Ben should have picked up the slack, especially when he knew how many hours Nora worked. His job was more flexible, since he was the boss and could set his own hours. Ben should have checked the homework and grades. As usual, he'd left her to juggle everything. Her job, the bills, the kids. Yet another reason why Nora wasn't answering his texts or heading home.

The kids climbed into the car, Jake talking a mile a minute, Sarah ignoring everyone. Nora engaged in a half-hearted conversation with her youngest while she drove, but her gaze kept flicking to Sarah. Her daughter had her backpack clutched to her chest, chin on the gray fabric, her face sour and sad.

Nora parked in the back of the bakery beside her mother's car. By the time she helped Jake unbuckle, Sarah had already gone inside. Ma was waiting at the back door when Nora pulled it open, her face expectant. Across the kitchen, Bridget was on the phone, taking an order. She had given the kids a quick hello, sent a wave in Nora's direction, and then went back to the call. Iris was mixing dough in one of the massive stand mixers, watching the arm revolve and giving the recipe nervous glances from time to time.

"Half day?" Ma asked, with a judgmental arch of her brow.

Just once, Nora wanted to walk in this building when she was having a bad day and not be subjected to an FBI-worthy interrogation. Just once, she wished her mother would give her a hug and leave her alone.

"Something like that." Nora told Jake and Sarah to go out front and pick a cookie. When the kids were gone, she turned to her mother. "Can we, uh, come stay with you tonight?"

"Stay with me? Why?" Colleen's gaze narrowed, and she leaned closer.

"Ben is...uh...finishing up the kitchen renovation. I won't have a sink or stove while he's doing that, and the house will be a mess. With the kids, it's just...tough."

In the space of twenty-four hours, she'd lied to her sister, a nun, her kids, and her mother. She was pretty sure she'd just bought herself a one-way ticket straight to hell. Do not collect two hundred dollars. Do not pass purgatory.

Ma cocked her head and studied Nora for a moment. It was like being in front of the headmistress all over again. Nora held her ground, keeping that fake smile on her face until her cheeks hurt. "It'll be nice to spend time with my grandchildren," Ma said. "And since you're busy here and I have a little free time in the afternoon, why don't I get them from school tomorrow so they won't have to go to that day care?"

"That would be great." One less bill to pay, a bill Nora couldn't afford anyway. "Thanks, Ma."

The assessing look returned. Ma put a hand on Nora's cheek. "Are you okay? You look a little pale. Are you sleeping enough? Eating enough?"

"I'm fine, Ma. Just fine." The immortal phrase used by everyone in the O'Bannon family. A phrase that had become Nora's mantra. If she kept saying everything was okay, then maybe by some weird law of attraction or last-minute miracle, it would be.

Iris wasn't entirely useless. She was quiet, so quiet that Nora forgot she was there. She did whatever Bridget or Nora asked, with minimal questions. They kept her on simple tasks—mixing dough, filling baking pans, washing dishes. Around three, she asked if she could leave. Iris toed at the floor for a second and spoke more words than she had since she'd arrived. "Is it okay if I go now? My friend has a doctor appointment 'cause she's, like, pregnant, and she broke up with her boyfriend because he, like, plays Xbox all day and treats her like crap."

Ben might have been far from perfect as a husband, but he had been there for every OB appointment and had been there to hold Nora's hand, rub her back, and talk her through the labor and delivery with that calm, quiet voice of his. She could only imagine how hard the road ahead would be for Iris's friend. "Iris, if your friend needs some baby clothes, I have plenty left over from the kids. I'd be glad to put together a box."

"That's really nice of you," Iris said, her face bright with surprise at the offer, which made Nora wonder what kind of world the girl lived in where this kind of thing was a shock. "She's on, like, food stamps, and baby things are expensive."

Nora didn't have the heart to tell Iris that those expenses only grew as the kids did. Not to mention the stress. A box of hand-me-down onesies and bibs was about all Nora could offer right now.

"No problem on leaving early, Iris," Bridget said. "When you come in tomorrow, we can set up a more official schedule."

"Okay. I...I appreciate it. I'm trying to help my mom out."

"Well, as long as you keep working out like this, you'll have a job," Bridget said.

"Okay." Iris lingered a moment, worrying her bottom

lip, as if she had more to say. Instead, she took off her apron and headed out the door, with only a quiet goodbye sent in Colleen's direction. As Iris exited, she stepped to the side, making room for a tall man in jeans and an old Stones T-shirt to enter.

Ben.

For a second, Nora's heart forgot everything that had happened. She saw the stubble on his cheeks, the one untameable wave of hair, the rippled muscles of his arms, and the solid wall of his chest. Ben had worked in construction since he was fifteen, and even though he had his general contractor's license now, he preferred to be hands-on, transforming a pile of wood and plaster into a celebrity-worthy bathroom or gourmet chef kitchen. The defined muscles and flat plane of his stomach showed how hard he worked, and despite everything, Nora's body still reacted to his. Damn it.

She wanted to hate him, and maybe a part of her did. The part that felt betrayed, the part that had been alone and sobbing on the bathroom floor, waiting for a husband who was on a three-day bender of slot machines and roulette wheels. That anger simmered beneath the surface, like a tsunami behind a dam. She'd never talked about it, never told Ben about that night. Instead, she kept those emotions tucked deep inside the crevices of her mind.

Sarah and Jake broke into a run, barreling across the shop's tile floor and straight into Ben. "Daddy!"

"Hey, guys!" Ben chuckled and scooped up both kids, one in each arm. "What are you two doing here?"

"Mommy said we got to get outta school early, 'cause we're having a fun day," Jake said. "And tonight, Gramma's making us cookies, and we're gonna watch a movie at her house."

"Are you coming to Gramma's too, Daddy?" Sarah asked.

Ben lowered the kids to the ground and put a hand on Sarah's shoulder. "Let me talk to your mom about that, okay?"

Nora cut her gaze away from the question in Ben's face, the hope in the kids' eyes. "Ma, could you watch the kids for a minute? I want to talk to Ben…without little ears around." She kept her tone light, as if they were going to talk about something mundane like Sarah's birthday party, not the end of their marriage.

"Sure, sure." Ma bent down to her grandkids. "Who wants to help me finish putting up the Halloween decorations? I think we need more cobwebs, don't you?"

Nora left her apron on the counter and headed out the front door with Ben. They walked a little while in silence, ambling down the sidewalk and away from the nosy stares on the other side of the plate glass windows of the shop. A part of Nora wanted to let the silence linger because then she wouldn't have to talk about the rest, all those things about their relationship that she hadn't faced as the bills stacked up and the stress threatened to overwhelm her. But doing that had left her with a dying marriage, an empty bank account, and a repossessed house.

"I'm not coming home, if that's what you're here to ask me," she said finally. "Either way, there's no home to go to."

"Home is what we make it, Nora."

She scoffed. "Let me get you some linen so you can embroider that into a little sampler and hang it on the wall."

"Can we talk about this without the sarcasm, please?" Ben's face pinched into a scowl. "I want you to come home, Nora. You and the kids."

"Home? What fucking home, Ben?" She shook her head. "Home is a place you can depend on, a place you know your kids are going to wake up in every day, a place you are sure they will go to sleep in every night. Our home is on the auction block. It's not ours anymore."

They skirted a planter filled with chrysanthemums, blooming bright yellows and oranges. Georgi, the owner of the flower shop next door to the bakery, gave Nora a little wave as she passed. She nodded in return, pasting a smile on her face. That everything-is-fine smile she had perfected since childhood.

Ben ran a hand through his hair and sighed. "I don't know what you want me to do, Nora."

"It doesn't matter, Ben. It's too late. I think..." She drew in a breath, let it out again. She couldn't keep lying to herself or to Ben. The truth had been right there in front of her on all those nights she sat home alone, and in all those moments when she looked at the man she thought she used to know and realized he'd become a stranger. "I think we should separate. Officially."

He stepped in front of her. His body blocked the sun,

and a cool shadow dropped over her. "Are you asking me for a divorce?"

She looked up into eyes that used to be filled with love and understanding, not the cold distance she saw now. She caught the scent of his cologne on the breeze, a mix of warmth and sawdust. They might have had something wonderful once, but every disappointment, every hurt, every loss had whittled away what was left of their relationship. She was tired of fighting. Tired of hurting. Tired of hoping. "Yes, Ben, I want a divorce."

He stared at her for a long, long time, his features hardening. "So you're giving up."

"No, I'm not. I'm accepting reality. Maybe you should try that sometime."

He threw up his hands and started walking again, his steps hitting the pavement with hurried, angry thuds. "What the fuck do you want out of me, Nora? I'm working as hard as I can, going to meetings, groveling—"

"Groveling? Really? You fucked up our lives, Ben." She grabbed his hand and spun him back to face her. "*You* lost tens of thousands of dollars. *You* didn't pay the bills. *You* didn't stay involved with the kids, and now Sarah is probably going to be kicked out of St. Gregory's for fighting—"

"Sarah got into a fight?" Concern erased the anger in Ben's face, and for a second, he was her husband again, the man who had held her hand in that delivery room and calmed her when the pain got too hard to bear. "Is she okay?"

She refused to fall for the look in Ben's eyes again. He

might have been in that delivery room, but he had also deserted her when she needed him most. "She's fine. I took care of it, Ben. Like I have taken care of everything else from the day we got married. And don't worry, I'll take care of the divorce too."

THREE

On the nights when the panic set in and sleep eluded Nora, she would lie on the couch under a blanket her grandmother had knitted, watching shows about gold miners or hoarders or strange medical procedures. One night, between infomercials for acne medicine and rotisserie ovens, there'd been a documentary about some woman who had a rare disease that could only be treated in a hyperbaric chamber. She'd lain in that glass coffin, breathing extra-oxygenated air, while medical staff sat outside, watching her every breath.

That was what being at her mother's house was like. Ma had intuition that would make Sherlock Holmes jealous, and she'd sensed something was up from the minute Nora asked if they could stay there for the night. The renovation excuse was as thin as rice paper, but it was all Nora could come up with.

After Ben left, Nora went back to baking and frosting, using the repetition of work to keep herself from thinking.

She'd told the kids their father had to go back to work and would call them later. Jake had pouted until Ma put him to work turning the stand mixer on and off as she whipped up more cake batter.

Sarah just gave Nora a harsh stare and curled into one of the chairs in the corner of the shop, her nose in a book. Nora came out to the front of the shop, asking Sarah what she was reading, if she had any homework, if she was hungry. Sarah gave bare-minimum answers.

When her kids were born, Nora had lain in the hospital bed with each one, while their tiny fingers curled around hers, and she had vowed to be a good mom. An involved mom. The kind who colored pictures and applauded like a lunatic at the school plays. She had whispered all these promises to Sarah and Jacob, her heart full and her intentions good. For a long time, she had been that mom. She'd existed on a handful of sleep, but she had been at every event, sat down with every homework assignment, exclaimed over every macaroni masterpiece.

Nora could pinpoint the exact moment she had unplugged from her kids. She'd been sitting on a cold concrete bench on a biting winter afternoon and faced the fact that she'd been fooling herself for years. A good mom protected her children. A good mom held her family together. A good mom put that above—

Above everything.

So Nora immersed herself in work and tried to pretend Sarah's iciness was normal third-grader behavior. Around three, Ma took the kids to her house, and Nora followed along after the bakery closed at six. On her lunch break, she'd picked up a copy of the paper and scanned the classifieds for affordable rentals. Apparently the words *affordable* and *Boston area* didn't go together. The best she could come up with that fit her budget was a fifth-floor one-bedroom apartment in an iffy neighborhood in Roxbury.

She had to find a home for her kids. The longer she put this off, the more suspicious her family would grow. Eventually, she would have to tell them the truth. That the always perfect, never failing Nora O'Bannon Daniels had failed everything. Failed her marriage. Failed her children.

If she could get some kind of solution in place in the next week or so, the transition for the kids would be easier. She could tell her family something about downsizing and leave all their questions and buttinsky tendencies for another day.

As soon as Nora got into her car, she let out a breath, and the stress of feigning happiness left her in a whoosh. She checked her email and saw one from Sister Esther that said just what Nora had expected—Sarah was suspended from school for the rest of the week.

What had happened to her life? Even a year ago, Nora would have sworn on a Bible that she had a great family, good kids. But it had all been a house of cards, an illusion of *fine* that toppled with one big gust of wind.

Nora tossed her phone onto the passenger's seat. It bounced off her purse and tumbled to the floor.

Then the tears hit. They rolled down her cheeks, blurring her vision as she drove across Dorchester to the neighborhood where she'd grown up. Everything she passed—the deli that served those amazing corned beef sandwiches that Ben loved, the newsstand they'd visit every Sunday to buy the paper, the movie theater he'd taken her to on their first date—reminded her of what used to be and what she had lost. The gambling, the fights, the money, all of it stones thrown at their marriage until it crumpled.

She cried for all of those things and then pulled over a few blocks from Park Street, wiping away her tears and the smeared mascara on her face. She pinched her cheeks to give them some color, swiped on some lipstick, and ran a comb through her hair. If no one looked too close, they'd suspect she was tired, not that she'd spent the last twenty minutes sobbing. Yet another façade. She was practically a pro at this now.

When Nora walked into the house, her mother and kids were at the kitchen table, eating a chicken casserole. Well, Ma and Jake were eating. Sarah picked at her food, moving it around just enough to make it look like she'd eaten a few bites.

Nora slipped into one of the chairs, dished up a plate of food, and then bowed her head for a quick, silent grace. She wasn't sure God was even listening to her, considering how He'd answered her prayers about saving the house from foreclosure. "Amen," she whispered, and hoped God heard all the silent prayers in her head.

"Did you start on the cupcakes for that open house?" her mother asked, launching into work mode before she even passed the rolls. "And that retirement party cake for the judge?"

"Yes, Ma, I did." Nora ate some chicken, the food barely registering on her taste buds. She had no appetite and no desire to sit here in this suffocating dining room. She'd skip dinner entirely if it wouldn't raise a red flag with her mother.

"I'm worried about us making that deadline," Ma said. "We have so much going on, and the judge is an important client."

"It'll be fine, Ma. Don't worry." Nora had learned long ago to couch the words she used with her mother. After Dad had died, Ma had been so overwhelmed and so quick to irritation that Nora had begun glossing over the truth. She'd hidden the occasional bad grade, the missed home-work assignment. She'd covered for her sisters when they'd scraped a knee or skipped a class, small lies that kept the peace and eased the tension. Maybe that was where the "everything's fine" line had begun, some kind of well-meaning conspiracy to keep the shadows of the truth from sneaking in.

She'd done the same thing when she got married. With her family, her friends, her husband. Little white lies that smoothed over the rough edges and kept up the illusion of the American dream.

"Mommy, can we call Daddy after dinner?" Jake asked. "I want to tell him about how Sister Mary hung my picture on the wall. She said it was the bestest one ever."

"Best," Nora corrected. "That's great, Jake."

"I drew a picture of a puppy," Jake said. "Can we get a puppy? I'll walk it, Mommy, I promise."

Jake's little face, imploring, yearning. Nora had been a little older than him when she'd sat at this very table and asked her mother the same question.

And received the same answer. Because a puppy needed a yard. A place to sleep. She couldn't even offer that to her own children right now. "Not right now, Jake. Maybe someday."

Sarah snorted. "What she means is no, Jake. Because Mom never lets us have what we want."

Ma shot Nora a sharp glance. Nora took another bite of chicken casserole. She didn't have the energy to deal with Sarah or the disappointment on Jake's face. Ignoring them all seemed the best course right now.

"Nora, are you going to say something?" Ma asked.

"Do we have any bread?" There. She'd said something.

Ma handed Nora a basket of rolls with a side of judgment and turned to her granddaughter. "At my table, Sarah, daughters do not talk to their mothers like that. You need to apologize."

Sarah kept her gaze on her plate and mumbled, "Sorry."

Ma pursed her lips but let it go. Thank God.

For a while, Nora ate and considered her options. She didn't have a home to go back to. She didn't have enough money to rent an apartment. Which left her mother's house. The kitchen remodel lie was going to work for only so long and Nora had to come clean if she wanted to stay here.

Besides, how bad would it be to rely on Ma for a while? Even if Nora was a thirty-year-old with two kids who had to run home to mommy to bail her out of her own bad decisions.

Then she noticed the lines in her mother's face, the shadows under her eyes. Normally vibrant, strong, and opinionated, Colleen O'Bannon was a washed-out version of her usual self. The stress of running the bakery, worrying about her own mother's failing health, and the four grown daughters that would forever be little girls in Colleen's mind, was clearly taking its toll. Guilt rolled through Nora. She'd dropped the ball at work more and more as her own life unraveled, and left those responsibilities on the shoulders of her mother and her sisters. She needed to step up, to be more present, not ask for more.

"How's Aunt Mary, Ma?" Even though Ma's sister Mary had revealed last year that she was actually Colleen's mother—a lie perpetuated almost seventy years ago as a way to protect young Mary's reputation and the scandal of an out-of-wedlock pregnancy—everyone still called her Aunt Mary.

"Getting there. You know her. She refuses to admit she's hurting at all, but thank goodness that doctor has been firm with her," Ma said. "She'll probably be in the hospital another few days, and then she'll come home and stay with me."

Nora ate a bite of casserole. Sarah was still pushing her food around, but Jake was winning the clean plate award. "What about her house in Revere?"

"She should sell that thing, given how often it sits empty. Mary is a lot of things, but frugal isn't one of them. She'll have all these medical bills now, and Mary has never squirreled anything away. All I can say is that it makes me thankful that you and your sisters have been smart about your money. Well, Bridget had a little incident"—which was how their mother referred to the fact that Bridget's late husband had blown almost all their money on a child he had with another woman—"but she's got things back on the right track now."

If there was one lesson their mother had drilled into them over and over, it was the value of frugality. Colleen O'Bannon could make a dollar stretch until it begged for mercy, while also diligently giving one-tenth of everything she made to the church. Part of that had undoubtedly been due to being a widowed mother of four girls under ten, where almost everything was a hand-me-down or a share-me.

Nora had lived by those principles until Ben bankrupted them in the space of a few weeks, and everything she had so carefully squirreled away went to keep them afloat. Ben kept promising that the next contracting job, or the one after that, would be the one that would finally put them on top. Money in the bank—she had none of that. But empty promises—those she had aplenty.

"Mommy, are you gonna watch *Moana* with us tonight?" Jake danced in his seat. "Gramma says we can make popcorn and eat it on the couch!"

"You're letting them eat in the living room, Ma?" Nora said. Never in her life had she or her sisters been allowed to take so much as a cracker and eat it outside of the kitchen or dining room. "Isn't that the first sign of the Apocalypse?"

"We do not joke about the end of the world, Eleanor." Her mother's lips pressed into a thin line. "And Jake and Sarah know to be careful."

In the year and a half since Bridget's husband had died and their fractured family had come back together, Ma had changed, mostly in good ways. She'd welcomed Abby and her new wife, Jessie, into the family fold and started to relax, by degrees, some of her rules and strict guidelines. They played music in the bakery while they baked, there was a weekly family potluck dinner, and now, apparently, she was allowing food on the couch.

"Mommy, are you gonna watch with us?" Jake asked again.

"Sure," Nora said, if only because sitting on the sofa watching a cartoon would delay the hours she'd spend alone in her old bed and the thoughts that would crowd her mind. The guilt that seemed like a shroud.

"When you go into work tomorrow, you should start on the cake for that wedding on Saturday." Ma gathered up her plate and got to her feet. "Lord only knows why someone would have a zombie-themed wedding—"

"It's Halloween, Ma."

"Still not a reason to combine the living dead with a sacred institution." Another pursing of the lips and apologetic glance heavenward. "Regardless, they're expecting three hundred guests, so make sure you—"

"Get an early start and leave enough time for the decorating. Yes, Ma, I know." Nora sighed. For the first time in a long time, she didn't want to go to work. Didn't give a shit about decorating a cake for somebody's *Walking Dead* wedding or how many scones she was going to need for the people at Prudential tomorrow. She wanted to crawl into a corner, far away from the mail and the calls and the yellow notices waiting for her and just hibernate until she found her strength again.

Except Nora O'Bannon didn't do that. Nora was the one they all depended upon, the one who kept her shit together and kept the bakery and her family functioning as smooth as a Rolex.

Ma disappeared into the kitchen with her plate. The kids followed soon after, while Nora tried to make it look like she'd made a dent in her meal. After two bites, she gave up and brought her plate into the kitchen. Ma was filling the sink, while Jake and Sarah were putting the leftovers in the refrigerator. "Go sit down, Ma," she said. "I'll do the dishes."

Her mother hesitated. Even giving up control of the dish sponge came with reluctance. "That's a very sweet thing to do. Just make sure you use the good dish detergent and wring out the sponge when you're done. Also—"

"Wipe down the counters and dry off the sink. This isn't my first time in your kitchen, Ma." So her mother had changed only a little. Considering she was sixty-three, any change at all was probably a miracle.

"Sarah and Jake, will you finish clearing the table, please?" Ma said.

"Okay, Gramma!" Jake bounded off to the dining room, at that age where helping still seemed like fun, not a chore. Sarah dragged her feet behind her brother.

Nora turned off the faucet. In the warm water and bubbles, she found a moment of peace. She could concentrate on the task of washing, rinsing, and drying and not have to think about her life, her bills, or the state of her marriage and her family. Washing was simplicity, dipping the sponge into the warm soapy water, circling it around the ivy-bordered plate, then over the back. Running warm water over the porcelain until the bubbles swirled down the drain and the plate gleamed. She nestled it among its partners, then picked up the next one. Lather, rinse, repeat.

Ma and Jake left to take the trash to the curb. Sarah slunk into the kitchen and put her dish on the counter. "Wait, don't leave yet, honey." Nora dried her hands on the towel and then turned to her daughter. Sarah's chipmunk cheeks and wide eyes made her seem so much younger. The protective side of Nora wanted to avoid the conversation, to protect her child from the tough subjects, but doing that had brought them to the principal's office. "We need to talk about today."

"I didn't do anything." Sarah threw up an immediate defense with a sullen attitude.

"Sister Esther said you were beating up Anna. I thought she was your friend."

Sarah scowled. "She's not my friend. I don't like her anymore."

Didn't like Anna anymore? Since when? As far back as

Nora could remember, Sarah hadn't mentioned anything negative about Anna. Was it just some squabble over a favorite book or a boy or another friend? "Did something happen?"

Sarah shook her head and stared at the floor. Her hair swung in front of her face like a curtain.

Maybe it was something small, a fight that would blow over as quickly as a summer storm. Mortal enemies one day, BFFs the next. Nora tried to think back, but the last year and a half was a blur, all those months blending into one another while Nora tried to forget and move forward at the same time.

"Well, either way, it's wrong to fight. You know that, and you also know there are consequences to bad behavior." Nora lowered herself to Sarah's level. "Sister Esther emailed me and said you are suspended for the rest of the week. You also have to go to an antibullying class after you get back on Monday and spend your next couple weeks of recess in the library."

"That's not fair!" Sarah crossed her arms over her chest and pouted. "Why do I have to go to that stupid school anyway?"

"It's a good school, and you're lucky to go there." Though Nora wasn't sure she could afford the private school tuition anymore. Her pay from the bakery would be enough to cover renting a small apartment and most of the bills if she was careful, but tuition—that was out of her budget. Ben's income had been an inconsistent roller coaster, especially when he'd been gambling, so she knew better than to count on that. If she filed for divorce, there'd be a separation agreement and—

Nora shoved those thoughts to the back of her mind. It was too much, too many things. Besides, she could see Ma was a second away from being back inside the house. The last thing Nora wanted was her mother offering her two cents on finances, parenting, or marriage. Hell, if Nora wore pink instead of coral, her mother had an opinion about it. She'd argue the color of a rainbow with God Himself and then tell Him that He had made it too thin or too short, to boot. The last thing Nora wanted right now was advice—aka criticism—from her mother.

"Go get your pajamas on, Sarah," Nora said. "We will talk about this later."

"But—" Sarah glanced back at her mother, scowled, and then cut off her protests. "Fine."

Sarah trudged off, and Nora went back to the dishes. To the peace and quiet of running water and soft bubbles and the satisfying order found in taking something dirty and making it clean again. If only she could do the same with the rest of her life.

Ma had always done the same thing. Whenever Ma was stressed or worried, she ironed, she vacuumed, she dusted. Setting her world to rights again, she called it. When Nora was three, someone had given her a toy vacuum for her birthday, and she'd slipped into place beside her mother, running straight lines up and down the carpets, straightening the fringe on the hall rugs, removing and dusting every one of the Hummels in the corner cabinet. With each cherub-faced figurine, this weird peace would fill Nora. As she got older, washing, ironing, and dusting became her escape. Sometimes she stayed late at the bakery just to clean—and to breathe in the quiet and order.

As Nora was putting the last dish away, her mother came into the kitchen, and the easy peace Nora had recaptured disappeared again. Ma had that look on her face, the one Nora and her sisters had come to dread. It was the look that said *I have something to tell you and you're not going to like hearing it.*

Sort of the same look Ma got on her face when she dispensed cod liver oil to anyone with a bellyache. Now Ma leaned against the counter, watching Nora dry the casserole dish and stow it in one of the lower cabinets. "It doesn't go there," Ma said.

Nora sighed and straightened. Instead of *Thank you for doing the dishes*, there was criticism. "Okay, then where does it go?"

Her mother came closer and peered up at her. "Are you okay? You seem a little...short with me. You barely noticed your children, never asked them about their homework, never checked to see if they finished their dinner. And you let Sarah talk back to you. None of that is like you."

"Well, maybe I'm changing." Nora slid the damp dish-towel over the oven's handle to let it dry. "I'm not up to dealing with a million questions tonight, Ma, so can we drop it? I'm...tired."

Her mother placed a palm on her forehead. "You're not warm, so I don't think you're sick."

But Nora was sick. Sick of the problems. Sick of the bills. Sick of trying to find answers she didn't have. "I told you. I'm tired. I'm going to go to my room."

"Nora, your children—"

"Will be fine with their grandmother and won't even notice I'm not there to watch the movie. I'll come back when it's time to put them to bed." Nora turned to leave the kitchen. She could hear the strains of a Disney song coming from the other room and the ebb and flow of Jake's excited chatter as he gave Sarah a play-by-play of a movie they'd seen a hundred times.

Before Nora could escape, Ma grabbed her arm. "Something is not right with you."

"I'm fine, Ma. Just…fine." Nora even threw in a smile for good measure.

Ma pursed her lips and then shook her head. "All right, then. If you insist. Go ahead and go to bed early."

Nora headed down the hall to the bedroom she'd grown up in. The walls were still painted a pale pink, the twin bed on the far right covered with a newer version of the white comforter Nora had as a girl, and the same braided rug sat in the center of the room, an imaginary lake between her bed and Magpie's when they were kids.

Nora threw on an old T-shirt and climbed under the covers. Exhaustion weighed down her arms, her legs, and her chest, like a heavy woolen blanket, begging her to succumb, to just…let go. Sleep for a week, a month, until the kids turned eighteen. The best she could manage right now was a catnap before she had to put the kids to bed. Or answer Ben's voice mails and texts.

Before she could doze off, her phone vibrated, and Magpie's face lit up the screen. Her closest sister, the one who knew Nora best and the person Nora missed most. Over the years, she'd gotten used to Magpie's infrequent visits and calls, but a part of her longed for the days when they had shared this very room and stayed up long into the night, whispering secrets and dreams. "Hey, stranger," Nora said when she answered. "Where are you now?"

Her youngest sister laughed. Magpie—no one called her Margaret, not since the day she'd started to talk, chattering like the namesake bird—traveled the world writing for magazines. She was the only one of the O'Bannon girls to eschew working at the bakery. She jetted from country to country, unencumbered by a man, a family, or a mortgage. There were days when Nora seriously envied Magpie's life.

"Actually, I'm on my way back to Massachusetts for a quick vacation. I was thinking maybe we should spend some time together. Now, before you say no, hear me out. A friend gave me the keys to one hell of a nice beach cottage up in Truro. Right on the beach, isolated from the tourists, and even though it's fall and likely to be a bit cold, the Cape is still gorgeous. I have a rare week off, and I was hoping I could convince you to come up and stay with me. Just for one night, if you can't get more time off. And if you want to bring the kids—"

"Yes."

"I know it's hard, because you're so busy with the kids and work and—" Magpie stopped. "Wait, did you just say yes?"

"I'd love to get away to the Cape for a few days." Sarah had four days of suspension coming her way. Nora could pull Jake out for those days—he wasn't exactly missing rocket science in kindergarten—and finally take all those vacation days she'd let stack up. It would give her time to think, to regroup, without her mother breathing down her neck.

And without Ben a few minutes away. Far too easy to call. Far too easy to foolishly rely on again.

"When can you be here?" Magpie asked. "I get in tonight, and I was going to go up there and air out the house, zip over to the grocery store, that kind of thing."

"I can be there tomorrow," Nora said. "Me and the kids, if that's okay."

"That's awesome, Nora. Really, really awesome. Maybe we can get Bridge and Abby to come down on the weekend, if the bakery isn't too busy. Have a barbecue or something."

Nora laughed. "Are you getting domesticated, Magpie?"

"I wouldn't go that far." Her sister paused. In the background, the Charlie Brown teacher voices of a busy airport droned. "But I am thinking about...and don't tell Ma this...but I am thinking about maybe staying put for a little while. Actually living in that apartment I pay an un-godly amount of rent for every month. Seeing you guys more than once a quarter."

"Magpie staying put?" Nora said. Her sister was never one to tie herself very long to one place or one person. The fact that she'd even rented an apartment—really just a holding space for things she bought on her travels—was a miracle. "There's got to be a full moon or something, if both you and Ma are acting out of character."

"Probably so." Magpie laughed. "What's Ma doing different?"

"As we speak, she is letting the kids eat popcorn. On the couch. In the living room."

Magpie let out a low whistle. "I better reread Revelations. I think the world is coming to an end."

Nora laughed and held the phone closer to her ear. Her youngest sister could breathe life and joy into the darkest of days. Spending some time with her would be good, very good. "Magpie, I've missed you."

"Don't go getting all soft and mushy on me now," her sister said, but there was a slight catch in her voice. A second later, she brightened again, all traces of emotion gone. "They're calling my flight. I'll see you tomorrow. And, Nora?"

"Yeah?"

"I've missed you too." Then she said goodbye, and the connection was gone.

Nora lay in her old twin bed, staring at the ceiling and holding on to her phone. The time away was only a few days and yet another way to put off the inevitable, but right now, it felt like a lifeline.

FOUR

The beach house came into view, short and squat and weathered to a soft gray. It was nestled between spindly scrub oak and pine trees and plump green bayberry bushes, with a long sandy path leading to the front door. If Norman Rockwell had painted a beach cottage vacation scene, this would be it. The house had a quaint, welcoming air to it, as if it were saying, *Come, stay with me, and you'll forget all those troubles back in the city.* Nora turned off the car and waited while the engine ticked and cooled. "We're here, kids," she said.

Jake, who had fallen asleep almost as soon as they got out of Dorchester, roused. He lifted his sleepy head and rubbed his eyes. "Can I go swimming, Mommy?"he

Nora chuckled. Her youngest child, who went from zero to sixty in two-point-four seconds, then crashed just as quickly when the fun was over. "After we get unpacked and say hi to your aunt. Okay?"

Jake leaned over and nudged his sister. He bounced in

his booster seat and pointed at the cottage. "Sarah, we're at the beach!"

Sarah elbowed Jake. "I'm not stupid, Jake. I can see that."

Nora bit back her hundredth sigh of the day. "Sarah, be nice to your brother."

"I don't even want to be here. Why did we have to come?" Sarah scowled down at her tablet. She'd had her head buried in that thing for the entire two-hour ride, barely speaking to her brother and not at all to her mother.

Nora sighed. "Because I think we all need a little bit of a break."

"I'm gonna miss the class party." She gave the screen an angry swipe. "And trick-or-treating. And I want to see Daddy."

"We will still celebrate Halloween, I promise." Nora didn't address the question about Ben. This morning, she'd taken the coward's way out and texted him when he was at work to tell him she was taking the kids to the Cape and would let him know when they were settled.

Less than twenty-four hours ago, she'd asked her husband for a divorce. Maybe she should be talking to a lawyer or filing for a separation or something. But the mere thought of all that paperwork and questions and court appearances pressed the air out of Nora's lungs.

She got out of the car, opened the back passenger door, and unbuckled Jake. Then she went around to the back, popped the trunk, and grabbed their bags. Jake bounded out of the car and ran up the stairs with Sarah trudging along behind him, dragging her backpack, the straps snaking a path in the sandy walkway.

Magpie burst through the front door and down the stairs. Her long, dark hair flowed behind her like a veil, as flowy and loose as the maxi dress that swirled around her legs. Magpie was tall and thin, almost willowy, and as unconventional as spaghetti for Easter dinner. "My favorite niece and nephew! Come here, you two!" She bent down and the kids ran into her arms. Sarah's grumpiness disappeared a moment later as she told her aunt about the new kid at school, how far she'd gotten in *Plants vs. Zombies*, and which One Direction singer was her favorite. Jake butted in from time to time with stories about the classroom bunny and the Tooth Fairy's recent visit. "Whoa, whoa. You all have been super busy! Let's get inside and you can tell me all about it over some ice cream. Sound good?"

"Yeah!" Jake punched one arm in the air. "I love ice cream."

"Why don't you two pick out your rooms first," Nora said. She waved the kids up the stairs and into the house. Later, she'd mention the insanity of starting this trip off on a sugar high. For now, she'd take the peace some mint chocolate chip could buy.

As soon as the front screen door banged shut behind Sarah and Jake, Magpie put an arm around her older sister. "Nora, what the hell happened to you? Because, and forgive me for being direct, you look like you got run over by a Mack Truck."

"The usual. Working too much. Sleeping too little."
And lately, from trying to dodge Ma's prying eyes and
questions. Nora had broken the news about her vacation
first thing this morning, which had gone over about as
well as peace negotiations in the Middle East. Ma wanted
to know why her daughter was in such an all-fired hurry to
get out of town, why the kids could afford to take so much
time off from school, and most of all, why Ben wasn't
part of the packing list. Nora had held her ground and
loaded the car, ignoring her mother's disapproving scowl
and complaints about her desertion of the family bakery.
On the way to Truro, Nora had called Abby and Bridget,
who had both told her it was about damned time she took
a few days off.

Yeah, the usual sounded like it about covered the why-
she-looked-like-shit question.

"Let's go inside," Magpie said, taking one of the bags
from Nora's shoulder. "For the adults, I bought a whole lot
of wine. And good chocolate."

Nora laughed. "I'm going to need it." She needed a lot
more than a bottle of pinot grigio, but for now, the thought
of getting totally smashed and passing out sounded like
heaven to Nora. Maybe she could wake up from her wine
coma and all the nasty details of her life would have been
sorted out by some fairies. And maybe a meteor was going
to hit the ground in the next ten minutes too.

The beach house had a slight musty scent but Magpie
had already opened the windows, letting in a gentle cross
breeze and the *shush-shush* of the ocean. The kids had

peeled off toward the bedrooms, and the sounds of a squabble over dibs carried down the hall.

"Don't fight, guys." Nora's voice sounded weary to her own ears. She put the bags on the floor, then sank into a chair. It wasn't just her voice that was weary; it was all of her. She was tired of arguing, tired of fighting, tired of losing. Tired of trying to figure out what to do next.

And most of all, tired of pretending she had it all under control.

Without a word, Magpie took Nora's bags and brought them down to one of the guest rooms. She returned, opened a bottle of white wine, and poured a generous glass. Then she kicked an ottoman over by Nora's chair and plopped down. Magpie held out the glass and waited for Nora to take it. "Here. You need this."

"It's only ten in the morning, Mags."

"It's vacation. Drink."

"You're a bad influence, you know."

Magpie grinned. "That's what you were counting on when you came down here."

Nora noticed Magpie had only brought one glass into the living room. "Aren't you joining me?"

"I'll have some later," Magpie said. "Right now, I just want you to chill out before you make me stressed."

Nora took a long sip of wine. It was a smooth, dry chardonnay with hints of pear. Perfect. She couldn't remember the last time she'd had a glass of wine. Alcohol hadn't been part of her food budget in a long, long time. She took a second sip, a third. "Thanks, Mags. You know me well. It's been a hell of a week, and it's only Tuesday."

"Is it just turning thirty?"

Nora scoffed. "Turning thirty is the *best* thing that happened to me this week. And that's saying something."

"You want to talk about it?"

Nora took another sip of wine. She'd skipped breakfast, and the alcohol was already filling her head with soft fuzzies that tempted her to confide in Magpie, to let her family see inside the mess that had become her life. But Nora had held on to the lie of her perfect marriage and perfect home for so long that she couldn't seem to find a way to let the truth unravel. "It's not a big deal," Nora said while her next sip of wine dimmed the panic whispering behind every thought. "Just a stressful few days."

Magpie studied Nora for a second and then got to her feet and put out a hand. Down the hall, the kids were now arguing over the bed choices. "Come on, Nora, let's go outside."

"But the kids—"

"Will figure it out, just like the four of us did. We all survived the war of who gets to ride shotgun without killing each other, and Sarah and Jake will too." Before Nora could argue, Magpie grabbed her elbow and led her out to the back deck.

The French doors of the beach house opened onto a wide, shaded deck that offered an unobstructed view of the bright blue Atlantic. The neighboring houses were tucked behind trees, just out of view, making it seem as if they were the only people in the world. A sandy path flanked by a wood and wire fence wove through beach grass and down to the water. Gulls cried to each other as they circled over the sand, fighting over whatever scraps littered the edge of the water.

Nora drew in a deep breath of salty air. "It's gorgeous here."

"Isn't it? When Charlie told me about this place and offered to let me stay here, I couldn't say no." Magpie wrapped her arms around herself and leaned against one of the posts. "You know, I've been all over the world, but the Cape is still my favorite place. 'Till, in sheltered coves and reaches of sandy beaches, all have found repose again. Ever drifting, drifting, drifting on the shifting currents of the restless heart.'"

Soft, melancholy tones colored her sister's voice. Nora wondered if maybe she wasn't the only O'Bannon pretending to have it together. "That's beautiful, Mags. What's it from?"

"Longfellow. Thoreau quoted that poem in *Cape Cod*." Magpie sighed. "I do so love it here."

"So...who's Charlie? I've never heard you mention him before."

"No one special. Just a friend." Magpie turned, took Nora's empty glass from her, and set it on the railing. "Let's grab the kids and walk the beach."

A conversational diversion, Nora was sure, because any guy who gave a woman keys to a beach house like this was surely more than no one special.

Nora waited to ask again until the kids were with them and charging down the beach. She and her sister had kicked off their shoes and strode down the cool, soft sand. "He must be one heck of a friend to trust you with this place."

Magpie shrugged. "Charlie knew I needed a vacation, and that was enough reason for him."

Charlie. Nora could count on one hand the number of men Magpie had bothered to mention. "You want to talk about it? About why you, the one who never sits still, need a vacation? I've never known you to take so much as a sick day, Magpie."

Magpie let out a short bark of a laugh. "When has anyone in this family ever wanted to talk about anything important? Besides, I'm fine. Perfectly fine."

"Aren't we all?" Nora let the words drift away until all that was between them was the cry of the gulls and the gentle song of the water.

FIVE

The words refused to come. Magpie stared at her Mac-Book, the screen casting her room with a soft bluish-white glow, and couldn't think of a single thing to write. She'd stared at his email for over an hour, started and stopped writing a reply a hundred times, before settling into inaction. For a woman who had been on the go since the day she got her first pair of Stride Rite sneakers, being still did not come easy.

I want to see you, Charlie had written. *You left without a word. Why?*

Because Charlie was the first man she'd ever dated who wanted more from her than a few nights of distraction. Magpie didn't do commitments, didn't do long-term. The longest tie she'd maintained was a lease on an apartment in Charlestown, and she could count on one hand the number of nights she'd spent there in the last six months.

Magpie closed the laptop lid and set the computer to the side. She swung her legs over the bed and padded barefoot out to the kitchen. She'd left the windows open, and the ocean whispered on the breeze. It was so peaceful here, so quiet. So unlike her usual life.

For years, she'd avoided the quiet. It gave a girl altogether too much time to think. To realize how alone she really was.

Magpie was reaching to get a bowl out of the cabinet when she noticed Nora sitting outside on the top step of the deck. She had her arms around herself, even though she was wearing a thick sweatshirt.

The hunch in Nora's shoulders, the stress in her face, worried Magpie. And scared her. Nora had always been the backbone, the one everyone could depend upon. Right now, Magpie needed that, which was why she'd asked her sister to come. She'd hoped that, after a few days at the cottage, she could draw the strength she needed from Nora to make a decision about her future.

I love you, Charlie had written. *I know that's crazy because we barely know each other, but I love you.*

Another girl might be thrilled to hear those words, to see them in print, but Magpie was not another girl. She loved her freedom, her life of traveling the world. The busyness that filled her every minute. And in her experience, "love" led to unhappy endings, like Bridget's lie-filled marriage to her late husband, like Nora's occasional troubles in paradise, and like—

Like Dad dying a week before Magpie's fifth birthday.

Magpie closed the cabinet door, grabbed a jacket from the hook by the door, and slipped outside. "Hey."

Nora turned. "Hey. What are you doing up?"

"I could ask you the same thing." Magpie shivered against the cold and zipped the jacket shut. The fleece carried the scent of Charlie's cologne, spicy and sharp. For a split second, she missed him and wondered if she'd done the right thing by running instead of staying put. By avoiding instead of answering. "I shared a room with you for almost eighteen years. Every time you had a big test or an important event at school, you'd sit by the window and stare up at the moon."

"And you'd come and sit with me," Nora said.

"Because you looked so lonely there. Like you do now."

Nora sighed. "I just have a lot on my mind, that's all."

Magpie settled on the top step beside Nora and drew her knees to her chest. Her bare feet shone pale and bright in the dark. "You know I'm always here if you want to share."

"Sharing doesn't make the problems go away." Nora tightened her sweatshirt against her chest. It was an old Patriots sweatshirt, oversized, faded, and frayed at the edges. One of Ben's, Magpie was sure, because the fabric dwarfed Nora. Was her sister thinking of her husband just now, missing the feel of him in the bed beside her?

Magpie thought of her own problems, the things she wasn't facing or accepting. The burden she carried, all alone. A burden she had hoped she could share with Nora because the choice she had to make was too big for one person to decide. But right now, she couldn't seem to push the words out of her mouth.

If Magpie ever doubted her DNA, this moment reminded her of one common O'Bannon trait—avoiding all hard topics.

The two sisters sat there for a moment, watching the water swoosh in and out, the moon dancing off the tops of the waves. The breeze had kicked up a little, riffling across the beach grass and up the steps. Neither said anything, but that was okay. If Nora wanted to talk, she would, but more often than not, Nora would be the one to pull herself together and get the job done, regardless of what was happening in her life. She'd been back at work ten days after she had Sarah, a week after she had Jake. She'd come in every time someone got the flu, stayed late for every rush job. So whatever was bothering Nora was surely a temporary ripple. If any of them had it together, it was Nora.

Magpie envied that. She had always felt like she was in a vast ocean, scrambling from float to float, none of them sturdy enough to reach dry land. But Nora had it all—a husband, kids, a house. Maybe she had some stress about things lately, but overall, she lived on the kind of solid foundation Magpie had never found. Never really wanted. She wasn't built for that kind of thing, not like Nora was. She was the flighty one, the one who didn't commit, didn't settle down, didn't make long-range plans.

"Don't worry about me, Mags." Nora let out a long breath. "We have a lot of bills and not enough money. It's the American dream, right? So Ben and I have been arguing a little more than normal."

"Well, that's to be expected. I mean, you have credit cards and a mortgage. I'm sure kids add pressure too."

"Yeah." Nora took another sip. "Anyway, I'm sure it'll all be fine. These few days away are exactly what I needed. A little R and R."

Magpie sensed Nora was holding something back, painting over the truth with a dirty brush. Her sister's reticence grated on Magpie. Their relationship had always been so one-sided, with Nora serving as a de facto mother when their own mother checked out, an overwhelmed widow with too many kids and not enough hours. Magpie, younger than Nora by four years, was only four when their father died. Even now, at twenty-six, they treated Magpie like a china doll, too fragile to handle any real weight. "You know you can talk to me, right? I mean, about anything. You don't always have to be the strong, independent one."

"I'm fine. Really. Just...tired."

Magpie reached out and took Nora's hand, giving her fingers a squeeze. Two decades ago, Nora had been the one doing that for her little sister. When Magpie got scared at the movies, or when she was hesitant to cross the road, Nora's hand and steady voice were always there. *I believe in you*, Nora used to say. *You can do it.* Even now, whenever Magpie traveled somewhere far and unsettled, she'd call Nora, just to get that little extra boost of confidence. It was why she had invited Nora here. Because if there was ever a time when Magpie needed to hear those words, it was now.

She wished she could turn around and do the same for Nora, but the truth was, even if Nora did decide she needed someone to lean on, Magpie's life was a bit of a disaster right now, and she was the last person who should be offering advice or support. "Do you need anything?"

Nora's eyes glistened with tears, and her smile wobbled. "My sister."

Magpie drew Nora into a hug. That she could do, and do well. Later, there'd be time to talk about her own mess. For now, she could hold Nora's hand. "You got it."

SIX

The girl was better than she'd expected. Colleen O'Bannon had had her doubts when Roger sent Iris to work at the bakery, but Colleen could see glimmers of talent—when the girl stopped doubting herself and actually took a chance. Bridget had done her best to encourage Iris along, but with Nora out, most of the workload in the bakery had fallen to Bridget and Abby, leaving them little time to do more than bark orders. Iris shied away from the harsh, hurried words like a leery stray cat.

Iris came in through the back entrance, so quiet Colleen would have missed her except for the click of the door. The girl—dressed all in black again with her eyes rimmed like a raccoon's—hung her ebony sweatshirt on the hook by the door and slipped an apron over her head. Without a word, she started loading the dishwasher with the dirty pans from Abby's earlier bread baking.

Colleen marched over to Iris and shut off the water. "You and I are going to work together today."

Iris blinked. "Uh...okay."

"You could be doing a much better job than you are."

"I'm sorry, Mrs. O'Bannon. I'll try harder, I promise." Iris stepped back, seeming to shrink into herself.

"And we will start with that." Colleen waved a hand over Iris's too-thin frame. Good Lord, the girl looked like she'd barely eaten in a year. Tomorrow, Colleen was going to start bringing extra leftovers for lunch and make sure Iris had some meat and potatoes. Michael, God rest his soul, might have died two decades ago, but Colleen still cooked like she had a family of six at home. This skinny girl could use a bowl or two of a hearty potato soup. Some starch for her body and a little starch for her spine too. "You are working at the O'Bannon family bakery. Which makes you an honorary O'Bannon. And all the O'Bannon girls are strong and confident."

"But you just said I was screwing up—"

"I said no such thing. I said you could be doing a much better job than you are. That doesn't mean anything other than what it says." Colleen slid an apron over her head and knotted it in the back. She'd spent too much of her days taking orders, calling suppliers, and meeting with customers, instead of here, in the kitchen she loved. "Now, first thing we are going to do is decorate the wedding cake on the counter."

Iris backed up a little. "Wait. Me? I don't know how to decorate."

"I have seen you doodling on that pad of paper of yours when you're on break. That takes artistic skill. I suspect you can apply the same to a piping bag." Colleen marched over to the cake and slid the tub of white buttercream frosting across the counter to Iris. "First thing we are going to do is the crumb coating, which is a thin layer of frosting that sets for a bit in the refrigerator before we start decorating."

"Why do you do that?"

"It gives the decorative coat of frosting a solid base to work from. Also gives the cake itself a little strength. It's amazing how a simple mix of butter and sugar can turn something soft into something much firmer," Colleen said. "Now, you take that long, flat knife, scoop up some buttercream, and smooth it over the outside, like this."

Colleen picked up a second offset spatula, scooped out some buttercream, and slid it over the top of the cake and then down the side. "You rotate the cake as you do the sides, so you get a smooth, even coat. The base coat is the foundation of everything this cake will become. That's why it's so important to get it right."

Much like the daughters she'd raised, soft and tender at first. Then, as the layers of life—the joys, the tragedies, the challenges—filled them, they'd grown stronger. Into young women Colleen was secretly very, very proud of.

She glanced over at the young girl beside her. Definitely still rough around the edges. It made Colleen wonder about her family. Did she have a mother who cared? A mother who made sure she had a jacket on cold winter days and a warm meal in her belly before bed? Colleen hadn't asked much about Iris's family. It hadn't occurred to her to care about anything other than the girl's work habits. But now, standing beside this too-thin, too-quiet girl, she did care.

Colleen nudged Iris's arm. "Go on. That cake isn't going to frost itself."

"Um, okay." Iris mimicked Colleen's movements, but as she spun the turntable, the spatula gouged the cake and sent a chunk tumbling to the counter. "Oh, God. I'm so sorry, Mrs. O'Bannon. I'll make another one."

The foolish girl was shrinking again, as if she thought Colleen was going to do something silly like hit her. Colleen put a hand over Iris's, preventing the girl from backing up any more. What had happened to this girl that made her draw into herself like a gopher disappearing into his hole? "You'll do no such thing. Crumbs happen, and all we do is cover them up." Colleen slid the spatula across the outside of the cake, and in an instant, the gouge was gone and the side was smooth again. "Now you try. Go slow. Better to take your time now than to have regrets later."

Iris tried again, her moves more cautious. She turned the cake, sliding the spatula along the edges and then swooping the frosting up and over the top. A second spin, smoothing the edges. Then another time across the top before she stepped back. "How's that?"

There were a few lines in the crumb coating, a couple of places where the layer wasn't consistently even. With her girls, Colleen would have criticized and made them do it again until the cake was perfect. As they'd grown up, her daughters had become amazing bakers and artisans,

but that criticism had nearly cost her the close relation-
ships she held dear. Perhaps it was time to soften a bit,
to leave some room for errors. Some dents in the cake,
smoothed with the frosting of understanding, or some
other such silly metaphor. Goodness, maybe she was just
getting old if she was waxing poetic like this. "It's perfect,
Iris. Just perfect. Now let's store it in the cooler and start
the next one."

A smile bloomed across the young girl's face. The first
genuine smile Colleen had seen on Iris since she started
working here. The kind of smile that took root in her
cheeks, her eyes. The kind of smile filled with a sense of
wonder and pride.

"Thank you, Mrs. O'Bannon," Iris said, her voice soft.
As she turned away to store the cake, the smile lingered,
and if Colleen wasn't mistaken, it seemed that Iris was
walking a little taller.

Nora laced her shoes and did a quick toe touch stretch.
It had been at least two years since she had gone for a
run, and even then she'd only been doing short distances.
Before Sarah was born, Nora used to run six miles every
morning before she went into the bakery. The runs cleared
her head and helped erase some of the calories she consumed at work. Then her life had become cluttered with
late-night feedings and early-morning bakery days, and
running had taken a backseat.

Back in the old, prekid days, Ben had often joined
Nora on her runs. They'd have long conversations about

things that seemed so deep at the time—endangered animals, global warming, rising tensions in the Middle East. Now Ben ran alone, and Nora...

Well, she did everything but take care of her own needs. The running shoes she'd randomly grabbed from the closet when she'd packed were hardly used, still stiff and slow to yield when she walked out the door. Pretty much the same as Nora's legs, already twinging at the thought of putting one foot in front of the other.

The sun was just cresting the Atlantic, casting the house in a soft gold color. The long, winding road to the beach house was quiet, most of the houses vacant. It was the kind of neighborhood with price tags that spelled second home, which meant the neighborhood was all but dead during the week.

She started out with a slow jog, easing into the rhythm, the pace. Her legs protested, little nagging aches and pains trying to urge her to head back to the couch. But she kept moving, and as she rounded a bend, she found her stride again, and her legs picked up speed.

Her feet hit the ground, *slap, slap, slap* against the pavement, her thoughts staccatoing at the same pace.

Ben's smile, just before he kissed her on their wedding day. The way they'd laughed on the way out of the church, dumb and in love.

Decorating the Christmas tree and lying underneath it with the kids—Sarah only four, Jake a newborn—their family of four cast in sparkling light. When all seemed hopeful and perfect.

Waking up at two in the morning to find the bed empty and cold. Again. The suspicions that had chilled her spine.

Finding the credit card statement, filled with cash advances at the casino, pushing even the minimum payment over what they could afford. The shock that broke her.

Running out to the cold. Tears freezing on her cheeks. Crumpling to the bench, overwhelmed by a sense of loss so big, it almost drowned her that day.

The fights with Ben. The promises, the hope, and then the devastation when it happened again. And again. Until Nora stopped hoping and Ben stopped talking.

And then the auction notice, hanging on the door of the house they'd celebrated buying nine years earlier with an apple juice toast because Nora had been two months pregnant with Sarah at the time.

All of it gone. Just...gone.

Faster, faster, she pounded the pavement, until her breath was coming in short jerks and her calves burned. Another hundred yards, another, and finally the exertion broke that wall of stress in her chest, and endorphins rushed in to fill the space. Nora bent over, heaving in deep gulps of air, while her heart thudded in her chest and sweat beaded on her brow.

And for the first time in months, her mind finally went blissfully and sweetly blank. One brief millisecond of peace. She wanted to catch that moment and stuff it in a bottle, save it for the dreaded days and moments ahead.

"Here." A bottle of water, attached to a male hand, appeared in her line of vision.

Nora jerked into a standing position. A man stood in front of her wearing paint-speckled jeans and a loose-fitting, wrinkled pale blue dress shirt. His feet were bare, and he had a short beard that was a shade lighter than his dark brown hair. He was about her age, handsome in that careless, rolled-out-of-bed way.

"Don't worry. I'm not a crazy stranger, and it's not poisoned." He grinned. "Bottled right here in Massachusetts."

"Thanks," she said, taking the water from him. She uncapped it and guzzled half.

"I saw you running. The way you were attacking that road, it looked like you were running from something. Last I checked, there weren't any bears or wolves here, just so you know. And the sharks tend to stay in the water."

She smiled at the jokes, her breath still coming in heaves. "Just...working off some stress."

"You should try painting," he said. "It's better than any antidepressant out there."

She glanced at his jeans, mottled with a rainbow of paint dots. "I take it you do that?"

He thrust out his hand. "Will Gibson. Artist in residence, which really just means I'm the only one crazy enough to stay here for the winter."

She shook with him, his grip warm and sure and...nice. She let go and thumbed toward the beach house. "Nora O'Bannon. I'm just here for a few days, staying with my sister at her friend's house. I think she said his name is Charlie?"

"I know him well." Will grinned. "Charlie's house is

great. I've been over there before. And you came at the right time of year, after the tourists are gone."

She smiled. "It is quiet and peaceful here. Such a change from Dorchester."

"I grew up in Mattapan, so I know what you mean." Will shoved his hands in his pockets and rocked back on his heels. "Hey, I'm having a barbecue tonight. Just a few of the neighborhood diehards, if you and your sister want to come by. Make a few friends for the next time you're here."

"Oh, I don't think…"

"Come on, it'll be fun. Besides, you probably burned a thousand calories on that run and could eat all the burgers you want." He gave her a grin, and she found herself wondering how sweaty she looked. If her hair was a disaster. If her inside emotional mess showed on the outside.

Nora shook her head again. "My kids—"

"Bring them. My friend John has three, and my sister, who lives down the road, has two. It's a kid-friendly barbecue and did I mention fun?"

Fun. She couldn't remember the last time she'd had any of that. Still, she should probably stay home and crunch some numbers or go through the classifieds to find an apartment. Instead of putting all that off. Again. "I'll think about it."

Will reached in his back pocket, pulled out his wallet, and extracted a business card. "Here's my cell. I just live over there"—he pointed to a periwinkle cottage on the corner—"but feel free to call me if you want some sandcastle-building tips."

She laughed. "Is that also part of your job?"

"That and greeting all the beautiful women in our neighborhood."

Beautiful women? Surely he didn't mean her. She was a sweaty mess, with a slight belly from two kids and a butt that hadn't seen a squat in years. The same shyness that had persisted in her high school years returned. It was Tommy's basement all over again, and Nora's nerves made her words stumble and her cheeks heat. "Uh...thank you."

He flashed her another grin. "See you tonight. Around six. And don't worry about bringing anything. We have more than enough food to feed the entire town."

He turned to go. Nora stood there, in the middle of the street, stunned and confused. Had he just asked her out? Was it a date if they were in a group? And what about that flirting? The last person she'd flirted with had been Ben, and that was at least twelve years in the past. She should call after Will, tell him she was still married, say she couldn't make the party. Instead, she said, "Thanks for the water!"

He turned, gave her a wave and a grin, and headed into his house. Nora stayed there a moment longer, feeling a strange mix of guilt and elation, and then jogged back to the beach house and all the responsibilities she'd been avoiding, the business card tucked in her sports bra.

SEVEN

Going to the barbecue only intensified the basement party déjà vu. She'd been out of the dating game for so long—not that she'd ever really played to begin with— that Will's clear interest when he smiled at her from across the yard left her disjointed and confused.

Nora stood to the side of Will's house, nursing a soda in a red Solo cup while the kids played in the yard. Jake had blended in with his new friends as seamlessly as pouring water into a pitcher, but Sarah lingered on the sidelines, talking to John's daughter, who was a year or two older. Their dark heads were pressed close together as they whispered about whatever secrets third- and fourth-graders held.

Magpie hadn't arrived yet. She'd told Nora she had a headache and needed to lie down for a moment. Her sister had looked pale, a little tired, and as much as Nora wanted a wingman to keep her nerves at bay, Nora had gotten her little sister a cool washcloth and a box of crackers and then headed down to Will's with the kids, promising to be home early. She wouldn't have gone at all, but Magpie had insisted.

That's what she got for telling her sister about meeting Will. "You should go," Magpie had said. "Have a few beers and some conversation that doesn't revolve around pie crusts and potty training."

In the end, it had been the kids who'd made the decision for her. Sarah had looked out the window, seen the other girl arrive at the house across the street, and for the first time since she'd arrived at the beach house, expressed interest in something other than her iPad. Maybe a night out would help erase Sarah's distance and bring back the cheerful eight-year-old Nora missed so much.

Will strode over to her, a beer in one hand. He had on a fresh pair of jeans and a dark gray Grateful Dead T-shirt. His hair was a little long and shaggy, and with the beard, he had that air of rock band guitarist about him. "I have to admit, I wasn't sure you'd come."

"Neither was I." Because if he was flirting and if this was some version of a date, then Nora was playing with fire.

Will leaned against the house beside her. Not close enough to touch, but close enough for her to be aware of him. It felt wrong, but intoxicating at the same time. "Then why did you?"

"I don't know." It was the first honest thing she'd said in a while. She was still married. Flirting with another man was wrong. Go-straight-to-hell wrong. She could almost hear the admonishments of Father McBride, the lecture after confession, his disappointment clear in the tense air of the tight wooden booth with the dark mesh screen separating her from the priest.

She could just imagine her mother's pursed face, the judgment in her eyes. Ma had never remarried after her husband died, because she took the married-for-life part of her vows pretty damned seriously. Nora wondered if her mother had ever had moments of doubt, moments when she felt like she was married to a stranger, moments when she wanted to walk away. When the man who had pledged to be by her side forever abandoned her for a roulette wheel on the darkest day of her life.

"You're overthinking it," Will said. He pressed a finger to her forehead for a second. "I can tell by that little wrinkle in your brow."

Damn. He'd touched her. A momentary contact, but still, it sent her thoughts into that same *What-am-I-doing?* spiral. "I overthink everything."

He chuckled. "And I tend to not think at all before I leap. Maybe it's the artist in me."

Nora traced the condensation on her cup. "What's that like? Not agonizing over every little decision?"

"Well, considering I've never been the agonizing type, I'm not sure my answer will help you. But I can tell you that I don't worry about the small stuff, and I don't have a bunch of medications lined up in my cabinet."

"And you have the painting antidepressant."

He grinned. "Works like a charm, every time. As soon as I put brush to canvas, my mind sinks into the colors, the shapes, the slight whoosh as the paint glides across the surface. I forget to eat; I forget to pay the bills; I forget the world exists outside my studio. Which is both good and bad."

Nora knew that feeling well. How often had she used the work escape hatch from life? "I get that. I work in my family's bakery with my sisters and my mother. I'm the head decorator, and when I'm decorating a really elaborate cake, an earthquake could open up beneath me and I wouldn't notice. I get completely wrapped up in my work."

"So you're an artist too."

"I don't know if I'm an artist." She shrugged, but inside she warmed at the compliment. "It's just frosting."

"Ah, but I would wager that your 'just frosting' creates elaborate flowers and lace patterns and intricate swirls. That's art, dear Nora the Neighbor, in one of its most natural forms."

The pet name had notes of endearment in it. Already, Will was too familiar, too close, too attractive.

"I'm married." The words just blurted out of her, popping into the air like two overinflated balloons. "I'm sorry... I just thought you should know that."

He studied her, a half-smile tugging on his lips. "Are you married-married, Nora the Neighbor, or just sorta married?"

She wasn't sure. She'd asked Ben for a divorce but had not filed. They weren't together right now, but they weren't technically apart either. She was enjoying this stranger's attention, maybe too much, but feeling guilty about even standing here. "What's the difference?"

"Married-married means you're with the love of your life, the man who fills every nook and cranny in your heart. Sorta married means you're hanging in there, hoping it's going to get better but knowing deep down inside that you're going to leave someday." He paused, took a sip of beer, and eyed her over the rim of the cup. "Maybe someday soon."

Once upon a time, she'd thought Ben was the love of her life. His smile, his touch, had filled every part of her. Now she was holding on to that history by threads woven out of lies and mistakes. "It's . . . complicated."

"Ah, the ambiguous blend of the two." Will tossed his empty cup into a nearby trash can, laced his hands behind his back, and looked out at the yard. "Let me see if I can put it together. He used to be the love of your life but things have been rocky lately, and you're on the fence about what you want."

"Is it that obvious?" Was it disloyal to admit her marriage was on the rocks? Not to mention to admit that to another man?

"I get it. I went through a tough divorce myself a few years ago. And in case you were worried, all I really wanted was to invite you to my barbecue. It's not a date, Nora. Just one neighbor having dinner with a bunch of other neighbors."

"Good. Because I shouldn't . . . It's just all up in the air right now." And either way, the last thing Nora needed in her life was one more person wanting anything from her. She couldn't figure out where she was going to live or how she was going to break any of this news to the kids. If anything spelled wrong timing to think about another man, that did.

Plus, she did still love Ben, in a way. And they weren't divorced and . . .

It was complicated. Complicated as hell.

Will held her gaze for a long time. He had nice eyes. Soft, kind, warm. "I know I don't know you that well yet, but if you ask me, any man who lets a woman like you get away is a fool."

She didn't know what to say to that. She sipped her beer and avoided speaking.

Then he pushed off from the house and gave her the friendly *I'm just a neighbor* grin. "Tell me, Nora . . . how do you take your burger?"

EIGHT

Thursday morning dawned dark and gloomy. A storm was moving in, and the wind started to kick up, catching the sand and peppering it against the glass. The kids were still sleeping, so Nora shrugged into sweatpants and a sweatshirt, pulled her hair into a ponytail, and poured herself a cup of coffee before she stepped out onto the back deck.

The wind whipped around her, nipping at her legs, chasing under her sleeves. Angry waves rolled through the ocean, crashing into each other in great foamy white explosions. Rain started to fall, coming at an angle with the wind, hitting the deck with a hard, fast patter. The droplets spattered Nora's bare toes, the edges of her sweatpants.

She'd barely slept last night, dealing with a different storm, this one inside her head. The guilt over going to the barbecue when she should have been focused on finding a way out of this mess. Regret that she had let them end up in this situation in the first place, thinking she could juggle the bills and the creditors and somehow turn negatives into positive numbers. Guilt over how she had failed—her family, her children, herself. And most of all, a flood of deepening, impotent frustration.

Maybe if Nora had been honest that day with Ben, none of them would be here. Maybe he would have stayed home and everything would have been different. Maybe she would have been standing at a barbecue with his soft brown eyes staring into hers, instead of a stranger's. And maybe she wouldn't be thinking right now how easy it would be to start over again with another man, instead of trying to fix the mess with the man who had let her down one too many times.

Magpie came outside, bundled in a rain jacket, her hands cupped around a mug. A bolt of lightning cracked overhead, and Magpie flinched. "Trying to get yourself electrocuted?"

"I've always loved storms. They're just so...unexpected."

"And dangerous and unpredictable. Everything you aren't, right?" Her little sister laughed.

"Maybe it's everything I wish I had been," Nora said softly. A woman who was dangerous and unpredictable would have flirted back last night instead of taking her burger to go and heading home thirty minutes after she'd arrived. A woman who was like a storm wouldn't have let her home slip away. She would have moved heaven and earth until the bank came back with a workable solution. A woman like that wouldn't have been caught unawares by her husband's gambling and the shambles her marriage had become, and she sure as hell wouldn't have painted a pretty picture over the ugly truth.

Nora took a sip of coffee and watched a forgotten beach ball tumble down the shoreline, the bright colors rolling over each other like a runaway rainbow. "Did you ever wonder what might have been if you took a different path?"

"You know me, I don't second-guess anything. I just dive in and save my regrets for retirement."

Nora couldn't even imagine living like that. But Magpie had none of the ropes that tied Nora to that whirling circle of worries and decisions. A house, a husband, kids. Responsibilities—like keeping children clothed, warm, and fed, not to mention teaching them to be considerate people—loomed over Nora every minute of the day. Even here, standing on the deck while the storm raged around her, a part of her mind worried about Sarah and Jake. Were they awake now? Scared by the noise? Would they be disappointed to have their beach day canceled? Was she giving them too little of her time? Of her heart? Would they one day grow up and look at her with anger and disappointment in their eyes? *How could you let us lose our house, Mom?*

"Are you wishing you had a do-over?" her sister asked.

"No, no, of course not." Nora took one last look at the storm and then turned back to the house. She pulled open the thick glass deck door. "My life is what it is. I wouldn't change any of it."

Except that was another lie. The dishonesty was stacking up like bricks between her and Magpie. Nora hated that, but she'd always protected her baby sister. Magpie had enough to worry about, and besides, how could she possibly understand the stress of being a wife, a parent, and a soon-to-be-ex-homeowner?

Nora had kept so many secrets so close to her chest for so long, she wasn't even sure where to begin. Lies she'd told her family. Her husband. Herself. Better to not burden Magpie with things that were beyond her control. It was a vacation, and Nora was determined to keep it that way for the kids and for her sister.

They went inside. Nora poured a second cup of coffee, and Magpie hung up her jacket. Then she curled into one of the kitchen chairs, her knees up to her chest. "I know you say everything's fine, but it might not hurt to step out of your comfort zone a little."

"I step out of my comfort zone once in a while. I did it when I went to that barbecue at a perfect stranger's house. And there was that time I quit working at the bakery, in solidarity with Bridget." Nora sprinkled some sugar into her coffee, added a dash of cream. She watched the white liquid swirl into the dark brew and felt a little pang of regret that she'd left Bridget, Abby, and Ma in charge of the bakery. None of the cake orders required complicated decorating jobs, but still, she should have been there. Maybe she should go back early—

Except that meant dealing with that whole where-to-live question sooner. In this little beach house, she had a reprieve from all that. She could pretend her life wasn't totally screwed up and that she didn't feel a constant panic in her chest.

"Those are great things but not exactly life-changing. I love you, Nora, but you've always been so...uptight," Magpie said. "Such a stickler for the rules. Even here, you get up at the same time, go to bed at the same time. The kids have the same routine every night—"

"Schedules are good for kids. It helps them know their world is predictable." Except being homeless negated all of that predictability. Her world was about to turn upside down, and everything her children had known all their lives would be ripped away.

"For as long as I've known you, you've run every part of your life by a watch. Maybe it's time you did something else. Like throw your watch into the ocean—well, not really, because it isn't good for the fish—but symbolically. You are on vacation, after all." Magpie leaned forward, her eyes bright with mischief. It was a look Nora knew well because it usually meant Magpie was going to propose something Nora wasn't going to like. "Why not take a vacation from your worries too?"

"What is this, a Bill Murray movie? I can't do that, Mags. I have kids. I can't just abandon all my responsibilities." And because all a vacation from her worries did was put off decisions that had to be made. She'd done that when she'd gone to the barbecue, and all it had done was give her a sleepless night and a mountain of guilt. She needed to get back on track, needed to find a solution. Ben sure as hell wasn't going to do it, which put all the responsibility of finding four affordable walls in Nora's hands.

"You can abandon all that while I'm here," her sister said. "I'm fully capable of feeding my niece and nephew and getting them to bed on time."

Nora snorted. "You. Temporary mom."

Magpie dropped her gaze and whisked a forgotten crumb off the table. "I may not look or act it, but I'm more domesticated than you think."

"I'm sure you are, but, sweetie, cooking dinner? I love you, but seriously, you could ruin a bowl of cereal." Of the four girls, Magpie had been the only one who never wanted a baby doll or played with Barbies. She didn't set up house or pretend to make dinner in the cardboard boxes the girls had fashioned into a fake kitchen. Magpie had been the one exploring creeks and climbing trees and writing in her journal. No one had been surprised she grew up and wanted nothing to do with the bakery.

"Okay, so I can't cook," Magpie said. "That particular gene seems to have skipped me. But I am fabulous at ordering takeout and being the cool aunt who lets them watch *Frozen* six hundred and seventy-two times. Which means you can go vacate."

There was a reason Nora had twenty-two vacation days saved up. The best time to take a few days off never seemed to coincide with the kids' or Ben's schedules. When spring break rolled around, the bakery was overrun with orders for Easter and spring baptisms and weddings. When summer break came, she was knee deep in family reunions, corporate picnics, and meetings with fall brides. The thought of a day without a schedule, without a plan, nearly made her hyperventilate. Magpie was right, though. Even here, on "vacation," Nora had kept to a schedule with bedtimes and reading time and meals. "It's been so long since I had a day with nothing to do that I don't know what I'd do," Nora said. "As it is, I'm already itching to get back to work. I shouldn't have left the bakery shorthanded. There's the Collins wedding and—"

"Nora, you have been more responsible for that bakery than all of us combined. You've given most of your life to that place." Outside, the storm began to pick up, winds hitting the flagpole next door and making the cable clang. "I think it's about damned time you took a few days for yourself."

She'd heard the same lecture from her other sisters, usually on a monthly basis. Nora couldn't remember a time when she hadn't worked at the bakery, a time when she had thought about nothing but herself. Once she became a mother, thinking of herself first was impossible. Every decision she made, every thought in her head, every free hour on the calendar, circled around the kids. "That's pretty much what Bridget and Abby said."

"There, it's official. You're outvoted." Magpie grinned. "So go into town today, and leave the kids here with cool Aunt Magpie. Treat yourself to a big breakfast, a new dress, or just go shopping for shit you don't need. I don't care if you curl up in the library with a book. Just get out of here and do something *just for Nora*. If you come back with a gift for me or anyone else, I'm confiscating it. Got it?"

Nora laughed and shook her head. Magpie knew her well. Chances were good without that warning that Nora would have found some trinket for the kids or a thank-you gift for her sister. "I haven't done anything like that..."

"Ever. Even when we were kids, you were the most responsible one. Who made sure my shoes were tied and I had lunch money? Who never forgot me at school and even now, when I'm a grown woman, checks to make sure I arrived safely?"

She shrugged. "That's just being a sister."

"No, honey, it's more than that. It's being *everyone's* mom." Rain pelted the windows, and the darkening clouds cast the house with a dim light. "I agree, Ma could have been more involved, but she was juggling the bakery and raising four kids on her own. But that didn't mean you had to do it."

"When Dad was gone, someone had to help her," Nora said. Bridget had been busy with school, Abby devastated by the loss of their father, and Magpie too little to understand. Nora had stepped in, using the vacuum and the dust rag to avoid her own grief.

Magpie put a hand on Nora's arm. "I don't think you've had a single moment of your life where you were selfish. Hell, you've never even taken a spa day. But you did give all of us one for Christmas last year."

Nora started to protest, but instead shut her mouth. Her mind reached back, and in her memories she saw herself, on the sidelines, the one who made the dinner or did the dishes or sewed the costume while everyone else lived their lives, went on their adventures. She'd filled in for her sisters' sick days and vacation days, come in early to do extra prep, stayed late on busy days. In the in-between time, she'd been room mom and served on the PTA, sold the Girl Scout cookies, and hosted the play dates.

She'd done everything for everyone else, telling herself it was because it was easier. And where had it left her? Was it selfish to pretend, at least for today, that she didn't have a family? To abdicate the breakfast and bath time battles to someone else? She'd have a taste of what it would be like to be on her own, doing things entirely for herself without worry about other people, because she'd gone straight from mothering her sisters to being Ben's wife.

Magpie dug in her pocket and pulled out a few bills. She pressed them into Nora's hand. "Now don't say a word about not taking money from me. You have taken care of me all my life. You've put me up in your house when I needed a place to stay, you've fed me when I was hungry, and you've nursed me through the flu twice. I can't do any of those things, but I can watch your kids for a day and order you to treat yourself to a pedicure."

"Mags, I can pay for my own pedicure." Nora tried to push the money back, but Magpie just put her hands behind her back and shook her head.

"You can, but if I know you, you won't. You'd use the last dime of your allowance to buy a teddy bear just because you wanted to put a smile on your sister's face."

Magpie's eyes shimmered, and the shared memory flowed between them. Nora remembered finding Mags crying in their room about a month after their father had died, inconsolable because he was going to miss her first day of kindergarten. He'd told his youngest daughter many times that he would be there. He'd take the day off from work and walk his little girl into school, just as he had all the others. Nora had shaken the few bills and change out of her piggy bank, dashed down to O'Donnell's Sundries, and bought a teddy bear from Mr. O'Donnell. Years later, she was sure the kindly man had charged her far less than the sticker price, but at eight years old, all Nora knew was that the stuffed animal Magpie had noticed a few days earlier was the one thing that would ease her tears. In her first-day-of-school picture—taken by Ma, who had filled in for their late father—Magpie held the dark brown bear to her chest, beaming. "You left that bear outside my door and told me that the fairies had brought it for me from Dad. I carried that little guy everywhere for years."

Nora shrugged. "You needed it, Mags."

"And you need this. So go on, get out of here."

Nora drew her sister into a tight hug. "I hate you for being right."

Magpie laughed. "That's a new one, isn't it? Magpie the wise O'Bannon." She waved at Nora, ushering her down the hall and into the guest bedroom. "Now shoo. Go get changed into something that makes you feel fabulous and head into town. Take my Miata"—she tossed Nora a set of keys—"and live a little."

The little red car zipped along the roads, hugging the curves like a lover. The engine hummed when she was cruising and let out a deep, growling roar whenever she sped up. Nora had never driven anything like the Miata, and although it took a few minutes before she was comfortable behind the wheel, the temptation of a mostly empty Route 6 won, and before she knew it, she was pushing the little car well past the speed limit. The rain had stopped, leaving behind only dark, threatening clouds and brisk winds.

Downtown Truro was anchored by the Highland Light, standing tall and proud in its acclaim as Cape Cod's first ocean beacon. Locals had dubbed it the Cape Cod Lighthouse and gladly recounted its storied history of saving lost travelers and ships caught in storms. In the bedroom where Nora was staying, there was a painting of the same lighthouse, a throwback image to the days when massive wooden ships made the dangerous cross-world journey to bring people and cargo to the fledgling United States.

Truro was the sleepier cousin to bustling Province-town, just a few miles down the road. Unlike some of the more crowded and tourist-centered towns on the Cape, the few shops in Truro were largely converted saltbox houses, quaint and cozy. The businesses blended in so well that it almost seemed like there weren't any.

She parked in front of a little deli and headed inside. She inhaled the scent of freshly brewed coffee, mixed with the sweet aromas of muffins and pastries. The deli bustled with business, people filling almost every table, the hum of their conversations creating an undertow to the alternative rock playing on the sound system.

Nora ordered a coffee and tucked herself into a corner table with a forgotten copy of the *Cape Cod Times*. She skipped past the stories about a hit-and-run crash and another about the dip in tourism dollars, and settled on a lifestyle piece about a couple renewing their vows on a fisherman's trawler and tried not to feel both envy and a certain amount of *you're crazy for getting married* while she read.

"Let me guess. Coffee to offset your vicious single-beer hangover?"

Nora looked up. Will stood before her, wearing a non-paint-spattered pair of jeans that drew her eye along his lean legs and up to his face. She blushed, both at the unexpectedness and the ironic reference by another man to her drinking at parties. If she was the kind of person who believed in signs, she might see one in that comment, so eerily reminiscent of Ben's twelve years ago. "Will. You surprised me."

"I seem to have a habit of doing that." He gestured toward the empty seat across from her. "May I?"

"Sure." She folded the paper and set it aside and grabbed her mug, suddenly unsure of what to do with her hands. For a second, she wished she'd taken more care before leaving today. She'd pulled on jeans, a pale pink T-shirt, and a faded blue hoodie that had *comfortable but frumpy* written all over it.

Will settled into the chair and leaned against the wall so he was half turned toward her. He had on another concert T-shirt—the Stones, in gray today—and she could see red and yellow paint freckling his arms. He took a sip of coffee from a paper mug. "So, what brings you to town on this rainy day?"

"You want the truth?" She leaned forward, lowered her voice. "My sister kicked me out. She said I needed a day on my own, to do whatever I wanted. But... I don't know if I should."

"And what's so wrong with that?"

She glanced out the window, at the gray day and the bustle of traffic going by. People hurrying to destinations, to people they loved, things they had to do. "I haven't had a day to myself in so long, I don't know what I want. I thought I'd just sit here, read the paper, then go home."

"That would be one sad, sad day off, and absolutely not the way anyone should spend their time on the Cape. Ever." He got to his feet and put out his hand. "Come on, let me show you Truro the way I see it."

She cocked her head and studied him but didn't take his hand. "The way you see it?"

"Through an artist's eyes. It's a beautiful place, if you know where to look." He lowered his hand to his side but kept talking, without any hint of disappointment or annoyance that she'd ignored his offer. "First stop, the art gallery, to see everyone else's impressions of the town."

A dangerous and unpredictable woman would go. She would see the adventure and leap on it with both feet. But Nora O'Bannon didn't do unpredictable. Didn't do adventures. "I probably shouldn't..."

"It's not a date, if that's what you're worried about. Think of me as part of the tourism board."

"Just doing a community service?"

"That's it, ma'am." He tipped an imaginary hat her way and extended his arm toward the door. She looked at the café table, the newspaper, the coffee, all those predictable, boring, *sad* remnants of her day off, and then again at the door and the possibilities that lay beyond it. "Come on, Nora the Neighbor. Let's explore this town and find out exactly what you want."

Find out exactly what she wanted. Somehow, it seemed a few hours strolling around a beach town with a handsome stranger was only going to muddy the waters.

NINE

Will knew the town of Truro like he'd been born with the map in his head. As they walked, he gave her a history lesson, one far more interesting than any she'd had in that hot second-floor classroom at St. Gregory's. The cozy town traced its roots as far back as the rest of the coastal Massachusetts towns. "Not many people know this," Will said, "but the Pilgrims landed here first, in November of 1620."

"Really? Is there some famous disappointing rock they stepped on too?" She'd gone on a field trip to Plymouth Rock in the third grade, thinking the landmark would be some giant boulder, a mini-mountain the Pilgrims saw from the sea. It turned out to be an oversized stepping stone that looked like the hundreds of others around it on Plymouth Bay.

Will chuckled. "No. But there was fresh water, which the Pilgrims desperately needed after all that time at sea. They sent out an exploratory group, which found a spring and acres of corn, and they started to think, hey, this might be a great place to live. Except the Pamet Indians already lived here, and they weren't looking for new neighbors. There was a fight, and the Pilgrims decided it would be best to retreat. So they got back on the *Mayflower*, sailed straight across Cape Cod Bay, and ended up in Plymouth."

"I never knew that, and I've lived in Massachusetts all my life."

Will shrugged. "Probably because it's not good for tourism to say 'Hey, this is the place where the Indians told those invading Pilgrims to take a hike.' We all like that happy ending, even if the truth is smudged a bit in the process."

She kicked at a stone in her path. It skittered to the edge of the sidewalk and disappeared down a storm drain. "Or repainted to look happier than it really is."

Will shot her a glance but didn't say anything. Instead, he led her across the street and down a narrow avenue. On the right sat a bright yellow Cape Cod house that had been converted into an art gallery. Dozens of rainbow-colored wind chimes hung from the roof of the porch, partnering with the breeze to sing a soft musical greeting. Metal sculptures peppered the front yard, lined the edges of the driveway, and marched across the roof of the detached one-car garage.

Inside, the house had been opened up, walls removed, ceilings lifted to create an airy, bright space for paintings and sculptures. Will and Nora wandered the space, looking at a hundred different variations of beach scenes—

impressionist, modern, abstract, neon, pastel, watercolor, acrylic. He told her about the artists, most of whom he knew. Which one was a closet drinker; which one had an iguana he took everywhere, claiming it was a service animal; which one had once been featured at the MFA and had a breakdown from the pressure of such fame. "There's a story behind every single one of these paintings."

"Like the cakes we bake." Nora's favorite part about the business—hearing why the customer wanted the cake and what event it would celebrate. They had the regular run-of-the-mill birthday and retirement cakes, but every once in a while, Nora received a memorable order. On those days, she put a little extra effort into the work, as if her heart were part of the filling. "There's the nightmare bride who micromanages every detail, and then there's the baby shower for the couple who tried to have a child for ten years. And the get-well cake for the toddler who beat leukemia or the thank-you cake for the woman who donated thousands of dollars to a scholarship fund for underprivileged kids. Sometimes, it's more fun to take the order and hear the story behind the dessert. Then, when I'm decorating, I feel like that emotion comes through in the design. Or at least, I'd like to think it does."

"I'm sure it does. What we feel in here"—his hand hovered over her heart and her breath caught—"is always translated into here." He drifted his fingers over her hand, a flutter of a touch, but it cracked the strong hold she had on her composure.

She hadn't been touched by a man other than Ben in

more than a decade. Part of her wanted to flinch away—
this is wrong; what about Ben?—but another part of her was
flattered. Curious. Even though Will had said this wasn't a
date, it sure felt like one. The undercurrent of attraction,
the flirty glances and words, the way he brushed against her
every once in a while. She liked him—a lot—and wondered for a second what it would be like to live here, in
this quaint artists' town with a man who added color to his
world.

Instead, she turned and pointed to a painting of a
school of fish and asked some inane question about how
the artist got the paint to look so shiny. All the while, her
heart was beating like a jackhammer, and her mind was
swirling with questions.

What was she doing here? Where did she think this
was going to go?

Nora was the one who followed the straight-and-
narrow path. She'd never broken curfew, never failed a
test, never snuck out to sleep with a boy. She'd done everything that had been expected of her, everything the church
and Ma dictated, staying true to her family, her children,
her husband.

And where had that gotten her? Homeless, almost pen-
niless, and soon to be divorced. She'd done all the right
things ninety-nine percent of her life and ended up with
the wrong result. There were days when she wondered if
this was the price God was making her pay for that winter
morning when she'd exploded at Ben. One day, when she
had lost control and everything fell apart.

Was that what she was doing now? Losing control of herself, her priorities? Or was it just a simple moment of enjoying some attention from a handsome man? If there was a ranking of sins, basking in a little flattery had to be far less bad than kicking her husband out of the house in the middle of January.

Her phone buzzed. "Excuse me," she said to Will. The call gave her an excuse to avoid those thoughts. Bridget's face filled the screen, a happy image of her sister captured on a sunny fall day last year. In the last year and a half, Bridget's old vivacious spirit had returned with every step she took in her new life. The smile in her photos now looked larger, realer than the one in the years before her husband died.

"Hey, sis, just checking to see how the vacation is going," Bridget said.

"Great. The kids are having a blast." Well, Jake was. The jury on the vacation was still out in Sarah's mind.

"And you? I hope you're relaxing."

Relaxing? No. The stress still hung on her shoulders, and now it was compounded by a strange blend of guilt and anticipation. "How are things at the bakery?" Nora asked.

Bridget laughed. "I hear you trying to change the subject. Don't worry about how things are here. Just worry about how things are there. Did you get to do some sightseeing? Shopping?"

"That's what I'm doing right now." Nora forced a bright tone into her voice, slipping back into the place where she felt most comfortable, smack dab between Denial and Deception. "It's been storming off and on here today, so it's a good day to spend inside the shops. The tourists are mostly gone, and it's quiet and peaceful in Truro."

"Good. I'm glad to hear it. That Iris girl, by the way, is working out really well. She picks up quick and seems to really love working here. She's quiet and keeps to herself, but I think she's really liking the job."

"That's great." Nora listened as Bridget went on about the bakery, and then Ma and an update on her complaint of the week—something about the cookies being too small, and then finally segueing into news about Garrett, the man Bridget was dating. But Nora's mind lingered elsewhere, in the shadows of the life she was avoiding. The texts and calls from Ben she hadn't answered. The massive problem of where she and the kids were going to live. Bridget had sold her big house and moved into a cozy rental cottage, so that was out. Ma had enough room, but living with her mother would make Nora homicidal within a week. Abby and Magpie both lived in one-bedroom apartments, too small for three extra residents. Which left finding a rental and a miracle check that would give her first, last, and security. Not to mention enough to pay all the other bills.

"Mags asked me if Abby and I could come to the Cape for dinner on Saturday night," Bridget said. "But we have this big wedding order that came in at the last minute, and we'll be working late that day to finish."

Guilt washed over Nora. "I should come back. You guys shouldn't have to handle that without—"

"We can and will handle it, Nora. You deserve a few days off. Plus, I bet the time away will make that handsome husband of yours miss you like crazy."

She doubted Ben was thinking of her with anything other than annoyance right now. "I'm sure you're right," Nora said. "I can't wait to see him."

It was a wonder God didn't strike her with a bolt of lightning right here in downtown Truro. She glanced over at Will, and her guilt multiplied. He flashed her a quick smile, then went back to admiring a painting of two children playing on the beach, a leaning sandcastle half constructed between them.

"Hey, Nora, I hate to let you go, but I've got a meeting with a bride in a few minutes. Give those kids a hug from their aunt Bridget and be sure to have lots of fun with Magpie!"

"I will. Talk to you later, Bridge." Nora tucked the phone back into her pocket and turned to Will.

"Everything all right?" he asked.

Not even close. But Nora put on her lying smile and said, "Yup, everything's great. It was one of my sisters, calling to see how I was doing."

"How many sisters do you have?"

"Four. I'm the second oldest, and Magpie, the sister I'm here with, is the youngest. We're a big, noisy Catholic family from Boston."

He chuckled. "Nothing clichéd about that."

A hunched woman in her late eighties came in from a room in the back and greeted Will with a warm hug and a kiss on each cheek. The old woman was wearing a bright, multicolored dress that hit at her knees and a floral headband settled into her short, gray curls. Bright pink cat-eye glasses matched her fuchsia lipstick and nails. "William. So good to see you. How's my favorite artist?"

He chuckled. "You say that to everyone who exhibits here."

"Ah, but you're the only one I say it to and mean it." She glanced up at Nora. "And who is this lovely young woman with you?"

"This is Nora," Will said, shifting into position beside her. "She's staying at the Duncan place down the street from me. Nora, this is Beverly, the best gallery owner on the Eastern seaboard."

Beverly laughed. "You're just buttering me up so I'll make you the headliner at the next show." She gave him a smile that spoke of a long friendship filled with affection. She turned to Nora. "Charlie Duncan's place is a lovely home. Did you know you have a piece of Will's hanging in that house?"

"I do?" Nora glanced at him. "Which one?"

"The one of the lighthouse," Beverly answered. "I believe it's still hanging in the back bedroom. I sold it to the house's owner a couple years ago. His sister loved it, so he hung it in the guest bedroom."

"That's the room I'm staying in. I love that painting." The first night she'd stayed in the beach house, Nora had lain awake in bed, watching the moonlight dance across the swirls of paint. In the dark, it almost seemed like the water was moving, the oil-created ocean rolling in over and over again. The sky was much like the one today—dark, forbidding, a storm whipping at the water. The white-caps of the waves multiplied on one another until it looked like thick fog. And in the center of it all, the Cape Cod lighthouse, a white beacon drawing one lone sailor back to a safe harbor.

"I love the juxtaposition in it, the contrast between danger and possibilities. The storm is on its way in, but you don't know when, or whether the boat will make it back in time," she said. "When I look at that painting, I almost want to hold my breath and wait to see if the captain manages to reach the harbor before the storm rolls in. But the lighthouse is there, promising safe passage and something the captain can depend upon."

Good Lord, she was rambling. What was wrong with her? It was just a painting, and he was just a man. An ordinary man.

But then he gave her a shy grin and she was glad for every word she'd said. "Thanks."

"Ah, this one, she gets it." The old woman smiled. "You have quite an eye for art, young lady. Are you a painter too?"

A three-year-old had more artistic abilities than Nora did. She shook her head. "Oh no, I'm just a baker."

Will leaned toward the old woman and cupped a hand around her ear, feigning a secret. "Don't let her fool you, Bev. This woman has created some cakes that I think should be works of art of their own."

Nora blinked. "How do you know that?"

"A little determined Googling. I knew your name, knew you baked cakes, and knew you were from somewhere in the Boston area. Took me a minute, but I found an article about this cake the mayor ordered for his birthday party, and in the picture there was one Nora O'Bannon who works at Charmed by Dessert and who looks suspiciously like my new friend Nora the Neighbor."

That cake replica of the Boston skyline had taken her three days to complete. The intricacies of the skyscrapers and the molding of the tiny street details had been time-consuming, backbreaking work. She'd missed Sarah's school recital and come home so exhausted that she'd barely been a part of her own family that week. Was that the kind of thing that had eroded her relationship with her daughter? Was that all Sarah wanted—more time? "That's my sister Bridget's recipe. She's the chief baker, and she's always making something amazing out of thin air."

"I saw some of the cakes on the shop's website, and I'd have to disagree and say you're the one creating amazing things." Will smiled.

Her face heated, and a little thrill ran through her. How long had it been since a man complimented her? Ben used to, back in the days *before*. Before the gambling. Before the bills. Before she fell apart. Before their lives disintegrated. But as the years went on and the chasm between them widened, Ben stopped asking about her days at work, and she stopped asking about his. Their conversations became perfunctory, focused on the kids—*Did you check Jake's backpack? Sarah has a recital Tuesday night. Don't forget to be at the parent-teacher conference.*

"Could I interest you two in a cup of tea?" Beverly asked.

Will glanced at Nora and then back at the shop owner. "Maybe another time, Bev. I'm going to show Nora the artist's view of Truro."

Beverly put a hand on Nora's arm and smiled up at her. "Oh, I envy you, young lady. If I was thirty years younger, I'd fight you for the chance to spend the day alone with this handsome man."

Nora wanted to rush in and explain that this handsome man wasn't her man, that this wasn't a date, but Will was already saying goodbye and leading them out of the gallery. He stopped on the sidewalk outside the little Cape and turned to her. The air had thickened, promising another storm sometime today. "I apologize for Bev. She's a really enthusiastic supporter of local artists, and if we stayed much longer, she would have tried to sell you the entire William Gibson collection."

"Given the one example I have, I'd say the William Gibson collection is probably worth buying."

That shy grin swept across his face again. She imagined he was about as comfortable with praise as she was. There was a reason Nora worked in the back of the bakery and not up front.

"Okay, on to the rest of the tour before we get caught in the weather," Will said. "And as much as I envy that sporty little roadster of yours, I think we're best off taking my Jeep."

"Oh, that's not my car. It's my sister's. I drive a Buick. Four doors, practical, boring. A mom car." Which is what she should be remembering. She was a mom. A married mom. She shouldn't be getting into anyone's Jeep right now. She should be working on a way out of the mess she was in.

But Nora was tired of doing the right thing. Tired of shouldering all the burden. Tired of holding her cards close to her chest, alone in her pain and loss. Ben should be the one finding a home for his kids. Ben should be worried about first, last, and security deposits. Maybe in her absence, he would have no choice but to step up. And in the meantime, Nora was going to stop following all those rules and expectations that hadn't gotten her anywhere. Nora was going to be dangerous and unpredictable, at least for one afternoon.

"Mom car or not, it gets you from A to B, so there's nothing wrong with that." He pointed to a black Wrangler in the parking lot. An older model, with a removable hard top and roll bars. "There's my ride. And if you want to give Beverly or the deli owner a heads-up, I won't be offended."

"A heads-up? About what?"

"That I am taking you away in my car, possibly for nefarious purposes." He arched a brow and did his best villainous leer.

Nora laughed, really laughed, and realized how good it

felt to do that again. "Do you have a nefarious purpose in mind?"

"Nope." He pressed a hand to his heart. "Scout's honor."

"Then let's go. Before it gets too dangerous." She climbed into the passenger seat, unsure if she meant the impending storm or the time alone with Will.

TEN

The second round of storms rolled over Truro just as Nora was getting home. She pulled into the beach house driveway and saw Will park in his own driveway. He sent her a quick wave before he dashed inside. She sat in the little red sports car as the storm pounded the roof and the moment of being dangerous and unpredictable wore off.

What was she thinking?

She hadn't been. She'd been caught in the rush of Will's flirting, the excitement of stepping outside those lines of her life, and craved more of that sense of doing something wrong. A part of her thought she deserved it. After all she'd put up with, all she had endured, all the times Ben had abandoned her. Didn't she merit a little flirting and smiling once in a while? The day had thrilled her, a roller coaster of emotions that had left her heart racing.

Nora reached for the door handle and paused. Was that how Ben felt every time he'd put another ten-dollar chip down on red? Had walking into the casino given him that same punch of excitement?

Regardless, spending an afternoon looking at art and a few cool architectural features around Truro didn't put their family into financial distress. It was hardly as irresponsible as what Ben had done. But that didn't stop the flickers of guilt that ran through her as she hunched into her sweatshirt and ran the short distance from the driveway to the house, rain pelting her and soaking through the cotton fabric, chilling her skin. Wind blew the door inward and nearly yanked it from her hand. Nora shut the door, lowered her sweatshirt, and whisked the worst of the water off her clothes. "Whew. It's wet out there."

Magpie, Jake, and Sarah stared at her from the living room, the three of them standing side by side. Jake was grinning, Magpie looked guilty, and Sarah was smiling. A suspiciously happy smile.

Despite the smile, Nora was pretty damned sure this wasn't good news.

"What?" Nora asked.

"We found something," Magpie said, putting up her hands. "And before you freak out, just hear us out."

Nothing good ever came after *before you freak out.*

"What *exactly* did you find?" Nora lowered her purse to the floor and hung her wet sweatshirt on a hook, with a little sinking dread in her gut.

"This." Magpie grinned like she'd hit the lottery and then stepped to one side, the kids to the other. And there, behind them, sat a wet, bedraggled dog.

Don't freak out. Yeah, easier said than done. Nora could barely afford to feed the *people* she had in her life. Surely the kids didn't expect to keep this dog? Even if he was admittedly kind of adorable. In that little-orphan-Annie-rescue-dog way.

His scrawny body had light brown fur, short pointy ears, and a tail that swooped across the floor in hopeful, friendly arcs. A cute dog, sort of a ragamuffin mutt with a little terrier in him.

Don't freak out. Even though everything in Nora wanted to scream, *Get rid of it! We can't afford it. I don't need one more thing to worry about.*

Jake came running forward first. He latched on to Nora's hand, pumping it with excitement as he talked. "Mommy, can we keep him? He was all wet, and he was cold, and we gave him dinner, and he loves us!"

She shook her head, hating the disappointment that filled Jake's brown eyes. Why did she have to keep being the bad guy? Why wasn't Ben the one standing here, saying no to a lost mutt? Because Ben wouldn't say no. Ben would adopt the dog without a second thought, then do something big, like build a doghouse in the backyard or whisk everyone off to Petland to lavish the stray with chew toys and dog bones. Nora was the realistic one, the one who looked at all the angles and ramifications, the one who remembered that paying the mortgage and feeding the humans in the house came first. "Jake, we can't keep a dog. He probably belongs to someone who is missing him, and—"

"He doesn't have a collar. We checked. And he was sad, until he saw us. Now he's happy. See?"

"Jake's right. We found him, just wandering the beach, a real mess," Magpie said, giving the mutt an ear rub. "He needed a bath, something to eat, and a place to crash for the night. I swear, the silly dog is smiling now."

The dog did, indeed, look happy. But that was probably mostly due to his full belly. Nora saw the remains of the leftover burgers they'd had for dinner last night scattered on a paper plate in the kitchen. The stray had dined pretty well. "Jake, this isn't our house, and—"

"We can take him home. We have a big yard." Sarah laid a protective hand on the dog's head. "Mom, he's a really nice dog. And Daddy loves dogs. He'll say yes."

Damn it. Even Sarah was finally talking to Nora again. If she said no, the kids would be crushed. They'd already had so much disappointment in their lives, with even more devastating news to come soon.

How was she supposed to tell the kids there was no house and no yard to bring the dog to? That as soon as this little vacation from reality was over, they were going to have to move into a new, strange place? A place that probably wasn't going to allow a dog, assuming Nora could even afford to add a pet fee to the growing list of expenses for moving.

An overwhelming sense of failure threatened to swamp her. Her life was a mess, her kids were about to be home-less, and she'd been out on a not-date date, looking at art with a stranger all afternoon. Instead of working or calling the bank or *something* productive.

The dog let out a little bark, and his tail wagged some more. Undoubtedly, someone was missing this dog. They could keep it for tonight, and in the morning, she'd look up the local vet, bring the dog there, and he'd reunite it with its proper owner. That would delay the disappointment, at least for a few hours. "He can stay tonight—"

The kids cheered. Jake did a little dance, and Sarah hugged the dog's neck.

"But tomorrow," Nora added, always the bad cop and hating it, "we're going to find his owners."

Jake's face fell. Sarah's gaze dropped to the floor. If there was a Worst Mother of the Year award, Nora was a shoo-in. Once again, she cursed Ben and his decision to put horse races and blackjack games ahead of providing for his family. He was the one who had brought them to this place, brought her to this horrible position of having to disappoint her kids. Again.

"Who's ready for dinner?" Magpie said, before the kids could start to cry or beg Nora to change her mind. Nora sent her sister a grateful smile. "Why don't you guys go get cleaned up, and I'll order a pizza? You guys want pepperoni or cheese? Or both?"

Once Jake and Sarah were out of the room, the dog slid onto the floor and laid his head on his paws. He let out a sigh, as if to say, *Whew, dodged that bullet.*

Nora sank into a chair. She ran a hand through her damp hair. Yet another mess in an already complex life. "A dog, Magpie? What am I going to do with a dog?"

"I know, I know." She dropped onto the ottoman. "But

Sarah got super excited when she saw him. She's been so sad ever since she got here, and I saw her perk up, and I just couldn't say no."

Ever since the meeting with Sister Esther, Nora had been trying to figure out what was going on with Sarah. Dropped grades, angry looks, and playground fights were completely out of character. Could a dog turn her daughter's attitude around? Was it really that simple? It was an awful lot to ask of something with four legs and scruffy fur.

Maybe later, when they all were settled in a home again, Nora could get the kids a dog. But right now, she didn't even know where they were going to sleep when they got back to Dorchester. "I can't keep a dog. They need too much...just too much."

"That's what Ma used to say whenever we asked for a dog." Her sister got to her feet and crossed to the kitchen counter. The dog padded over to her and raised his head for attention. Magpie gave his ears an absentminded rub. "Remember how many times we begged to get one?"

"I asked Santa for a puppy every single year," Nora said. When she'd been too little to write, she'd drawn a picture. But all Santa had brought her was a stuffed dog that she'd named Rags. "Ma always said a dog would be too much work, between the bakery and us girls and everything."

"And we never got a dog." Magpie dropped down beside the mutt and buried her face in his fur, whispering nonsense words. The dog's ears perked up, his tail wagged, and Magpie's face lit with pure joy. The youngest of all of them, Magpie had maintained that wonder and appreciation for the world that Nora had lost somewhere between her marriage vows and dropping Ben off at rehab.

A part of Nora was jealous and wished she could recapture those feelings. Except she wasn't sure she'd ever lived with that kind of wild abandon. The minute her father died, Nora had stepped into a pair of practical, sensible shoes and worn them ever since. How would her life have been different if her fun-loving, rule-breaking father had lived?

"We almost got a dog," Nora said softly.

"When?" Magpie rose. "I don't remember that."

"You were so young, and Ma never mentioned it after..." Nora's voice trailed off. "Dad was going to get us a dog."

"Really?"

Nora nodded. "He loved dogs. Remember how he'd pet every single one he saw? Or look for an excuse to walk Mrs. O'Neill's Great Dane?" She glanced down at the stray and knew her father would have loved that dog like a fifth child. "How he was always over at Dan Murphy's house, playing fetch with his Lab? One night when he was putting me to bed, he told me about this spaniel he had when he was a kid and how that dog was his best friend for years. I snuck out of bed for a drink of water and I overheard him telling Ma that he thought we were old enough to take care of a dog, and he was going to buy us all one for Christmas. But then..."

"He died." Just two soft, sad words.

Even though it had been twenty years, the sudden

death of their father still echoed in Nora's heart. One minute the six of them were sitting down to dinner, and the next, their father was crumpled on the floor, clutching at his chest. A week later, the four girls had held hands as they stood around the casket, too young to understand the permanence of that hole in the ground.

"Then why not get a dog now?" Magpie asked. "Like, in memory of Dad?"

If her life had been going in any other direction, Nora would have agreed. Her kids were old enough to help out, and a dog was the kind of thing that seemed to complete the two-point-five kids suburban home picture. Except right now, Nora didn't own a single part of that American dream. "It's not as easy as you make it sound."

The dog slid down beside her sister's feet and let out another sigh, quite the drama queen for a mutt. Magpie studied Nora for a long moment, her lips twitching like they did whenever she was puzzling on something. "Well, like you said, his owners are probably looking for him anyway. For now, your kids are happy, the dog is happy, and we can deal with all the rest later."

"Dealing with the rest later is what got me into this mess in the first place," Nora muttered. The dog got to his feet, ambled over, and pressed his head against Nora's leg, his tail beating a breeze into the room.

The storm raged on into the night, intensifying after midnight, battering the small beach cottage with howling winds and heavy rain that shook the windows and drummed on the roof. Nora lay awake in the unfamiliar bed, scrolling through her phone, scanning a rental app for affordable apartments. At this point, she'd settle for a cardboard box with indoor plumbing. Given the sky-high rent in Boston, a cardboard box was pretty much all she could afford.

She set her phone on the nightstand and started to curl into her bed when she heard a soft whimper from the room next door. She waited, heard it again, and then swung out of bed. Pulling on a pair of sweats with the T-shirt she was wearing, she ducked into the kids' room.

The dog lay at the foot of Jake's bed, curled into the comforter. He gave Nora a quick glance and then went back to sleep, as if he knew full well no one was going to kick him out of the bed. Nora heard the whimpering sound again and realized it was coming from Sarah's bed. Moonlight cast a dim glow in the room, enough for Nora to circumvent the hazards of forgotten Legos on the floor and cross to Sarah's bed. Her daughter was curled into a ball under the covers, clutching her favorite stuffed bear to her chest. The muted light glinted off the tears that dampened Sarah's cheeks.

Nora sank onto the bed and put a hand on Sarah's thin shoulder. "What's the matter, honey?"

"I...I wanna go h-h-home. I wanna go h-h-home *now*."

"It's the middle of the night, so we can't go now, but we will in a couple days." She started to tell Sarah about Ben's offer to take the kids trick-or-treating but stopped herself.

What if he got sidetracked by work or a bad decision? Even though it had been a year since Ben quit gambling, Nora lived in fear of the moment when she'd get that call. *Honey, I screwed up.*

So she didn't make promises she couldn't keep. And she didn't count on a man who had stopped being dependable a long time ago.

"I thought you liked vacation," Nora went on, in that happy Mom voice she'd perfected during the terrible twos. "You've been swimming and playing on the beach with Jake, and you met this great dog."

Sarah shrugged. "Yeah. I guess."

Nora brushed back a damp lock of hair from Sarah's forehead. In the dark, her daughter looked so frail, so vulnerable. Nora wanted to scoop her up and hold her close, like she'd done when Sarah was a baby and she'd fall asleep on Nora's chest. Nora would lie on the sofa, still and quiet, watching her newborn breathe, her delicate eyelashes fluttering as she dreamed. That sweet, fresh baby scent would fill the space, and a deep, warm contentment would wash over Nora. The naps always ended too quickly, and as Nora worked more and Sarah spent her days in day care, those sweet, magical moments became few and far between. "Before you know it, you'll be back at school and wishing we could go on vacation again."

Sarah shook her head. "I don't wanna go back to St. Gregory's."

"Why not?"

"I just don't wanna."

"Is it because of that fight with Anna?" Nora pressed her hand to Sarah's cheek. "Because if you want, I can talk to her mom and—"

Sarah jerked away from her mother's touch. "No! I don't want you to. You'll just make it worse."

Nora could understand Sarah being embarrassed or maybe even reluctant to have the mothers intervene, but sometimes that was the easiest way to head off a ruined friendship. Surely whatever had happened between the girls could be cleared up with a conversation. "Honey, I know what it's like to fight with a friend. I'm sure if Anna's mother and I talked, we could help you two work it out."

"Anna's not my friend anymore." Sarah buried her face in her pillow and shook her head again. "I don't want you to talk to her mom."

"Oh, come on. You guys have been friends forever." They'd gone to preschool and kindergarten together, been in Girl Scouts, practically lived at each other's houses. There'd been sleepovers and camping trips and long afternoons spent at Build-A-Bear or Chuck E. Cheese's. "When we get back to Dorchester, why don't we call Anna, and I'll take you two to Boston Garden for the day? Maybe ride the swan boats? And see the *Make Way for Ducklings* sculpture? You've always loved that, and I'm sure Anna would too."

She shook her head. "I don't want to. Just leave me alone."

"Sarah." Nora reached for her daughter, but as she did, Sarah twisted away and put her back to her mother. She put a hand on Sarah's shoulder, but her daughter remained burrowed in her pillow, the stuffed bear hiding most of her face. "Honey, come on, talk to me."

"No. You don't understand. All you do is make it worse."

"Make what worse?"

But Sarah refused to answer. The more Nora pressed her, the more Sarah pulled away.

When had this divide opened between them? She'd always thought that she and Sarah were close. Told herself that she was a good mother.

Maybe she was fooling herself about that too. Maybe she'd spent too many hours at work to see that her entire family was eroding. Guilt squeezed Nora's heart, and she vowed that going forward, she would take more time off and be there more for the kids.

A second chance, Lord, Nora whispered in her head. *That's all I need. Give me a chance to do it right and be the mother You want me to be.*

Nora leaned over, gave Sarah a tender kiss on her temple, and then whispered, "I'm just next door if you need me, okay? Good night, honey. I love you."

Nora waited a long time, but there was no answer from her daughter. She told herself Sarah had already fallen asleep and stepped out of the room. But she left the door ajar, just in case.

ELEVEN

The moon reflected off the white column of the Cape Cod lighthouse, dancing along the solitary landmark in a turbulent painted ocean, the ship's captain caught in a perpetual battle to reach solid ground. The pillar glowed in the dark, almost like it was meant to be a beacon for her too. Nora lay in the dark bedroom, her heart heavy, her worries a burden she could barely hold. Sarah had stayed in her room, resolute. The more Nora tried to figure out what was upsetting her daughter so much, the further she got from an answer.

Nora missed her husband. Missed the partner she used to have. The friendship. The beach house bed seemed cold and empty, a vast cotton iceberg without Ben beside her. Even though it had been two years since they had shared a bed, she'd never gotten used to the empty space.

Nora picked up her phone, swiped across the screen, and opened the photos app. She scrolled back, two, three, four years. And there, in those photos of their trip to

Disney World, the weekend camping trips, the afternoons spent on Wollaston Beach, was the life she used to have. Ben, hoisting each of the kids onto his broad shoulders, a trio of wide smiles reflecting in Nora's camera lens.

She switched to the messages app, sliding her finger down until she got to Ben's name. **Nora, talk to me,** he'd written earlier today.

Her finger hovered over the Reply button. Three little dots popped up in a pale gray bubble, meaning Ben was awake now, too, and typing another message. She waited, her heart in her throat, both aching for his words and dreading them. They had lost what they once had, and like the house, she didn't see any way to get it back.

I can't sleep without you here.

She thought of Ben alone in that big house, empty of the voices of the children, of the dinners and squabbles over toys and TV channels. Her heart ached, and the space in the bed seemed to quadruple. **Me neither,** she wrote.

His response was immediate. **You're up? Can we talk?**

Before she could type yes, her phone was ringing and Ben's face was on her screen. It was one of her favorite pictures of him, from three years ago, before it all started going south. He'd been sitting across from her at dinner, and she'd raised her camera to take his picture. He'd smiled, one of those soft, intimate smiles that seemed meant only for her.

She pressed the green button and put the phone to her ear. "Hey."

"Hey." The word had a hint of surprise in it, as if he wasn't sure she'd answer. "How are you and the kids?"

"We're good. They're having a great time." She didn't mention the dog. Didn't tell him about everything going on with Sarah. Maybe because a part of her didn't want Ben to know she couldn't handle this on her own. That she was screwing up and was as beleaguered as the captain in the painting. Only she didn't have a lighthouse to tell her which way to go, how to fix this deepening mess. And as much as she wished she could depend on Ben—and ever since he'd gotten out of rehab he'd been insisting that she could—Nora's trust for her husband still hovered in the negative digits.

"I'm glad."

She pressed the phone tighter to her ear, wanting him to say those words—*I can't sleep without you here*—one more time. Because here, in the dark alone, with the world crashing down on her, she needed him. Needed them to be a team again. She didn't care about the debts or the divorce. She would open up to him and tell him what had happened that morning, and maybe they could get back to where they used to be. She missed him. Missed them. Just for a minute, maybe they could...pretend. "Ben—"

"We need to talk about how we're going to divide things up." He cleared his throat, and the softness disappeared from his voice. "I think we can do this amicably, Nora. Then there's not as much disruption for the kids."

Divide things up. Do this amicably. She blinked away tears. "I, uh, thought you didn't want to get divorced."

"I've been thinking about it since you left, and I think you're right. We've grown apart, Nora. And the best thing to do is split up what little we have and go our separate ways."

She'd been angry when she said it, frustrated, sure that nothing could ever return to what it once had been. Across from her, the lighthouse stood against the storm, solid and immovable. She'd once thought she was like that lighthouse, the one her family, her kids, could rely on to be strong, but now she was like a swing on a frayed rope. One gust of wind away from falling apart. "But I thought ... your message said you were lonely in the house without me."

She hated the vulnerability in her voice. The fear.

"Insomnia isn't a reason to save a marriage." His words were cold, as harsh as the ones she had thrown at him the day she walked out the door.

"You're right. It isn't." The tears brimmed and then spilled, sliding down her cheeks. She drew in a breath, forcing the sorrow out of her voice. She refused to let any more weakness show or to be the one who crumpled. "I'll, uh, write up a list of the furniture and stuff I'd like to keep, and you do the same. If there's anything we disagree about, I'm sure we can find an equitable solution."

"Good." Silence filled the space between them for a moment. Then Ben cleared his throat again. "And, Nora, one other thing—"

"Yeah?" Hope still fluttered in her chest, damn it.

"I'd like to pick the kids up on Halloween and take them trick-or-treating here. That way they can have one more Halloween in this neighborhood."

She wanted to believe in him. Wanted to trust that he

would show up, that he wouldn't let the kids down. Again. But years of disappointment said otherwise. "That would be great," Nora said, a part of her angry at that little flutter of hope. Why had she been stupid enough to wish for a happy ending in a story that had already finished? "If you actually do it."

"Damn it, Nora, I'm trying here. I know I haven't been the most involved father," he said. "I've let work and my own issues get in the way of being there for you, for the kids. But I want you to know that I will be totally hands-on whenever I have custody, and if you ever need anything, I'm just a phone call away."

I need you now, she thought, *but you're already on the other side of my world.* "I'll keep that in mind." Then she said goodbye and shut off her phone. She lay in the dark, staring at that lighthouse until her tears blurred the image.

TWELVE

The lone vet in Truro, a tall, skinny man in his seventies with soft blue eyes and a ready smile, shook his head. "Sorry, Mrs. Daniels, but I don't know who this dog belongs to. I've never seen him here before, and pretty much everyone in town brings their pets to me. Maybe some summer renter left him behind." He sighed. "It happens more than you'd think. Damned tragedy, if you ask me."

Nora pointed to the dog's scruff. "Isn't there one of those chip things in his head?"

"Nope, sorry. I checked that first thing. You can call the police department, see if anyone's missing a dog. And you're welcome to put a flyer up on my bulletin board, but I'm afraid we're heading into the off-season, so I won't have that many people through that door for a few months. If some family left him behind, I doubt they're coming back anytime soon. Or ever." The vet ran a hand down the dog's flanks and *tsk*ed under his breath. "He looks like he's been

129

on his own for a while. He's pretty skinny and malnourished. He found you all just in time."

Nora thanked the vet, paid him money she didn't really have, and took home a dog she didn't really want.

When she walked in the door of the beach house, Jake scrambled to his feet, abandoning the Legos he was playing with his aunt, and then ran up to the dog, dropped to his knees, and wrapped the mutt in a tight hug. "You're gonna be my puppy, Chance! Yay!"

"Chance?" Nora laid the leash she'd bought at the vet's office on the counter and set her purse beside it. God, now they'd named the dog? Nora had hoped maybe the connection would have lessened after the first night, but if anything, Jake seemed more invested in the mutt. Thank goodness Sarah was outside on the deck playing dolls and didn't hear or see the whole *you're my puppy* thing.

"Yup. That's his name," Jake said. "Aunt Magpie said it was 'cause he took a chance when he came here, and we gave him seconds."

Magpie came over and ruffled Jake's hair. "A second chance, you mean."

Jake tugged the dog over to his Legos pile to explain the house he was building. "Come on, Chance! Let me show you the house I'm building for you and me and Mommy and Daddy and Sarah!"

Magpie watched him with a wistful look on her face. She had always been the one who believed in signs and instant miracles. The dreamer of the family, who didn't have the realities Nora had to deal with. Her little sister didn't know how hard it was going to be to leave the dog at a shelter now that the kids had named it. Encouraging them would only make the whole loss more painful. "Mags, we don't name the dog we aren't committing to," Nora whispered. "That just makes it worse."

Her sister waved that off. "It'll be fine. Come on, we were just about to make ice cream sundaes for lunch."

"That's not a healthy lunch. Let me throw together some turkey sandwiches and—"

"Nora, this is *vacation*. In case you have forgotten the definition of vacation, it's when you do all the things you aren't supposed to do. Like stay up past your bedtime. Eat breakfast for dinner. Get drunk and stumble home at four in the morning." Magpie grinned. "Which, by the way, I decided not to let Jake do. Sarah might get a pass."

Nora's jaw dropped. "You did not—"

"Oh, for God's sake, of course I didn't. I'm the cool aunt, but not *that* cool." Magpie leaned against the counter and crossed her arms over her chest. "What's up with you lately? You are totally stressed. Like more than usual."

"I'm fine."

Magpie snorted. "This is me you're talking to. If there's anyone in this family you can't bullshit, it's me."

"Will you get off my case?" Nora shook her head. "Jesus, Mags, just leave me alone."

The brightness disappeared from Magpie's face, and her eyes turned icy. "You know, Nora, you can be a real b—"—she glanced at the kids—"witch when you want to be. I'm trying to help you, in case you haven't noticed."

"I have. I'm sorry."

"You're too damned worried about what's going on with you to even think there might be other people in this house who are going through something too." Magpie turned on her heel and headed down the hall and into her room. The door slammed shut.

Things other people in the house were going through? Had she missed something? Been too self-absorbed to be there for Magpie?

Nora gave it a few minutes before going down the hall. She knocked on her sister's door, but Magpie told her to go away. Nora stood there a moment, thinking back over the last few days, trying to figure out if there was anything different about her little sister. She seemed a bit run-down, but that was likely jet lag.

For most of her life, Nora had been exactly what Magpie accused her of the other day—the surrogate mother to her sisters. She'd learned to make dinner at age ten, to set her own alarm to get up earlier than her sisters on school days, and to keep a running list in her notebook of what everyone else had to do, from science projects to soccer practice. How had she lost track of her little sister?

A little sister who was, Nora reminded herself, a full-grown adult who didn't need a mother to make sure she ate her green beans and went to bed at a decent hour. After a while, Nora went outside and tried to engage Sarah in a conversation, but Sarah just said she was tired and went inside.

Okay, so she was batting a thousand. For a woman

who was used to juggling all the balls and doing it success-fully, these past months of failure—and accepting that it was partly because she'd deluded herself about how good her juggling act was—had started to wear on Nora. She thought of all the decisions ahead and figured she better get her shit together pretty damned soon or she was going to screw those up too.

The doorbell rang, the Chinese food arrived, and after Nora got the kids set up with their sweet-and-sour chicken, she carried a plate of General Tso's chicken down the hall and knocked again. "Mags, the food's here."

A pause, then the sound of the door unlocking and opening. "I'm only taking this because I'm hungry."

Nora smiled and handed her sister the paper plate. "Good thing your stomach isn't mad at me too."

Magpie sank onto her bed and gestured for Nora to sit beside her. She looked down at the plate in her lap for a minute, her long straight hair spilling down the back of her maxi dress and dusting against the comforter. "I'm sorry for what I said before."

"No, I'm sorry. You're right. I'm so wrapped up in my own shit, I can't see anything else." Nora sighed. "I've been doing that for a long time and am just now realizing it."

"You gonna tell me what is going on? Because I've been around you long enough to know that this isn't normal Nora behavior. Plus, Sarah's kind of a mess, and your tem-per has a shorter fuse than Wile E. Coyote's dynamite."

That made Nora laugh. "Is it that obvious?"

"Only to people who know you well." Magpie's hand

covered Nora's. "And only people who spend more than a few hours at work with you. You've always been pretty good at covering up the tough stuff."

Nora sighed. The burdens on her shoulders seemed ten times heavier in the last few weeks, hell the entire last year. She'd gone through all that...

All of it alone. She'd told herself it was for the best, because telling Ben wouldn't have changed anything. Maybe if she opened up to her sister—a little—that heaviness would ease. "Ben and I have been having money problems," she said. "It's nothing, really. But it's made me a little more stressed than usual."

Okay, so that was barely telling the truth, but it was a start.

"Then this vacation came at just the right time." Magpie's gaze swept over Nora, and her eyes narrowed. "Anything else bothering you? I don't want to pry, but it seems like Sarah's pretty pissed at you too."

"Sarah got a few bad grades and she's been in trouble." *Way to keep on minimizing the truth, Nora.* So, losing her house became a couple's money problems and her daughter almost being expelled was a handful of Ds?

"I'm so glad it's nothing big," Magpie said. "You'll bounce back. You always do. You're like the most stable one in the family."

If they only knew the truth. Nora hadn't felt anything close to stability in a long time. But just seeing the relief in Magpie's face that her older sister—the one she'd always depended upon—was okay reminded Nora why she didn't dump her problems on her family. She got to her feet and crossed to the door. "I should get back to the kids before they eat all the egg rolls—or feed them to the dog."

"Nora? Can I ask you something?"

Nora turned back. "Shoot."

Magpie dropped her gaze to her plate again. "When Sarah and Jake were born, like, how did you know what to do?"

"Meaning how to be a parent?" That was an odd question coming from her firmly-forever-single sister who had expressed almost zero interest in having a family.

Magpie nodded. "I'm just asking because I want to be a better aunt, and I think, even with Sarah's grumpiness this week, that you're doing a great job."

A mother doing a great job didn't take the risks Nora had taken. A mother doing a great job put her children before a fight, a man, everything. The only thing Nora seemed to be doing a great job at was beating herself up.

"There are days when I think the complete opposite." Nora clutched the door frame and reached back in her memory, to those early days when Sarah was born and she and Ben had been filled with overwhelming joy, even when they were operating on fumes after late-night and early-morning feedings. Sarah had seemed like such a miracle to them, with every burp, every movement, every smile. But Nora also remembered feeling overwhelmingly lost and terrified of making a mistake. "I think you just do your best. No one gets it right all the time."

Magpie picked at the edge of the comforter and let out

a long breath. "Sometimes I wish Dad hadn't died. Ma was great and loved us a lot, but he was like the perfect parent. I was so little when he died, but I remember the piggyback rides and trips to the park and ice cream on Wednesday nights. I loved him so much."

"Me too. And he loved all of us like we were the sun and moon in his world." Nora often wondered what her father would say if he could see her now. Would he be proud? Disappointed? Would he have seen through the careful façade she had maintained for all those years and given her a shoulder to lean on? "Mags, I guess the key to being a good parent is to think what Dad would do and run with that."

"That sounds like good advice."

"It is." And all Nora had to do was follow it.

The next morning, Nora laced up her running shoes and shrugged into a sweatshirt. The storm a couple days earlier had left behind cold weather and a brisk wind, but she opted to brave the low temps anyway. She'd woken up craving the run, after another sleepless night and hours spent surfing real estate sites, looking for a place for them to live. She could feel the clock ticking down, like a bomb waiting to explode.

Nora crossed to the front door, just as the dog ambled in front of it. "Hey, dog, you have to get out of the way."

Chance sat there, wagging his tail and looking up at her. He let out a little yip.

"Shhhh. The kids are still asleep." She bent down and

patted his head. Okay, not quite a pat, but if Nora started petting this dog, the thing would get more attached, and that path wasn't going to lead anywhere good. "Now shoo. I have to go before everyone gets up."

The dog didn't move. This time he let out a whine. He looked up at her with big, brown pleading eyes. His tail gave a hopeful wag.

"Do you want to run with me? Is that it?" At the word *run*, Chance jumped to his feet, his tail beating a staccato against the door. Nora laughed. "Okay, okay, but if you pull on the leash or trip me, you're coming right back home. Deal?"

Chance waited for her to clip on the leash, but as soon as she opened the door, he lunged forward, eager, rushing. They stepped into a brisk October morning, and into a quiet, still-asleep world. The sun had just barely risen, and the beach neighborhood lay mostly in shadow.

Nora wrapped the end of the leash around her hand and started to jog. She expected the dog to take off, but instead he matched his gait to hers and trotted alongside her. Nora wound her way down the street, then down another one, clicking off a mile, then another, before she paused, walked a bit, and turned around to jog back. Her pace was nowhere near what it had been nine years ago, but she was surprised that she could slip back into running with relative ease. Had to be all those hours on her feet at the bakery, which by the end of the day often felt like she'd run a marathon.

All the while, the dog stayed by her side, slowing when

she slowed, stopping when she waited to cross a street. He would look up at her from time to time with something that looked suspiciously like a grin on his face. He was...happy out here, running.

She had to admit he was a good dog. Kind of cute and well mannered. If she had a running buddy like him, she might just get out on the roads more often.

"You're just sucking up to me," Nora said, the words slipping out between breaths and steps. "Pleading your case so I'll keep you."

The dog's tail wagged.

"But I can't have a dog, not unless I find a rental house with a—" Nora stopped.

This time, Chance didn't pay attention and ran a couple steps before the leash made him halt. He looked back over his shoulder at her, panting.

"I totally forgot. I know a house I can rent," she said to him. Good Lord, now she was talking to the dog? "Buy a little time, maybe come up with a plan before my family gets all involved and crazy."

She fished her cell phone out of the inside pocket of her sweatshirt and dialed her aunt, trying to remember what Ma had said about when Aunt Mary would be released from the hospital. Her heart troubles had returned over the last year, and she spent more time resting and less time traveling. It was sad to see, given how vibrant and busy Aunt Mary used to be, but at the same time, all those weeks spent in Massachusetts had given Ma a chance to bond with the mother she'd never really known.

Nora had always loved Aunt Mary. Though Magpie was the closest in personality, with her flitting around the world and aversion to being tied down, it was Nora who had spent the most time with Aunt Mary when she was a little girl. Her aunt would come home from Africa or Europe and invite her nieces over for the afternoon, undoubtedly to give Ma a break from four little girls, and nine times out of ten, it was Nora who ended up in the kitchen with her aunt, fixing lunch or making a simple dessert for them all to share.

Nora admired her aunt, the way Mary took life on her own terms and lived with few regrets. Even after she revealed last year that she was Ma's mother, she was clearly proud of the daughter she had helped raise and was relieved that the truth was finally out and they could be an honest, open family. Maybe a part of Nora envied Aunt Mary, too, in the same way she envied Magpie and her life free of the ties that bound Nora so tightly.

"Hello?" Aunt Mary's voice was a little weak but still held the familiar chipper optimism. After her recent stay in the hospital to repair a blocked artery, it was good to hear traces of heartiness still in Mary's words.

"Hi, Aunt Mary, it's me, Nora."

"Oh, Nora! So nice to hear from you! How's the beach? Your mother said you took some time off. About damned time if you ask me."

What was with her family? It was as if they all had the same script. "The beach is great, and the kids are having a good time, although it's getting cold now. Anyway, I'm coming home Sunday afternoon. And I...I wanted to ask you a favor."

"Sure, sweetheart, anything."

She shuffled from foot to foot. The cold air snuck under her jacket and chilled her chest and waist. "Ben's still working on the kitchen, and I have no idea when it's going to be done. I was hoping we could crash at your house while you are staying with Ma. It won't be forever, just until we get things together at the other house." The lie slipped out of her with a practiced ease that made Nora wonder how she'd become this person who lied to her family, lied to her children, lied to herself.

Good old-fashioned Catholic guilt heated her face. Good thing she was on a phone, miles away from her aunt, who would surely see through Nora's words in person.

"You're more than welcome to stay at my house," Aunt Mary said, no hesitation, no questions. "I've been there so rarely over the years, what with all my traveling, that the old girl will be glad to have some company. And I'm staying at your mom's now while she hovers over me and warns me not to stay up past my bedtime."

Nora laughed. "Some things never change."

"Indeed. But that's what makes them good, dependable. Anyway, you are welcome to my house and to stay as long as you like."

Forever? Nora wanted to ask. *Or until I hit the lottery and can afford a home again?* "Thank you, Aunt Mary. You have no idea how much of a relief that is."

"I do, my dear. I truly do." She paused a beat and then

lowered her voice. "Now, I take it you don't want me to tell your mother about this."

Nora stood there, silent for a second, her breath frosting in the chilly air. How was she supposed to respond to that? Chance lay on the ground beside her, his head on his paws.

"I know you're having troubles, Nora," Aunt Mary went on. "I know you lost the house, and I know you're teetering on a very fine line with everything else. And I want you to know that whatever you tell me is confidential. You tell your mother and your sisters in your own time, not on my timeline."

"How did you find out?" And if Aunt Mary knew, who else knew? That overwhelming sense of failure threatened to drown her. If her family realized how far Nora had let her life slip away, they'd be disappointed, ashamed even, but not as ashamed as she was of herself for letting it get to this point.

"Now, don't be mad, dear, but Ben came to me," Aunt Mary said.

"Ben. My *husband* Ben? Came to you?" Ben, who rarely visited her family? The same husband who had skipped family dinners and barbeques to go to the track?

"He knows you and I are close, and he came to visit me in the hospital on Wednesday. He was a broken man, I have to say. I've never seen him so upset. We talked for a long time. I like that boy, Nora."

Well, Aunt Mary was alone in the Ben Fan Club right now, at least out here on this quiet street in Truro. His visit to Aunt Mary came as a surprise. *He was a broken man.* Could Ben be as upset over this as she was?

If so, he had lost that feeling by the time they talked Wednesday evening about dividing the furniture and splitting custody. Nora wanted to ask, wanted to know what her aunt had meant by *broken*, but was afraid she already knew the answer. Ben had had a moment of vulnerability, like he had on the phone the other night. That was all. "What did you say to him?"

"Well, I offered to help you two out with some money, but he wouldn't have any of that. He said he wants to do this on his own, which I have to admire."

"He can't do it on his own," Nora said. "If he could, he would have done it by now. All he's done is let me down. Let his kids down."

"Now, now, I know Ben hasn't been perfect. No man is. But he is trying, and you have to give him credit for that."

Nora let out a long breath. How many times had she thought the same thing and taken Ben back? Trusted in his words, thinking his actions would match, and they never did. She was done doing that. "We've both been trying, Aunt Mary. And still we ended up here. With the house up for auction and our lives in total disarray."

"A life making mistakes is far more honorable than a life spent doing nothing at all. George Bernard Shaw said those words, and I happen to agree. You've made mistakes; he's made mistakes. The key is to go forward together."

Apparently, Ben hadn't told her aunt everything. Like that she and her husband weren't going to be going anywhere together in the future. Like how he'd left her a thousand times to place a bet. Like how she had been lying to him for over a year. A lie of omission, but still, a lie.

"I appreciate you letting us stay at your house, Aunt Mary. If you're okay with it, we might have an extra stowaway. The kids found a dog wandering on the beach, and if I don't find his owners before I leave, I might have to take him with me."

"I think that's an excellent idea! A dog is wonderful for a family. And my little Pedro will love to visit."

Her aunt's Chihuahua was practically a child in Aunt Mary's eyes, so Nora wasn't surprised she'd agreed to the dog resident. As for the rest, she needed to be honest about the state of her marriage. She didn't want Aunt Mary thinking there was going to be some ride off into the sunset. "Before you say yes to letting me move into your house, there's something you should know." Nora drew in a deep breath, let it out. "I'm not so sure we're still going to be a family at the end of this. Ben and I are talking about breaking up."

"My dear niece, take heart and believe in the love that brought you two together." Aunt Mary's voice was soft, understanding. Even though her aunt had never married, she did have one great love when she was young, and she understood the intricacies of that emotion better than most. "I know you have had money problems, but remember it's always easier to halve a potato with love."

Her family and their Irish words of wisdom. Most of them were about as useful as boots on a cat. "Okay, I'll, uh, keep that in mind."

"Good. Now, will you be at family dinner on Sunday? Your mother is expecting you and the children. And Ben, I might add, so you might want to call him."

"The kids and I will be there." If she didn't mention Ben, maybe no one would notice he hadn't come or just assume he was working. Nora clutched the phone and let out a long, deep breath of relief. She had a home to go to on Sunday. A home for her children. "Thank you again, Aunt Mary."

"No need to thank me with words, my dear. Just do it with your deeds. If there's anything I have learned in this past year, it's the importance of keeping a family together. It takes work, but it's work worth doing."

Only if there is work left to do, Nora amended silently.

THIRTEEN

Colleen headed into the converted white two-story house that held the headquarters for Sophie's Home, carrying a paper bag in each hand. There was a chill in the air, a sure sign that fall was making room for an early winter. Every year, Colleen vowed to move to Florida or Arizona or anywhere warmer than Boston in the middle of winter. But every year, she stayed put and suffered through the cold because her family was here. Her kids. Her grandkids. Her friends.

And now this charity. She'd been helping Sophie's Home for over a year now, bringing them extra baked goods, collecting clothing and children's toys, and now hiring Iris. Roger O'Sullivan, who had started Sophie's Home about a decade ago, had done wonderful things helping women who were down on their luck. Many of them were now employed, living in homes of their own, and emerging like butterflies out of the desperate situations they had been in before they arrived on this very doorstep.

When her husband died two decades ago, leaving Colleen to raise four kids and run a business alone, she'd thought her life had been tough. But it was nothing compared to what some of these incredible women went through—and still emerged to come out on top.

As Colleen entered the building, Roger came down the hall. When he saw her, a wide grin took over his face, and that sent a little flutter through her stomach. "Colleen! So glad to see you!" He took the bags from her hands before she could protest, hefted them into one arm, and held the door to his office for her.

Such a gentleman, even though she didn't need him to be. Colleen could take care of herself, but every time she reminded Roger of that, he upped the chivalry, so she'd stopped protesting. "Thank you."

"I made hot tea for you," he said. "I bought that Irish tea you like so much and made sure I had some fresh honey to go with it."

He was always doing thoughtful things. Brewing her favorite tea just before she arrived or walking her home at the end of the day. Every time, she insisted she was just fine, but Roger had this stubborn Sir Galahad side.

A part or her might—*might*—like that about him. Her late husband, God rest his soul, had been like that, and there were days when Colleen missed being treated like a lady.

She walked into his office and shrugged off her coat, laying it carefully over the back of a chair before taking a seat. In the year she'd been coming here, Roger had upgraded the ragtag furniture in his office to comfortable armchairs, bought a small refrigerator, and outfitted one corner of the room with a countertop and a couple of cabinets. He had the teapot on a hot plate with two mugs waiting beside it.

"It's not really necessary for you to go to so much trouble. I'm sure you have a busy day ahead of you." She perched on the edge of the chair, thanking him again when he placed a warm mug in her hands.

"Ah, but you do so much for Sophie's Home. I'm happy to do it. And I do like you an awful lot, Colleen O'Bannon. So I'm hoping the tea and the honey and everything else starts swaying you into my corner, sooner rather than later." He shot her a smile over the rim of his mug.

She set the cup on his desk, beside a photo of his daughter. She was a dark-haired, happy girl, about seven in the picture, with a wide smile and a missing front tooth. She didn't know much about his daughter—he rarely spoke of her—and she got the feeling it was a sensitive subject. Regardless, his commitment to changing the lives of the women in the Dorchester area was something she liked very much.

Well, respected. *Liking* would imply things like swaying into his corner. "Roger..." She took in a breath. "We have had this conversation many times."

"And I'll have it several more times until you agree to go to dinner with me," he said.

The man gave *persistent* a whole new meaning. Why couldn't he see she was too old, too set in her ways, to think about getting involved with a man again? If that was even the term these days. "I like our arrangement as it is."

"Well, I don't." He got to his feet and stared at the floor for a moment. When he raised his gaze to hers, his brown eyes softened with sadness. "Colleen, I'm afraid I'm going to have to end our alliance if you won't go out to dinner with me."

She cocked her head and studied him. "Is this blackmail?"

"Only if it works." The sadness gave way to a smile, and the momentary panic she'd had when he said he was ending their friendship eased. "Is it working?"

She had to admit that it was a clever way to get her to see his side. And something she might have done herself. "Well, it seems I have no choice."

His face fell. He sighed.

"I will go to dinner with you." She put up a finger when Roger's features brightened. Saying she'd go to dinner with him didn't mean she had to do it immediately. Maybe this would be enough to cease his endless asking. "But only once, and only to prove to you that we are not compatible romantically and I'm not this vixen you keep claiming I am." He'd called her that a couple of times, though Lord only knew what the man saw in her practical shoes and no-nonsense clothes that said vixen. Perhaps the man needed a vision test.

"You have made my day, Colleen," Roger said. "I will pick you up tonight at six."

"Wait. You want to go to dinner tonight? But it's Halloween and that's so quick and—"

"And at our age, we don't have the luxury of millions of hours." He sat back in his seat and took her hand in his. He had a warm grip, not too tight, not too soft. Secure. Comfortable. "I don't want to wait a day or a week to take you out and get to know you outside of this office. So, I'll see you at six?"

Nora counted her lucky stars that she had Magpie here on this vacation. If there was one thing Magpie excelled at, it was transforming a bad moment into a fun adventure. Nora had known the minute Mags asked her to come to the beach house that it would be a fun time, despite everything she was going through, because her sister had done it before.

When Nora was ten and Magpie was six, the girls had gone exploring in the woods near their house. They'd set out to find a pot of gold after spying a rainbow in the sky. Nora didn't much believe in leprechauns or pots of gold, despite the tales woven by her grandmother and her aunts, but Magpie did, so Nora went along, carrying a velvet bag they'd snuck out of their mother's bedroom.

The day had started out sunny, the two of them holding hands as they wandered down a well-trod path and deeper into the woods. From time to time, the leaves above parted enough for them to see the rainbow, arching above their heads like a beacon. Magpie hurried forward, tugging Nora's hand, not even noticing when dark clouds blotted out the rainbow, and a second round of storms moved in, the rain falling so hard and fast that it slapped the leaves and bounced off the ground. In seconds, Nora and Magpie were soaked and miserable. And lost.

Instead of complaining, Magpie had found a hollowed-out tree, and the two of them hunkered down. She gathered a pile of rocks, drew a square in the soft, sandy earth, and they played a makeshift game of checkers until the skies cleared and they could make their way home again. The stormy afternoon Nora had expected to be a disaster became one of her favorite memories with her sister.

Nora came in from her run, releasing Chance from the leash. The dog beelined for his water bowl while Nora crossed to the fridge and grabbed a bottle of water.

Magpie leaned against the counter, sipping a cup of tea. "Hey, in case you forgot, today is Halloween," she whispered, nodding toward the kids, who were sitting at the bar, eating cereal while the living room TV played cartoons.

Halloween meant costumes. Meant trick-or-treating. Meant Ben was supposed to get the kids and take them back to their old neighborhood. He hadn't texted or called since their late-night conversation, or even replied when Nora sent him the Truro address. Nora didn't know whether to take that as a confirmation that he'd be here or a sign that he wasn't. But either way, the kids were going to expect to trick-or-treat.

"Shit. I forgot the material I bought back at the house," Nora said. "I was going to make a princess costume for Sarah and a superhero one for Jake."

Mags parked her fists on her hips and arched a brow.

"You were going to sew two costumes, from scratch, just days before Halloween? In all your free time?"

"I could have done it." Okay, so even she had doubted her ability to get those costumes done before Halloween. She'd only bought the material because it had seemed so normal, so nothing-is-going-wrong-in-my-life. A little escape from reality found in Jo-Ann Fabrics.

"Listen, Nora, I know everyone in the family thinks you are superhuman, given the number of hours you work and how much you cram into that time, but even you can't create a thirty-hour day. Either way, there's not enough time to run to your house, get the material, produce a sewing machine out of thin air, and sew a princess costume, so we'll have to improvise." Magpie grinned. "If there's one thing I can do well, it's improvise. Nothing like getting caught in monsoon season in Thailand in some jungle and needing to come up with an inventive way to use a flak jacket for shelter."

"Wait…you camped under a jacket? During a monsoon?" Nora shook her head. "Why am I not surprised? I still remember that time we huddled in the tree and played checkers. You amaze me, Mags."

"I'm stronger than you think. At least when it comes to storms." Magpie's fingers drummed against the refrigerator door, something she only did when she was nervous or scared. What could Magpie possibly be nervous about? "In fact, I think it would be good if we had some time to talk tonight after the kids go trick-or-treating."

Magpie was the one who avoided the hard topics.

Sometimes, Nora thought that was half the reason her sister traveled so much—to run from the things she didn't want to deal with. "Talk? About what?"

"Just…girl stuff. No big deal. Sister time and all that." Magpie brightened, erasing the faint traces of vulnerability. Before Nora could press the question, the kids came in from the living room, done with their cereal.

"Can we put on *Frozen*?" Jake asked.

Nora put their bowls in the sink and added a little soapy water. Normal mundane actions that made everything else seem far away. "Yes, but only for a little while, then I want you guys to play outside. It's a beautiful day."

"Okay, Mommy!" Jake gave her a quick hug before dashing off to the living room. Sarah ambled behind him, quiet and sullen again. A moment later, Elsa was singing and the kids were settled on the sofa, Jake plopped in the center with Chance's head on his lap, Sarah nestled into one corner, buried in her iPad, as withdrawn as a hermit.

Nora sighed. "I don't know what to do with Sarah. She won't talk to me."

"I think she's angry with you. I don't know why because she wouldn't open up to me either, but she's mad. She told me that much the other day, when I was alone with the kids." Magpie shrugged. "Maybe you should find some quiet time, just the two of you, to sit down and talk."

"I've tried. I'll try again. Thanks, Mags." Nora sighed. Telling her sister about what was going on with Sarah would only worry Mags more. There wasn't anything her little sister could do about it anyway, although a part of

Nora was envious that Sarah had opened up, even a little, to her aunt instead of her mother. Maybe it was as simple as Magpie said—putting aside some time to walk the beach or sit on the back deck and try to get her to talk. It had to be about more than the fight with Anna, but what more, Nora wasn't sure.

"You're doing great, Nora. You're a really good mom, so don't beat yourself up about an eight-year-old's momentary attitude. We've all had one of those at one time or another." Magpie poured herself a bowl of cereal and handed the box to Nora, who did the same. They added some milk and then crossed to sit at the kitchen table. "But I do remember the four of us got pretty awful with Ma after Dad died. It's like we were angry at her, even though there was nothing she could have done to prevent what happened."

Dad's death had punched a deep, dark hole in their world, and the girls had been as shell-shocked as Ma. The fun-loving father who played catch in the yard, took them on impromptu ice cream runs, and got down on the floor to play baby dolls was gone. They were left with a stressed mother who spent weeks angry at God for taking her true love away.

In the light of adulthood, Nora understood what her mother had gone through. How incredibly tough it must have been to get up in the morning and keep putting one foot in front of the other. But when she was eight, all she'd known was that one day she'd woken up and nothing was the same ever again.

"I think we were just too young to understand how

death worked or what a heart attack was. And after he was gone, we all missed Dad so much." She shook her head. "He was always so much fun. The best dad ever, I think. I still miss him. He'd love having grandkids."

Nora had no doubt her father would have loved Sarah and Jake and spoiled them rotten. She wondered sometimes how her life would be different if their dad had lived, been there to temper Ma, to shoulder half the load. Maybe Nora would have had more of a childhood, wouldn't have felt the need to step into shoes that were far too big for a little girl to fill.

"Because half the time he acted like a ten-year-old himself. Ma would complain about how Dad never took any responsibility and left her to be the bad guy. Maybe he did." Magpie shrugged. "Do you remember how much fun we'd have playing those late afternoon soccer matches in the backyard?"

That was the kind of dad Ben was too. The fun kind, who played with the kids in the yard or horsed around in the living room. He built the blanket forts and roasted the s'mores and made the kids laugh. Nora had been the one to enforce bedtimes and routines, the bad cop in an uneven parenting team.

She realized she'd turned into her mother. The stern one, with rules and judgment aplenty and fun sorely lacking. Was that all it would take to get her kids back on track? Some impromptu fun times?

"Those soccer games were great, weren't they?" Nora smiled. "He even got Ma to play a few times."

Magpie laughed. "That was something to see. Her in her sensible shoes, trying to kick that ball. But at least she was a good sport."

"Then. Not after Dad died."

Nora ate a bite of cereal. "It must have been really difficult to raise all of us without him around. Now that I have kids of my own, I understand it, I really do."

"Ben's a big help, though. Right?"

"Oh yeah, he is. He's fabulous with the kids." Nora dipped her head and ate some more cereal. Fabulous at the fun times, not so fabulous at providing for them or being dependable or shouldering half the hard stuff.

"He's the kind of husband and dad that all of us wish we had. Even I'd settle down with a guy like that." Magpie sighed, the kind of dreamy sigh Nora used to have when she'd first fallen in love with Ben. She wanted to tell her sister that reality rarely matched the fantasy. "You really picked a keeper, Nora, and you guys have such a great life."

Nora pushed the cereal around in her bowl. "So, Halloween. We really should figure something out. The kids have been pestering me and I didn't have an answer for them, because I'm not so sure I can count on Ben to show up. If he doesn't, I'll take them trick-or-treating here, but either way, they need costumes. I don't know what we can make with what we have here. Maybe I should go to the store." Not that she had the money to buy costumes a second time. She shouldn't have bought them the first time, even if the twenty dollars she spent on fabric wouldn't make a blip in the debt they owed the bank.

"We can totally come up with something cool with what we have here," Magpie said. "Between your craft skills and my overpacking, I bet we can put something together. How about we get the kids on board after lunch? We'll take them to the beach this morning and let them look for shells, then eat and make costumes. It'll be fun."

"As much fun as playing checkers in a tree?"

Magpie grinned. "Even more fun. I promise."

FOURTEEN

Magpie sat on the beach, her knees drawn up to her chest while the incoming tide swirled icy water around her toes. The sun was on its downward journey, still a couple hours from sunset. The sky was washed in tones of pale orange, a soft contrast to the green-blue Atlantic. It would have been a beautiful sight—if she'd focused on it for more than a half second.

Inside the house, Nora was getting Jake and Sarah ready for their Halloween adventure. Any other time, Magpie would have joined in but tonight she just... couldn't. She'd done her best earlier, then made up an excuse about needing to call her editor, just to slip outside and be alone. The more time she spent here, the more the pressure to make a decision grew.

She slid her thumb over the little green symbol for the phone app, took a deep breath, and pushed the fifth number on her Favorites list, below the numbers for her sisters and her mother. The other end began to ring, and Magpie hesitated, about to push end when she heard, "You are one hard woman to get in touch with."

Charlie's voice. She'd missed the sound of it, deep yet edged with laughter. He was the kind of guy who didn't take life seriously, who didn't take anything seriously, not even his job. That was what had made him the perfect sorta-boyfriend. A casual relationship with good sex and no expectations. Exactly how Magpie liked things.

"Sorry. I've been working a lot since I got here." Which wasn't true. She had barely been able to write five words in the last two days. "And helping my sister with the kids. Just busy." Too busy to return texts. Too busy to answer calls. Too busy to make decisions she didn't want to make.

"You're just using me for my beach house, aren't you?"

She worked up a laugh. "You know it."

"Good. I want you to. And I want you to have a good time while you're there. Speaking of which, how about I join you?"

She froze. "Join me?"

"Yep. As in I catch a flight out of here and come spend a few days enjoying fall on the Cape. It'll probably be the last time I get out to the house before I have to button it up for the winter."

"I...I thought you weren't going to be back in the States until December." She had met Charlie when she'd been on assignment for *Redbook*, researching a piece on women entrepreneurs in India who had started a university for girls. Charlie had been there to write about the school's innovative medical program. He mostly wrote about medical news while she focused on stories about women being empowered, and they'd found a commonality in their shared world of crazy editors, insane deadlines, and the heady rush of jumping from place to place, always chasing that last elusive detail.

"My editor changed his mind about the piece on that heart machine. Turns out the guy who invented it was brought up on some kind of corporate espionage thing from his previous employer. Now they're sending me to Cleveland to do a piece on some new cancer treatment and then over to Boston on Sunday night to do a thing on stem cells. If you're in town, great, if you're at the beach house still, I'll shoot down there. Since I'll be a couple hours away, I figured I could spend a couple days with you before I have to fly to Denver and let you refresh my memory of how that pink bikini looks on you."

"It's too cold to wear a bikini." Like that was a valid reason to ask him not to come? *How about telling him the truth?* her conscience whispered.

"You're still beautiful, Maggie, even when you're bundled up in a parka with the snow falling around your face in the middle of Leningrad." A voice sounded in the background, and Charlie called out, "On my way...Sorry, but I have to go. I've got a meeting to wrap things up here; then I'll be on my way. I'll see you soon."

Before she could say, *Please don't come. I'm not ready to see you,* the call was disconnected.

*   *   *

Nora sat on the ottoman, with the same leggings and shirt she'd been holding for the last twenty minutes, trying to cajole a defiant eight-year-old into cooperating. All the parenting books would tell her she was failing at Mom 101, that she should lay down the law or nix Halloween for Sarah, but the part of Nora that was swimming in guilt over the house couldn't bring herself to play bad cop.

"Sarah, we need to finish getting your costume together so you can go trick-or-treating." Ben had texted after lunch, saying he'd be there around four, to be sure he got back to their house in time for the start of trick-or-treating. They had less than a half hour until he was going to be here, and Sarah had yet to put on a single item.

"I want to be a princess." Sarah crossed her arms over her chest and repeated the same argument she'd been using all afternoon. "You said you were going to sew me a princess costume."

"I'm sorry, honey, but I left all the stuff for that back at the house."

"You lied! You said I could be a princess! I hate you!" Sarah spun on her heel and ran out of the room.

Nora followed, giving Sarah's door a perfunctory knock before she entered. "Hey, kiddo, that wasn't nice. You know better than to yell at your mother."

Sarah raised her chin. "I don't care."

Nora sank onto the bed beside Sarah but didn't touch her. Everything about Sarah screamed closed off, needing space. The wall between them had grown every day they'd been here, becoming more solid, less yielding. "Honey, I'm really sorry about the costumes. Sometimes things don't work out as we plan, and we have to create a new plan."

"I don't want a new plan." Her daughter's face was tight and pinched. "I don't want to be a superhero. It's dumb."

"Well, it can be cool, too, because we're inventing your costume. That means you can be any superhero you want." Nora affected her best *this is awesome* face. She wished Magpie hadn't left to walk the beach. Since they had arrived in Truro, her sister had been the one who could almost always coax Sarah out of her bad mood and had often run interference between Nora and her oldest child. "How about Supergirl? You used to love Supergirl."

"That was when I was a *baby*. I'm not a baby anymore." She planted her feet and gave Nora that *I dare you to disagree* face. "Daddy would have let me be a princess. He would have taken me to the store and bought me a princess costume and not made me wear this baby one. Daddy wouldn't make me be a stupid superhero."

Nora sighed, her heart fracturing. In Sarah's face, she saw the sweet infant she'd welcomed into the world eight years ago. It seemed like just yesterday when Sarah used to curve her whole body into Nora's lap, like a baby bird settling into its nest. She would fall asleep, her head on Nora's chest, the sound of her mother's heartbeat a soft lullaby to a little girl who was scared of the dark.

Where had their relationship derailed? And how had Nora missed the signs?

Maybe it was all the upheaval with being away from

home. The new setting, new bed, new routine. And maybe Nora was lying to herself about this too.

"Honey, I know this sucks, and I know it isn't what you wanted, but you will still have lots of fun trick-or-treating with your dad and Jake. I'm really sorry about your princess costume, but maybe"—Nora touched Sarah's cheek and waited for her daughter to face her—"we can get creative and make a princess superhero."

"There's no princess superheroes."

Nora gave her daughter a smile. "There's one right here. I think you're a strong, smart, amazing kid. And if you ask me, that's what makes for the best kind of princess and the best kind of superhero."

Sarah considered that for a moment, her watery eyes locked on Nora's. "Okay...I guess."

That was going to be about as much of a concession as Nora was going to get. She'd take it because it was a step forward, and that was better than all the steps backward they'd been taking. She rooted through their suitcase and Magpie's, and a few minutes later came up with some options.

One of her sister's long pink skirts became a dress on Sarah. A sparkly beach cover-up became an improvised cape. And a handful of rhinestone butterfly barrettes clipped onto a headband became a crown. Nora added some usually off-limits makeup to give her daughter pinker cheeks and lips before curling Sarah's long hair. Sarah stood in front of the mirror in her room, her mouth twitching from side to side as she assessed her mother's work. "I do kinda look like a princess superhero."

Nora leaned down and hugged her daughter. It took a moment, but then Sarah yielded to the embrace, relaxing against her mother. "You do indeed. And you'll be the most special one because no one else will have the same costume as you."

Sarah lifted her gaze to Nora's in the mirror. Her lower lip trembled, and the sweet little girl that had been hidden behind a wall of defiance reappeared in the softening of Sarah's features, the shimmer in her eyes. "Do you really think I'm strong and smart, Mommy? After I got in all that trouble?"

"I do, honey, I really do." God, she loved her daughter. And oh how she had missed the sound of the word *Mommy*. Nora pressed a kiss to Sarah's head and held the moment for as long as she could.

Jake burst into the room, his homemade cape spinning in a wide arc behind him. Sarah stepped away from her mother, the moment broken by Jake's exuberant entrance. "I like being a superhero! I look like Batman!"

Magpie had used a short black skirt for Jake's cape and used a pair of Sarah's leggings for tights. Her creative sister had even printed out the Batman symbol to affix to Jake's black T-shirt. Jake, the easy one, had been as pleased with his homemade costume as he would be if Batman himself dropped off a replica.

Jake buzzed ahead of them down the hall and into the kitchen, his arms in front of him, the makeshift cape fluttering behind him. "I'm gonna fly to every house. And I'm gonna get lots of candy!"

"All right, kids, let's take some pictures," Nora said. But before she could grab her phone, the doorbell rang. Ben. With impeccable timing, as always.

Sarah pivoted in an instant, beat Jake to the door, and flung it open. *"Daddy!"*

Two syllables, dancing with joy. Everything about Sarah shifted the second she saw her father. Her eyes lit, her arms went out, and a smile exploded on her face. She clung tight to Ben when he lifted her up, burying her face in his shoulder as if she hadn't seen him in a century.

No one could deny the love that Ben had for his kids and they had for him. Nora shouldn't be jealous, shouldn't wish that the kids would run to her like that, but she was. That little moment with Sarah in the mirror had been a blip, over and done already.

Ben hugged Sarah tight for a long moment, then swung her onto one hip and put out his free arm. "Hey, who's that in the cape? I think that's Batman!"

"It's me, Daddy! Jake! And I can fly! Watch me!" He ran forward, arms outstretched, making a *whoosh-whoosh* sound, and leaped into Ben's embrace.

Nora stood, not twelve feet away from her own family, and watched them as if they were on the other side of a glass wall. The outsider, the one who had fractured their little quartet. For a moment, she wanted to take it all back, to tell Ben to forget the divorce, forget the auction. Just go back to the house and live in a cloud of denial until the sheriff kicked them out.

Except she'd been living in that cloud for years, and it

had brought her here. To a daughter who hated her, a husband who didn't love her anymore, and a home that had disintegrated.

Ben lowered the kids to the floor. "Let me talk to Mom for a second, okay?"

"Okay! I'm gonna get my bag for all my candy!" Jake buzzed across the room with Sarah hurrying behind him.

Ben shifted his weight and met Nora's gaze. For a second, she thought he was going to say what she'd been thinking—forget the divorce and the auction and just go back to where they were before all this.

"Do you mind if they stay with me tonight?" Ben asked instead. "It's a long ride up here, and I was thinking it might be nice to have some one-on-one time. We still have the house for like three weeks, and I haven't moved anything out yet, so it'll be like normal to the kids."

"You don't have...someplace else you're going to go on a Friday night?" Wherever he'd been going on Friday and Saturday nights for the last few months. All those nights she'd spent alone, her mind picturing one worst-case scenario after another.

Ben held her gaze. "No, I don't." He paused, just long enough for a weird flutter of hope to run through her, and then he added, "At least not this Friday night."

So...nothing had changed. Why did she even care anymore? He was entitled to his life, a life that would soon be unencumbered by a wedding ring.

Standing with him, here in the foyer of the beach house, with a spattering of sand at their feet and the soft sound of the ocean in the background, echoed their honeymoon. They'd gone to Ogunquit Beach in Maine for four days, staying in a little inn that sat right on the beach. Every night, they'd gone to sleep with the sound of the ocean and a gentle breeze blowing in the open French doors. It had been a magical, amazing honeymoon, and for a second, she wanted to ask Ben if the sand under his feet made him think of that time too.

"So, is it okay, Nora? I'd really like to spend some time with the kids. You've had them all week."

The icy words jerked her back from the beach in Maine and into the present day, where she no longer had a house and she was getting a divorce. Reminiscing was only going to make this harder. She cleared her throat, past the damned lump there, and called down the hall. "Kids, grab some pajamas and your toothbrushes. You're going to stay with Dad tonight."

"Thanks," Ben said.

"No problem." Nora stood in the foyer, awkward and unsure with the man she had slept beside for a third of her life. The clock on the wall ticked the seconds away, each click sounding as loud as a gunshot.

Ben cleared his throat. "You doing okay here? Need anything?"

"Three hundred thousand dollars?" The joke fell flat and Ben's face soured. "Sorry. I shouldn't have said that. Anyway, we're fine. Having a great time."

"Good. I'm glad." He toed at the floor. "You needed a vacation, Nora."

She couldn't tell if he was being sarcastic or nice. Ben's face, once as familiar to her as her own, had become something she couldn't read, couldn't interpret. It was as if their marriage had become a high-stakes poker game, and neither one of them wanted to betray what they were holding. The irony of the thought nearly made her laugh. "Thanks. Uh...how's work?"

"Busy. I got the Harcourt project. Well, part of it. They're going to see how it works out with the first couple houses."

"Oh, good. I'm glad." Ben had been courting Harcourt Builders for a long time, hoping to get a chance at handling some of the building for their new subdivision going into Newton. It meant good money—when the project was done. Too bad he hadn't worked this hard before, when it would have made a difference.

For weeks after he got out of the gambler's rehab program he'd gone to, Ben had sat around the house, despondent and frozen, as if the verve had gone out of his life when he'd quit gambling. It was only in the last few months that Ben had gotten back to a normal schedule.

He shifted his weight again. "Well, traffic might be bad going back. I should probably hit the road. Kids? You ready?"

The kids came back, bags slung over their shoulders, and slid into place on either side of Ben. This was how it would be, she realized, after the divorce. An awkward handoff in some foyer with neither of them having much to say.

Nora pasted a bright smile on her face. "Have a good time, kids," she said, her voice high, rushed, filled with faked happiness. "Be sure to listen to Daddy and don't cross the street without him."

Sarah rolled her eyes. "I know, Mom. I'm not a baby."

"Then that means you can help your dad watch out for Jake. Okay?"

Sarah shrugged. "I guess so."

"She'll be great, won't you, Sarah Bear?" Ben ruffled his daughter's hair, and she beamed up at him. That little flicker of jealousy ran through Nora again. "Well, we better get going if we're going to get back to Dorchester in time," he said. "I'll see you tomorrow morning. Bye, Nora."

The kids bounded out the door with their father, Jake in flying mode, Sarah chatting a mile a minute about how she couldn't wait to go to the houses in their neighborhood. The three of them went down the walkway, climbed into Ben's car, and left, without so much as a backward glance or a goodbye.

And Nora realized something had indeed changed. She'd been shut out of her own family.

FIFTEEN

By six o'clock, Colleen had changed her clothes three times and finally opted for one of her church skirts and a sweater. She'd slipped on hose, then the long gray wool skirt, paired with a pressed white blouse and a navy cardigan, along with the gold cross her mother gave her when she graduated high school. In the mirror, she didn't look like a vixen at all. More of a dowager edging her way toward a rocker on the porch. Perhaps now Roger would give up this silly idea of dating her.

She was just adding a handkerchief to her purse when the squat white phone on the hall table rang. Colleen was one of the last holdouts to keep a rotary phone, caving to the handheld type under duress. She still used the landline far more often than that itty-bitty cell phone the girls had given her two Christmases ago. When the cable man came to the house to repair a broken line last winter, he'd told Colleen he hadn't had to install a telephone line in at least five years. "Most folks don't bother with that kind of thing anymore."

"I like tradition," Colleen told him. "And things I can depend on. When a storm hits or the power is out, those fancy cell phones quit working. This"—she'd patted the now-dusty white phone with the mile-long corkscrew cord that she could still see wrapped around the doorway with one of the girls on the other end, whispering to a friend or a boy who had called—"will always be there when I need it."

Colleen picked up the handset and said hello, half expecting Roger to tell her he had changed his mind. Instead, she heard Mary's chipper voice. Ever since Mary had told Colleen that she was her real mother, Colleen had switched to calling her Mary instead of "my sister" or "my mother." At her age, the moniker probably didn't matter much anyway, but Colleen was a woman given to tradition and not partial to change. Hence the rotary phone and the regular schedule with Mass and family dinners.

"Are you okay?" Colleen didn't bother with a hello back or any small talk. All those things did was clutter a perfectly fine conversation. "Do you need a ride home from your friend's house?"

"I'm fine, just fine. Stop worrying," Mary said. "Gloria said she will drive me home after we are done playing bridge so I won't be walking in the dark, although I'm more than healthy enough to traverse three blocks on my own. I tell you, it feels good to be back out and among the living again."

Even though Mary made light of her heart condition, the precariousness of her health worried Colleen. Mary had always been a person who did her own thing, set her own schedule, traveled at her own pace. Three weeks of convalescing in the hospital and then at home had given her some serious cabin fever, blowing up her social schedule with lunches and card games and shopping trips. Short of sprinkling some Unisom in her afternoon tea, Colleen had yet to find a way to get Mary to follow the doctor's advice of resting and recuperating. "I do hope you aren't overdoing it."

"I'm sitting at a kitchen table, holding a deck of cards. That's hardly overdoing it." Mary chuckled. "Anyway, my dear worrywart, I called to see if you wanted to join us. Carolyn doesn't think she can make it, and we really need a fourth."

"I can't." She paused. "I have...plans."

"Plans? Like with another person?"

"You say that like I'm some kind of friendless hermit. Yes, Mary, with another person." Colleen moved in front of the hall mirror, gave her hair a pat, and then checked for lipstick on her teeth. Goodness, why was she trying so hard? This was hardly a date.

"Wait...are you going out with that Roger? He's very handsome and clearly keen on you, Colleen. I think he'd be good for you."

"We are discussing the shelter over dinner. That's all." Colleen crossed herself and whispered a "forgive me" to the ceiling. This man had her fibbing to her family. Yet another reason she shouldn't date him.

"Well, I think you should throw caution to the wind

and go all in, my dear daughter. Life is too short to spend your days alone and miserable." Mary sighed. "I know that lesson too well."

The sadness in Mary's voice spoke of the years she'd spent away from her family and the love she had lost long ago. Colleen could sympathize—the loneliness she had felt in the two decades since her Michael died had been almost palpable. Perhaps that was what drove Mary to fill her days and nights with friends and adventures. "Speaking of making plans, perhaps you should make some of your own to actually listen to your doctor."

Mary laughed. "The busy workaholic daughter giving her busy social-holic mother advice to slow down? If I do that, Colleen, I'll be underfoot all the time."

"Having you stay here hasn't been too much of a hardship," Colleen said.

"Which is your way of saying you like me living with you, you softie. It has been good, I admit. Gives us plenty of time to rebuild that connection we missed. Speaking of mother-daughter connections, have you spoken to Nora?"

Colleen noticed Mary's quick conversational segue. On any other day, the inquisitive detour might have annoyed her—she'd been parenting on her own for two decades, after all, and didn't need anyone else to point out her mistakes—but truth be told, Nora's recent decisions had spurred some worry. Nora was usually so calm and steady and happy, but in recent weeks her daughter had been subdued and distant, not to mention the way she just up and took off on a trip. "I talked to her a couple times on the phone. She seems to be having quite the busy time on vacation. Though it still surprises me that she did that at the last minute. Nora's always been such a planner."

Mary paused. "I wouldn't want to butt in, but I think doing so is a requirement in this family, so I'm going to be a buttinsky, like it or not. Nora needs you right now, Colleen, more than she'll say."

The hairs on the back of Colleen's neck stood up. She should have tried harder to talk to Nora instead of being so consumed by this shelter business. Yet another reason why dating anyone was a ridiculous proposition. "Why? What's going on?"

"She's having a rough time, and you know her, she's never going to speak up about it. So I think you should reach out and talk to her. Don't tell her I said anything. Just be there for her. And for God's sake, be gentle."

"I'm always gentle."

Mary let out a hearty laugh. "Colleen, you are about as gentle as a porcupine with a heart of gold. Your intentions are great but your approach is prickly."

Colleen scoffed but knew Mary had a point. It wasn't one that Colleen liked to acknowledge, but it was true. For three years, she and her middle daughter Abby hadn't talked, after a family fight at Bridget's wedding. Then Bridget had pulled away, dropping out of the bakery and then family dinners. In the past year, Colleen's daughters had come home—literally, with Magpie in Massachusetts again for longer than a split second—and Colleen didn't want to risk losing any of them ever again. Their amends had been in fits and starts, a recalcitrant engine trying to travel a bumpy road.

This week, Colleen had chalked Nora's quick departure up to stress. The main responsibility of their busy bakery had fallen on Nora's shoulders for years, as Colleen stepped back in her old age and gave her daughters more free rein to helm their inheritance. Yet the more she thought back over the last few months, the more she realized Nora had seemed distracted, moody, unlike herself. Colleen couldn't imagine why. Nora had a wonderful husband, great children, and a lovely house.

Colleen knew she sometimes put too much on Nora. When Michael, God rest his soul, had passed away, Nora had stepped in as a second mother hen, who got all the other ducklings in a row when Colleen was too tired or overwhelmed. Of the four girls, Nora was the most like Colleen—stubborn, independent, and the last to complain or ask for help. Maybe Nora simply needed a few days' rest. "I'll call her first thing tomorrow, or tonight, if it's early enough when I get home."

"I hope you *aren't* home early enough to make a call. Besides, it's Halloween. The kids will be out trick-or-treating, so Nora will be busy."

"I forgot about that." Even though she'd spent most of her day selling orange frosted cupcakes, her brain had let that detail slip. Well, it was all due to that Roger. Every time she got around him, her mind went fuzzy. Yet another reason to be clear with him that this was not a date. She didn't need another person in her life or another demand on her time. Her daughters still needed her, clearly.

Mary said something to the other people in the room and then returned to the phone. "I have to go. Ernestine Wickman is coming to play instead. That woman drives me crazy, the way she clacks her dentures every few seconds. Dear God, it's like playing bridge with a snare drum. Pray for patience for me."

Colleen laughed. In a few words, Mary had lightened the cloud hanging over Colleen. It really was good to have Mary back. "Just give her some extra-strength Poligrip. And keep her away from the crunchy food. Have fun tonight."

"Only if you promise me that you will too."

"I just saw headlights in the driveway. I'll talk to you later, Mary." Colleen replaced the handset in the cradle before Mary could ask any more questions or offer more advice that Colleen didn't need.

The doorbell rang, and even though Colleen had been half expecting Roger to come to the door for her, the sound still startled her. She caught her reflection one final time—determined she was sufficiently dowager-like—before pulling open the door. Roger stood on her porch, wearing a pale green button-down shirt, a blue-patterned tie, and dark gray trousers under his black overcoat. He held out a bouquet of white daisies wrapped in dark green paper. "Your favorite, if I remember right."

"They are." She'd only mentioned that in passing. Quite remarkable of him to remember. She took the flowers and inhaled their sweet, light fragrance. "'Black bees on the clover-heads drowsily clinging, where tall, feathered grasses and buttercups sway; and all through the fields a white sprinkle of daisies, open-eyed at the setting of day.'"

Roger smiled. "I like that. What's it from?"

"A poem by Abba Woolson. I remember reading it in high school, and it's stuck with me. I do think daisies are like that, don't you? A sprinkle of white happiness in a field, open-eyed even when the sun is going down."

"Why, Colleen O'Bannon, I daresay you are a romantic."

"I am no such thing. Reciting a poem doesn't make me any more romantic than a fencepost." The man was looking for signs of some great love story when there were none. One stanza from a poem, that was all it was. She led him inside and down the hall to the kitchen, where she retrieved a vase from under the sink, filled it with water, and arranged the daisies. "Regardless, we should leave before the restaurant gets busy. And thank you for being prompt. I appreciate people who are on time. If you ask me, it's ill-mannered to be late."

"Actually, I was ten minutes early, so I drove around the block a few times." Roger chuckled. "Guess I was a little nervous. I haven't been on a date in a long time."

For some reason, that pleased her and also made her wonder why a nice man like him hadn't been scooped up by some predatory widow. Colleen grabbed her purse, tucked it under her arm, and readied her keys. "Let's go, then."

As they walked down the hall, he put out his arm, but

she ignored it, using the excuse of locking the door. "You look very pretty tonight, Colleen," Roger said. "That blue sweater brings out your eyes."

"Now who's the silly romantic?" She nodded toward his car, hoping he didn't see the blush that heated her cheeks. "Before I get inside that car, are you a good driver?"

"The state of Massachusetts and Allstate think so." He grinned as he opened her door. A moment later he got in on the other side. "Sit back and enjoy yourself, Colleen."

She tried to do just that, but every nerve inside her was buzzing. Roger drove a practical four-door sedan, maybe eight years old, without a lot of fancy gadgetry in the dash. A cross hung from his rearview mirror, and the backseat was filled with canned food donations for the shelter. The car was clean and neat, tidy. He pulled away from the curb and headed down the street, well within the speed limit. At the four-way stop, Roger came to a complete halt before turning right, and Colleen allowed herself to relax a bit in the passenger seat.

He took her to a small Italian restaurant a couple miles from her house, a place she'd wanted to try since they opened a year ago. Roger had made a reservation, and they were seated in a booth almost as soon as they walked inside. The cozy atmosphere was less *Sopranos* and more Pavarotti, with elegant chandeliers for lighting and dark blue seat cushions.

The waitress, a friendly, too-skinny girl in her twenties, dropped off some menus and left them alone. Colleen fidgeted in her seat. She'd never been good at small talk, and even worse at date talk. Michael had been the third man she'd dated, and he'd been so full of life, she'd never had to say more than a handful of words with him.

"Iris is doing well," she said. "Thank you for sending her to me."

"You're welcome. I'm glad to hear she's working out." Roger glanced over his menu at her. "Has she told you her story?"

Colleen shook her head. "I haven't asked either. I'm not much for prying. I always assume if someone wants me to know, they will share the information. She is quite the withdrawn young girl, though. And she often seems...troubled. But she doesn't share." The young girl had warmed a bit to working with the family, but she still had a tendency to go quiet. And there'd been a couple times Colleen had found her talking on her phone in angry whispers.

"She doesn't talk much about it, but I think it will help you understand her." Roger laid his menu to the side and folded his hands on the white tablecloth. "Iris has been on her own since she was sixteen. Her mother has been in and out of jail and rehab for drugs, and Iris has been on her own, between places, more than she's been in a stable home with her mother. She came to us a few months ago, and we got her set up with a high school and a tutor. She was...angry for a long time, getting into trouble on the streets and in and out of schools. All of it understandable, after what she's been through with her mother. But we've seen a nice change in her since we brought her into the shelter and enrolled her in the school in her old neighborhood and she reconnected with a very good friend of hers—"

"The unwed mother."

Roger frowned. "You say that as if it's a terrible thing. Sometimes, Colleen, it is far better for a woman to raise her child alone than with a man who is abusive or drug addicted."

"True. But still…the church discourages that. They, and I, think children need stable homes." Colleen thought of her own mother, who had pretended to be her sister, all to protect the family reputation. There were circumstances, of course, that could explain such a choice, but far better for young people to wait and be settled before adding children to their lives.

"You were essentially a single mother yourself, and your daughters turned out quite well."

"Well, yes, but I was married when I had them and was blessed with Michael as their father for more than a decade." She might not have remarried, but her children had had a strong foundation with a good father.

"All I'm saying is try not to judge Iris's friend—who is a very nice young woman, struggling to do the right thing— by a set of rules that aren't meant to fit everyone. Grace is about giving people understanding and compassion, regardless of the choices they make."

Roger did have a point. She'd almost lost Abby because of her stubborn views, and her steadfast commitment to the rules set in place by the church centuries ago. Like the diocese, Colleen had begun to soften in some of her attitudes, trying to be more welcoming and less judging. It was new thinking, new ways of responding, and the one thing Colleen hated was change. The more predictable her days were, the easier it was to deal with the waves. "I shall think about it," was all she said to Roger.

"Good. Because that girl is a very important part of Iris's life. When Iris was seven, her mother would lock her out of the house so she could turn tricks to pay for her drugs. Monica lived next door and took Iris in, any time of the day, and kept that girl from ending up on the streets or worse. She's the one stable thing Iris has, and she's a good influence on her." Roger took a sip of water.

"Do you"—Colleen drew in a deep breath—"trust Iris? I mean, a girl with a background like that?"

"I wouldn't have sent her to you if I didn't trust her." Roger studied Colleen. "Why? Has she done something to make you mistrust her?"

"No, not anything in particular." The whispering into her phone and the periods of withdrawal didn't necessarily mean anything, but they still raised the hairs on the back of Colleen's neck.

Roger let out a long breath. "It would be nice if you loosened a few of those rules and standards you live by, Colleen. People can surprise you, in a good way, if you do."

"And sometimes it's the opposite," she replied. She re-settled her napkin in her lap. "Well, regardless, for now, Iris is working out, and I'm glad to give her a job. Perhaps it can change her future a little bit."

"It already has. She says such wonderful things about you and the bakery. She looks happier than I've ever seen her."

What a life that young girl had endured. Colleen whispered a silent prayer of gratitude that her girls had never ended up living on the streets. All four had turned out to be responsible adults, and that alleviated a lot of the worry on Colleen's shoulders. How sad that Iris had never had a mother who worried like that, or sisters to wrap their arms around her. The friend was, indeed, a blessing. "That surprises me that Iris is telling you about the bakery. She hardly talks at work."

"I sent her to you because I knew you'd be able to connect with her. And most importantly, that you'd be good for her."

"Me? Why?"

"Because you've experienced loss and being on your own, and yet you didn't quit or give up, or let your anger at what happened with your husband get in the way."

She'd only been doing what had to be done and had never seen any of that as a hardship. It was merely her life, and her job was to live it as God intended for her to do. Wallowing in her grief would have only hurt them all. Still, the praise warmed her. "Well, I had four girls to raise. I didn't have time for anger."

"Ah, you make it sound so easy, Colleen. When I know sometimes it is harder than hell to let go of your anger at God for taking someone you love too soon."

His voice held notes of sadness and grief, two things Colleen could relate to. She might have hauled herself out of bed every day to run the business and raise her girls, but late at night, when she was alone in her bed, she had railed at God and cried the tears she couldn't shed in front of her daughters.

"I understand that, Roger," she said softly. "I think we all have been there before."

The waitress dropped off two glasses of chardonnay. Colleen thanked her and took a sip, noting Roger had good taste when it came to wine. The white was smooth and refined, with a hint of pear. "You've never told me how Sophie's Home came about—I mean, not entirely. You said you were looking for a purpose after you got divorced, but it seems like a big change for someone who was working in management. Why did you open it?"

"That's a story not many get to hear." Roger splayed his fingers across the base of the wineglass. He stared into the amber liquid as if there were some truth to be found there. "It's not a story I tell often either. Even all these years later, it's hard to speak the words."

"You don't have to tell me if you don't want to." She prayed he would, though. Ever since she'd met Roger, she'd wondered about his background. About why a man with a promising career in banking would give up everything to run a nonprofit shelter. About why this man had once been as angry at God as she had been.

She did care, Lord forgive her, about this man. He had become more than a friend over the last year, and even on this date that wasn't a date, she wanted to lend him her shoulder.

"Sophie was my daughter," he said after a while, his voice soft and sad. "She was the light of my life. The best thing that ever happened to me."

Was. Already, Colleen could feel his pain. She hadn't lost any of her children, but like any mother, that fear lingered at the edge of every good night, every missed call, every stormy day. "What happened to her?"

He didn't say anything for a long time. The soft jazz on the sound system and the murmur of conversations filled the silence. Colleen waited. She knew too well that some subjects required patience and space, and so she gave his thoughts room to breathe and bloom.

"Sophie was a beautiful girl, inside and out. She was so light and happy when she was little, always singing and spinning. She loved to spin, and she'd wear these dresses that flared out when she did, like a ballerina." His face softened at the memory, and Colleen could almost see the little dark-haired girl in the picture in his office dancing. "Nori, my wife, and I did our best with her, but with the divorce and shared custody and both of us working too much and home too little, she was left on her own far too much. When she got to high school, she got...lost. That's the best word for it."

Another fear Colleen knew well. Abby had done the same for a while, but then she'd joined the softball team and that had redirected a lot of her teenage anger. Thank God. "Did Sophie fall in with a bad crowd?"

Roger nodded. "By the time Nori and I realized Sophie was in trouble, she had gone from pot to heroin. We sent her to rehab. Three of them. But that damned drug had its tenterhooks in her and wouldn't let go."

Colleen had seen those addicts on the streets of Dorchester. Most days, she almost saw through them, because they were such a common sight. The church had an outreach program, of course, and Colleen had donated to that, but never had she put a face to the drugs. She thought again of that young girl in the picture, that missing front tooth in a smile as wide as Boston Harbor. She couldn't imagine how painful it would be to see one of her girls descend into that world. They'd been faced with temptations, as all children were, but thank God her girls had made smart choices. It was times like this that reminded her how very blessed her life had been. "Oh, Roger, I'm so sorry."

"She ran away from home a dozen times, and twice we found her in the hospital. Beaten, raped, strung out. Lord, it broke my heart every time, and I tried, God knows I tried, to save her. But she was stubborn and the drugs were stronger than her faith in herself. The third time, she didn't come home." His eyes filled and his voice thickened. His hands trembled against the glass, and Colleen's breath caught, knowing in her heart what was coming next, wishing Roger wasn't going to say the words. "My sweet Sophie died the day before her seventeenth birthday."

"Oh, dear Lord, Roger. That is terrible. I'm so very sorry, and I know that doesn't even begin to touch the grief you have felt, but I am." She covered his hand with her own and gave his fingers a squeeze.

He gave her a weak smile. "She was sober, you know,

for six months before that third time. God, I had such hope then. I really thought she could do it that time, you know? She moved in with me, and she was going to school and saying all the right things, and I started to believe. To trust that God had her in His hands and she would be okay.

"One night, we were sitting on my back deck, and I swear, it was just like having my happy little girl back again. She was wearing one of those flare-out skirts she loved so much, and she was humming along with the radio." His smile wavered. He drew in a deep breath and held it a moment before he spoke again. "The sun was going down, and I remember she sat beside me, reached across the chairs, and took my hand. We'd been talking about the garden, about how she wanted to plant some flowers come spring. She loved flowers, all kinds. Roses, orchids, daisies—like you, Colleen."

He paused, and she sat there quietly, waiting. Giving Roger the room he needed to let the long-hidden painful words trickle forward.

"Then she turned to me and said—and I'll never forget this moment, the way her eyes were so bright and intent, the conviction in her voice—she said, 'Dad, I want you to know that the one thing that kept me going was knowing home would always be here. That *you* would be here. It gave me hope, too, that someday I could have a different life. The life I wanted before I took that one wrong turn.'

"I damned near started to cry right then. Instead, I just gave her a hug and told her how proud I was of her. How I believed in her. She cried a little, too, and then whispered words to me that I have heard in my heart every single day since she died. 'Promise me, Dad,' she said, 'if anything ever happens or I screw up again, that home will always be here. And so will you.'"

Colleen's heart squeezed, and she blinked away her tears. The mother in her ached for Roger, for the lost life that could have been something amazing. His grief filled the space between them and drew her closer, in that shared language of parents who knew heartache. "She must have loved you very much."

"Not nearly as much as I loved her." He shook his head and swiped away a tear. "It was ten years after we buried her before I stopped being angry at God and decided to do something. I realized, if there had been a place like Sophie's Home around when my daughter was lost and on the streets, maybe she could have found shelter, safety, support. These girls need a place they can depend on, a place that will give them the security they need. So I quit my job and bought that house and poured everything I had into it."

"I'm sure Sophie is looking down on you, proud of her father for all the lives he has helped."

"Ah, but it's never enough lives, is it? I'm always worried about the teenager who hasn't come to us or the mother who is living on the streets and doesn't know we exist."

Colleen vowed to make it her mission to spread the word about Roger's shelter. To help even more than she already did and bring in more donations. Maybe starting with her bridge group or those ladies down at Saturday night bingo. She could start a trickle that would hopefully someday turn into a river, giving him the resources he needed to help even more girls and women. He was an amazing man, doing an amazing thing, and that drove her to want to make a difference. For the first time in a long time, stirrings of excitement danced in Colleen's belly. Something new to put her passion into, her energy. "That is an incredible story. I can see why you are so passionate about it. And it makes me want to help even more. What else can I do?"

"Just get Iris on the right path. She's a lost girl, too, and I don't want to lose another one."

Colleen gave his hand another squeeze and realized touching him had become natural at some point. "I can do that."

SIXTEEN

Five miles later, Nora was sweating, exhausted, and no less stressed than when she started her run late that Saturday morning. She had less than twenty-four hours left in the Truro house, which meant getting back to reality and, more, dealing with that reality. She hadn't hit the Megabucks or found a pot of gold in the last five days, so that meant the problems she'd left behind were still waiting for her, like mice in a shadowed corner.

Nora walked back toward the house, uncapping the water bottle she'd brought with her and taking a long drink. As she rounded the corner, she saw Will in his front yard, adding a sea life scene to his plain black metal mailbox. The vivid colors of saltwater fish and a soft blue-green ocean almost seemed real in those depths of color and shadow.

"Looking good," she said. Though she wasn't sure if she meant the artwork or the man. Will was the kind of man who made jeans look like a sin, even today, with spatters of paint and an old Grateful Dead T-shirt. Damn, he looked good. If she was any kind of a Catholic, she'd be whispering a Hail Mary for committing mental adultery.

She didn't.

Will dropped his paintbrush into a Folgers coffee can and gave her a grin. "I could say the same about you. Have a good run?"

"Yes, thank you." She held up the water bottle. "And this time I didn't need rescuing."

He rose and brushed the grass off his knees. He placed the coffee can on the post holding the mailbox. "Pity. I was hoping for an excuse to see you again."

Damn it. Why did that comment make her take two steps closer to him? Coaxing a smile out of her on a day when she was overwhelmed and stressed and a little panicked. And made her wonder what it would be like to kiss him, to feel his chest against hers. His smile was a little lopsided, and a part of her found that endearing. Sexy. Tempting. "That's really nice of you to say, Will, but I—"

"Is this why you left me? For him?"

Ben's voice froze Nora's sentence. She turned, the move seeming to take a century, until she was face-to-face with the man she had once pledged her life to. He was a statue, steel ice, and a hot wave of guilt washed over her, even though she was doing nothing wrong. Except she had been sinning in her mind, in the way she looked at Will. She'd been thinking about kissing and touching another man, a man whose eyes reflected interest, not condemnation. A man who hadn't left her more than a quarter million dollars in debt and homeless. She'd been imagining what her life could be like without Ben, and with this man instead. "No, Ben, this isn't why I left you. And this isn't what you think."

Will stepped forward and thrust out his hand. Nora wanted to tell him to stop, to not make it worse, but Will moved faster than she could find her voice. "Ben, is it? Nice to meet you. I'm Will—"

"I don't care who you are." Ben leaned into Will's face. Ben was a good three inches taller than Will, and his shadow loomed over the artist. "Stay the fuck away from my wife."

Will put up both hands and took a step back. "I swear, man, nothing is going on between us. We're just temporary neighbors."

Ben's gaze darted between Will and Nora. His eyes connected with his wife's, and in the moment they connected, it seemed as if Ben could read every thought she'd just had about Will. Ben's anger flickered, then yielded to hurt, and Nora wanted to erase the entire moment. But there were no words that would mend this rift. No bandage she could put on the marriage that had died two years ago.

She thought of all those Friday and Saturday nights he'd been gone until the wee hours. The secrets he'd kept. The money he'd wasted. The snowy day he had left her alone and scared. She knew that sense of betrayal, knew it well. How dare he accuse her of anything. Ben was the one who had abandoned her, who had checked out long ago.

His mistress had been a pair of dice, the affair housed in a dark, smoky casino. "Ben—"

"The kids are inside with your sister. I left their stuff in the hall." He turned on his heel. "I'm done here."

Nora broke into a run and caught up with him just as he reached his car. She touched his arm, but it was like connecting with a steel post. Her emotions roller coasted, rising and falling between anger and hurt, bottoming out into fear. "Ben, stop. There's nothing going on between Will and me."

Ben spun around, and for the first time, she noticed the lines in his face, the shadows dusting his eyes. "So you're on a first name basis with the 'temporary neighbor'? Funny, we lived next door to the Monahans for five years, and I don't think you could have told me either of their first names."

"The Monahans weren't our friends." And she'd never been home. She'd been working or volunteering at the school or shuttling the kids to different places. There'd been no time for neighborhood block parties or inviting them over to play cards. She'd been doing the job of two parents, because Ben had been too busy sending their money down the drain.

"And this man you've known for what, a week, is?" Ben said. "I find that convenient, considering you asked me for a divorce just the day before you went on your impromptu *vacation*."

She threw up her hands. "God, why do you have to make every single fight we have into something like this?

Something huge, over the top? Is it the gambling? Are you still jonesing for that high? Because that's what you do, Ben. You go big, in everything you do, regardless of what it costs us."

He pointed down the street, to Will's half-finished mailbox, standing alone since Will had gone inside. "I'm not making it into anything. I saw you with him. I saw the way he looked at you—"

"Which is nothing I can control."

"And the way you looked back at him." Ben took two steps closer, his face unreadable. He had two days' worth of stubble on his cheeks, and his dark hair was long enough to need a trim. "You used to look at me like that." His voice broke a little and her heart cracked.

But she couldn't let him in again. Couldn't let that whisper of vulnerability in his words tempt her to return to something that had already taken its last breath. "Since when have you cared how I look at you? I've been looking at you like that for a dozen years, and what did you do with that look?"

"Here we go again." He cursed. "Jesus, Nora, when are you going to stop making me pay for my sins?"

"When they stop ruining our lives."

"You think I did that single-handedly, Nora? It takes two to make a marriage and two to break it."

She shook her head. When was he going to see that he was the one who had plunged them into a crater of debt so deep they had no hope of climbing out? That it was him at that roulette table, not her? She'd been at home, trying to hold on to the very thing Ben had left, as if his family was just another game of chance. And when she *had* tried to make it work, that one last-ditch effort to turn their lives around, he'd left her again for Foxwoods.

She shivered in the warm Cape Cod sun, as if she were back on that bench while the snow fell around her and her dreams ebbed away. It had been over a year, and still the pain was a dagger. "I'm not having this conversation again, Ben. We have argued about what happened a thousand times. You don't see it. All that therapy and meetings and you still don't see what you did to us."

"I do see it, Nora. It's why I kept trying."

She let out a sharp, short laugh. "Trying? You call leaving me to do everything trying? Unplugging from your family when I needed you most? You left me, Ben. You walked out the door and..." Nora shook her head and drew in a breath that headed off the threat of tears.

"What are you talking about? I never left you, Nora. I've been here, the whole time."

A part of her wanted to tell him, to just unleash all the words she had kept inside. The hurt was like a giant wall of water, held back by a flimsy piece of plastic. If she nudged it, she was afraid it would drown her.

Either way, it was too late. They were done. "Why can't you just accept this and move on? Let it go?"

"Let it go? You're my *wife*, Nora. Those are *my* kids in there. This is *our* family. I can't let that go."

She wanted to reach out, to touch his unruly hair and tell him she didn't want to let go either. But then she thought of the bills, the auction notice, the stress that had been thrust on her shoulders days ago, and most of all, of that cold winter day when he'd driven away and she stayed where she was. "That's not what you said the other night."

"Yeah, well, news flash—I'm also not superhuman. I get hurt and depressed and angry, and I lash out and say things I don't mean sometimes too."

She sighed. Why did he have to waver so much? To keep resurrecting this hope in her, that maybe he had changed? He'd whispered all the right words that night a year ago, and she had believed for a moment that there was still a chance, that the man she'd fallen in love with over a plastic cup of ginger ale was still there. "Do you think I didn't mean it when I asked for a divorce?"

He closed the gap between them. If she inhaled, she'd catch the scent of his cologne, a fragrance as familiar as her own name. "Yes, that's exactly what I think."

"Then you don't know me very well, Ben." Nora stood stock-still, a tin soldier fortifying herself against weakening to a whiff of cologne and the memories the scent awakened.

He studied her for a long time. The softness in his gaze hardened. "No, I guess I don't." Then he climbed into his car and left.

Sarah sat in the kitchen chair, arms crossed, face defiant. "I didn't do anything."

Nora sighed and sat in the opposite chair. The second

she'd entered the house after Ben left, she'd heard yelling in the kitchen, with Magpie trying her best to referee. Now Sarah was in a time-out, and Jake was on the back porch with Magpie, his little shoulders hunched. "You got into a fight with your brother. And you broke his truck."

Sarah shrugged. "He started it."

"Maybe so, but that doesn't give you permission to fight with him or break his toys. You're the older one, Sarah, and you should know better."

Sarah cut her gaze to the floor. The chair was low enough for her feet to touch the tile, and she swung her bare toes back and forth against the cool melon-colored surface. "Why are we here?"

The question surprised Nora. "I thought it would be fun to go on vacation. Aren't you having fun?"

Sarah shook her head. Tears brimmed in her eyes. "I want to go home. I want to see Daddy."

Nora sighed. At some point, she had to tell the kids the truth. Was it wrong to want to keep them in the dark a little longer? To not disrupt their world right away? "We will, soon. And you just got back from seeing Daddy."

Sarah shrugged. She gripped the side of the chair and lifted her teary eyes to her mother's. "Why were you fighting with Daddy? Why can't you just be nice to him?"

God, had Sarah seen their argument in the street? Nora should have thought before she'd said anything to Ben, especially in full view of the house. All she'd seen was white-hot anger. She hadn't thought about front-facing windows and two kids on the other side. *And for the sec-*

ond week in a row, Worst Mother of the Year goes to . . . Nora Daniels.

Nora's first response was to lie again, to pretend she and Ben weren't fighting. But kids picked up on the subtleties, the tension that sparked the air. On the rare occasions when her parents had an argument, she'd known. Ma would be working on one side of the house, Dad on the other, a wall of silence thickening the air.

Over the last two years, the kids had asked her a couple times why she was sleeping in the guest room, and she'd made a joke about Daddy's snoring. She'd hoped they were young enough not to question that reasoning.

"Your father and I are going to argue sometimes. All people argue, even you and me," Nora said. "Daddy and I don't agree on everything, but we agree on how much we love you both."

"Then why isn't Daddy here? How come he didn't stay with us? He needs a vacation too."

"He couldn't get time off from work." Another lie, because she hadn't even asked Ben.

"But Daddy's the boss. He can give himself a vacation."

Eight years old and already so wise, and so aware of all the nuances of the lives of her parents. Nora tried to think back, but all she remembered from her eighth year was the death of her father. She'd grown up in an instant after that, slipping into a role of responsibility before she was even old enough to know her times tables.

Ben's availability to go on vacation was not a conversation that Nora wanted to have right now. Nora had danced around the subject of Sarah's fight with Anna for days, partly because she was reluctant to add to the tension between her and her daughter. She'd hoped maybe she and Sarah could bridge this gap, maybe have a Mom and Me movie night or a game night to reknit some of those fragile threads, but if anything, things had become more strained, with the elephant in the room sitting smack in the center.

"We really need to talk about what happened at school with Anna and why you were picking on kids in your class," Nora said. "You'll be going back to St. Gregory's in two days, and that needs to be settled before you start school again."

"I don't want to talk about it." Sarah leaned back in the chair and crossed her arms again.

"I'm sorry, Sarah, but you don't get a choice. Sister Esther is going to ask about all this when you go back to school and so will Anna's mother. Why did you two get into a fight?"

"Anna said mean things to me."

Anna had always been a kind, polite child. Nora couldn't imagine what the sunny blonde had said that was mean. Although even good kids became cruel sometimes. *Sarah is the bully.* Kids like her own child. She thought back to the parenting articles she'd read over the years, always with that smug *not my kid* thinking in the back of her mind. Bullies sprang from troubled backgrounds and abusive homes. Sarah had none of that, yet she had still raised her fists to a friend. "What kind of mean things?"

Sarah paused for a long moment, fiddling with the

string bracelet on her wrist. "Are you and Daddy really okay?" Her lower lip quivered, and when she spoke, her voice was low and hoarse.

How could Nora possibly tell Sarah the truth? Nothing was set in stone yet, and maybe she was being cowardly, but until there was a court date and some paperwork, she wanted to preserve Sarah's world as long as possible. "It's all going to be okay, honey. Don't worry."

And yet another generation learned the *I'm fine* O'Bannon method of coping.

Sarah gnawed on her bottom lip. "Can I go now?"

Nora debated pushing the subject of the issues with her classmates, the fight with Anna, but she could see tears threatening in Sarah's eyes again, and the mother in Nora couldn't bear to make her daughter any sadder. "Okay, but you need to apologize to Jake. And tomorrow, we're going to the store to buy Jake a new truck with the money you got for your birthday from Gramma."

"That's not fair!"

Life isn't fair, she wanted to say. *Sometimes the house you planned to grow old in is lost forever, and sometimes the man you marry turns out to be someone you don't really know. And sometimes you do the best job you can for your kids and you still screw it up.* "Please be more careful with his toys. Now go outside and apologize."

Sarah hopped off the chair and headed out to the back porch with Chance hot on her heels. She stood beside Jake and mumbled a reluctant apology. Jake jumped up, hugged his sister, and asked her to play in the sand with him. That was Jake, the boy she'd called *bouncy* when he was little, because nothing ever seemed to faze or upset him for long. Sarah, on the other hand, had the brooding temper of her father. Nevertheless, she grabbed the shovel and pail, following her brother down to the beach. Nora watched as they dropped onto the beach beside each other and started excavating a foundation for a castle.

Magpie came back into the house and hung her sweatshirt on the hook by the door. "How'd it go?"

"Let's just say I'm dreading the teenage years."

"That bad, huh?"

"Worse." Nora put her head in her hands. Every time she tried to make things better, they went sideways. And she had yet to break the news to the kids about moving into Aunt Mary's house. Duck and run from honesty, that was becoming her specialty. "Am I being a terrible mother?"

"You're a great mother, Nora. A great wife. God, all of us admire you and wish we could hold it together half as well as you do," Magpie said.

Nora scoffed. "I'm not as great as you think, Magpie. And I'm not really holding it together. The whole thing is shadows and duct tape."

"Then talk to me," her little sister said. "Tell me what's going on."

I screwed up my life. I screwed up my marriage. I couldn't even manage to be a good mother. "Nothing. Sorry. Just a stressful day. I'll be fine in a little while." Nora even managed to work up a smile to put frosting on her lie.

Magpie arched a brow. "Come on, Nora, this is me. Don't feed me the family bullshit. Talk to me."

There was too much, piled up over years and years of keeping everything to herself, that explaining what was going on to Magpie would mean unraveling a Gordian knot of lies. Exposing secrets she hadn't even shared with her husband. "There's nothing to talk about. Really. It's just...being a mom sometimes comes with a lot of problems and things you didn't expect."

"If you say so." Magpie fiddled with the knit place mat. "How did you know you wanted to be a mother? I mean, not that I'm thinking of it or anything, just wondering what made you say, yes, I want a couple people depending on me for food and shelter for eighteen years."

It was the second question about parenting that Magpie had asked in as many days. Maybe it was because she'd been around the kids so much or had seen Nora's struggle. From the time she was born, Magpie had made it clear she never wanted to be tied down, not to a husband, not to kids, not to one place. She'd lived vicariously through her niece and nephew, spoiling them often with trinkets she brought back from her trips. Ma would nudge Magpie from time to time in the direction of settling down, but her little sister would deflect the attention to the already-married Abby and Jessie or Bridget, the latter of whom was getting relatively serious with Garrett now. If Nora had to wager a guess, she'd bet Abby and Jessie would be the first to bring another grandchild into the O'Bannon family fold.

"I guess I always wanted to be a mother. Even when I

was little, I wanted to get married, have a family, and teach them how to make cookies." Nora laughed. "When you're ten, you think the key to happiness in life is a few chocolate chips."

"Hell, you think that at twenty-six too." Magpie kept fiddling with the edge of the place mat, lifting, smoothing. "Is there anything you wish you did differently?"

"You mean about getting married and having kids? A thousand things, Mags, but I can't look back. All that does is drive me crazy." And gave her insomnia that left her watching bad reality television shows in the middle of the night.

"Things like what?" Magpie asked. "You know, in case I ever get whisked off to another planet and forced to marry Jabba the Hutt or something."

"And this is why you are the writer and I'm the cake decorator." Nora laughed and shook her head. "I could give you the standard answers. I wish I'd saved more. I wished I'd spent more wisely. I wish I'd waited a little longer to get married. But really, the only thing I wish I'd done was... pause."

"Pause?"

"I married Ben because he asked. Because I was head over heels in love. I didn't take a breath and look down the road. I just did it. And over the years we've been married, I've spent too much time buried in the minutiae. In trying to get from A to B while getting X, Y, and Z done. I haven't taken enough time to pause and look at what's happening in the meantime. Or even pause to enjoy the good moments. And process the bad." Maybe if she had stopped and paid more attention, she would have seen the end coming sooner. Or she would have acted instead of pretending everything was fine.

Magpie cocked her head and studied Nora. "Was it the money problems that you and Ben were fighting about earlier? Because if you need some money, I'd be glad to give you some."

"We're fine." Nora covered Magpie's hand with her own. "Seriously. I'm just spouting off. He annoyed me this morning. That's all."

"Which is exactly why I don't live with a man. The only one who can annoy me is me." Magpie grinned.

The mask Nora wore about her life and marriage began to slip. She could feel the tears nudging at her eyes again. She glanced at the kids, still playing in the sand outside the beach house. Soon they'd be inside again, wanting lunch. "Hey, didn't you mention you wanted to talk to me? We have some time now, while the kids are playing."

"It's no big deal. It can wait. I'm hungry," Magpie said, too fast, too easily. Again, Nora wondered about her little sister, but then Magpie smiled and any doubts disappeared. "I'm going to go make us some lunch. Leftover pizza okay?"

"Considering I think that's the only thing you can cook, that's great."

Magpie got to her feet. "All my life, you've been the one I've gone to for advice and support, Nora. I hope you know that you can come to me when things get tough for you." She paused by Nora's chair and gave her a quick hug. "I understand more than you think."

SEVENTEEN

Sunday morning brought a bright sunny day and a return to reality. Nora got up early and started packing. She hurried the kids through breakfast, one more trip to the beach and a rousing game of tag in the yard with their aunt and the dog. Then she stood on the back deck and watched her children, happy, laughing, enjoying their last bit of vacation in a naïve bubble.

For a second, she allowed herself to imagine the future that had never happened. A third child in the mix, toddling between Sarah and Jake, eager to learn the world, carve out a space of his or her own. Maybe a dog, too, a flash of fur weaving in and out of the children. And finally, Nora and Ben, holding hands or leaning against each other, proud and content with their family, their life, the home they had built.

Tears stung Nora's eyes, and her throat closed. She shut her eyes and drew in deep breaths until she erased the images in her mind. That future was never going to come to pass. Dreaming of it only resurrected a pain it had taken her months to bury.

Nora kept procrastinating when she really needed to decide what to do about her future. She'd never been the kind of person who put things off, but the thought of all those changes, all those decisions, swamped her.

Just dealing with the dog was a mountain she didn't want to climb. No one had called about Chance, and no one had reported a dog like him missing. He was Nora's, for all intents and purposes. She liked the mutt, and if things were different, she would have kept him. But it was too much, one more burden she wasn't prepared to handle.

Magpie came up the stairs and leaned against the porch post. "Geez, those kids wear me out. I need a nap."

Nora laughed. "Kids have more energy than you think."

The dog came up and pressed his snout to Magpie's leg. "And more than this guy." Magpie rubbed his head. "He's a good dog."

Nora sighed. "He is. It'll be a shame to give him away."

"I thought you said we could keep him forever."

Nora hadn't even noticed that the kids had stopped playing. Sarah was standing at the foot of the path, her fists on her hips, her jeans coated with sand.

Jake was beside her, tears welling in his eyes and his lower lip starting to tremble. "Mommy?"

Damn. Nora had screwed up yet again.

Nora started down the stairs toward the kids. "Guys, I know you love Chance, and he's a great dog, but we don't really have the time or room for a dog. He needs to go to a good home, and after we get back, I'll make sure he finds the best home ever—"

"You always break your promises! I hate you!" Sarah ran past Nora, up the stairs, into the house, and down the hall. A bedroom door slammed.

Shit.

Nora dropped to her knees and took Jake's hands. He was so little still, so black and white in his view of the world. She hated breaking his heart, hated all of this. "We'll get another dog someday, I promise."

"I want this one, Mommy. I love Chance, and he loves me, and he needs us." Jake's lower lip sucked in and out, in and out, and the brave face he tried to hold began to crumple.

"I have an idea," Magpie said. She put a hand on Nora's shoulder and met her sister's gaze. "I've still got a few days off. Why don't I take Chance back to my house and let him have a sleepover there? You guys can come visit him after school. And that gives everyone some time to..." She glanced at Nora.

"Come up with a plan," Nora finished. It wasn't the truth—she couldn't afford her kids and herself, never mind a dog—but it bought her some time. And maybe she could do the math again and find a way to stretch her budget a bit further. "I'm going to go talk to Sarah."

"No problem. The Jakester and I are going to take one last look for cool shells." Magpie ruffled her nephew's hair. "Sound good, buddy?"

"Okay." As he walked away, he started talking about Chance, telling his aunt all the dog's favorite tricks and treats, the happiness restored in his world.

Nora headed inside and found her daughter lying on Nora's bed, crying. Across the wall hung Will's painting of the perpetual storm, an apt image for Nora's life right now. The bed creaked as Nora sank onto the mattress beside her daughter. Sarah rolled a little toward her with the added dent in the mattress but kept her face hidden. "Honey, we worked something out with the dog." Nora put a hand on Sarah's back. "Aunt Magpie's going to take him for a few days, and you and Jake can visit him whenever you want."

"I don't care." The pillow muffled her words.

Nora rubbed a gentle circle against the small of Sarah's back. When she was a baby, that had been the only way to get her to stop crying. Nora would pace the kitchen floor, shush-shushing a teething Sarah, and rub gentle circles until sleep eased the pain. "Talk to me, Sarah."

It took a moment, but finally Sarah rolled over. Her face was blotchy and tear-stained. The defiance glittered again in her eyes. "I don't wanna talk. I hate you. I want Daddy."

The words sliced an artery in Nora's heart. *I hate you.* When Sarah was four, they'd gone on a family vacation to Canobie Lake Park. Six months pregnant with Jake, Nora thought the trip to New Hampshire would be one last "just the three of us" opportunity. From the second they arrived, Sarah had glued herself to Nora, insisting Mommy do everything, from cutting up her food to helping her in and out of the stroller. Every time Sarah said "but I want Mommy," Ben's face had taken on this pained expression. Every ride, every restaurant, every exhibit, Sarah had insisted on being with her mother. At the time, Nora had felt frustrated and a little annoyed. The second trimester had left her exhausted and cranky, and Sarah's clinginess had been overwhelming. When Ben told her how much it hurt him that his own daughter wanted nothing to do with him, Nora had barked back that she would have paid good money to have a day when Sarah didn't want her. *Be careful what you wish for.*

I hate you. Did Sarah really mean that? "I'm sorry, Sarah, but Daddy isn't here right now."

"Because you're divorcing him?"

Silence filled the space between them. There was a yip outside—Chance racing down the beach probably—but no other sound except the faint ticking of a clock. "Where did you hear that?"

Sarah's fist curled around the edge of the white comforter, crumpling the cotton into a thick ball. "I don't know."

"Sarah, where did you hear that?"

Sarah worried her bottom lip, averting her gaze.

Nora cupped her daughter's chin, but still Sarah wouldn't meet her eyes. "Sarah, where did you hear that?"

Another minute passed. "Anna told me," Sarah said in a voice so low that it was almost a whisper. "I told her she was a big liar, and she got mad, and we got in a fight, and we got in trouble at school, and Sister Esther said I was being mean, but it wasn't me. It was Anna. She said it every day, and I got madder every day and told her to shut up, and I didn't want to fight her, so sometimes I was mean to other kids. Then she said it in front of everyone at school and I...I hit her."

So that was the bullying the school had talked about. An ongoing battle with Anna, over information the other little girl shouldn't have. Who had told Anna that Nora and Ben were breaking up?

"Then I saw you fighting with Daddy." Sarah's eyes widened. "Are you divorcing him? Are you leaving us?"

"No, honey, I'm not leaving you." How the hell had Anna found out about her marital troubles? Now the fight at school made sense, and the way Sarah had been acting for days. The avoidance, the hostility, the reluctance to talk. A child's greatest fear, she'd read once, was that their home would be broken and uprooted.

Exactly what was happening to Sarah.

The urge to shield her daughter a little longer rose stronger in Nora's chest. Someday, she'd have to sit them down—hopefully she and Ben would do it together—and tell them Mommy and Daddy weren't going to live to-gether anymore.

That day wasn't today. Nora didn't have the heart to speak those words.

She thought of her mother, and the incredibly difficult conversation Ma had had with the four of them. They'd all been sitting on the couch in the formal living room, while the sun streamed through the windows and danced on the oval rug. Four girls under ten, fidgeting and squabbling, until Ma knelt before them. Dark shadows rimmed Ma's eyes, and she was shaking as she spoke. She looked so fragile, Nora was afraid her mother would fall apart like the porcelain doll Nora had dropped on the sidewalk.

"Your father died," Ma said, and even though Nora was too little to comprehend the permanence of dying, the impact losing Dad would have, she remembered feeling as if the earth were shifting beneath her. A wide crevasse of the unknown opened under the girls, breaking the perfect world they'd always known.

The irony that Sarah was also eight and that Nora was debating about telling her own daughter that her world was falling apart, didn't escape her. Even if it was just a divorce and not a death, Sarah's world would never be the same.

Tomorrow morning, Nora was going to call Anna's mother and find out where that rumor had started. Even if it wasn't a rumor at all. Until then, she wasn't going to rock Sarah's world. "You don't need to worry."

Sarah took in that information with a tentative nod. "Daddy's going to be excited when we come home, and maybe he can make a fence for the dog."

Nora could feel Sarah watching her, waiting for the only answer she wanted to hear. That they were going home after this and everything was going to be okay. Just like it was before. Nora drew in a deep breath. It was past time she started facing the truth—and admitting it to her children. "Honey, we aren't going home to that house. We're going to go live at Aunt Mary's for a little while."

"Why?"

"Because Daddy and I don't have enough money for that house anymore and we need to find another one." Not exactly a lie but not exactly the truth.

"But... but I love that house. I don't wanna move."

"I love that house too." Nora swept Sarah's bangs off her forehead. Her little girl was growing up, faster than Nora wanted. All these losses and changes were hastening that process, and Nora hated that. If she could rewind the clock, take them back to the days before—before Ben started gambling, before they went broke, before her marriage fell apart—she would. "That house is where Daddy and I brought you home from the hospital. We painted your room pink, and we built a white crib, and we put those glow-in-the-dark stars on your ceiling for you to see at night."

In those days before their first child was born, Nora and Ben had been a happy team. She remembered painting the walls, the two of them working side by side, their rollers completing each other's swipes of paint. They'd laughed, they'd kissed, they'd dotted each other with paint, and then they'd made love on the floor, while the paint dried and the sun set.

A watery smile spread across Sarah's face. "I remember those stars."

"We didn't want you to be scared at night, and Daddy told you that the moon and stars were always watching out for you. That the angels sat on the edges of the stars and made sure all the little kids were okay."

"And Daddy drew an angel on one of the stars. And he said he made it look like you, because he thought you were an angel. Just not the dead kind."

Ben had said that about her? She remembered the night he'd brought the stepstool into Sarah's room to pencil an angel at the edge of one of the stars. Later, he'd gone back and traced the drawing with a Sharpie, making the image more permanent. The stars and the angel had stayed until Sarah turned six and wanted a big girl's room with princess wallpaper and a ballerina lamp. Nora had spent an entire Sunday afternoon peeling the stars off the ceiling and painting over the spots where the glue had stuck. She'd erased the constellation and the angel with a few swipes of white paint, working alone this time. By then, those moments of laughter and kisses had been replaced by late nights beside a roulette wheel.

"I don't want a new house," Sarah said, and the tears started again, sliding down her cheeks in slow, sad rivers. The cold maturity that had filled her face earlier yielded to the pain of a little girl who was losing everything she knew. "I want my house, and I want Daddy to draw me another angel. I want everything to stay the same."

Nora drew her daughter into a hug. She rested her head on top of Sarah's, inhaling the sweet strawberry scent of her shampoo. Even that wasn't the same. At some point, Nora had changed brands, and she couldn't remember why. "I do, too, honey. I do too."

EIGHTEEN

Magpie curled into the leather armchair in the corner of her living room, with Nora's dog asleep at her feet, and looked out over a sparkling nighttime city. She loved this apartment, a fifteenth-floor space in a busy neighborhood that had a clear view of the Mystic River, and just beyond that, the northern side of Boston. She'd rented the space two years ago and spent so little time here that her neighbors greeted her as a stranger every time she came home.

Home. It was a funny word, Magpie thought. A word she didn't really understand or know. The only home she'd ever really had was the one she grew up in, that triplex on Park Street with her sisters and her mother. After her father died, home had become a place with a hole in it, a space no one could fill. The first time she got on a plane and headed to Texas on a magazine assignment, she became a wandering vagabond and told herself that was the life she wanted. She'd gobbled up assigned trips to far-flung

212

places like they were Xanax, using the constant travel to ease the gnawing unrest inside her.

Her apartment was bare bones, filled with furniture from a single marathon shopping trip to IKEA and a smattering of mementos she shipped to herself, most of them still in boxes, waiting for her to be here long enough to unpack them and settle the vases and handmade bowls and artisan mirrors on some shelf where they'd gather dust and wait for her to return.

Her cell phone began to ring, dancing across the glass of the end table. Charlie's name and face lit up her screen, but Magpie didn't answer, just like she hadn't answered the last few times. She didn't have an answer for him, and if she knew him like she thought she did, not answering would eventually make him give up. Charlie would move on to the next challenge, the next girl in the next city.

Chance got to his feet, came over, and laid his head in her lap. "Silly dog. Don't start depending on other people. You're better off alone, you know." Magpie rubbed his head. The dog sighed, content with the simple love.

Her phone lit again, texts from her sisters wondering why she hadn't gone to their family dinner. She texted back and told Bridget she was feeling under the weather, worn out from the days on the beach.

She lied.

All those days in Truro with Nora and she'd never brought up the real reason she'd asked her sister to go with her. Maybe because she'd hoped it wouldn't become real if she didn't talk about it. Or maybe because she didn't want to see that look of judgment and disappointment in Nora's eyes. Nora had been the one who had encouraged Magpie, told her to go after her dreams, travel the world. What would she think if Magpie told her sister that those very dreams were about to end?

So many times, Magpie had come close, dancing around the edges of the topic, thinking maybe she could speak the words, but then she'd seen the struggle in Nora's face, the stress that her sister was dealing with, and she'd changed the subject. Avoided it, was the truth.

"Maybe you and I should run away together," she said to the dog. "Go to Africa or Japan or Costa Rica. Somewhere far, far away from . . . everything." Chance wagged his tail and leaned into her touch. "Or maybe we should stay right here and deal with shit. What's your vote, puppy?"

A set of chimes sang. It took a minute for Magpie to recognize the sound as her doorbell, not surprising given how infrequently she'd been home. She got to her feet, which made the dog sigh in disagreement.

Through the peephole she saw a familiar face. A face she didn't want to speak to right now.

"I know you're home," Charlie said. "Your car is parked in the carport."

Damn it. Magpie pulled open the door and leaned against the jamb. He looked good, damn him, wearing a blue chambray shirt and a pair of faded jeans. Charlie had warm brown eyes and sandy blond hair that brushed along his brows and a grin that could charm the coat off a bear. "Why are you here, Charlie?"

He frowned. "I have to say, that's not the greeting I was expecting after flying twenty-three hours to get here."

"Don't pretend like you flew back to Massachusetts for me. You have an assignment."

"Exactly. Two birds. One stone." He put his hand above her head and leaned closer. That grin widened and lit his eyes. "What's up with you? Why are you so pissed at me?"

Magpie shrugged. Chance came up beside her, nosing at the door. She shifted to block the dog from getting out, though a part of her wished Chance had more guard dog in him than lover dog and that he would be intimidating enough to chase Charlie away. "I told you. We had a great time, but now it's over. We'll be friends, maybe hook up once in a while."

"That's what you want. To hook up once in a while." The words weren't even questions. His gaze flattened, and his grin dropped.

"Well, depending on where both of us are. I mean, you might meet someone else, and I—"

"I've already met the woman I wanted to. A woman I don't want to just hook up with."

She sighed. How many women had he used that line on? She'd known what she was getting when she'd first gone back to Charlie's room in a tiny hotel in Leningrad, but now he was acting like those nights they'd had were more than a momentary salve for loneliness. "Come on, Charlie, don't make this into some Nicholas Sparks movie. You were the one who said you were in it for a good time. I was cool with that. We had the good time; now we move on."

"Move on. Huh." He leaned in closer, his eyes meeting hers with that twinkle that had first attracted her to him. Charlie was the kind of guy who loved a woman for a week or a month, then found another. She had the same commitment allergy and had gone out with him because she thought he knew and understood the rules. No I love yous, no long commitments, no promises. "You really want to move on?"

He was so close she could feel the warmth of his skin, see the flecks of gold in his eyes. Tempting. And wrong. Magpie pressed a hand to her stomach, and there, in her gut, she knew the right answer. She stepped back. "Yeah, Charlie, I'm moving on. Thanks for coming by."

Then she shut the door and went back to her chair and her view of the city. Chance lay down beside her, his tail arcing against the floor as if he was happy with that answer too.

The soft sugar paste yielded easily under Nora's fingers, curving into petals that hugged the pink conic center mounted on a thin wooden stick. Three dozen pastel molded roses stood at attention in the box beside her, hardening in the air. She repeated the process over and over— roll the sugar paste into a flat circle, then cut out concentric floral shapes that gradually stepped down in size. She'd slide a cone through a stack of three of the shapes and then dampen her fingers and work each petal up and around the center, layering rose petals one on top of the other, tweaking the edges with a slight crinkle. A set of modeling tools sat on the shelf before her, but Nora preferred to fashion flowers by hand, giving each one its own unique look.

Her fingers moved fast, spinning magic with each touch, transforming pale pink paste into replicas of Mother Nature. Later, she'd dust them with the airbrush, adding hues and shadows to create depth.

Like Will did with his paintings. Even the simple one on his mailbox. Thinking of him reminded her of her cowardly exit yesterday morning. She'd ducked out of Truro without stopping by his house. When she'd glanced in her rearview mirror, she'd noticed that he had finished the mailbox, adding a quartet of seahorses cavorting in the seagrass.

Across from her, Bridget was piping Bavarian cream into golden puffed shells. She hummed along to the radio, to an old Chicago song about love and missed opportunities. Ma was out front, in a consult with a woman planning a family reunion. Abby was in the back of the kitchen, unloading baked loaves of bread from the oven before sliding in the next batch of dough.

Life was back to normal, at least within the bakery. The routine and schedule settled the rolling anxiety inside of Nora. For at least eight hours a day, she could create faux flowers and decorate wedding cakes and control what happened.

"Those are beautiful. Can you teach me how to do that?"

Nora glanced over at Iris. The girl had tamed her Goth look since the last time Nora had seen her, edging away from Marilyn Manson and closer to Joan Jett. Bridget sang Iris's praises, telling Nora that Iris often showed up early and stayed late and was always eager to learn. As much as Nora wanted to just be left alone in her perfect, controlled world of sugar flowers, she couldn't resist Iris's clear interest. "Sure. Sprinkle some powdered sugar on your work surface first. Then grab that little rolling pin and a ball of the sugar paste."

Iris did as Nora instructed. "Okay. Now what?"

"Remember how you roll out a pie crust? Same principle here, though you want to get it thinner. Flowers are delicate, and making them is a delicate process. Too thin and the flower crumples, too thick and it droops."

"How will I know when it's right?"

"Trust your gut. If I had to give you one piece of advice, that would be it. Do this often enough and you'll just *know* when it's right or when to start over." Or when to throw in the towel and admit defeat.

Last night, long after she'd put the kids to bed in the twin beds in Aunt Mary's guest room, Nora had lain awake, Googling "divorce in Massachusetts" and "renting after foreclosure." Every Web page she visited made her more and more depressed. The dream she'd had that bright summer day she'd married Ben was dying a slow and painful death.

Actually, that dream had died last winter. She just hadn't faced the truth until now.

She was exhausted, and if she could have, she would have crawled into bed and stayed there for a month, hiding under the covers in a cave of denial. But someone had to be responsible and someone had to pay the bills, and as always, that someone was Nora. So she got dressed, went to work, and pretended everything was fine.

Nora started working on another rose while watching Iris work the tiny rolling pin and press the pink paste into a circle. The young girl rolled a few times, stopped, checked the thickness, rolled some more, checked it again.

Nora could see herself in Iris's hesitant movements. The need to please, to earn those rare words of praise. Twenty years ago, that had been Nora. Too short to stand at the counter, she'd sat on a metal stool between her mother and grandmother, listening to them chat about the neighbors or the weather while their fingers created magic out of little more than shortening and sugar.

"Is this good?"

"Perfect," Nora said. She handed Iris the trio of petal cutters. "Cut out one set of three different sizes."

"Just enough for one flower? Why not do a bunch at a time?"

"The sugar paste dries too quickly. You need it to be pliable to create the flowers, then allow it to harden before putting them on the cake, so they'll last." She watched Iris wriggle the plastic cutters into the paste and set the shapes aside. "Now take that little bit left behind and roll it into a ball." Nora demonstrated with a scrap of sugar paste. "About this big. Once you have a ball, form one end into a point."

Iris did and then stepped back to marvel at the tiny cone. "Ah, that's the center of the flower."

"Exactly. We always work from the inside out."

"Sort of like working on yourself," Iris said softly. Her bangs swept across her forehead, hiding her eyes.

"I never saw the metaphor in sugar flowers, but yeah, I think you're right." Was that the point she had missed in all the busyness of working and raising children? That she hadn't worked on herself? Hell, she barely had a self after she had kids. In an instant, life's focus shifted to this tiny, vulnerable human being who depended on her for everything. Perhaps that was where all those midlife crises came from. Women who had set their selves aside while they raised their children and too late realized they were staring at a stranger in the mirror.

"It's something your mom said to me." Iris shrugged. "I mean, we all have shit—sorry, crap—that we need to deal with, and the best way to do that is by starting on the inside. Like, with believing I can do something like this. I kinda have issues with that self-esteem thing."

"We all struggle with that," Nora said. "Believing we can handle the challenge before us. Believing we are strong enough. Believing we won't fail again."

Which was why Nora had sought solace in the bakery today. Here, at least, she didn't fail. Here, she controlled her environment and knew what was coming, day after day. Three of these flower cutouts would come together to create a thing of beauty, every single time she made one.

"Yeah. My friend Monica and I were talking about that. She's the one who's, like, pregnant. And she's really scared about screwing up her kid." Iris began rolling another set as she talked. "Monica is super poor and she's got to buy diapers and baby food and stuff. And the baby is gonna be here like any day."

"There's aid for that kind of thing, right?"

Iris nodded. "Roger's helping her out, too, but she's still worried. You have good kids, like, what would you tell her to, like, help her be a good mom?"

Nora scooped out some more sugar paste and rolled it into a ball in the palm of her hands. She thought of Sarah's little hand, then Jake's, tiny infant fingers that latched on to Nora's from the minute they were born. Trusting and needing parents who wouldn't screw it up. "You just do your best," Nora said. "And then you pray the kids turn out okay."

"Well, some moms don't even do that." Iris finished the first piece, so she took the ball of sugar paste from Nora and began to flatten it with the rolling pin.

Would Nora's kids grow up and say the same thing to a woman they barely knew? Would they look back on this year and see it as the year their mother failed them? Or would they understand she had done the best she could, that she had tried so hard to hang on to their world?

Nora slid thin wooden sticks into the flower centers and handed one back to Iris. "Poke this through your smallest flower cutout. Then we'll start forming the petals."

Work instead of talk about good mothers and healthy parenting. Work instead of thinking about how she was back in Dorchester now and she could run into Ben at any minute. Work instead of wondering how the hell she was going to afford to give her children the life she had promised them when they'd put their tiny hands in hers.

Nora took the set of modeling tools off the shelf and started to explain how to use the bone tool with its fat and skinny bulbous ends to press the petals into flutes. Iris looked down at the sugar paste and then back up at Nora. "Can you teach me to do it the way you do? 'Cause you didn't use those. You did it with your hands."

Nora hesitated and heard her own voice asking her grandmother the same thing. Ma had told Gramma that Nora was too young to learn the delicate process and handed Nora the same set of modeling tools. But when Ma left the kitchen, Gramma had bent down beside Nora, covering her granddaughter's hands with her own thin, cool ones, and helped her change the flat circles of sugar paste into roses, daisies, sunflowers. That had been the moment Nora fell in love with cake decorating, with the magic of transforming simple ingredients into majestic creations.

"Okay. Start with dampening the petals just a bit, so they're easier to work. Then you sort of pinch and roll at the same time, working them up and around the cone. It takes patience and a light touch, so don't rush this." She worked a few petals on her flower, moving closer to Iris and slowing her movements.

Iris's first two attempts were clumsy, and the petals folded like a blanket over the cone. She let out a long breath. Then she squared her jaw and tried again. The third time, the petal fluttered into place. Iris looked up, her face bright with surprise and pride. "I did it."

"You did." Nora set her flower in the drying box. It sat among the others, a close enough twin that only a practiced eye could tell the difference. "You really have a talent for this, Iris."

"Thanks." The girl blushed and toed at the floor. "I've, uh, never really been good at anything before. And to take this"—she spun a ball of sugar paste—"and turn it into this"—she waved her hand over one of the roses—"kinda shows me that you can make something beautiful out of something that isn't. Like people, huh?"

"Most people, I guess." Nora started working on another flower while Iris did the same.

"It's like my mom. She's screwed up twelve thousand times, and I know I should hate her and cut her out of my life, but there was this time"—Iris let out a sigh—"that I used to see the flower in her. It's still there. I believe that."

Nora stopped working. "Why? Why believe that? Why not walk away instead of getting hurt by her again?"

"Because she hasn't stopped trying." Iris's eyes welled. "How can I give up on her when she hasn't given up on herself?"

NINETEEN

Nora ducked out early from work to pick up the kids from school, partly happy to be in the old routine and partly wishing she were back in Truro where the biggest thing she had to worry about was tracking sand inside the house. Nora found Anna's mother waiting for her own daughter in the parking lot. Joyce was sitting in her Benz, an iPad resting on her leather steering wheel while she fiddled with letters in Words with Friends. Nora had always liked Joyce Stanford, who was one of the few people she considered a friend. "Hey, Joyce."

Joyce glanced up and her brown eyes widened. She seemed startled, almost nervous. "Oh, hi, Nora. Uh...how are you?"

"Fine." Nora swallowed. "Can I talk to you for a second?"

"I was hoping you would." Relief flooded Joyce's face, as if she'd been waiting for Nora to approach first. "Anna's really upset that Sarah is so angry with her."

"Sarah told me that Anna said something. I'm not quite sure where Anna came across this information." Nora glanced toward the school. Three minutes until the bell rang and the kids were released so she had to have this discussion fast. A discussion she didn't want to have, but it was like ripping off a bandage—do it quick and it would be over and she could move on. "Anna told Sarah that Ben and I were getting divorced."

Joyce's face colored. "Oh...uh, I'm sorry about that."

"What do you mean, you're sorry about that?"

"I didn't think Anna was listening. I thought she was in bed." Joyce shifted in her seat and let out a long breath. "Ben came over one night and we got to talking—"

"Ben, my *husband* Ben? You were alone with him? At night?" Was that where Ben had been spending his Friday nights? With this woman she thought was her friend?

How much of her life had she been clueless about? Ben's gambling, their finances, Sarah's grades and fighting, and now this? Had she buried her head in work too much, using that as an excuse to hide from the messes in her family?

Then again, hadn't she kept a few things from her husband too? Had all those lies and secrets piled up between them and created an impassable wall?

"He was upset, Nora. He needed someone to talk to, that's all," Joyce said. She put a hand on Nora's and her eyes pleaded for understanding. "And he thought I would be the best one because I know you so well."

Jealousy flared inside of Nora, white-hot and fast.

"What exactly did you talk to *my* husband about late at night, Joyce?"

"Well, what all has been going on between you two. He's really worried, and he was afraid that you might divorce him."

Nora jerked her hand away from Joyce's window. This woman was her friend, and she'd kept all this a secret. Because she didn't think Nora could handle it? Or was there more? And why had Ben been going to Aunt Mary and Joyce instead of coming to her? "When did he say this?"

"A couple weeks ago. He said he knew the bank was going to come down hard and if the two of you lost the house, he was pretty sure you'd leave him. He said he'd screwed up too many times, and this would be the last straw." Joyce turned to Nora. "Was it?"

"That is none of your damned business. And for the record, the next time my husband wants to know what I'm thinking, tell him to ask his fucking wife." She spun on her heel and stalked back to her car, just as the bell rang. The kids exited the building like a swarm of bees, and Joyce and her Benz were lost in the frenzy.

The bakery was quiet, in that nice lull of Monday afternoons when no one was rushing to a wedding or a baby shower or panicking over a last-minute need for rolls and dessert. Colleen loved this time of day, when the air was still, the pressure was off, and she could take a moment to enjoy the quaint little shop she'd spent most of her life in. Nora had left early to pick up her kids and Abby went home to catch some sleep before her predawn shift the next morning.

Bridget emerged from the kitchen. "Hey, Ma, we're all cleaned up back there. Mind if I leave early? Garrett and I are going to a show at the Wang Theatre, and we were hoping to grab some dinner first."

"Go ahead." Colleen set the cleaned cookie display back on the counter, ready to be filled tomorrow. "You've been spending a lot of time with that man."

Bridget's smile burst like sunshine on her face. "He's a pretty special guy."

It was nice to see her daughter this happy after the years of unhappiness with her late husband. A part of Colleen envied that and wondered if maybe she'd done herself a disservice by staying true to a man who had been dead for twenty years. Then again, Michael had been a pretty special guy, too, and not one who could be easily replaced. She'd loved him in a way she'd never loved anyone else. He'd been so fun, so easy to be with. He'd brought a lightness to her heart, one that she was afraid she'd never find again. Maybe theirs had been a once-in-a-lifetime love, the kind that once gone could never be recaptured. Or maybe she had left that empty place at her dinner table for far too long.

Colleen pressed the Open Drawer button on the cash register, at the same time the day's total sales receipt printed. As she had done a thousand times before, she added the checks, the credit card receipts, and the cash, subtracting the hundred dollars they left in the drawer for starting cash. She compared the two numbers, then looked over at the pile of cash. "Hmm. That's odd."

"What's odd?"

"I didn't get the same number. I must have added wrong." Colleen pulled out the adding machine she kept under the counter, turned it on, and repeated the process, this time double-checking every number before she typed it in. The adding machine jiggled as it spat out a total. "Bridget, did you pay the delivery guy with cash today?"

"Nope. With the company credit card, as I always do." Bridget leaned over her mother's shoulder. "What's wrong?"

"I'm two hundred dollars short." In all the years she had run this bakery, the register had never been off by this much. There'd been the occasional transposed number on a transaction, and the time Magpie filched three dollars to buy candy her mother had told her not to, but never had the day's total been off by so much.

"Maybe something got entered wrong. If you want, I'll take all the receipts home and go through them."

"Thank you, dear. Maybe you'll see something I missed." Colleen passed the pile over to Bridget, then added the two register tape totals. She tucked the cash into the night deposit bag and stowed it in the safe in the office. As she returned to the front of the store, she cast another glance at the register and ran through the day in her mind. "Let me know what you find out, will you?"

"Sure, Ma. I will. Don't worry. I'm sure it's nothing."

Bridget kissed Colleen on the cheek before hanging up her apron and leaving through the back. Colleen straightened the tables in the front, gave the glass case one more swipe with cleanser, and turned the sign to closed.

Just as she did, she saw Roger's familiar face on the other side of the door. She unlocked it and ushered him in, closing the door quickly against the November chill, but not before a brisk wind swept under the transom. She shivered. "I swear, these winters get colder every year."

Roger blew on his cupped bare hands and nodded. "Makes a man think about moving to Florida. Especially if a man knew someone else who would love the warm weather too."

A little part of her flared with jealousy. Who was he thinking of moving to Florida with? And why did she care? "I hope you don't mean me, because I would certainly not shack up with you and move to another state."

"Who said anything about shacking up?" Roger hung his coat on the hook by the door and took off his hat. He wore one of those old-fashioned fedoras, which on most men looked like a costume but on Roger looked…jaunty. "I'm thinking a week in Florida to start, see if we like the heat in the winter. If we do, maybe we buy property down there, a place to sit out the New England winters."

Colleen blinked at him. Had he said "we"? More than once? A second ago, she'd thought he was making a joke about taking her to Florida, but now he seemed earnest. "Are you asking me to go on vacation with you?"

"No. I'm asking you to marry me, Colleen." Roger

stood before her, his hat still in his hands, and gave her a smile.

"Roger O'Sullivan, do you have early-onset dementia? Marry you? Seriously?" She waved the idea away. "That is the stupidest thing I've ever heard."

She started to turn away when he grabbed her hand and stopped her. "Why?" he asked.

His hand on her arm was warm and gentle. They'd touched so rarely that every time he brushed against her or put a hand on her shoulder, she felt this odd little trembling deep inside. But that didn't mean anything other than he'd startled her, Colleen told herself. "Because we have only been on one date, which wasn't a date at all. We discussed work the whole time. I hardly know you."

"You and I have seen each other at least three times a week for the last year. We sit together at Mass almost as often. I have taken you to coffee, and you have brought me pie. I think you know me quite well."

This was all treading far too close to the thoughts she'd just been having. Thoughts that felt like sins, with her Michael looking down from above. She'd promised to love him until she died, and she intended to do so. Loving another man—loving Roger—didn't fit into that equation, no matter how much a part of her wished it could. Wasn't it Paul who had written in the Bible that a woman must never separate from her husband? And if she did, and couldn't reconcile with him, it was far better to remain alone?

Yes, she had gone to coffee with Roger and, yes, she

had brought him pie and, yes, she had thought about him far more often than she should. But that didn't mean she should push Michael's memory to the side and move another man into her heart. "Those are things you do for friends. Or people you admire."

"And is that how you feel about me, Colleen O'Bannon?" Roger arched a brow. "Like I'm another friend? Some acquaintance you admire?"

Goodness, he was standing so close to her. That little tremor started in her veins again, and she wondered if it was a heart attack about to take her down. Or maybe there was a part of her that wanted him to kiss her, just so she could prove to herself that she wasn't attracted to this man at all. "This is a pointless discussion. I'm not getting married again."

"Because your heart is still pledged to a man who has been dead for two decades." Roger shook his head. "Just because Michael died doesn't mean you have to as well."

"I've done no such thing."

"You've gone through your life on autopilot, working, raising your girls, then going home to an empty house that you keep meticulously clean because that helps you forget how lonely you feel and how quiet the night is without someone snoring beside you."

"Snoring is irritating." She scowled. "I'd sooner smother you with a pillow."

He laughed. "Maybe you will grow to love the sound of me sleeping beside you."

"And maybe you are a crazy old man who needs to get

a dog." She took a step back, inserting a respectable distance between them. They were alone in the bakery, and even though it was still daylight, it seemed as if the rest of the world had disappeared.

"I don't need a damned dog, Colleen. I need you." He shook his head and cursed. "You are the most infuriating woman sometimes."

"Good. That alone is a reason for you to give up this silly notion that you are in love with me."

Roger leaned in, close to her. "You are like a prickly cactus alone in the desert, so afraid of anyone getting close to you because you don't want to hurt again. Life hurts sometimes, Colleen, and sometimes it is full of joy. Don't keep living in the shadows because you are afraid of feeling again." Then he narrowed the gap and, just like that, drew her in for a kiss she wasn't expecting. It was a sweet kiss, a tender kiss, and for a second, she froze, so unused to that kind of affection that she forgot what to do. Just as quickly, Roger drew back. He plopped his hat back on his head. "January first through eighth, I'll be on a beach in Fort Myers. And I hope you'll be there beside me." He shrugged into his coat again, pulled an airline ticket out of his pocket, pressed it into her hand, and then left the bakery.

The little bell over the door tinkled a goodbye.

TWENTY

By Friday, the kids had settled into Aunt Mary's house. More or less. Jake took the change much better than Sarah did. He was his usual adaptable self, asking only if they could go back to the old house to pick up his Legos. Sarah had remained mostly silent, not complaining but not celebrating either. There'd been no more incidents at school between her and Anna, and for now, things seemed to be on an even keel.

Nora whispered a silent prayer to God every time a day went by without drama or tears. Maybe this could go smoothly—or as smoothly as a divorce and relocation could go—and the kids would be okay.

Ben had picked them up after school a couple times, kept them overnight once, and delivered a lot of their clothes and toys when he brought them home. He'd done the drop-off quickly, saying he had to get back to work. She didn't ask him about Joyce, didn't ask him how he was do-ing. They kept their conversations short and entirely about the kids. Duck and avoid—she was becoming an expert at that.

They'd decided to tell the kids that Daddy was working on the house, and that's why he was staying there. Sarah had been suspicious but didn't ask any questions, and Jake did what Jake did—went along as happy as a clam in a tide pool.

Magpie had been scarce in the last few days, and Nora kept meaning to call her sister but then figured Mags was doing what she always did—dashing off to some unknown destination, chasing after the next story. Nora pulled into the driveway, unloaded the kids and a couple bags of groceries before heading inside. Chance scrambled to his feet, dashing over to greet the kids with tail wagging and face licking. Jake giggled and dropped onto his knees to hug Chance, but the dog wriggled free of Jake and pressed his nose to Sarah's hand.

In the end, Nora had relented about the dog too. Part of that keeping-the-kids-happy-until-she-dropped-the-divorce-bombshell thing. And, a part of Nora liked the dog. Sort of like a delayed birthday gift, from when she had her father around.

A smile bloomed on Sarah's face, and she turned to Nora. "Can I go outside and play with Chance?"

Nora was about to say *Don't you have homework?* but realized that was what the old Nora used to do. Enforce the schedule and *then* allow room for fun. She'd lived her whole life that way, thinking the more she kept things in order the easier it was to predict the detours in the road.

She'd been wrong.

Maybe if she had loosened up a bit, dropped the reins from time to time, she and Ben could have communicated more. She could have kept that close relationship with Sarah. She could have been honest with her husband that winter day. And she wouldn't be feeling so lost and adrift now. "Sure. You can do your homework after dinner."

Surprise lit Sarah's eyes, and she lingered a moment, as if sure her mother would change her mind.

"Be sure to keep your coat and hat on," Nora said. "It's cold out there."

A second later, both kids were in the yard with Chance running laps between them, barking his joy at playing fetch. Nora watched from the kitchen window and realized this would be her life now. Just her and the kids. No one to turn to and say, *Hey, look at how much fun the kids are having.* No one to share the milestones with. No one to lean on when the days were dark.

Not that Ben had been much of any of that. He'd unplugged from his family when he'd been gambling. After rehab, he'd tried to reintegrate himself, but he'd been absent from their quartet for so long that it was like trying to add another peg into an already full box. Nora had been reluctant to trust him or rely on him because he'd let her down too many times before. And now...

Now the kids were going to be shuttled from one house to another. There'd be a division of birthdays and holidays and awkward conversations at school plays.

"Nora?"

She turned at the sound of Ben's voice, wondering for a second if she was hearing things, filling in the silence in the house with her husband. But no, there he was, standing in the foyer. Tall and trim, and handsome as hell, even now. There were shadows under his eyes and several days of stubble on his jaw, but a part of her heart still leapt at the sight. "What are you doing here?"

"I didn't mean to barge in, but I rang the doorbell a couple times and you didn't answer. I didn't know if you were out back or busy or what."

She waved him into the kitchen. "Sorry. Just daydreaming."

Ben grinned. "You? Daydreaming? You're the one who hardly takes five minutes to sit down and eat dinner."

A rehash of her faults was not on Nora's agenda for the day. All that did was lead them into fights, and right now she was 5 and 0 on the no-drama scoreboard. "Why are you here, Ben?"

"I wanted to see my kids."

A little crack of hurt went through her when she realized he hadn't said he wanted to see her. God, why couldn't she make up her mind? Why was a part of her still holding on to something that had already died?

She drew in a deep breath and straightened her shoulders. No drama, no tears, just a calm, businesslike discussion. "If you can wait a minute to see them, I'd like to talk to you about the furniture. On my break today, I started making a list—" She opened her purse to pull out a piece of paper.

Ben put his hand over hers, the touch still familiar and warm, even after everything. "Can we not talk about that now?"

"Ben, the house is being auctioned off in eighteen days. We don't have much time to get the furniture out of there. We still have to figure out how we're going to pack up the stuff, move it to some storage unit or something—"

"We have time, Nora."

"You act like we have months, not days. Jesus, Ben, face reality, will you?" She shook her head. "Why did I think you had changed? You're reliable one time, on Halloween, and here I stupidly go thinking you're going to be responsible and supportive and stop burying your head in the sand. You know what, Ben? Don't worry about the list." She waved it at him before shoving it back into her purse. "I'll figure it out. Just like I have everything else for the last two years. I should have learned my lesson last year about depending on you."

"I'm not saying I'm not going to work on this with you." He took her hand, his touch warm and encompassing and sure. "I'm saying we have time. Things could still turn around—"

She yanked her hand away. He still didn't get it. "God-dammit, Ben, will you quit gambling with our lives? I swear, it's like you think our home—*our children's home*— is one more blackjack deal or craps roll. Nothing is going to turn around. They stapled a damned auction notice on

237

our house, and we are losing *everything*. Face the facts. Our house is gone, and our marriage is over."

"Nora, you have some nerve—" Ben's gaze went somewhere behind her and his face crumpled. "Sarah. Oh God, Sarah."

Nora spun around and saw her daughter standing in the open doorway of the kitchen, tears streaming down her face. How long had she been there? What had she heard? Nora took two steps toward her. "Sarah—"

"Don't talk to me! Don't touch me! You promised me, Mommy! You promised me you weren't divorcing Daddy and we were going to be okay!" She spun out of the kitchen and burst out the door. The screen door slammed shut, the dog started barking, and Sarah disappeared.

Nora and Ben spent an hour combing Mary's neighborhood, calling for Sarah. Ben went on foot while Nora waited for her sister to come and watch Jake. Magpie hurried in the door ten minutes after Nora called, saying only that she needed her there immediately. Those ten minutes lasted an eternity while Nora paced in the front hall and held a finger over the Send button for 911.

"Hey, what happened that you needed to drag me away from my lame evening at home bingeing on Netflix?" her sister asked as she hung her coat on the hook and stuffed her hat in the pocket.

"Sarah heard Ben and me arguing and she took off." Nora pulled on her coat and grabbed her car keys from the hall table. "Will you stay with Jake? Don't say anything to him, please. I don't want him to worry."

"No problem." She gave Nora a quick hug. "It'll be okay, Nora."

"That's the problem, Mags. None of this is going to be okay. And it hasn't been okay, not for a long time." She hurried out the door, climbed in her car, and started to search, scanning the streets, pausing at shadowy backyards. She and Ben texted and called each other as they made their way through Mary's neighborhood. She lived on the southwestern side of Revere, near Winthrop Avenue and Route 1A, in a neighborhood peppered with triplexes and apartment buildings. Her little two-story, single-family saltbox was a lone holdout against the towering multifamily homes.

It was a neighborhood Nora barely knew, but Ben had worked several jobs here and knew it well. So she took his direction, forced to rely on his knowledge. They were almost like the partners they used to be. Before...

Before everything went to hell in a handbasket.

Nora and Ben worked in a crisscross pattern, with Nora driving the longer main roads and Ben walking the connecting side streets. Nora kept her window down, calling Sarah's name every few seconds, keeping the car moving at a snail's pace.

As she drove, her frustration and anger mounted. Everything that had happened in the last two years had led to this moment, to Sarah running away. The gambling, the house, the fights. Sarah getting into trouble in school, the scuffle with Anna. Nora and the kids living in a house that wasn't theirs. Their ruined lives, ruined family.

She reached a cross street and saw Ben standing at the corner. He gave her a little wave and started walking toward her, as if nothing was wrong, nothing was different. In an instant, the anger inside her erupted. She slammed the car into park and then got out, leaving the door open and the engine running. "This is your fault!"

"Mine? All I did was try to see my kids. You were the one who started in on me about the gambling. Again. The last time I gambled was a year ago. *A year.* You won't fucking let it drop, Nora."

"Because that gambling is still affecting us now, Ben, in case you haven't noticed. You make it sound like you put down the dice and, in an instant, everything was perfect." She waved at the house in the distance, the house that she lived in that wasn't home. "Look at our family, our lives. We're losing our house, our daughter is getting into fights at school, and you're off telling Joyce how unhappy you are." Jealousy surged, a white-hot rush. She told herself she didn't care who Ben was with, didn't care that he had confided in another woman.

"You want to know why I went to Joyce?" Ben said. "Because my *wife* hasn't been there for me in so damned long, I'm not even sure she cares that I'm alive."

"What is this, feel bad for Ben day?" she scoffed. "I've been busy working, taking care of the kids, the house, the bills, all the shit you didn't want to do. I don't have time to pick you up off the floor when things get crappy."

"The things I didn't want to do? Or wasn't allowed to do? Perfect, efficient Nora did everything. Every time I tried to do anything, you made me feel incompetent. I'm surprised you didn't give me directions on how to take my own kids trick-or-treating." Ben shook his head. "The truth is, Nora, you're just as screwed up as I am. You just refuse to admit it."

"Me? I'm not blowing our mortgage on a freaking white ball, Ben."

"Go ahead, keep blaming it all on me. I can take it. I'm a big boy." He smacked his chest. "But just remember who deserted who when I went to rehab."

"Deserted you? I never left us, Ben."

"Are you implying that going to rehab was leaving you? Leaving our family? I did that to save us, Nora. To save me. And you did leave me, the day I checked into that place." He took a step closer, and she could see the shadows under his eyes, the stubble on his jaw. "You never called. Never visited. Didn't write me a single damned letter. When the therapist asked you to come up for a couples' session, you said no. When I asked you to go to a meeting with me, you said no. You left me, Nora, to do this all on my own, when I needed you. I needed you, damn it." His voice thickened.

Every instinct inside her urged Nora to reach out to Ben, to apologize, smooth it over, make it better. But then she thought of that winter morning and the many, many nights and days he had left her when she needed him, and she turned around and got back in the car.

"Right now, our daughter needs us. That's all that matters, Ben."

He looked off into the distance for a second, as if gauging his words. "You want to tell me what happened in Truro?"

"Does it really matter, Ben?" She shut the door, put the car back in gear, and headed down the road. She spent another twenty minutes driving up and down the streets, calling for her daughter.

Should she call the police? Would they do anything about a child being gone for such a short period of time? And then Ben's number lit up her cell, and for a second, the fight was forgotten. They could circle back to all that later, after Sarah was safe. "Did you find her?"

"No."

"It's getting dark. Maybe we should just call the police. What if someone took her?"

"Nora, we'll find her." Ben's voice, steady and calm, carried over the cell connection and eased the racing fear in Nora's heart. "Trust me, okay?"

For two years, she hadn't trusted her husband. He'd lied to her over and over again, taken money without her knowledge, spun wild tales to cover his tracks. He'd abandoned her when she needed him most. But in this moment, in the dark interior of her car on a cold fall night, she chose to trust him. Because she needed to hold on to that, to him, if only for a moment. "Okay, Ben." She clutched the phone and closed her eyes. *Please let him be right; please let us find her.*

"Wait...I have an idea. Where are you right now?"

She leaned out the window. "Uh...Campbell Avenue."

"Okay, good. Turn right on Walnut. A couple blocks down on the left there's a playground. I think she might have gone there. Meet me there? I'm close to it."

"Me too." Nora kept the phone connection open until she got there, pulling into the parking lot at the same time Ben came running in. She jerked the gearshift into park and tumbled out the door. The two of them broke into a run, calling Sarah's name. They circled the playground, trying to see past the shadows, the darkened spaces under the tables and seesaw.

And then, inside the orange tower at the top of a bright blue climbing structure, she saw a familiar pink coat. Nora's heart lurched and relief washed over her in a tidal wave. "That's her," she said to Ben. "Sarah!"

The two of them scrambled up to the tower, Nora opting for the ramp, Ben grabbing the outside poles and swinging himself up. He reached their daughter first, crouching until his broad frame nearly filled the small square space. "Sarah! Thank God. Are you okay? Are you hurt? We were so worried about you."

Sarah plowed into Ben's arms and broke into hard, heaving sobs. "I'm sorry, Daddy, I'm sorry."

Nora started to cry, too, deep sobs of relief, of gratitude, of regret. She watched her husband hug their daughter, and all those hours of searching and worry evaporated. They'd found her. Thank God, they'd found her.

Nora had already lost one child. She couldn't survive losing another.

Ben ran a hand down Sarah's long brown hair, pressing kisses to her temples. She squeezed tighter and sobbed into his shoulder. "It's okay, honey. It's okay. We've got you." Then he reached out and grabbed Nora and pulled her into the circle.

TWENTY-ONE

After they got home, Sarah was too tired to eat more than a couple bites of a sandwich. Nora told her and Jake to get ready for bed and then she hugged Magpie, thanking her sister and promising to call later. Mags seemed off, not quite herself. Nora made a mental note to check in with her sister later.

Ben lingered in the kitchen, still wearing his coat. The betrayed, angry part of Nora wanted to kick him out, but the parent in her, who knew how scary those hours had been and how troubled their little girl was, couldn't shut Ben out. He loved Sarah as much as Nora did, and it wouldn't be fair to let their argument get in the way of him spending time with her.

"Why don't you stay and help me put the kids to bed?" Nora said. "I think Sarah would like that."

"Thanks." He seemed grateful for the small request, and she felt like crap for not including him more in the last couple weeks. Ben loved his kids—keeping him from them would only hurt the kids.

She busied herself folding Sarah's sweatshirt because it kept her from having to see the surprise and gratitude in her husband's eyes. After they were divorced, they would be constantly doing this dance of holding on to the shreds of a family while still keeping that dividing line between them. Already, Ben's presence had a degree of awkwardness. Part of it was the simmering tension from their argument; part of it was the environment. This wasn't their house—wasn't her house either—and this was no longer the family they used to have. Maybe someday she'd get used to that feeling of being out of place, but right now, she felt like she'd stepped into another country where she didn't know the language or customs.

The two of them fell into step together as they walked down the hall to the guest bedroom. Years ago—before the poker and the horse races and the lies—putting the kids to bed together had bridged the gap between being Mommy and Daddy and shifting back into Ben and Nora. They would sit on either side of Sarah's bed or stand beside Jake's crib, giving kisses and stories and last-minute glasses of water and then tiptoe out and shut the door.

Then it would be just them again, and more times than not, Ben would take her hand on that return trip down the hall. Anticipation would build inside her for those moments on the couch when she curved into him. They'd watch a movie or split a bottle of wine or head to bed early to make love and fall asleep wrapped together in a human bow of legs and arms.

Those moments had eroded bit by bit until they were gone altogether. A part of Nora grieved that loss, missed the simplicity of those years. What had driven Ben to the casinos instead of their living room? And what had made her turn a blind eye, ignoring his distance, his mistakes, instead of confronting him? By the time she had finally said something, the money was gone and the damage done.

That day when she'd confronted him, she had lost everything. Her husband, her marriage, herself. She'd sat on the cold bench in the snow and watched Ben drive away, while the life inside her died.

The truth is, Nora, you're just as screwed up as I am. Ben was right. She was screwed up. She had screwed up. She'd ignored and skirted and avoided, doing her level best to put a fresh coat of paint on a wall moldy with lies. *You're a good mother,* Magpie had said. Ben had said the same thing more than once. They couldn't be more wrong.

Jake was already in bed, holding a book and a stuffed dinosaur. Nora pasted on a smile when she saw her son. "Can we read *Dinosaurs Sing* tonight, Mommy?"

"Sure. Sarah, want to come sit on Jake's bed and listen?"

"Is Daddy going to do the dinosaur voice?"

"Of course," Ben said. "Because I'm a good dinosaur." He bent his hands into claws and let out a "Rawwrr."

Jake laughed and shifted to the side. Sarah climbed in the middle and Nora sat on the edge of the bed by the nightstand. Ben pulled up a chair and sat on the opposite side. Nora's gaze connected with Ben's across the divide of their children. He looked away first, nodding toward the book. "Let's see what the dinosaurs are up to tonight."

"Yeah, sure." Nora opened the book, extending her arms so all four of them could see it. And so that she could read the book through blurred vision. "Once upon a time, there was a family of dinosaurs who lived in a big, deep, cool cave. There was a Mommy dinosaur and a Daddy dinosaur and a little baby dinosaur named Barry."

Jake laughed. "Barry is a silly name."

"I've never met a dinosaur named Barry," Nora said as she turned the page. "Barry liked dinosaur school until one day when their music teacher, Mr. Brontosaurus, came in the classroom."

Ben leaned forward and affected a deep, rumbly voice. "Children, today we are going to learn to sing. That way everyone will know we are nice dinosaurs."

Sarah giggled. "Daddy, you are the best dinosaur ever."

"Say it again, Daddy." Jake bounced in place. "Please?"

The rest of the book went that way, with Nora narrating and Ben in recurring roles as every dinosaur in the story. By the time they finished, Sarah had curled up against her brother and Jake was nodding off.

"Let me put her in bed," Ben said. He scooped Sarah up and transferred her to the twin bed across the room. He settled her on the sheets and then drew the pink and white plaid comforter to her chin, tucking it around her waist and legs. *Like a burrito*, Sarah had said when she was little.

Ben pressed a tender kiss to Sarah's forehead. "Good night, princess. Sleep tight."

Tears stung Nora's eyes. She crossed to Jake, settling the covers around him, knowing her restless, always busy boy would kick most of them off by the middle of the night. She kissed each of the kids, then tiptoed out of the room and leaned against the wall.

She could hear Ben whispering good night to Jake before he clicked off the light. Ben lingered in the room, and she could see him in her mind, the loving father watching over his children, cementing their sleepy faces in his heart. How many nights had they done that together? Holding hands, marveling at the amazing humans they had created.

When had it shifted? When had they stopped putting the kids to bed together? The chasm in their marriage had opened a little at a time. One night, she'd put the kids to bed alone, and a month later, she was doing it every night. Ben was "working late" or "caught in traffic" or any of the hundreds of excuses that covered for his stops at the off-track betting parlors and casinos.

"They're down for the count," Ben said. He left the door slightly ajar and then walked back down the hall with Nora.

She avoided the living room and swung right, into the kitchen, instead. Delaying saying goodbye to him but not wanting to re-create those nights in the living room together. "Do you want some coffee?"

"Yeah, that would be great. Thanks." The words were as distant as a stranger's.

She kept her back to him as she filled the carafe, added the grounds, and set the pot to brew. Too late, she realized offering coffee meant at least five minutes of waiting. The dishes were done, the countertops clean, and the options for avoiding Ben were minimal. A part of her hadn't wanted to let go of the moments she remembered, and now she was stuck, caught between bittersweet memories and harsh reality. "Thanks again for helping tonight."

"I'm her dad. Of course I'd help find her." He shook his head. "Do you really think I'm that bad of a father?"

"No, no. I just…" She sighed. She was screwing up a simple thank you. "I don't know what to say right now, Ben."

"Neither do I, Nora."

The coffeepot *glub-glubbed*, and the rich scent of fresh-brewed coffee filled the air. Just enough to pour one mug, so she started with Ben's, if only to have a reason to turn away and gather herself together. She could go back to their argument, but a part of her was so tired of fighting, of trying. Maybe it was best if she just kept things civil and simple. "How did you know Sarah would be at that playground?"

"That's a story I've never told you." He accepted the coffee from her and took a sip. "Thanks."

Nora retrieved the cream from the refrigerator and took the sugar out of the cabinet before leaning against the counter to wait for the next cup to brew. "What story?"

He was quiet for a moment. The dog curled up at Ben's feet and shut his eyes. "Do you remember that weekend you had to work an all-nighter? I think Sarah had just turned five and Jake was one. I was in charge overnight, for the first time."

She nodded. "I remember that night. I accidentally dropped a five-tier wedding cake and had to stay all night at the bakery to make another one in time for the wedding. We cut that so close—I was literally wheeling the cake into the reception hall at the hotel while they were saying their vows outside on the lawn."

Ben wrapped his hands around his mug and stared down into the cup. "Sarah ran away that night too."

Anger roared through her. Typical Ben, keeping the truth to himself. "Why didn't you ever tell me that? Jesus, Ben, that's not the kind of thing you should keep from me."

"That's *exactly* why I didn't tell you. Because I knew you'd freak out and tell me I was completely inept as a father."

Hurt shimmered in his eyes, and the anger that had peaked so quickly ebbed again. She, of all people, had no right to call him a bad parent. She poured her own coffee and sat across from him at the table. "That isn't fair. I never told you that you were inept. Yeah, I took over for some things, but I didn't want you to—"

"Do it wrong. You've always had trouble letting go of the reins, Nora, of letting the rest of us try and maybe even fail. You kept such a tight leash on everything in our lives that there was never any room for me."

"What are you talking about? You were always there." *Until you weren't,* she added in her head.

"I was there, but I was an outsider." The hurt flickered

in his face again, in the wry smile that disappeared as quickly as it had appeared. "Frankly, I'm surprised the kids are as close to me as they are. You did *everything*, Nora. The laundry, the cooking, the baby care, working full-time, then running the baths and reading the stories."

"It was just easier that way." That was what she had told herself over and over again as she ran the wash or loaded the dishwasher. That it was easier to do it herself than to trust someone else. And now, she realized in an ironic twist, she was the one feeling like an outsider every time the kids asked for Ben or ran to him. Tonight was the first time in a long time that she'd felt included, wanted, by the kids. By Ben.

"Easier for who?" Ben said. "Because to me, you were always exhausted and crabby and busy. I had a family with you because I wanted it to be a *family*. The kind of family that lets the dishes stack up because we're too busy playing in the yard. The kind of family that doesn't care about a little mud on the floor or a bathtub overrun with bubbles. Because those things meant we were having fun. We didn't have fun, Nora."

"We had fun. We did stuff. We went on vacations." Did he have different memories than she did? Different videos and pictures in his phone? Because she remembered trips to amusement parks and days at the museum and picnics in the park.

"Fun? We took one-day trips that were so well planned, they could have been executed by a four-star general. You wrote up itineraries and budgets and printed out the damned map, as if I was incapable of driving us to the aquarium. So it was never actually fun, Nora. We never truly got to just be and go with the flow."

The argument they'd had earlier was still simmering at the edges of his words. All it would take was a couple cross words and they'd be right back there. She got to her feet and added more cream and sugar, just to avoid looking at Ben for a moment. "You still haven't told me how you knew where Sarah was."

He wrapped his hands around his mug and stared down into the coffee. "When she took off that night I was watching her, I found her at that playground down the street from us. Wasn't much as playgrounds went, but Sarah loved it there. She was swinging when I found her, with a smile on her face the size of Texas. She told me she ran off because she wanted to have fun instead of do whatever it was that was on that list."

Of course. Here it was—the blame-it-on-Nora excuse. If she'd been more fun, if she'd been more relaxed...

Didn't he understand why she needed to keep things under control? Why she couldn't let go?

"So basically you're saying I'm a shitty mom, and that's why our daughter is so angry that she ran away." Nora cursed, got to her feet, and poured her coffee down the drain.

Ben set his mug on the table and rose to cross to her. He stood there, waiting until she turned away from the sink and faced him again. Ben's eyes were soft and kind, not judgmental or hard. They were the eyes she had fallen in love with, the eyes that still knew her better than any-one else.

"I'm not saying you are a bad mom, Nora. Not at all. You're a way better mom than any mom I know, includ-ing my own. You're there for the kids when they need you most."

I'm not, Ben. I'm not at all. "How can I believe that? They're homeless now—"

"They're not homeless. You're living here; they have beds to sleep in. You did that; you made sure they had a place." He waved toward the rooms above them, where their children were all tucked in and safe. "And all isn't lost with our house."

She shook her head. Just when she started to fall for him again, he went right back to the impossible odds argu-ment. He kept betting on their future—and losing. "Good Lord, Ben, when will you give up? They are auctioning the house off in two weeks. It's over. Let it go."

"I'm not giving up, Nora." He shifted closer to her. "You are."

"I am not. I'm facing reality." The reality that she had failed as a mother, failed as a wife, failed in general. Her daughter had run off not once but twice, because of what Nora had done. And the baby—

Guilt chased up her throat and caught on a sob. "It's over, Ben. I...failed."

"If anything, I did. I let all of you down. We had that night last year when we thought we'd try again, and, Lord, did I want to turn things around. I was going to quit gambling and be there for you and the kids. We even talked about having another baby, remember?"

She nodded, mute. Tears burned in her eyes.

"And a month later, I was back gambling again, like a fool. We had that huge fight and you told me to choose my family or the gambling and what did I do?"

"You left me, Ben. You left me there. And I..." She shook her head. What good would it do to tell him now? To resurrect the past? Nothing had changed. Nothing was going to change.

"You what?" He touched her, a tender caress along her hand, before his fingers rested along hers. His thumb skated back and forth over hers. "Tell me, Nora. Please, just tell me. Because even though I made the wrong choice that day, I started making the right ones the next day, and it was all because of what you said to me."

Maybe once he knew, he would give up and see that there was nothing here to save. That they were done, their family was done, their future gone. That it was true—she was screwed up, and there was no fixing what had gone wrong.

"That night a year ago when we thought we'd try again..." It took her a minute to pull the words out of her gut, words she had buried so deep because she had never planned to speak them. They burned on the way up, scraping her throat, opening a wound that had barely scabbed. "I...I got pregnant."

A flicker of joy danced in Ben's eyes, then disappeared as he clearly realized a year had passed, and there was no baby. Ben, who had always wanted a big family. Who had told her once he wanted a house full of kids with her. "Why didn't you tell me?"

She blew her bangs out of her face. "Why would I? You were never there, Ben. Not then, not when I finally decided to tell you. It was a month after I took the pregnancy test, and you'd been begging me to trust you again. That night, you came home from Foxwoods or wherever you were, and you had blown your entire paycheck at the casino. Again. You promised me you wouldn't do that. You *promised* me, Ben. And I trusted that. Trusted you."

"I'm sorry, Nora. I didn't—"

"And I was so angry with you," she said, the words coming faster now, that cold winter morning as fresh in her mind as if it were yesterday. "So, so angry. I chased you out of the house and I told you to leave and never come back, and you got in the car and you left. And then I changed my mind, because I still loved you, and I ran after the car and..." The tears spilled over her eyelashes and streamed down her face. The words scraped past her throat, and she knew, just knew, that her husband would never look at her the same way again after she said the rest. "And I slipped on the ice and...I...I lost the...the baby."

Ben stood there for a long moment. His face crumpled and his eyes welled, grief for a child he'd never known existed until now. "You...you lost it?"

"It was my fault and I shouldn't have gotten mad and I shouldn't have run and—" She shook her head. "I can't do this again, Ben. I can't be what you want me to be. I'm not that woman. And I don't want to be."

He didn't say anything for a long time. The kitchen was silent, save for the dog scratching his neck and settling down again. "What happened in Truro?" Ben asked again.

"Nothing." That wasn't entirely true, but it was close enough.

"I don't believe that. And if you do, you're lying to yourself." He shook his head. "You keep saying I'm the one who ruined our marriage. But you're the one who stopped trying. You're the one who gave up. I didn't." He cupped her jaw and met her gaze. As much as she wanted to pull away, the part of her that still cared deeply about him, still remembered what it had been like to be held by him, loved by him, couldn't move. "Do you really want to throw all of this away? Over a loan?"

It would be so easy, too easy, to say, *Let's try again.* To pick up where they had left off, as if the past year had been nothing more than a short detour.

"There you go again, taking years of issues and problems down to one simple thing. This is about more than the mortgage, and you know it. Ben, please just…stop trying to fix what is broken." *Please don't tempt me to fall for you again when I'm just learning how to let you go. I can't go through this again.*

"Nora, if you would just try—"

She shook her head. It was too late. The wheels were already in motion. And when Ben had some time to think about it, he'd realize that they wanted different things from the future. "I can't, Ben. Just let it go. Let us go. Please."

His face hardened, and the brown eyes she loved so much turned icy. The warmth in his touch disappeared. "If that's what you truly want, then I will. Goodbye, Nora."

Ben had said goodbye a hundred times in the years she'd known him. But never had that one word held the same meaning that it held tonight.

TWENTY-TWO

N ora woke up Sunday morning and noticed the quiet in the house first. The rooms sounded empty, echoing back her own footsteps, the closing of closet doors, the opening of drawers. She pulled on a robe and then sat in the kitchen, nursing a cup of coffee and waiting for the sun to rise.

Ben had stopped by to pick up the kids the night before, all businesslike and distant. He'd stood in the foyer, exchanging the bare minimum of words with her while the kids grabbed their backpacks. A new wall had gone up between them after her admission the other day about the miscarriage and their decision to proceed with the divorce. She kissed both kids, reminded Sarah to read some of her chapter book and told Jake to be sure to bring home his art project. Nora shut the door before she could see them get in the car. And before any of them saw her tears.

Her mother had texted this morning before church, saying the bakery was going to be slow today because of some unexpected road construction that would shut down the street for most of the day so Nora didn't need to come in. It was a rare day off—at exactly the wrong time. She needed to stay busy, to keep her focus on anything other than the gnawing hole in her life.

She called Magpie, surprised when her little sister answered on the first ring. "Are you turning into a morning person?"

"God, I hope not. I just had trouble sleeping last night. Not used to my own bed, I guess."

"I know what you mean. It was weird being here the first few days but now I think I'm getting used to Aunt Mary's house. Believe it or not, but I got up, accomplished nothing more than drinking a cup of coffee, and crawled back under the covers."

"Okay, the Apocalypse is surely on its way now. That's the third sign."

"Hey, I'm not that bad."

"Nora, the last time you slept past six in the morning, you had the flu. And even then you got your shit together and came to work to do a consult at ten that morning. You're like superhuman."

"Hardly." A superhuman woman wouldn't be in the boat she was in. A superhuman woman would get dressed and out the door even when she was depressed as hell and the future looked as bleak as the sky on a winter day. A superhuman woman wouldn't be on the edge of a sob every minute of the day. "Ma said the bakery isn't busy today and I was wondering...do you think your friend would mind if we went back to that house in Truro? It's a nice day for November, and I doubt we'll get many more of those for the next few months. Do you want to come with me?"

Nora told herself she just wanted to walk the beach one more time before the cold settled in for a months-long stay. That this was about rejuvenation, not about finding out *what if.*

"I'm not up to going today," Magpie said. "I'm sure it's totally cool for you to use the house today. The spare key is under the terra-cotta planter on the front porch."

"You're not up for an adventure? Are you feeling okay?"

"I'm...I'm tired. Lots of writing this week, that's all. Enjoy the beach for both of us, okay?"

Magpie sounded not at all like her usual energetic, wild self. Nora debated running over to her sister's apartment and checking on her, but just the thought of caring for one more person made Nora want to stay in bed for a month. She'd stop by after she went to Truro. Whatever was bothering Magpie couldn't be that serious anyway. Her sister lived a life that could be a Bob Marley song. No commitments, no worries, no stress. "Are you sure, Mags? It won't be the same without you."

"Yeah, yeah, it's fine. I have some work to get done anyway. And you're right, this is way too early for me to be up." Magpie's laughter was closer to the carefree sister Nora knew well. "I'm probably going to need a nap later. Maybe two."

"All right. Well, just let me know if you need anything later." Nora lingered in bed for a little while after she hung up the phone. She had to force herself to stay at first, because everything inside her said, *Get shit done*. Laundry, dishes, bill paying, robbing a bank...

Instead, she took a long, hot shower and spent time drying and curling her hair, leaving it down instead of in its customary ponytail, and then put on some makeup. She slid into some jeans that fit more loosely than they had a couple weeks ago. Apparently becoming homeless and getting divorced was a good way to diet.

She let the dog out, setting him up with a couple of toys and a chewy bone, and then drove to Truro on deserted roads. Most people were either sleeping or in church, and with the tourist season for the Cape a couple months in the past, the hook end of the state had a much-needed breather. As she drove, she fiddled with the radio, if only to let the noise distract her from her ever-churning mind, filled with questions she couldn't answer—*What am I going to do about a long-term living situation? What am I going to do about Ben? Are Sarah and Jake going to be okay through all this? Am I going to be okay?*

When the B-52's classic "Love Shack" came on, Nora bumped up the volume. The song pulsed in the car, the beat thumping against the floor and the seats. When the B-52's were pounding on the door, wanting to get in on the party inside, Nora turned up the radio a little more, rolled down the windows, and sang along at the top of her voice. She sang about Chryslers and shimmying, huggin' and dancin', and thought of all that she had skipped in her life.

She'd never had those years of partying that her friends and sisters had. The midnight beach bonfires, the beer pong challenges in mildewy basements, the two a.m. hookups with boys who didn't even know her last name. She'd skipped from high school to marriage, jumping right over dorm life and sowing her oats like she'd been playing Life Monopoly and had drawn the Skip Ahead to Marriage without Passing Go card from the Community Chest.

The song wound to an end, and the radio announcer started talking about the band's chart history. Nora went to roll up the windows but decided to leave them down, to let the wind whip at her hair. She couldn't remember the last time she'd sung along with the radio and driven too fast on the highway. The rare times she was alone in the car, she was usually making plans for the bakery, returning phone calls about school events, or dictating lists to Siri.

How had her life gotten to this dull, predictable place? No more, Nora vowed, no more being the one who missed out on life. If the B-52's were to be believed, the secret to happiness was found in being a little wild and unpredictable. She'd literally let her hair down today by taking out her perpetual ponytail. Maybe she should do it in other ways too.

As she swung her car in front of the beach house in Truro, the radio was pounding out "You Give Love a Bad Name." She closed her eyes, leaned back against the headrest, and sang along with the chorus at the top of her lungs until Bon Jovi finished singing about being shot in the heart.

"And yet another of your many talents, Nora the Neighbor."

Nora jumped at the sound of Will's voice as if she'd been caught looting the cookie jar. She turned off the radio and tried not to look like an off-key idiot. "Will! You scared me. I didn't even hear you come up."

His sunglasses hid his blue eyes, and that same lock of dark hair swooped across his brow. A long-sleeved dark green T-shirt hugged his muscular chest and tapered into jeans that skimmed along his legs. He was one hell of a good-looking man, the kind that GUESS jeans would plaster on a billboard in Times Square. Damn.

"A herd of elephants following the Notre Dame marching band could have passed by your car and you wouldn't have heard them." He grinned and nodded toward the interior of her old Buick. "What the hell kind of speakers does this thing have anyway?"

Nora turned off the car and got out. "Sorry. I didn't mean to disturb the whole neighborhood."

"Darlin', the whole neighborhood right now is me. Everyone with any sense has left before winter sets in. I'm the only bear that hibernates on this street." He leaned against the rear door of her car and crossed his arms over his chest. "Why are you here? I thought you were never coming back. And by the way, you should have stopped by to say goodbye."

"I'm sorry. I had to get back to work." Not exactly the truth. The whole encounter with Ben and Will had left her shaken, and a part of her had felt guilty even though technically she'd done nothing wrong. So, in her best ostrich with her head in the sand imitation, she'd avoided all of it and left without telling Will.

"I'm glad you're back, though. How long are you here for?"

She tried not to hear the words *I'm glad you're back* and take them for anything other than friendship. "Just for the day."

"Then I say we make the most of it." He grinned. "How about a picnic on the beach in an hour?"

She hadn't thought about food and had forgotten to eat before she left. That was her excuse for saying, "Yes, that sounds like fun."

Deep down inside, she knew the truth. She'd been hoping she would see him. Then when he'd called her *darlin'* with that little flirty tone, she'd loved the attention. For two years, she'd slept in a separate room from a husband who had become a roommate. She'd forgotten what it felt like to look in a man's eyes and feel beautiful, desired, special.

And she might be going to hell for it, but she wanted just a few more minutes of that with one selfish picnic on the sand.

"Great," Will said. "I'll pack some sandwiches and meet you down there. See you soon." He gave her another smile before he crossed the street and a little rush ran through Nora.

She went inside the beach house and opened the windows, letting in the sounds of the ocean and the scent of the salt water. The soft *shush-shush* soothed her nerves and grounded her. This was just a lunch, nothing more. She had no reason to feel ashamed or nervous.

She stepped out onto the back deck and turned her face up to soak in the afternoon sun. The temperature had risen in the time she'd been driving, so Nora shed her coat and shoes, and headed down the sandy path to the beach.

She could almost fool herself into thinking she had reached the end of the world because there were no other human beings for as far as she could see in either direction. She rolled up the cuffs of her jeans and strolled along the shore, picking up shells and tossing them back, watching the incoming tide fill the dips and divots in the sand, and listening to the seagulls call to each other across the sky.

The moment reminded her of an early fall morning when she was seven and had stayed home sick from school. Her mother had gone to the bakery, and her dad had taken off work to stay home with her. By midmorning—and after a long nap—her fever broke, and she'd felt better. Instead of driving her to school, as Ma would have done, Dad slipped Nora's arms into a light jacket. "We're going to play hooky," he told her. "And go to the beach. Just you and me."

In a family of four girls, time alone with Dad had been a rare, treasured thing. When her father bundled her into the car and drove them down to Tenean Beach, Nora had felt more special than she ever had on her birthday. To a seven-year-old, the beach had seemed as big as the moon, with its colorful playground and view of the harbor. That day, the beach had been as empty as Truro was today, with parents at work and kids at school. Dad had bought some sandwiches on the way there, and they'd had a picnic. Then they'd dashed in and out of the water, laughing when the waves slapped their legs with cold water.

As Nora walked along the sandy shore of the Cape, she realized why that day was one of her most treasured memories. Because she'd had fun.

There'd been no expectations, no rules, no schedule. Her father had been the carpe diem parent, while Ma was the one who brought everyone back to earth. Then Dad died a year later, and the fun had died with him. Ma ran a tight ship, probably because there was no other way to function as a business owner and mother of four girls under the age of ten.

As much as she'd loved and admired her father and held that memory of the beach day close to her heart, in the end, the one she'd emulated had been her mother. She'd married a carpe diem guy. She didn't know if that made her an optimist or a fool. Because carpe diem guys didn't squirrel away savings or plan for rainy days. They lived moment to moment, until those moments caught up with them.

Just then Will loped down to the beach with a red plaid blanket tucked under one arm and a small cooler in his opposite hand. Nora stayed where she was, feeling all kinds of wrong, but at the same time rooted to the spot, anticipating, dreading, wondering. Was she embarking on carpe diem territory herself or making a massively stupid mistake?

When he reached her, his smile widened. "You came. I have to admit, I wasn't sure you'd be here."

She took the blanket from him and settled it over the sand. Even though the day had been unseasonably warm and sunny, the beach was still deserted, and that made their impromptu picnic much too intimate. "Honestly, I don't know why I'm here."

He set the cooler down and took a step closer to her. "Because you're as curious as I am about where this could go."

What happened in Truro?

Nothing.

Yet.

Was that why she'd come here? Why she'd gotten in the car and driven all those miles and let down her hair and affected this live-for-today attitude?

She was here alone in Truro. Ben had the kids, way back in Dorchester. No one, in fact, knew she was here except for Magpie. Whatever happened, no one would know, except Nora and Will. This could go anywhere—back to his house, or here on the uninhabited beach—and for a few hours, she could feel like she used to when Ben had first smiled at her. Beautiful. Sexy. Desired.

She could forget everything waiting for her back at home, push her guilt about the kids and the bills and the job to the back burner. All her life, Nora had been the one who played by all the rules, did everything right. She'd gone in early, stayed late, organized the classroom parties and hosted the sleepovers. And where had that left her?

Had it really been worth it to live her whole life on the straight and narrow?

The temptation to take the road never traveled was strong, whispering that she deserved this, that chances were good Ben already had someone else in his life, on all those Friday and Saturday nights he didn't spend at home. All she had to do was reach out and touch Will, to open that gate.

"I'm married, and I know I told you that already, but...I am." The words tumbled out of her mouth, because maybe if she reminded him and herself, she wouldn't forget that ring on her finger. If she stepped too far off that path, she was afraid she'd get tangled in the weeds and never make her way back.

"And is that a permanent situation?" Will asked. "Because from what I saw the other day, it didn't look like that."

She sighed and sank onto the blanket. "I don't know. I don't know where I'm going or what I'm doing. All I know is my life is a mess, and I have no idea how to clean it up."

He settled beside her, withdrew two beers from the cooler, unscrewed the caps, and handed one to her. Comfortable, easy, as if they'd been together dozens of times. "Three years ago, I was where you are. My life had fallen apart, my career was on the skids, and things got so bad, I was applying to work at the bank."

"You? Working in a bank? Sorry, but I just don't see it." His tattoos peeked out from under his shirtsleeves, and his hair dusted his collar. He didn't look like any teller she'd ever dealt with, but then again, if she'd had one that looked like him, she might have gone to the bank a lot more often.

He chuckled. "Neither did they, which is why I didn't get hired. I did, however, get hired to paint a mural in the lobby when the manager found out what I used to do for a living. The problem was, I had lost my desire to paint—hell, my desire for anything. My wife had walked out on me a month earlier, taking the furniture—and the next-door neighbor."

"Ouch."

"Yeah." He shrugged. "I was in this empty house, living next door to another empty house, and every time I tried to paint, all I heard were those echoes of failure."

"I hear those too." She thought of her kids, of the yellow notice on the house, of the hurt in Ben's eyes Friday night. Those images flickered in her mind all day, growing brighter and stronger when she was alone at night and regrets crowded into the bed.

"I sat down to start the mural—it was going to be seven twenty-by-forty canvases—knowing that getting it right was a big deal. It was my way back to my career. The kind of piece that could lead to more work and something approaching a steady income, which usually isn't associated with the word *artist*." He took a long drag off the beer and leaned back on his elbows. A trio of seagulls swooped down, found nothing to interest them, and left in a flutter and squawk. "I sat there in the bedroom I had turned into a studio for at least an hour and...nothing. Not a single damned idea. I've always been the kind of artist who had more ideas than time to paint them, but this time, I drew a complete blank. I was so angry, so sure my career was over. I kicked the canvas, which made it fall over and crash into my paints, which spilled in a nice, big Technicolor puddle on the tile."

She put a hand over her mouth to cover her gasp. "What did you do?"

"I had a damned fine pity party for the rest of the afternoon. Grabbed a beer, went outside, debated what kind of careers a washed-up artist that not even a bank wanted to hire could have. Turns out there aren't a lot of options." He chuckled. "Anyway, I sat out there the rest of the day, and when the sun started setting, I went back into the house to clean up the mess. And there, on the floor, I found what I needed the most. Inspiration."

"In paint on the floor?"

"The canvas had fallen into the paint, and there was a swath of oranges and purples across the front. This long swoop of color that streaked across the whole canvas. I looked up, and the sky, I kid you not, looked exactly the same. The sunset had painted the clouds in purples and oranges, with a peek of blue below, merging into the ocean. The water was calm that day and those amazing clouds were reflecting off the ocean. The pier down there"—he pointed a few hundred yards down the beach—"was kissed with just enough light that it seemed almost surreal.

"It was an amazing sight, and one that filled me with such peace and a sense of harmony with the world and myself again. I felt like I'd found my truth, know what I mean? And so that's what I painted. I don't think I've ever painted as fast as I did that night. I wanted to capture it before it disappeared."

Will tugged out his phone, scrolled through some photos, and then showed her the picture of the sunset, followed by ones of the finished project. The mural looked as real as the image he had captured and brought to life all those feelings of peace and harmony that he'd talked about.

"That is stunning."

"Thanks." He tucked his phone back into his pocket. "My career turned around after I finished that mural. Several other branches commissioned the same piece on a smaller level, and within a couple months, my house was furnished and my life was full. My point is"—he handed her a sandwich—"that sometimes you can find what you are looking for in the middle of the mess."

Her eyes met his, and warmth spread through her veins. Will had this way of looking at her that made her feel like the only woman in the world. "Do you really think so?"

"I've found what I've been looking for." He leaned closer, winnowing the gap between them.

Nora held her breath. The water, the gulls, the sand seemed to disappear. And then Will kissed her. Tender, sweet, slow, as if he were memorizing the feel of her lips. He cupped her jaw, and his fingers danced along her cheek.

Nora hadn't been kissed by another man in so long

that at first she remained stiff and scared. Then her body responded, desire quickening in her veins, and she yielded to his kiss. When she closed her eyes, the kiss was similar enough to Ben's that she could fool herself.

Will drew back and a slight smile curved across his lips. "You are as amazing to kiss as I thought you would be. And I would love to find out more—much more—about what it's like to be with you, but I think maybe we should just have lunch for now."

If he hadn't stopped the kiss, would she have? Nora didn't know, and didn't want to find out, because a part of her was still simmering with desire and still thinking about taking his hand and leading him up to that bedroom with the painting of the lighthouse.

If anything, kissing Will had made her life messier. Her decisions more complicated.

She unwrapped the sandwich and took a bite. Turkey, cheese, and lettuce, with a couple slices of bacon and some mayonnaise on toasted wheat bread. "I don't think my mess is going to be as easy to solve."

He leaned back on his elbows again and looked out over the ocean. "Maybe you just need to change your view, until it shows you your beauty and your truth. It's there, Nora, if you look hard enough. And look in the right places."

In some kind of poetic finale, the sun was just starting to set as Nora and Will headed back up the beach to the road. They had talked all afternoon, finishing up the lunch he had brought and eating the entire package of cookies he'd tucked in the cooler. He hadn't kissed her again, but he had found a hundred reasons to touch her—handing her a water bottle, taking the trash and stowing it in the bag, tumbling a pile of shells into her outstretched palm. Every single time, her heart zinged and her brain let out alarm bells.

Will stopped walking when they reached the beach house and set the cooler on the ground beside him. His hands captured hers, his grip firm and warm—

And not Ben's.

Ben's hands were slightly bigger, his fingers longer. When he held hands with her, he laced their fingers together and traced lazy circles over the back of her knuckle with his thumb. She couldn't remember the last time he had held her hand, but her heart remembered what it felt like. Damn it.

No matter how much she tried, she couldn't turn Will into Ben. Couldn't transform that amazing kiss from almost-Ben into actually-Ben.

"I had a wonderful time," Will said.

"Me too. Thank you for lunch."

"My pleasure. And I mean that." He gave her hands a squeeze and leaned closer, close enough for her to catch the woodsy notes of his cologne, close enough to kiss him again. In that second, she imagined a future with him. Making love in his bedroom, waking up in his arms, strolling along the street in the early morning. The temptation inside her strengthened, urging her to close that gap, to feel his mouth on hers one more time. "When will I see you again, Nora the Neighbor?"

She held on to him for a second longer and then released his hands and stepped back. She wasn't this person, and wasn't going to be. For better or worse, she was Nora O'Bannon Daniels, a little OCD, a little uptight, and a woman who, in the end, couldn't do the wrong thing. A woman who, despite everything, still loved the man who had put that ring on her finger. A woman who couldn't fully picture herself with Will, because he didn't fit right with Sarah and Jake and the life she already had. She wasn't ready for whatever could happen in Truro, and she might never be. "You won't."

He cocked his head. "Why not? I thought you had a great time."

"I did. But that isn't enough, Will. It's not enough to break the rules I live by. I thought I could, and to be honest, that's most of the reason why I drove down here today. I wanted to know what it could be like if..." She let out a long breath. "If I did something the old Nora would never do. I guess I thought if I lived my life differently, even if only for an afternoon, I'd get different results. But all this would do is make my mess even bigger."

He considered her words and finally nodded. "I can respect that. Doesn't mean I like it, but I can respect it." He reached up and cupped her jaw. "I hope he knows how lucky he is."

The days when Ben thought he was lucky to have her in his life had passed. "It doesn't matter if he does," she said. "I know who I am, and even if the person I am is far from perfect, it's a person I want to respect in the morning."

Because she hadn't been that person, she realized. She had been driving down the wrong path for a while. Now she needed to try to navigate that road alone, not with a man she plugged into Ben's place.

Will dropped his hand. "Well, if you ever want to do something you might regret in the morning, you have my number." He pressed a quick kiss to her forehead before he turned on his heel and disappeared into the dark.

TWENTY-THREE

God invented books for days like this, Magpie told herself as she settled into her couch and flipped through the stack of paperbacks on her end table. She couldn't remember the last time she had read anything longer than a magazine article. She loved books—always had—and frequently shipped new titles to herself from Amazon. Books that stacked up in that pile but never got read. Magpie was always too busy running from one place to another to be bogged down with a stack of paperbacks and a story line.

She'd begged off on family dinner tonight, telling her mother and sisters that she had a deadline to meet. But her laptop sat on the end table, the lid shut. She needed to get back to work, to answer emails, file this week's story. But she didn't do any of that. She sat on her couch, turning pages in the latest Harlan Coben novel. She lost the plot five minutes into starting the first chapter.

The apartment was quiet, the city winding down outside her windows. The dog had gone to live with Nora and the kids, and Magpie had to admit she kinda missed the furry moron. For her twenty-six years of life, Magpie had mostly been a loner, living out of a backpack as she traveled from assignment to assignment, never staying long enough in any one place to connect.

Except with Charlie. He'd been different somehow, more fun, less serious and less competitive than the other journalists she hung around with. Charlie lived by the seat of his pants, greeting every day as if it was a new adventure. He never took anything too seriously—which was something she appreciated.

Until something serious happened.

Her doorbell rang. She debated ignoring it and then heard Charlie through the door. What was he, Beetlejuice? Did the mere thought of his name deliver him to her doorstep?

"Maggie, you're starting to make me wonder if I need to buy new cologne or mouthwash," he called through the oak separating them. "Or maybe you think I have cooties? I assure you, I got my malaria shots."

She laughed. Damn that man for making her laugh and dissolving her resolve. Magpie swung off the couch and padded over to the door. When she opened it, there was Charlie, with a bouquet of flowers in one hand and a bottle of bourbon in the other.

"Let's make some bad decisions together tonight," he said, hoisting the Maker's Mark. His smile was tempting. Very, very tempting.

She shook her head. "I've made enough bad decisions with you."

He leaned in, his brown eyes sparkling, his smile warm. "And some pretty damned good memories. So let me in and let's have some fun."

"I'm not in the mood for that, sorry. Thanks for coming by." She started to shut the door, but he put his hand up and stopped her.

"What's up? Seriously. You went from sixty to zero with me. You disappear from the hotel without a word, barely talk to me in the last month and a half. Did I piss you off somehow and not know?"

He wasn't going to give up. The dogged determination that was at the core of his career success would mean he'd be on her doorstep again in a few days. When Charlie wanted something, he went after it. And right now, he wanted her. Magpie sighed and opened the door again. "Come on in. We need to talk anyway."

"Talk?" He gave her that charming, joking wink. "Since when have we done much of that?"

Magpie flicked on a light, muted the TV, and then sat on the sofa. Charlie laid the flowers on the end table before he headed into the kitchen. "Do you want yours on the rocks or neat?" he called over his shoulder.

"None for me, thanks."

Charlie stopped and turned back. "No bourbon? Did I just hear that from the woman who drank me under the table in Venezuela? And Turkey, if I remember right."

"I've got a drink, thanks."

He shrugged, grabbed a tumbler from the cabinet, and filled it halfway with bourbon before returning to the sofa. He sat down beside her, and Magpie shifted to put her back to the arm of the sofa and cross her legs on the cushion.

The humor dropped from Charlie's face. "I get the feeling this isn't a talk I want to have. Is this because I said all that *I love you* bullshit? Because we can just erase that, if you want, go back to the way it was." He made a hand motion as if wiping away the words. "I know that kind of thing freaks you out. I don't know what got into me. Maybe some kind of love bug when I was in Italy." His chuckle died into a sigh when she didn't join in on the joke.

Magpie wished she had talked to Nora first. There'd never seemed to be a good time when she was at the beach house. No, that was a lie. There'd been hundreds of opportunities. She'd chosen not to use any of them because talking to Nora would mean facing reality, and as long as she could, Magpie wanted to pretend none of this was happening.

But here was Charlie, in the flesh again and as eager as a new puppy, completely unaware of what had happened in Magpie's life. He deserved to know, regardless of what her decision would be. And maybe once she told him, he'd leave and she could go back to existing on her own. With no one to answer to, no one to worry about...

And no one to tell her what to do with her own fucked-up life.

She waited while he took a sip of the bourbon. "Okay, so, you know me. I'm not a small-talk, beat-around-the-bush kind of girl." She took in a deep breath, let it out. "Remember that night in Caracas? The party at that bar and all those shots we did?"

"In a foggy blur, but yeah."

She'd landed a major interview with Laverne Cox that day, a cover story that would showcase the *Orange Is the New Black* actress and her passionate fight for transgender people. The kind of story that would take Magpie's career up a few notches. She and Charlie had laughed and danced and toasted her success, while the band played and the liquor poured. It was hot, the bar one of those hideaway ones only the locals knew about, lacking in atmosphere and air-conditioning but filled with the real flavor of the city. One drink had turned into two, had turned into ten...

She'd lost count of how much she'd had to drink when she'd stumbled back to the hotel with Charlie. They'd ended up in her room, in a crazy rush to tear off clothes and finish what they'd started when they'd been grinding against each other on the dance floor. They hadn't thought—they'd just screwed.

"When we got together that night, we were both pretty drunk, and we didn't really think—"

"All I could think about was touching you." Charlie grinned. "You were wearing that short red dress, and my God, you were the most beautiful woman in the room."

"And when we went to bed," she went on, the words tumbling out of her, overlapping with Charlie's because if she stopped talking, she'd never say it, "we didn't use protection. And now I'm"—she blew out a breath and, with it, the last couple words she'd kept close to her heart all this time—"I'm pregnant."

Millimeter by millimeter, his grin faded. The light dimmed in his eyes. All the laughter and fun that wrapped around Charlie like a leather jacket ebbed away. "Pregnant?"

She nodded.

"And what are you doing about it?"

"I haven't decided yet." That was the truth. Ever since she'd seen the two pink lines on that stick a month after she left Venezuela, she'd been debating. The list of pros and cons was as long as an airport runway, but she'd yet to sway into one column or the other.

"Well, good. Then you can just get rid of it, and we can get back to business." He got to his feet. "I'll get you a glass. A little bourbon won't hurt now."

White-hot anger rushed through Magpie at the harshness of his words, the matter-of-fact, decision-is-done tone. "I told you, I don't want a drink. And I don't want to get back to business. Nor do I know if I want to get rid of 'it,' Charlie."

He came around to face her. "Honey, you and I live our lives out of carry-ons. We're rarely in the same place for more than a few days. You can't bring a kid into that. And besides, you always told me you were not the domesticated kind. That's part of what I loved about you. You were never going to ask me for a white picket fence and a Labrador."

"I never thought I wanted those things. I'm not sure I

do now." Her hand rested on her abdomen. She'd gained only a couple of pounds, the difference not even noticeable. It seemed impossible to believe there was a human being forming in there. She could almost convince herself it wasn't happening; it wasn't real.

Almost.

"You know I care about you," Charlie said. "I think you're awesome. But I'm not the kind of guy who does kids and a mortgage. Hell, I can barely take care of myself, never mind one or two other people."

"I'm not expecting anything out of you." But that was a lie. A part of Magpie had hoped for some Hollywood ending. Maybe she'd read too many novels or gotten caught up in her envy over Nora's nearly perfect life. Maybe that silly dog and the week with her niece and nephew had given her some kind of nesting-instinct thing. Or maybe it was seeing the way Nora had dropped to her knees and hugged Sarah to her chest after they'd brought the girl home. The relief and love and protectiveness that Nora had for her daughter—the same kind of support and protection her older sister had wrapped around Magpie in all those scary years after Dad died. That was where the reality was, not in the pages of the novels on her table.

"Uh, I don't want to be responsible," Charlie said. "I know that's a shitty thing to say, but, Maggie, you know me. If I have more than twenty dollars in my pocket, I figure I'm not living right."

A part of her had known all along that this was what Charlie would say. The same devil-may-care attitude that had attracted her to him made him a lousy partner outside of the bedroom. He was the opposite of dependable and thrifty and had no life plans beyond the next assignment.

She got to her feet, ignoring the flowers on the end table. They were roses anyway, the only flowers she despised for being such common clichés. They'd wilt in a matter of hours, be dead in a couple days. She'd told Charlie that more than once and realized it said something about the man if he didn't pay attention to her words. "I think you should go, Charlie."

"Hey, hey, I didn't mean to piss you off." He put a hand on her arm, and for the first time since she met him, his touch annoyed her. "Let's go have some fun and talk about this later. Besides, what better way is there to spend your Sunday night than with me?"

She pressed the bourbon bottle into his hands and then crossed to the door to open it. "I've got plans, Charlie. And they don't include you." She waved him out the door, then shut it against his protests. "Not anymore."

TWENTY-FOUR

Most Sundays, Nora enjoyed family dinner. Not just because it was a meal she didn't have to cook after a long week in the bakery but also because being around her sisters, with all their quirks and squabbles, reminded her of those years living at home, when there was nothing bigger to worry about than who was going to ask her to prom.

This Sunday wasn't one of those days.

Nora had driven back from Truro, stopped off to feed the dog and let him out, and then gone straight to her mother's house. Ben had texted to say he'd meet her there to drop off Jake and Sarah, which left Nora without something to keep her busy so she could avoid talking to her mother and avoid thinking about what had almost happened this afternoon.

The second Nora shed her coat, her mother pounced. "Nora, you look so pale. Didn't you get a lot of sun when you were on vacation?"

"I wore sunscreen, and that was last week. Besides, if I came back with a tan, you'd give me a lecture about skin cancer."

"Well, you do need to watch those moles. You never know when one might turn deadly." Her mother opened the oven, checked on the pot roast inside, and then straightened to stir the gravy. "Dinner is almost ready. I do hope my grandchildren get here soon."

Nora took the pan of mashed potatoes and loaded them into a serving bowl. "How is Iris doing?"

Ma tasted the gravy, made a face, and added a pinch of salt. "What do you think of her?"

"She picks up really fast. I think she's going to work out well." Iris was bright and eager, and only seemed to get more so the longer she spent in the bakery. The girl had come in early and worked late, never complaining about the long hours on her feet or the sometimes frantic pace.

Ma tipped the gravy and poured it into the white porcelain gravy boat that had sat on Gramma's dining room table for decades. Every time Nora saw it, it was like having her grandmother at the table again.

"Do you think she's...trustworthy?" Ma asked.

"Yeah, I guess so. I mean, I haven't worked with her as much as you and Bridget have, but she seems to be responsible."

"I didn't ask about whether she was responsible." Ma washed her hands and grabbed a dishtowel. She put her back to the stove as she dried her hands, silent for a moment. "Two hundred dollars was missing from the register several days ago. I ran the totals several times, then had Bridget double-check to see if we entered a credit card receipt wrong or something. Everything was correct—except for the amount of cash."

"You think Iris stole it?" The young intern had seemed so grateful for the job, so eager to learn and please everyone. It seemed completely out of character, but then again, Nora had seen the man she'd married act as far out of character as one could. No one who knew Ben would think he would gamble away his family's home and future, but he had.

"I don't know if she did it or not," Ma said. "I was about to offer her a permanent job before I discovered this, but now I'm not sure. What do you think?"

Nora stopped, halfway to transporting the potatoes to the table. "Are you asking my advice, Ma? About something to do with the bakery?" Nora could literally count on one hand the times her mother had come to her for counsel, and never about anything more serious than whether they should switch from big gift cards to small gift tags.

Her mother picked up the gravy boat and followed her daughter into the dining room. Ma was a small woman with the same fiery red hair from her youth, dyed now instead of natural, and she had a fiery personality to match. Nora expected a lecture or a criticism and braced herself.

"I won't be around forever," Ma said, "and I think it's high time I handed over the decision making to you. You have good business instincts and you've done a wonderful job with the bakery, Nora. I think it's time you . . . well, you were in charge."

Nora placed the back of her hand on her mother's forehead. "Do you have a fever? Are you drinking? Because I just heard you say you were going to give control to me."

Ma swatted away Nora's hand. "I'm doing no such thing. I'm tired and I want to retire and"—she pivoted back to the gravy—"I might want to go to Florida for a bit this winter."

"To Florida?" Her mother had never traveled farther than Martha's Vineyard. Her life had been tied to the bakery, her kids, and the small world she knew in Dorchester, and vacations were day trips, if she took one at all. "Alone?"

"I might go with"—Ma turned away, burying her face in the fridge to retrieve the butter—"Roger."

"Did I hear you say Roger?" Nora gaped. "You are going on a trip with a *man?*"

"Maybe. I haven't decided anything." When Ma turned around, her perpetual scowl was back in place. "And I hope you won't go telling the free world about my plans. I'm just thinking about it because we are friends and he is going to be there and offered to take me with him for a few days. As friends, so don't create some spurious motivations behind me wanting a little sun and sand. In the meantime, it would be nice if you stepped up. You've been gone an awful lot, and the business is suffering."

The old Ma was back again. Maybe that moment of weakness was a mini-stroke or something. "Okay. I will. I'm sorry I've been gone so much. I'm just…going through a lot."

Ma cut her daughter a sharp look. "Is everything okay?"

"It's fine, Ma. It's fine." Nora straightened a place setting that was already perfectly aligned. "Do you want me to talk to Iris?"

"I will. It could be nothing more than an innocent mistake," Ma said.

"I hope so."

"Me too," Ma said quietly. "I've taken quite a shine to that girl. She reminds me of the four of you."

Nora put a hand on her mother's shoulder. "I'm sure it'll all work out. Like you said, probably just an innocent mistake."

The doorbell rang, Bridget called out that she'd get it, and a second later, Jake and Sarah came running into the room, beelining straight for their grandmother. "Gramma! Can we have a cookie?" Jake asked. "Daddy says I gotta wait for dinner, but I am really hungry right now. Like a bear."

Ma laughed and ruffled Jake's hair. "No cookies before dinner. Why don't you and Sarah go wash up, and by the time you get to the table, we'll be just about ready to eat. And if you finish all your dinner, you can have two cookies."

The kids tossed their mother a quick hello and then hurried down the hall while Nora and her mother carried the pot roast and potatoes out to the table. Ben was talking to Abby and Jessie, so Nora, the Queen of Avoidance, ducked back into the kitchen. She washed the few dishes in the sink, cleaned countertops that were already sparkling, and folded a load of laundry.

Maybe if she kept busy enough, she'd forget about how she had kissed another man just this afternoon and that she had thought about doing much more. Forget about the difficult conversation with the kids that would be coming soon. Forget about the decisions she was going to have to make in the next few weeks—finding an attorney, filing for divorce, dividing the house...

Admitting her life was a failure of epic proportions.

"Hey, sis, what's up?" Abby breezed into the kitchen, depositing her coat on the back of the chair. Jessie, her new wife, followed behind carrying a basket of fresh-baked rolls. Tall, thin, and blond, Jessie worked as a lit professor at Brown and had the patience of Job. She meshed well with the more energetic, emotional Abby, and whenever they were together, both of them glowed.

"Hi, Abs. Hi, Jessie." Nora worked up a smile that she didn't feel. "How's married life?"

"Awesome." Abby grinned. "Even better than we expected."

"Definitely." Jessie put a hand on Abby's shoulder and looked at her with such love that Nora had to glance away.

You used to look at me like that.

Ben's words, echoing in her mind. They'd toyed at the edges of her thoughts the whole way home from Truro. When had her look changed? Was it the day she found out he was gambling? Or the day she'd lost the baby?

"Uh, we're all set in here," Nora said. Her throat was thick, and her eyes burned. She pretended to scrub an invisible stain off the countertop, her back to her sister. "So if you guys want to go keep Ma company and see the kids, go ahead."

Abby went off to finish setting the table, Jessie heading into the family room to visit with Colleen. Bridget arrived a few minutes later with dessert, and Aunt Mary came down the back stairs, looking a little pale but definitely better than she had weeks ago.

Aunt Mary opened her arms and pulled Nora into a warm, firm hug. "How are you, dear?"

"I'm fine." Far easier to say that into someone's shoulder than to their face. Nothing about Nora was fine, especially not after she'd complicated all of it by kissing Will.

Aunt Mary drew back, cupped Nora's cheek, and shook her head. "Sweetheart, you are far from fine. Do you want to talk about it?"

"I'm fine," she repeated, but there was a catch in her throat and her damned eyes kept burning.

Aunt Mary studied her for a moment, looking like she was about to say something, but she suddenly stepped back. "I'll leave you two alone."

Leave us alone?

Nora pivoted and found Ben standing in the kitchen. He had on the dark brown jacket she'd bought him two Christmases ago, the one that brought out his eyes. The suede was butter soft, and it still had that new scent because Ben so rarely dressed in anything other than work clothes. Her hand ached to run down the fabric, sliding over the hills and valleys of his shoulders, his arms, his chest. The thought of Will became distant, as if she'd been with the other man ten years ago, not a few hours earlier. "Ben. I thought you left already."

"I wanted to talk to you. Do you have a minute?"

She grabbed a stack of napkins and took a step toward the doorway. Could he see in her face that she'd gone to the Cape today? That she'd kissed another man? That she still had a trickle of guilt running through her even though very little happened? "Well, dinner's about to be served and—"

"It'll only take a minute, Nora."

She drew in a deep breath and put her back to the counter, clutching the napkins to her chest like some kind of shield. "Okay. Let's talk."

"I've been thinking a lot about what you said two weeks ago." He shoved his hands into his pockets and rocked back on his heels, something he only did when he was nervous. "And I think if you want a divorce, then I won't contest it. I won't fight you. We'll get it over with quickly and amicably and make it as easy on the kids as possible."

"Thank you for that." But hearing him say it aloud, with that finality in his voice, made her throat hurt. *We'll get it over with.* A dozen years of marriage being ended with all the enthusiasm of a toddler eating a bowl of brussels sprouts. But he was right—they wanted different things out of their future. All they'd been doing was fooling themselves for the last year.

"But if you aren't sure or you want to wait a bit, I'm willing to do what it takes for that too." He thumbed toward the dining room. "Those are our kids out there, our family. I don't want to break that up if we don't have to. My parents got divorced when I was Sarah's age, and it was the hardest thing I ever went through."

"Your parents fought a lot, though, Ben. That makes it harder." Even now, her in-laws argued at baptisms and birthday parties. It was a wonder they'd ever fallen in love, given how they hated each other now. She and Ben had fought, as all couples did, but never that no-holds-barred, expletive-filled nastiness she'd seen in her in-laws over the years. Half the time she thought they'd all be better off if the two of them went into a cage and had at it until there was only one victor.

"They argued like it was the Civil War every day, and that made a part of me grateful they got divorced." Ben sighed. "I meant the aftermath. When I had half my stuff at my dad's house, half at my mom's, I never felt like I had a home. Like I belonged anywhere."

She remembered him telling her about that before they got married. It had been part of why she married him, because Ben had talked about how much he wanted to put down roots, to buy a home where they would raise their children and welcome their grandchildren. She'd bought into that dream, and now it was gone. "We'll make it work with the kids, Ben. We just have to communicate."

She could hear the TV playing and the low murmur of conversation in the living room, which meant Ma was keeping the kids and the rest of the family out of earshot. Thank God. None of the people sitting in front of *Wheel of Fortune* knew that in another room, Nora's world was crumbling.

"When we bought that house, Nora, and we added Sarah and then Jake, I felt like I belonged. We had a family. We had a *home*." He took a step closer. She caught the scent of his cologne, the same scent he had worn as long as she'd known him. It was familiar and warm. And tempting. "We belong in that house. All of us."

"The house is gone, Ben. Why can't you accept that? What do we have, like twelve days until it's on the auction block? There's no fairy godmother coming down to save the day, no leprechaun showing up with a pot of gold. It's gone, and that dream is gone too. I don't want what you do anymore."

"How do you know what I want? You stopped talking to me, Nora. Maybe if we had talked more, we wouldn't be here."

"Talked about what, Ben? All I ever heard you say was that you wanted more kids. A bigger family. And at the same time, you're blowing all our money and destroying our future." She cursed and then, in a hot rush, everything she had stuffed deep inside her exploded. All those thoughts she had kept to herself, all those words she had never said out loud. Maybe it was the day on the beach, the kiss with another man, the breaking of all those stringent rules that finally unleashed the truth. "The truth is, a part of me was relieved when I lost that baby."

There. She'd said it. She had been secretly grateful for the miscarriage. What kind of mother felt like that?

A long moment passed, with only the sound of Pat Sajak and an overly enthusiastic audience in the background. "What do you mean, you were relieved?"

"I don't want any more kids, Ben." She let out a deep breath. "I want a life."

"We had a life together, Nora."

"Maybe you did, but I didn't. I worked, I raised the kids, I cleaned the house, but there was no me. All those days I was in Truro"—*with another man*, her mind reminded her—"I got back to me. I started running again and reading and not being...anyone other than myself. And I imagined a different future."

"With someone else?"

She waited a beat. The answer was more complicated than yes or no. She'd had what she thought she wanted in front of her a few hours ago, and she had pushed it away. "Just a different future. One where I have a life, Ben, outside of the kids and the housework and the bakery."

"I've never stopped you from that, Nora. *You* did that. You stopped talking to me. You shut me out of your life and out of your heart."

"Because I had to, Ben. You were destroying me. Destroying us." The bright kitchen seemed too happy, too chipper, to be the right place for this conversation. Maybe they should have gone in the basement or out into the dark evening, where the world was colder and grayer and more like the truth. "I hate what you did to us. How can you say you don't want to break us up, that you don't want to lose the house, when you were the one who gave our money to the fucking roulette table? You might as well have stood there and put the keys to our house on red twenty-one. I hate you for what you did. I hate that this is where we are."

Except for that winter day, she had tamed her words and her anger. Nora had buried it all in working long hours and organizing closets and dusting shelves—anything to keep from exploding at Ben. She told herself he was getting help, that a good wife would be supportive of those efforts and not keep rubbing his face in his mistakes. The psychologist she'd spoken to at the rehab place had told her over and over again that those early days of recovery were fragile. One little thing could tip the scale and send Ben back to the casino. So she'd put on a cheery face and pretended all was well and stayed in the guest room. Because even she couldn't maintain the façade when the lights went out and it was just the two of them in a queen-sized bed.

"I quit gambling a year ago, Nora, and yet you can't seem to stop beating me up about it. I got help, and yeah, I know we are still behind the eight ball financially, but we can salvage this—"

"God, you are delusional." She started to walk away. "This is a pointless conversation."

He grabbed her arm and stopped her. "You call me delusional? You're the one who kept pretending everything was fine when it wasn't. The one who refused to face reality. The one who has blamed me over and over again, instead of admitting your own mistakes. Remember last year when I asked if we could meet with a financial planner when things got really bad? You refused."

"Because I could handle it. Besides, why would we pay someone to tell us what we already knew? We were broke and in debt. There was nothing he could do."

"Maybe there would have been, but we'll never know. You wouldn't talk to anyone, wouldn't take any help, not even that free debt class they offered at St. Gregory's. You kept on spending money, living our life as if nothing had changed. You took over the bills. I couldn't even buy a loaf of bread without checking with you—"

"Because you would take that money and buy ten Megabucks tickets. Or stop at the OTB and bet on some horse named Lucky Shot."

"I *would have*. Past tense. But even after all the work I did, all the counseling and recovery, you still held those reins. What are you so afraid of, Nora? Why can't you just let go and trust?"

"Someone had to be in charge, Ben. I was just trying to hold our family together." And because she was afraid that he'd run right back to gambling if she gave him the checkbook. *I gambled because I needed some excitement in my life*, he'd said. And all she'd heard was *my life with you is boring*. Once he came home from rehab and they settled back into playdates and parent-teacher conferences and work, they were back to that same world that lacked excitement.

When the kids were acting up and the hot water heater was leaking, would he take that checkbook and go right back to finding his excitement elsewhere?

Like he'd been doing every Friday and Saturday night for a year?

Okay, so yeah, maybe she had kept spending money as if they didn't have a looming debt. But it wasn't like she spent thousands of dollars. It was twenty dollars for costume material, ten bucks for a pizza. All to preserve some sense of normalcy for the kids.

"Instead of trying to hold our family together, you just drove a wedge deeper into our lives," Ben said. "You thought you were helping me. Or helping us. Instead you were controlling everything, just like you always have. You control what time the kids go to bed, what we eat, but most of all, what people think of us. That image of the perfect family was so damned important to you, you refused to ask for help when we really could have used it. And you know what happens when you try to control everything? You end up controlling nothing."

She rolled her eyes. "Good Lord, spare me from your recovery group mantras."

"They're mantras because they are true. Control is an illusion, Nora. It's only by letting go of control and admitting you don't have your shit together that you find out what you really have."

"I did that with you. I told you when we got behind on the mortgage. I told you we were on the brink of losing the house. And what did you do? Nothing."

"You didn't let me do a damned thing about it." His voice started to rise, but then he took a breath and forced it into a harsh whisper. "I offered to call the mortgage company, and you said you would. I offered to negotiate with the bank—"

"You're not a negotiator, Ben. And having two people in the mix would have just made it worse." Ben was one of those friendly guys who would pay a higher price for some lumber because the yard owner told him he was putting a kid through college. He rarely bickered on pricing or quotes, saying that it all evened out at the end of the day.

"Listen to you," he said. "Two people? It's not like we're picking up a hitchhiker and bringing him to the meetings with the loan officer. This is you and me, husband and wife, trying to save our house. Together."

They had stopped making decisions together a long time ago, and they both knew it. "Why are we even talking about this? It's too late anyway."

"Because I'm still trying to save something." He closed the gap between them, his eyes softening just a bit. "Us."

How she wanted to believe that. To fall into the trap again of feeling like they were a team. But it was too late. It was far too late. So she steeled her spine and pushed out the words that needed to be said. "There's nothing left to save, Ben. I'm sorry."

"Nora, you can't throw away our marriage and our kids' lives this easily." His voice cracked.

Nora hated that her weak, foolish heart still loved him.

"You did that with your first bet, Ben. Why don't you go cry to Joyce? She seems to care an awful lot about what's going on with you. I have to go. My *family* is waiting for me."

It was a low shot, and she hated herself as soon as she said the words. She would have taken them back, but Ben stalked out of the kitchen, gave the kids a quick goodbye, and left.

TWENTY-FIVE

After the front door shut, Nora emerged from the kitchen, still holding napkins they didn't need. Magpie had arrived while Nora was talking to Ben. She looked a little tired, which was unusual because, of the four of them, Magpie was the one who could stay awake all night and perk up before her morning cup of coffee. This Magpie looked subdued, pale, and worried. Nora realized she never had had that late-night conversation with her sister; in fact, she'd forgotten entirely that Magpie had wanted to talk.

What was happening to Nora? Since when did she let her family down like that? It was all that conflict with Ben, she told herself. Once they were divorced—

Divorced. God, the word held a razor edge that stole her breath and ached in her chest. It equated to *failure* in her mind. She had done everything right—and still failed to keep her family together.

"Come on, everyone, stop lollygagging," Ma said, ushering everyone forward like a mother hen. "Dinner is going to get cold."

They all sat down, with one vacant chair. Nora expected to see a place setting, the same one Ma had set every night for two decades for the husband she had lost, but the space before the chair was empty. Nora pushed her chair back and got to her feet. "Did you want me to get Dad's plate, Ma?"

"That's not necessary." Colleen waved Nora back into her seat and shook her head. "I think it's high time I said something to you girls. I will always love your father, God rest his soul," she said, glancing at Bridget, Abby, Magpie, and finally Nora, "but I need to start moving forward. If you girls are okay with that."

"Of course we are, Ma." Bridget leaned over and hugged Ma. The other three sat there, all looking a little stunned. "We've all been waiting for you to do that. Is there a special someone you are moving forward with?"

Even as Bridget asked the question, the answer was obvious. Nora had noticed how much time her mother spent with Roger and how giggly she got when he was around.

"It's far too soon to think about anything silly like that." Ma blushed and cleared her throat. "Our dinner is getting cold with all this jabbering. I didn't spend all that time in the kitchen to eat cold pot roast. Let's say grace."

Aunt Mary met Nora's eyes across the table, a question in her face, probably wondering how things had gone with Ben earlier. Nora just dipped her head and waited for her mother to pray.

When Ma was done, the table erupted in chatter. Bridget started first, asking Sarah and Jake about their vacation. Jake gave a lively and long-winded account, ending with, "and we found a dog! And Mommy is letting us keep him!"

Bridget glanced at Nora. "You got a dog?"

"The kids found him," Magpie said. "Nora took him to the Truro vet but he didn't know who he belonged to and the dog didn't have a microchip."

"So he's *temporarily* ours," Nora added. Emphasis on the *temporarily*.

Jake and Sarah took turns talking about Chance and how he fetched a ball and slept on Jake's bed. Nora pushed her food around and tried to look happy and interested, but her mind was back in the kitchen, on Ben asking her if she wanted to work things out. On the kiss she'd shared with Will, the mistake she had almost made this afternoon. When had she gotten so off track?

"Nora?" Ma asked. "What's this about you staying at Mary's house?"

Nora jerked her head up and rewound the snippets of conversation she'd heard. Jake talking about the dog, about his bedroom, and then mentioning that he was sharing a room with Sarah, and Bridget asking why.

Crap. She hadn't thought about the kids talking about staying at Aunt Mary's. She hadn't even told them not to say anything. Yet another detail that had slipped past her.

"She's staying there while Ben works on the other house," Mary said, saving Nora from an answer. "My house is empty, so I thought it would work out perfectly."

"The kitchen renovation is taking that long? I thought it was already halfway done."

"It is. It was. It's..." She glanced around the table. At Bridget, Abby, Magpie, Jessie, Aunt Mary, her mother, her kids. She was surrounded by people who loved her. People who made her feel like she belonged. People she could trust.

Ma passed the biscuits to Abby. "It seems to be quite the project."

"Everything okay?" Bridget asked. "You look a little run-down, Nora."

"Everything's fine." She barely held on to her wobbly smile.

"Mommy, I'm done. Can I go get a cookie and play in the yard?" Jake asked.

"Bring your plate into the kitchen. You too, Sarah. Then you can both go outside, but stay in the yard." The kids did as they were told, with no argument. Sarah was still tentatively engaging with Nora, but it was better than last week. Progress. She'd take it.

Except once the kids went outside, it was a lot harder to hold the façade on her face. Ma sent her a sidelong glance, obviously suspicious. "You haven't been yourself in some time, Nora."

"Just stressed. You know how renovation projects are." She added a little laugh that made it sound believable.

"So did you pick a countertop yet?" Bridget asked. "I know you were talking about granite. But have you seen those new ones from recycled glass? They're pretty cool too."

Nora remembered when she and Ben had started the renovation nine months ago. She'd had her head in the sand, completely unaware that they were already teetering on the edge of financial ruin. Granite, marble, recycled glass, none of that mattered anymore. Someone else would finish that kitchen and live in the space she had loved.

Exhaustion hit her hard and fast, a rogue wave brought on by years of carrying a burden too heavy for her shoulders. All her life, she'd been pretending everything was perfect. She'd shouldered the worries for her mother, kept her in the dark when the girls had struggled after Dad died. She'd done it to Ben, too, she realized, taking over with the childcare, the vacation planning, even the grocery shopping.

She'd been the perfect daughter. The perfect mother. The perfect wife. And where had she ended up? Homeless and divorced.

You control what time the kids go to bed, what we eat, but most of all, what people think of us. That image of the perfect family was so damned important to you, you refused to ask for help when we really could have used it. And you know what happens when you try to control everything? You end up controlling nothing.

That was exactly how she felt right now, completely and utterly out of control. Like being on a bike without brakes, careening down a steep hill. She'd been feeling that way since she lost the baby, and even more so now that she had lost her husband and home. It was only going to get worse as she took the next steps. She wasn't so sure she was strong enough to handle what was coming, at least not on her own.

"The truth is..." Nora sighed, and when she exhaled the next words, some of the stress that had had a choke hold on her breath began to ease. Why not tell them? Why not trust them? Why not admit that she wasn't as perfect as she pretended to be? Truth was, it was pretty damned exhausting keeping up that smoke screen. "We're losing the house."

Bridget's jaw dropped. "What? How? You love that house."

"I loved the life I thought I had in that house." And that, she realized, was the heart of the matter. The kitchen counters didn't matter. The flooring didn't matter. The dream she'd had when she and Ben had first bought the house was what she was losing. What she had lost a long time ago when her husband cheated on her with a deck of cards. "But it turns out that life was..." She paused. All those years, she had pretended she had it together. Admitting the truth was harder than she thought. "Well, it was built on a very shaky foundation."

Nora waited a beat. Waited for the shock, the judgment. For them to be angry that she had lied.

Abby glanced at Bridget and Ma and then back at Nora. "But I thought Ben was working and making good money."

"He was. He does. And we were doing really great, but then..." Nora sighed. She'd kept all of it from her family, her kids, lying about Ben's month-long stay in rehab, lying about everything. "I've been lying to you guys."

The words came out and hung heavy in the air. Her sisters didn't say anything for a long moment. Ma laid her hands flat against the table. "And why would you do such a thing?" she said.

"Because I'm the one who's supposed to have it all together." Nora's face heated, and for a second, she considered taking it all back, pretending the whole thing was a joke. But where would that get her? "I don't. I haven't for a long time."

Magpie reached out and put her hand on Nora's. "Why...why didn't you say anything?" she asked. "We spent all those days together, and you didn't really talk about things."

"I'm sorry," Nora said. "I didn't want to worry you. Any of you."

Abby scoffed. "Have you met us? Worrying about each other is what we do best."

"Besides, it's about time you stopped being the family martyr," Bridget said. "In case you haven't noticed, we're all grown up and fully capable of remembering our lunch money. You don't have to protect us anymore, Nora."

"I guess that is what I've been doing. Protecting you guys, my kids, maybe even myself."

"From what?" Abby leaned forward, her dinner cold and untouched now.

"From...the truth." Nora's throat clogged, and the emotion she tried to keep hidden from everyone around her began to bubble to the surface. "That life sucks and good people die and husbands gamble away all your money."

"Ben? He…" Outrage flashed in Magpie's eyes. "He did what?"

"He started gambling a couple years ago. He spent almost a full year blowing his paycheck on slots and dog and horse races and kept the whole thing hidden from me. Then on my birthday last year, he called me, crying, because he'd given away his car to pay for a gambling debt. I had to pick him up at Foxwoods. And that was how I spent my birthday, not on a moonlit cruise around Boston Harbor like I told you all." The fiction had become so real in the telling that for a long time, even Nora had believed it. She could keep up this fantasy marriage in her mind and avoid facing the truth. But now the dam that held those lies back began to fracture, and the words spilled out of her almost faster than she could say them.

"Why didn't you say anything?" Ma asked. "Your family is here to help you, Eleanor. You should have come to us."

Nora fiddled with her napkin, her gaze on her lap, as if she were thirteen, not thirty, and had gotten caught cheating on a test. "I was so afraid you would all be ashamed of me for failing so badly."

"Holy shit. I never knew any of that happened." Bridget shook her head and let out a long breath. "And, honey, none of us are ashamed of you. We all have crap we don't want other people to know. Mistakes we wish we hadn't made. That makes us human, not bad people."

Nora gave Bridget a watery smile. Around the table, the rest of her family echoed Bridget's support. They were her family, imperfect as they were, and they loved her regardless. How could she have gone this long and not seen that? Not trusted them?

When she was younger, she'd done it to protect her grieving sisters, her struggling mother. But as Bridget had told her, they were all adults now and all had weathered their own storms.

Everyone but Ma. Her mother's expression was stern, unreadable.

"Ben went into a program for a month," Nora said, "and then did meetings, one of those twelve-step things, and as far as I know he's stopped gambling, but the damage was already done. We were too far behind on the mortgage to get caught up, and now"—she sighed—"they're auctioning the house off just before Thanksgiving."

"That's less than two weeks away." Ma put a hand to her chest. "Is that why you're staying at Mary's house?"

"Partly, yes. And partly to think." Nora fiddled with her silverware. In the reflection of the knife, her image was long and drawn, wavy. "I told Ben I want a divorce."

Magpie cursed, and for once, Ma didn't even correct her. "A divorce? Really? But I thought you guys were so happy."

"I thought we were too." And now the tears she had held at bay for so long began to fall. If she'd had to write down the recipe of those tears, she would say they were one part relief and two parts regret. She wasn't going to be able to make any of it prettier with fondant and marzipan. "I don't know what I'm doing going forward. How I'm going to pack up the house. What my next steps will be. I guess I'll start with talking to a lawyer. It all just seems too overwhelming."

"Divorce is not a thing to take lightly," Ma said. "I hope you have thought this through. Your children—"

"All I do is think about my children, Ma!" Nora got to her feet. "Why do you think I'm doing all this? I have to give my children a home and at the same time try to keep them from finding out that their parents fucked up and that's the reason they are losing everything they know."

Ma pursed her lips. "There is no reason to yell at me."

"Yeah, there is. I've done everything right, Ma. Everything you and the church and God told me to, and this is where I am. Homeless, broke, and divorced." Nora threw up her hands. "I give up. I just...give up. I'm sorry I let you all down."

In an instant, her sisters were on their feet, surrounding her, wrapping her in their arms. They held her and they cried, and they became the support dowel in a seven-layer cake. Nora needed that so badly right now because she truly felt like she was about to topple. "I need you guys to be there for me now, if that's okay."

"Of course. That's what we're all here for, Nora," Magpie whispered. "To hold you up when you want to fall down."

Only her mother stood to the side, her face cold and blank.

TWENTY-SIX

Colleen lingered long after the bakery closed on Monday. She paced the floors out front, fretting and worrying about her daughters. It didn't seem to matter how old they got—she worried as if they were still little girls. Nora's house had been lost; her marriage was falling apart. Things that had taken Colleen by surprise.

She'd always known that Nora was the one who held everything inside. She put on a brave face, worked herself to death, and rarely asked for help. Colleen had relied on that, perhaps too much, in those dark, dark days after Michael had died. Was that the reason Nora had felt compelled to keep the truth a secret?

Maybe if Colleen had been more open, more approachable, more of a mother to Nora. She loved her girls, Lord knew she did, but she'd never been the one they ran to when they scraped their knees or had a broken heart. When they were little, Michael, God rest his soul, had

311

been the one to put on the bandages and dispense the hugs. When the girls got older—

Nora had done that for her sisters. She'd stepped in and been the mother hen when Colleen had been too busy to do it herself. Plus, she had always found it hard to be expressive with the people she loved. Maybe it was her strict Catholic upbringing or some character defect, but being public with her emotions and affection was something Colleen never did.

She vowed to be more present for Nora going forward. Pitch in with the kids, give her a pay raise to go along with the increased responsibilities at the bakery. And pay more attention to all of her daughters, every single day.

After she flipped the sign to closed, Colleen ran the total sales report from the register and then began counting the money. This time the amount in the register and the sales tally came out even, as it had the day before and a million other times. But the missing two hundred dollars from the other day still hadn't been accounted for. Colleen had gone over the list of sales and orders from that day, and they had definitely sold that much. She'd talked to all the girls about it—

Except one.

There was a sound behind her. Colleen turned and saw Iris standing there. Lately, the girl had been leaving a little early to help her pregnant friend get set up for the baby, or so she said. A part of Colleen wondered if it was more about avoiding a conversation she didn't want to have. "Iris, I thought you went home already."

The young girl dropped her gaze to the floor. "I...well, I had some work to finish up."

"Work. Hmm." Colleen watched Iris shift from foot to foot, her gaze still on the floor. "Stay here a minute, please. I want to talk to you. You left too fast yesterday and the day before."

"Sorry. I had stuff to do."

The girl refused to raise her gaze to Colleen's. A part of Colleen wanted to skip this conversation and sweep it under the rug. If it had been two dollars, maybe she could do that, but not two hundred. She'd liked Iris when she first started working there and had enjoyed the lunches she'd shared with the girl. Iris was smart and eager, and a good worker. But not the person Colleen had thought.

"Iris." She waited for the girl to look up. "Would you like to tell me how two hundred dollars miraculously disappeared from this register? I have asked Nora, Abby, and Bridget, and none of them know what happened to it."

Iris shook her head. "It wasn't me, Mrs. O'Bannon."

"Then who took the money?" Colleen leaned in closer, looking for a shift in the girl's demeanor, some kind of tell. It was the look Colleen had given all her girls at one time or another, and ninety percent of the time that was enough to make them fess up to whatever rule they had broken. "Because I don't see anyone else here who could or would do it."

"Seriously? Are you just accusing me because I'm..." Iris's face reddened, and she stepped back, as if she was about to bolt. "Whatever. I knew this job wasn't going to work out. You're just like everyone else." Then Iris spun on her heel and ran out of the shop before Colleen could stop her.

Roger came in a few seconds later. He'd been making it his custom on nice weather days, when she didn't drive to work, to walk Colleen home, a gentlemanly gesture she enjoyed every time until today, when she needed to tell him something he probably didn't want to hear.

He thumbed toward the front of the shop. "Why was Iris running down the street? I called out to her but she didn't stop. She was all upset."

"Because she robbed me and didn't want to admit it." Colleen crossed her arms over her chest. Roger was the one who had put that girl into her shop, amid her family. The very thing that Colleen protected like a mama bear. "Why would you send me a thief?"

Roger's brows knitted in confusion. "Iris is no thief. I've known her a long time, Colleen, and I wouldn't put her in this job if I thought she would do something like that. Why do you think she stole from you?"

"The register was two hundred dollars short a few days ago. I've gone over all the receipts and orders, and we definitely had the sales. But the two hundred dollars is still missing." She held up the stack of money she had just counted. "I gave it some time, thinking maybe she would put it back and do the right thing, but no, that girl you sent me is a crook."

"You're judging her without all the facts, Colleen. You should—"

"Don't tell me what I should do, Roger. My business is

my own." She shoved the bills into the night deposit bag and grabbed her keys. "I have no desire to have some man boss me around. I've been doing just fine on my own for more than two decades."

He scoffed. "You really don't want to let anybody in, do you? Not me, not Iris—"

"That girl stole from me."

"Did she admit it? Did you catch her?"

"She tried to blame it on someone else. Typical thief behavior." Colleen shook her head. "Besides, her running out of here should be evidence enough. Someone who was honest would have stayed."

"Maybe she ran because she was hurt that you accused her. She was crying, Colleen. That doesn't scream guilty to me." Roger crossed to the window and stared out at the quiet street. "Do you always judge people so harshly?"

"I'm doing no such thing. There's two hundred dollars missing—"

"And there are a hundred other explanations besides Iris." Roger turned and put his back to the window. "I thought I knew you, Colleen O'Bannon. I thought all this"— he waved his hand in a circle around her—"prickliness was a cover for a soft heart. I guess I was wrong."

The shop door opened and closed again. This time, leaving Colleen alone in the bakery with her anger and her principles.

Nora sat in her car, staring at the big white and red sign staked in her front yard, the letters bold and public and ugly. In three days, a bunch of strangers would stand on this very lawn and bid on the house she loved.

She had tried calling the bank and gotten nowhere. She'd then contacted a very patient lawyer who offered her two hours of sympathetic and free advice. In short, there was nothing she could do, not unless she could walk in with a three-hundred-thousand-dollar check and set the mortgage to rights.

She pulled away from the curb, turning her back on things that were lost causes, and headed to work. Tonight she'd grab some boxes and pack up what she could. She needed to book a U-Haul truck and a storage unit, which would mean she could keep most of the things from the house. She'd texted Ben several times, trying to nail him down about division of property and when they would move everything. Ever since the family dinner, Ben had gone mostly silent. He took the kids once and other than that, rarely answered her.

She told herself to stop being disappointed. She'd known this was coming and hoping otherwise was foolish. Ben had let her down. Again.

For almost two weeks, she'd been making excuses for him with the kids, doing her level best to preserve the status quo. Sarah had started talking to Anna again, and her grades were inching up. The last thing Nora wanted to do was send all that forward momentum in the opposite direction.

The raise Ma had given her was a big help and would be enough to pay for the moving expenses and the storage unit—assuming Nora could hire some neighborhood kids to do the heavy lifting—but Nora had procrastinated on making a plan. Her sisters had offered a hundred times to help her out, but old habits died hard, and Nora brushed off their suggestions or changed the subject.

She'd always been the one to get things done. Make a to-do list, check off the items one at a time, and go to bed happy to have accomplished each task. But in the last two weeks, getting out of bed and getting to work was pretty much the sum total of her accomplishments for the day. What was it about those stages of grief? She'd aced denial, made a mess out of anger, failed at bargaining, but boy, did she get a gold star for depression.

She ducked in the back door of the bakery, called out a hello to Abby and Bridget, then skirted around her mother and grabbed an apron off the hook. "Hi, Ma."

"You look terrible."

"Thanks. Good morning to you too." She slipped the apron over her head and threw her hair into a ponytail. "I need to get to work."

"Will you let me loan you some money, Nora? Maybe I can help—"

Her mother had been trying to help Nora ever since the family dinner. For once, Ma hadn't criticized Nora or talked to her about her life choices. She'd merely come up to her, said *I've decided you deserve a raise*, and let the subject drop. Nora didn't know why, and she wasn't about to poke that hornet's nest.

"Ma, it's too late. And Ben and I have it under control." Ever since she'd told her sisters the truth, they'd been hovering over her as if she was going to fall apart at any second. So she went back to pretending everything was just fine because that was better than being treated like Humpty Dumpty. Her mother needed the money she had for her retirement, not to bail out her adult daughter. The raise would be enough; Nora would make sure of it. "Besides, Ben and I created this mess, Ma. It's on us to clean it up."

"Nora, I think this is a mess too big for two to handle."

She gave her mother a quick hug. "It'll be fine."

Ma gave Nora a disbelieving arched brow. "The offer stands, so let me know if you need me. And I expect to see you both at Thanksgiving dinner."

Nora nodded. She wasn't sure that she and Ben would even be together then, but that wasn't an argument she wanted to have with her mother right now.

"And if you think it'll be all right with the rest of the girls," Ma said, "I'd like to invite Roger to our table."

Nora grinned. "Roger, huh? Well, Ma, I think that is a great idea."

"Don't look at me like that. The man has no family in Boston, and it's a holiday for joining with other people." Ma grabbed a sponge and began wiping the counter, but she was blushing, and the mere mention of Roger's name had made Ma's eyes dance. "It doesn't mean anything except that he likes my turkey."

"I think he likes a lot more than that," Nora muttered.

"Nora Jean! More working and less talking."

"Yes, Ma." Nora laughed at the consternation on Ma's face. Seeing Colleen O'Bannon ruffled was as rare as spotting an antelope on Boston Common.

Bridget finished her conversation with a customer, hung up the phone, and slipped a new order under the top ones on the clipboard. "Guys, that was the mayor's office. They want to order the chocolate peanut butter cake that got written up in *Boston* magazine. There's some big networking event the mayor is hosting with a whole bunch of businesses looking to expand in Boston. Supposed to be a lot of press there, which should be great publicity for us."

The surge of publicity they'd had from the write-up last year had been great for the bakery. They'd ridden that wave most of the year, and this next boost would be just the thing Charmed by Dessert needed going into the holiday season. Business was already up thirty percent from last Thanksgiving, and if early orders were any indication, Christmas would be the same.

"That's awesome," Abby said. "I knew that cake was going to put us on the map. It's seriously one of the best cakes I've ever eaten."

"We should come up with some kind of promotion to run at the same time," Bridget said. "You're the master at that, Nora. What do you think?"

Nora's mind had already drifted away, circling like a vulture around the auction sign and the divorce. "About what?"

"What we were just talking about five seconds ago."

Bridget put a hand on Nora's shoulder. "Hey, you okay? You totally zoned out there."

"I'm good. Just…planning the weekend." She sighed and then looked at her sisters and her mother. They wanted to help, and she needed to get better at asking for and accepting that. She couldn't do it all alone, and frankly, she didn't want to anymore. "I need to move this weekend. If you guys—"

"Of course we'll help you, silly." Abby put an arm around Nora's shoulders. "O'Bannon teamwork. I think that's our family superpower."

Nora swiped away the tears brimming in her eyes. "Thanks, guys. I appreciate it." She sucked up the moment of emotions and grabbed the clipboard for the day's orders. She glanced around the kitchen and noticed one station open. "Hey, where's Iris today?"

"She will not be returning," Ma said.

"What? Why not?" Bridget hefted a ten-pound bag of confectioners' sugar into her arms and then dumped it into the stand mixer. "She was a huge help, and she was just starting to remember the recipes."

"She…won't be back. And neither, apparently, will my two hundred dollars."

"Iris stole the money?" Nora asked. "Wow. I never would have expected that from her."

"Me neither." Ma pursed her lips and went back to studying the purchase orders. Nora and Bridget exchanged a glance. Then they let it go.

Ma went to make a phone call, the oven timer dinged,

and Abby switched out the bread loaves while Nora leafed through the clipboard of orders. Back to normal.

Nora pulled the top sheet off the clipboard. She read the work order, and her heart stilled. For a split second, she was twelve years younger, surrounded by her family with Ben right by her side. She glanced up at Bridget. "Who placed this order?"

Bridget shrugged. "I don't know. It was in the mail slot this morning. Paid in cash."

"That's weird." Maybe she was feeling nostalgic or maybe it was seeing the sign in her yard, the finality of those block letters, but as Nora mixed up the batter for the sponge cake base of the Torta del Cielo, her throat got thick, and her vision blurred.

She whipped egg whites with salt and set it aside. Next she mixed the yolks, some sugar, and vanilla together. She added ground almonds, flour, baking powder, a little nutmeg, and a pinch of almond extract. The sweet, nutty scent of almonds filled the air as Nora folded in the beaten egg whites. The cake layers for the torta were light and airy, like almond clouds that embraced the creamy filling and sat below the meringue crown.

Nora's hands moved in delicate strokes, swooping up some batter, sliding it lightly over the egg whites. Pivot the bowl, repeat, pivot, repeat, the movements practiced and automatic. Which was a damned good thing because the tears she'd held at bay had begun to spill by the time she was pouring the batter into the springform pans.

As she was pouring the ingredients for the almond

cream into the mixer, she heard the ding of the bell that hung over the shop door. When her grandmother had died, she used to think every ring of that bell was a whisper from Gramma in heaven. Now Nora wondered what her Gramma would think of the granddaughter who could bake anything but had made a total disaster out of her life.

Sarah came into the kitchen and slung her backpack on the counter. Nora stopped the mixer. "What are you doing here?"

"Daddy got me at school. I didn't feel good." Sarah dropped into one of the chairs. Nora crossed to her daughter and put the back of her hand on Sarah's forehead. Her skin was cool and dry to the touch.

"You don't have a fever. Is your belly upset?"

Sarah shrugged. "I guess so."

Ben came into the kitchen, wearing a white T-shirt and scuffed jeans and his dark brown work boots that had weathered into a soft tan. He looked handsome as hell, and her traitorous heart skipped a beat. "Can we talk?"

"Sure. Uh, let's go outside. Sarah, why don't you get started on some homework? Aunt Bridget can get you some crackers for your tummy."

"I will," Bridget said. She bent down in front of her niece. "We'll keep each other company for a while, won't we, Sarah?"

Nora pushed on the handle of the back door, and she and Ben stepped out into the parking lot. She cleared her throat and turned to face her husband. "Actually, I'm glad you're here," she said, all business, no emotion. "We need

322

to make a plan for moving out this weekend. Did you look over the furniture inventory I sent you last week?"

"Sorry. I haven't had a chance, Nora."

Again and again, he kept letting her down. Letting their family down. "For God's sake, Ben, they are going to lock us out in three days! We have to do this now, not a month from now, not a year from now."

He put up his hands and took a step closer. "Hey, truce, okay? I didn't come here to fight or just to drop Sarah off, though I hope it's okay that she stays with you the rest of the day."

Nora nodded. "Then why did you come?"

"I would like to ask you for a favor."

She scoffed. "You want a favor from me? Ben, I've been trying to ask you simple questions for the last two weeks, and you can't even be bothered to return a text message. Give me one good reason why I should do you a favor now."

"Because you used to love me once."

The words stopped her argument cold. She closed her eyes, drew in a breath, and faced him again. She *had* loved him once, and God help her, just seeing him now had her wondering why she'd stopped. "What do you need?"

"Could you drop the kids off at your mom's after school today—I already asked her to babysit and she said okay—then meet me at the house?"

Finally. He was going to face reality and talk about the division of property. "Fine. I'll bring my list."

A wry grin crossed his face. "I wouldn't expect you to

show up with anything less." Then his gaze softened and held hers for a moment. She took in a breath, wanting him to stay as much as she wanted him to leave.

"Ben, we need to be realistic about—"

Before Nora could finish her sentence, Sarah burst through the back door, followed by Bridget. "Sorry, sorry!" Bridget said. "Sarah said she had to talk to you two, and she ran off before I could stop her."

"It's okay." There wasn't much more she had to say to Ben anyway. And a part of Nora was glad for the distraction, heading off another argument, another discussion she didn't want to have. All this talk about lists and property division had left Nora depressed as hell.

She bent down to Sarah's level. Her daughter's eyes were red, lashes wet with tears. "What's the matter, honey? Are you feeling sicker?"

Sarah fished in the pocket of her jeans and tugged out a thick pile of twenty-dollar bills. "I want you and Daddy to stop fighting and stop getting divorced."

Money. The one thing that had been a source of hundreds of arguments between them. Whispered fights late at night that they thought the kids couldn't overhear. Tight sentences shot at each other while passing in the kitchen, muttered comments spoken while the TV played. All this time, she'd thought her daughter and son hadn't noticed, but they had heard and paid attention.

Nora glanced up at Ben, who looked as pained as she felt. She brought her attention back to Sarah. "Where did you get this money, honey?"

"I..." She thrust the crumpled wad of twenties toward her mother. "If you have enough money, you can buy the house, and we can stay with Daddy."

Nora took the cash from Sarah's hands and flipped through it. Ten twenty-dollar bills. Two hundred dollars. Her stomach dropped. "Sarah, did you take this money from Grandma?"

Sarah toed a circle on the tar. "Yeah, but there was a lot of money in there. I only took some."

Nora and Bridget exchanged a look over the top of Sarah's head. The money that had been missing. The money Ma thought Iris took. "That money wasn't yours to take, Sarah," Nora said. "It belonged to Grandma, and the bakery."

"You can't just take money, Sarah," Ben said. "It's wrong. You know that."

Tears welled in Sarah's eyes. "But...but you're gonna get divorced, and we have to live somewhere else, and I don't wanna move. And if you have enough money, we don't have to do any of that." Sarah lifted her gaze to her parents. Her eyes shimmered with hope that this was the answer, the way to straighten out the whole mess. "Right, Mommy?"

Nora didn't have anything to say. There was no way to ease this wound, to cushion the truth that these changes were coming whether any of them wanted them or not. She couldn't turn back time, couldn't hit the lottery, and couldn't spare her children from any of it.

"Sarah, I know you don't want any of those things

to happen," Ben said. He dropped to one knee before his daughter, his tall frame casting hers in a shadow. "I wouldn't either. But sometimes we have to change our direction to get to where we really want to be."

"I just want to be with you and Mommy. In *our* house."

"The house isn't important, Sarah Bear. I know it seems like it is right now, but in the end, what's really important is your family. And you're not losing that." He brushed her bangs off her forehead with a sweet, tender move and gave her a lopsided smile. "No matter what, you're always going to have me and Mommy."

"Together?"

One word, asking a hundred questions about the future. Ben glanced up at Nora. Their gazes held, and as much as she wanted to give him a smile, a promise, she couldn't. Neither of them had any idea where they would be tomorrow, next week, next year.

"Even if we aren't together," Ben said to Sarah, "we'll both always be there for you. I promise."

It was the best answer to give. And it was apparently enough for Sarah, who reached out and gave her father a hug. "I'm sorry I took the money, Daddy. I'm sorry, Mommy."

"It's okay." Nora ruffled Sarah's hair. As much as she wanted to be angry, she couldn't. The last thing any kid wanted was their predictable life uprooted. "But I think you need to go inside and give it back to Grandma. And tell her that you're sorry."

"Am I gonna get in trouble?" Sarah's face crumpled. "I don't want Grandma to be mad at me."

"Don't worry, kiddo." Bridget put a hand on Sarah's shoulder and steered her toward the door. "I'll be a character witness for you."

"What's a character witness?" Sarah asked as they went back inside. The door shut behind them, leaving Nora and Ben alone.

"I can't believe she did that." Ben ran a hand through his hair and let out a long breath. "I hate seeing her upset like that."

"It'll get easier. Once the kids are settled." She told herself that, even if she didn't believe it.

"Maybe we can talk to both of them tonight. After you come to the house."

Oh yeah, the property division. It made sense to do that and then sit the kids down together and tell them about the divorce. Speaking the words aloud, delivering them to the children, would make it a done deal. No take-backs, no swaps. "Sounds like a plan."

When Ben was gone, Nora talked to her mother and Sarah again. The money issue had already been settled, and Ma, instead of lecturing and punishing Sarah, had given her granddaughter a hug. Ma always had been easier on her grandchildren than her own daughters. Maybe it was true that with age, people softened, because Nora was pretty damned sure if she'd done that when she was eight, she would have been grounded for life.

She got back to work, but the recipe had blurred and

she had to take a few minutes in the ladies' room to get herself back together. By the time she came back, Bridget was in the middle of assembling the torta.

"I've got this one under control. But there's a rush congratulations cake order that just came in," Bridget said, nodding toward a bright pink work order. "Can you frost one of the vanilla sheet cakes? I'll deliver it this afternoon. Oh, and we are out of cupcakes, and Ma said we need to start on the Edwards' engagement party cake because they moved the date up to this Wednesday. Then we have the rest of the Thanksgiving pies to finish up. It's going to be crazy busy here for a few days."

All ordinary conversation, and Bridget, who knew Nora well, carried on as if nothing had happened. Neither of them mentioned Ben or the shadows under Nora's eyes or the fact that she'd been crying. They didn't talk about Sarah or the money or any of the things Bridget had overheard. They worked, letting cake and frosting fill the silence in the kitchen.

TWENTY-SEVEN

Colleen O'Bannon could probably count the number of times she had had to deliver an apology in her life. And even fewer times that she had been so wrong about someone's character. The thought disturbed her, needling in her brain like a buzzing bee. Maybe Roger had a point about how closed off she had become. Maybe not.

She put on her coat, told the girls she'd be right back, then marched out of the bakery and got in her car. A few minutes later, she was pulling up in front of Sophie's Home. She got out of the car, then stood on the porch, for a second feeling lost without pastries to fill her hands and give her an excuse for stopping by.

She found Iris in the kitchen of the shelter, mixing batter in a bowl. Her head was bent over the task in concentration, and from the ingredients waiting on the counter, Colleen guessed that Iris was making an Italian lemon cream cake. "Be sure to spray the springform pan with cooking spray or your cake will stick," Colleen said.

Iris jumped and turned. "Mrs. O'Bannon. I...I didn't hear you come in."

"I didn't announce myself. Frankly, I was afraid you'd run if I did." She gestured toward one of the chairs. "Let's talk a minute."

Iris nodded. She set the batter aside, wiped her hands on a dishtowel, then sat across from Colleen. Iris's foot tapped a nervous staccato against the tile.

"I...Well, I..." This time it was Colleen's turn to stumble over her words. She cleared her throat and tried again. "I came to apologize to you."

Iris's eyes widened. "You did?"

"I was wrong to judge you without talking to you. I made an assumption, and it was wrong." She crossed her hands on the table. "If you still want to work for me, I would like you to come back to the bakery. If you don't, I...well, I would understand."

"I do like working there. You all have been so good to me."

Until I accused you of being a thief. "Until the other day, and I am very sorry about that."

"It's okay." Iris picked at the edge of a blue linen place mat. "I get it. I mean, my mom does drugs and I've been on the streets some. People look at me different because of that."

A crime Colleen had also been guilty of. Judging without thinking first. Colleen took a moment to look at Iris, really look at her. The girl was thin as a yardstick, as young as a new calf, and as sincere as anyone who sat in the pews at church. "Well, they shouldn't. You are a very nice young woman."

"Thank you, Mrs. O'Bannon." She smoothed the edge of the place mat before squaring it with the edge of the table. When she glanced up, her black-rimmed eyes were filled with tears.

Colleen drew herself up before she softened like butter in the summer sun. "Well, do you want the job or not? If you say yes, for God's sake, you better learn how to make buttercream frosting. You always add too much confectioners' sugar and it's a bit too stiff."

Iris gave her a watery grin. "Okay. I will."

"And promise me you will get your GED. It can be noisy here, so you are welcome to study in the bakery at the end of the day. Now, have you eaten today?"

Iris shook her head.

"Good Lord, you need someone to take care of you." Colleen got to her feet and buried her face in the refrigerator, pretending to look for food. The tears she had managed to hold back began to spill, and she allowed herself a moment of grief for a young girl with a good heart and a lot of bad breaks.

Iris's life was light-years harder than Colleen's had ever been, but she could tell the girl enjoyed working at the bakery. Even seemed to like Colleen, who knew she sometimes had a rather brusque approach to things.

Colleen poured Iris some iced tea and fixed her a chicken salad sandwich. She put both down on the table. "Here you are."

Iris had wiped away the tears and the muddy makeup, but emotional hesitation still hitched her words. "Thank you."

"It is not necessary to thank me every time I feed you." She folded a napkin and set it beside Iris's glass.

"I didn't mean thank you for the food. I mean"—she fiddled with the place mat again—"thank you for coming here and talking to me, and giving me the job. You're the first person who's ever believed in me."

"No, dear, I'm the second." Colleen patted Iris's hand. "Roger believed in you first. He thinks you can do amazing things."

Iris blushed. "He helped my mom get in a rehab program yesterday even though she didn't have any money. He's very nice."

"He is." Who would have thought that a man whose shoes didn't match his belt and who often forgot his glasses on top of his head could be such a kind and generous person? The first time she'd met him a year ago, she'd thought Roger was full of boast and bluster, but she'd soon realized all that was a nervous cover for the humble generosity in his heart.

"He likes you an awful lot, Mrs. O'Bannon. Whenever I see him, he asks about you, and he gets all goofy."

He did? She knew he liked her but had no idea he got "goofy" when he asked about her. In that moment, Colleen suspected her own cheeks held a bit of a blush too. "Well, we are quite good friends." She got to her feet and tapped the plate holding Iris's sandwich. "I will see you tomorrow morning at six. And on Sunday, I expect you at my house at five p.m. sharp."

"What for?"

"Family dinner." A lump formed in Colleen's throat, but she coughed and it went away. She was merely helping out a girl whose mother was away. It wasn't like she was adopting Iris or anything. "From now on, I think you should attend that. Lord knows someone needs to feed you."

The tears started in Iris's eyes again. "Thank you, Mrs. O'Bannon. I'd like that."

"Good. Five o'clock. Sharp. I don't like tardiness." Colleen crossed to the door of the kitchen, then took a right and headed down the hall, before she lost her nerve. She stopped outside of Roger's office. The door was open, and he was reading something on his computer. His hair was a bit askew, his glasses perched on top of his head, but something inside her softened a little all the same. "I am here delivering apologies," she said.

Roger pivoted toward her. "You are? I didn't realize you offered those at the bakery."

"Well, we don't." She stepped inside and shut the door. They were alone, and a part of Colleen was thrilled. Another part was as nervous as a new bride. "But maybe we should start. It turns out my granddaughter took the money. And before you say anything, I already apologized to Iris and offered her a job."

He got up and came to stand before her. "Is this a sign that you are softening, my prickly cactus vixen?"

"I'm doing no such thing. I'm merely admitting I was wrong, as anyone should do." She answered him with an annoyed scowl, but she had a sneaking suspicion it looked more like a smile.

"You are changing that girl's life," he said. "In fact, you already have."

"I'm helping her a bit, that's all." She raised her gaze. Roger stood a full head taller, and a few inches taller than Michael had been. She liked that he was tall. He reminded her of an oak tree, strong and solid in a storm. "She told me you helped her mother out. You are a good man."

A flush filled his cheeks. "I'm an ordinary man, trying to do some good."

Now that the words were on the tip of her tongue, Colleen couldn't seem to push them out. She'd never been a flirty woman and hadn't the foggiest idea how to seduce a man. It had been so long since she'd dated, that she was sure she would do it all wrong. "I've been thinking about your offer."

He arched a brow. "You're calling a marriage proposal an offer?"

"For one, if that was a marriage proposal, it was pitiful. When you ask a woman to marry you, Roger O'Sullivan, you should do it right."

He laughed. "I'll make a mental note for next time."

Next time? Did he mean to ask her again? Or ask someone else? "And you don't start off by trying to whisk her away to some other state. She'll get the impression you think she's cheap."

He shifted closer to her and placed his hands on her hips. He had wide, strong hands, and they settled nicely in that space. "I don't think you're cheap, Colleen. Not in the least. And I invited you to Florida because I thought you'd enjoy it. We can have separate rooms, if you want. I'd just like to spend some time alone with you."

"And in this alone time"—she drew in a breath, holding it for a second—"what did you think you were going to do? Exactly?"

"Play gin rummy."

"Oh." She must have read him entirely wrong. Heat filled her cheeks, and she started to step back. "Well, gin rummy is fine."

But Roger didn't release her hips. He smiled down at her, but now his smile seemed warmer, deeper. "I'd love to play gin rummy with you, Colleen, but I'd much rather kiss you."

"Well...I...well..." She swallowed. God, he had amazing eyes. She could stare at them for hours. "Well, all right, then."

Roger raised his hands to cup her cheeks, a soft, tender, cherishing touch. Then he brushed his lips against hers, gentle, slow. It was a kiss unlike any she'd ever had before. Sweeter, nicer—

Wrong. Colleen jerked back. "We...we shouldn't."

Disappointment filled his face, and he let her go. It seemed to get colder in the tiny shop. "Okay."

"I want to. I just feel...wrong. Like I'm cheating on Michael." She shook her head. "That's silly, isn't it? He's been gone for two decades. But I…I've been alone all that time, and well, I never thought I'd ever love anyone else, and I haven't kissed anyone else, and I…I don't want to do it wrong."

"There is no wrong, Colleen. And I'm willing to wait, if you want me to."

Why did Roger have to be so kind and patient and understanding? Why couldn't he be a big jerk so she could just push him out the door and never think of him again? Because she did think of him, more than she should.

"I never thought I'd love another man," she said again, "until I…well, until I met you. And though you annoy me and frustrate me and show up altogether too often—"

"You love me?" His grin widened. "You vixen, you."

She wagged a finger at him. "And that too. You can't call me a vixen. I'm the exact opposite of a vixen."

"The definition of a vixen is an attractive woman who tempts and lures you. And you, my dear Colleen, have done that from the day I met you and you refused to take my arm crossing the street. You are stubborn and grumpy and driven and a hundred other things that make me love you more every time I see you."

"And you are an idiot." But she smiled when she said it and found herself swaying back toward him. He caught her waist again, and this time, when he leaned in to kiss her, she stayed right where she was.

TWENTY-EIGHT

Ma came back around lunchtime, breezing into the bakery and the kitchen like she always did everything—abrupt, fast, and firm. "We are shutting down for lunch."

"Third sign of the Apocalypse," Bridget whispered to Nora.

And for the first time in what felt like forever, Nora laughed. "Better prepare to divide the Hummel collection."

Bridget grinned. "I already told you, Ma's collectibles are all yours, sister."

"I hear you two muttering about my Hummels. Just for that, I'll leave them to Abigail. She would appreciate the value." Ma tsk-tsked at her two daughters. "Anyway, if you two are done acting like twelve-year-olds, Magpie wants to take us out to lunch, and Abby is meeting us there. Since we are all in the same place at the same time for once, I think that is a fine reason to close the bakery for an hour.

The world will not collapse, nor will the *Apocalypse* come in that span of time."

Nora nudged Bridget. "You're in trou-ble," she said in a singsong voice.

"Ma…" Bridget said, stepping closer to their mother. "Is your lipstick smudged? And didn't you just go to the shelter? Did a certain director of said shelter kiss you?"

Unflappable Colleen O'Bannon turned as red as a beet. "We do not have time to sit around and share idle chitchat. We're taking a short break for lunch; then we are coming back here. We have a business to run. Now, get your coats."

A few minutes later, everything was out of the ovens, the sign went to closed, and they were heading down the street to a small diner on the corner. Magpie was already waiting in a booth big enough for six, with Abby on the opposite side. Nora slid in next to Magpie while Bridget sat with Ma and Abby.

The diner had opened in that corner location forty years ago, and most of the décor still sported the late '70s feel that had been there for opening day. The tables were green, the bar stools some kind of color halfway between yellow and avocado, and the jukebox in the corner bright red, seeming stuck in the era of Cher and Bon Jovi. But the food was good, the service was quick, and the diner was one of several area restaurants that ordered all their desserts from the O'Bannon bakery.

Magpie was drumming her fingers on the tabletop while her left leg tapped out a beat against the tile floor. The waitress, a girl they knew well, came by, dropped off drinks, and took their orders with a minimum of small talk and then left them alone.

"So tell us why you're springing for lunch," Abby said when they were alone again. "And why you're still in town. Not that I don't love seeing you all the time, but frankly, Mags, it's getting kinda weird."

The others laughed and made some jokes but Nora noticed her little sister only made a half-hearted attempt to join in. Under the green Formica table, she grabbed one of Magpie's hands and gave it a squeeze. Magpie's eyes shimmered with unshed tears. "Thanks," she whispered.

"Hey, I need to apologize," Nora said softly, and she vowed she would be more present going forward, regardless of how messy her own life got. "I know you wanted to talk back in Truro and I never got a chance. I've tried calling you and stopping by—"

"And I've been avoiding you." Magpie gave her sister a watery grin. "I didn't want you to be disappointed in me, Nora."

Nora squinted at Magpie. It was ironic how they both felt the same way. Nora had kept her secrets to herself because she didn't want to let her family down, and here Magpie was, doing the same. "I could never be disappointed in you."

"Okay." Magpie let out a shaky laugh. "I'm counting on that."

The diner was starting to fill and the low hum of conversation filled the air, punctuated by the occasional "tuna on rye!" call from the waitstaff to the kitchen. Every time an order was ready, the cook rang a bell, which at the pace he was moving was about every thirty seconds.

"Well." Magpie took in a breath and, this time, was the one to give Nora's hand a squeeze. "I guess I can't put it off any longer. I...well, I brought you all here to tell you something. And now that you're sitting at this table, I'm not quite sure how to say it."

"Do it the O'Bannon way," Abby said. "Fast and blunt."

The waitress came by and deposited their orders. Magpie ignored her grilled cheese sandwich and ran a finger back and forth along the edge of her plate. Once the waitress left, Magpie drew herself up and blurted out, "I'm pregnant."

A sinkhole could have opened in the center of the diner and not one O'Bannon would have noticed. Total silence descended over the table for a good thirty seconds.

Nora swallowed her hurt. All those days at the beach house and Mags hadn't said a word.

Except she had. She'd asked to have a girls' talk more than once, and Nora had been so consumed by her own problems that she hadn't followed up. Magpie had become a secondary worry, something Nora pushed to the shadows while she dealt with the stuff in plain view, a choice that had also cost Nora in her relationship with Sarah. All that time she'd spent with Will—chasing some foolish flirtation because she was feeling lonely—all time she could have spent with her kids, her sister. She'd tried to connect with Magpie after they came back to Boston, but the window had closed.

340

"Before you ask, I'm keeping it. I wasn't going to but then"—Magpie drew in a breath and placed her palm on her abdomen—"I spent all that time with Sarah and Jake, and I kinda thought it might be nice to have a kid of my own."

Bridget grinned. "That's awesome, Magpie! Congratulations!"

"Yet another kid I can buy drums for at Christmas," Abby said. "Nora's still thanking me for the ones I gave Jake. Aren't you, Nora?"

"Almost as good as the bugle you gave him for his birthday," Nora said. "I'm glad I only have one evil sister."

Abby laughed. "Wait till you see what I buy him and Sarah this Christmas. I'm thinking violins."

Nora leaned over and drew her sister into a hug. From now on, she'd be there for Magpie. For the doctor's appointments and the first steps and all the crazy, stressful, joyous days ahead. "I'm so excited for you."

Magpie met her gaze. "Are you really? I was so afraid you would be disappointed that I did something so stupid."

"You are going to be an amazing mom, Magpie." Nora hugged her sister tighter. "I mean it. You're going to be great."

"So, tell us more. When are you due? Do you know what you're having? Do you have names picked out?" Bridget asked.

"The doctor said around the middle of June. And no and no. I'm still figuring this out." Magpie's smile wobbled. She turned to face their mother, who, from announcement until now, hadn't said anything. "Ma?"

All four girls swiveled to look at their mother. Nora braced herself for the lecture about premarital sex, the sin of having a child out of wedlock, the whole fire-and-brimstone thing. Ma had mellowed over the years, but Nora didn't think she'd changed that much.

"I think"—Ma paused—"what you did was a big mistake."

Magpie sighed. "I know, Ma. I didn't think and—"

"Bringing a child into the world isn't a decision that should be made lightly. You have no idea what a responsibility it is."

"I don't. But I'm hoping all of you will help me." Magpie reached out, and the other O'Bannon girls grabbed her hands and assured her they would be there, especially Nora, who was the closest, both literally and figuratively. Just as she had when Magpie was little, she would protect and help her sister.

Nora knew how hard parenting could be. She knew the challenges ahead of Magpie, but she also knew the joys. She had seen Magpie with her niece and nephew and had no doubt that her younger sister, with her heart of gold and abundant love, would be just fine once her child arrived. Maybe this would be the thing that would keep the wanderlust-filled Magpie home for more than a few weeks.

"I'm sorry, Ma. I know you're disappointed and probably going to tell me that I'm going to hell," Magpie said, "but I love this baby already and I'm not going to—"

"But I also think," Ma interrupted, putting up a hand to stop Magpie's words, "that it's time I stopped judging people as harshly as a winter storm. And...it's about damned time another one of my girls had a grandchild for me to spoil." She reached across the table, took Magpie's hand, and smiled at her youngest daughter. "The road you're choosing is a hard one, Margaret. I've raised children alone. But you are strong and smart, and you have all of us here to help you. We're O'Bannons. That's what we do."

TWENTY-NINE

The closer Nora got to her old house, the deeper the dread sank in her gut. This was what she'd wanted, what she had told Ben she was going to do. Divide their possessions in a calm, equitable, and adult manner and then go their separate ways.

She pulled into the driveway, parking behind Ben's sedan. It was empty, which meant he must have gone inside. She sat in her own car for a minute, listening to the engine tick as it cooled, and thought of how she had been here just a month ago.

There'd been birthday flowers on her doorstep and a trio of pumpkins for Halloween. The kids' toys had been scattered around the yard, with Sarah's bike forgotten against the house. And smack dab on the center of the front door had been the bright yellow paper that turned everything upside down.

Now the lawn had browned as November took a firm hold. The flowers, the pumpkins, the toys, and the bike were all gone, and so was the auction notice. If she ignored the sign at the edge of the drive, she could almost believe the house was back to normal.

She drew in a deep breath before getting out of the car, carrying a pen and the list of furniture she'd made weeks ago. With any luck, she could do this quickly and without arguing with Ben.

The first thing she noticed when she opened the front door was music, coming from the toolbox-shaped boom box she had bought Ben three or four Christmases ago. Aerosmith, singing "I Don't Want to Miss a Thing." If she closed her eyes, she was back in Tommy O'Brien's basement, sitting beside Ben, joking about sugar rushes and ginger ale and wishing this guy with an amazing smile would kiss her already.

Why did that song have to be on right now? Why couldn't it be some Justin Bieber nonsense song she didn't even like? She figured whatever radio station was playing it had a sick sense of timing.

"Ben?"

"Back here," he called. "In the kitchen."

She took her time walking down the hall, drinking in the pictures of the kids hanging on the wall and the end table with a fine layer of dust and a collection of clay projects the kids had made. To the right was the living room with the dark blue sofa she and Ben had bought together when she was pregnant. They'd sat on it so long that she'd fallen asleep in the store and bought it half out of guilt.

When she'd left him a month ago, the living room

had been a mess of toys, laundry waiting to be folded, and stacks of junk mail on the coffee table. All of that had been whisked away, the space tidied, and now the room shone. She was surprised and grateful he'd cleaned, even if nothing was packed. At least not having to deal with stuff strewn everywhere would make moving easier.

This weekend, the pictures on the sofa table would be in a box. The pillows she'd embroidered during one crazy nesting urge when she was pregnant stuffed in another, and the jigsaw puzzle she and Ben had spent a rainy weekend assembling, gluing, and then hanging on the wall would be broken in pieces in the trash. All of this would be moved someplace else or sold. Her life, her children's lives, in boxes and on trucks.

A profound sense of loss washed over her. As much as she wanted to blame Ben for all of it, the truth was that she was just as much at fault. For burying herself in work, for thinking she could handle it all, and for refusing to ask for help when she was over her head. She'd thought she was taking care of everyone when in fact she'd been trying to hold back a tidal wave with a wall made out of cardboard.

She turned away and continued down the hall. She rounded the corner into the kitchen, expecting to trip over the lip between the wood floors of the hallway and the old tiles they'd been meaning to tear up. But there was no lip. There was only a smooth transition from wood to slate gray tiles.

For a second, all she could focus on was the tiles. Twelve by twelve, with swirls of blues and white that wove in and out of each other in a wild, unpredictable pattern. When she'd seen them on the wall in Home Depot, she'd told Ben they looked like the ocean on a stormy day. He'd promised Nora that someday she would walk in her kitchen and that ceramic sea would be beneath her feet.

Now it was. But for some other woman. Some other family, who would buy this house on Monday morning.

She raised her gaze, taking in the whitewashed birch cabinets, the pale granite countertops, the deep white farmer's sink with the oversized sprayer faucet. Every detail one she had chosen, imagined, dreamed of. It was the kitchen she and Ben had planned—done and ready and smelling like new beginnings.

Ben was standing by the sink, his hands in his pockets and his face unreadable. He had changed out of his work clothes and had on a clean pair of jeans and a freshly pressed pale blue cotton button-down shirt. Why did he have to look so damned good? And why did she still have to be so damned attracted to him?

"What do you think?" he said.

She swallowed the lump in her throat and willed the tears in her eyes to stay back until she left. "It looks great. Whoever buys the house is going to love it." She forced a brightness into her voice that she didn't feel. "Did you do the work?"

"Yup."

In the background, Aerosmith yielded to Elton John, another of her favorite artists, singing "Sorry Seems to Be the Hardest Word." She could hear the sounds of a school bus stopping out front and the roar of kids getting off and going home. "Why did you do all this work? I mean, they're auctioning the house off in three days. Surely the bank wouldn't care what the kitchen looked like."

"Well, when you go to get a mortgage, they want the house to have more equity, and a finished kitchen and deck and a renovated master bath are all things that increase the value." He pushed off from the sink and moved closer to her. "Makes it easier for a bank to agree to a loan."

"You finished the deck? And the master bath?" Both were projects that they had talked about, but he'd never started. She'd given up asking about them long ago, around the same time she'd given up on the two of them.

"Let me show you, Nora." Ben put out his hand, and without thinking, she took it and walked with him across the sea of tile to a pair of French doors so new they still had the sticker in the corner citing all the benefits of triple-pane glass. They looked out over an expansive deck with built-in bench seating and a pergola waiting for some ivy or clematis to weave in and out of the beams.

"It's gorgeous." That lump in her throat only grew, along with a tide of anger. She kept trying to push it down because yelling at Ben wouldn't accomplish anything. She needed to be strong and calm. Get through this tour of the house that was no longer hers, divide up the furniture, and make arrangements for custody going forward.

"Wait till you see the bathroom." He pivoted, taking the back way off the kitchen to the narrow stairs that led directly to the master.

Nora had loved this staircase, a throwback to the days of maids and butlers. Halfway up the stairs was a little nook, maybe for resting a heavy tray or an extra load of linens; she never really knew. The staircase was barely wide enough for her, and Ben had to turn a little sideways to navigate the cramped space.

Five steps from the top, she stopped and dropped his hand. She didn't want to round that corner and see the room she used to share with her husband. She didn't want to peek at the bathroom that used to hold his shaving cream and her makeup, and hundreds of mornings where they wove in and out of each other as they got ready, in a practiced dance only married people mastered.

"Ben, forget it. Let's just go back downstairs and go over the inventory list."

"Not until you see this, Nora." He reached for her hand again, but she pulled it back.

"What's the point? All it does is make this worse. I'm watching everything I dreamed about disappear like it was a mirage, and the closer I get, the less real it is. I don't want to know what some other woman's bathroom is going to look like. I don't want to picture her rolling out dough on granite countertops that *I* fell in love with in the store."

"Then don't." He turned away and continued up the stairs. Then he opened the door and stepped into their master bedroom.

She could go back downstairs or follow him. Leaving wouldn't accomplish anything. She was still carrying the damned list, with not a single check mark on it. Was he purposely trying to torture her? Drag it out until she cried uncle or something? The Ben she knew had never been malicious, but they said divorce brought out the worst in people.

The master bedroom was just as neat and tidy as the rest of the house. The bed was made, the half dozen decorative pillows she'd loved and Ben had hated stacked in a descending triangle down the front of the white comforter. The armchair that had been perpetually full of Ben's dirty laundry was ready for someone to sit in and pick up the novel sitting on the small cherry occasion table beside it. Her slippers were sitting beside his, two by two, as if they could step into them and back into their marriage.

The door to the bathroom was open, and she could see the dark cherry cabinets she'd picked out, the cream tile with the green diamonds joining the corners, the twin sinks with matching oval mirrors and the chrome sconces casting a soft light onto the countertop. The space where the floor met the cabinets glowed. Just like the kitchen, every single element was one she had remarked on, some in passing. Had Ben paid that close of attention? Or was this all some weird coincidence?

"You even put in the lighting beneath the cabinets," she said.

"So you won't trip at night if you have to get up."

Nora closed her eyes and shook her head. The tears, the anger, the frustration bubbled inside her, rising and boiling like a volcano. She didn't want to imagine herself washing her hands at that sink or slipping into her slippers because the tile floor was cold in the winter. "Why are you showing me this, Ben? I don't care. I won't ever be walking into that bathroom again."

"Indulge me for one more minute, Nora. Just one."

"No, Ben. This whole thing is a waste of time. Just check what furniture you want, and I'll get out of here." She tried to thrust the list at him, but he ignored it. "If you want all of our stuff, I don't care anymore. I just want to leave."

"One more minute. Please. Then we can talk about armchairs or sofa tables or whatever you want."

It was the *please* that got her, the note of vulnerability in his voice. He took her hand again and gently tugged her into the room and then around the corner.

The bedroom was a funky shape, sort of a rectangle with an extra square-shaped nook beside the closet. They'd talked about a hundred different ideas for that space. Expanding the closet or adding a vanity table, but the one that Nora had lobbied for over and over was a door and a balcony, with a tiny porch where she and Ben could sit outside at the end of the day and watch the sun set over the trees. Ben had argued about how much work it would be, talking about structural needs and building permits, but all she'd seen was that Romeo and Juliet balcony she'd always wanted when she was a little girl.

And there, as if merely remembering it brought it to life, was a glass door that led to a tiny porch with a railed balcony that looked out over the trees. A small café table sat in the center, flanked by two chairs. A familiar white box sat on the table.

She glanced at him, confused, half ready to run, half beginning to hope again. "Ben...what is all this?"

"What you asked me to do, Nora." He gave her a smile and led her onto the balcony with him.

Almost every day in November had been cold, another New England winter trying to get an early foothold with temps dipping into the thirties and forties. Today had been warm, with the sun bright and happy, and the pleasant temperature had held all afternoon. It was exactly the kind of day she had envisioned when she'd talked about adding the balcony. The view was just as she'd pictured it, too, high above the speckled autumnal trees, spanning the gray and brown checkerboard of rooftops, and in the far, far distance, the city of Boston, outlined in hazy gray.

"Ben, what is this?" she asked again.

He didn't reply. Instead, he reached over and lifted the lid of the box. The sides parted, as they were designed to do, revealing the cake inside. Ma had ordered those boxes from a specialty company because they reduced the hassle of lifting the cake out and smearing the frosting. Nora had watched Bridget put this very cake into that box just a few hours ago.

"You're the one who ordered the torta? Why?"

"Because it was the cake we had at our rehearsal dinner," he said, as if it was a matter-of-fact thing to re-create that moment, not something weird when they were meeting to discuss the division of their assets. "There were little fake diamond rings attached to the ribbons, if I remember right."

"I found some that looked like my ring and used them for a fun little gift for whoever got that slice." She could hear the laughter of her sisters, the chatter of her bridesmaids, the happy hum of conversation at the party. She remembered catching Ben's eye across the room when she was cutting the cake and seeing a deep, sweet love in those brown eyes.

This time she kept her gaze on the cake because she was afraid she'd see indifference if she looked into Ben's eyes. She was daring to hope, and that, Nora already knew, was a foolish, dangerous thing to do. "But this isn't a rehearsal dinner, and I don't need this trip down memory lane, especially when we're getting—"

He put a finger over her lips. Her heart stuttered. "Please pull the string, Nora."

A long gold ribbon spiraled out of the center of the cake. She hadn't put it there, and she didn't remember Bridget doing so. Ben must have added it himself after he picked up the cake, though she couldn't fathom a single reason. She realized now why he'd asked her to go get Jake from school and drop the kids at Ma's—it had probably given him just enough time to stop by the bakery before he came here and set up this elaborate tableau. The urge to flee, to resist this desire to believe in him one more time, rose inside her again.

"Don't you want to know what's attached to it?" Ben asked, as if he'd read her mind and knew she was about to bolt.

Okay, so a part of her did want to know. If only to get to the bottom of what he was doing and why he had gone to so much trouble. Then again, this was Ben, who did everything in a big way. Even, it seemed, their divorce.

Nora tugged the ribbon. It slid easily out of the cake, landing with a soft clang on the metal table. She stared at the object for a second, confused. "That's a house key."

"Yes, it is." Ben wiped the almond cream off the key and then handed it to her. "In fact, it's *our* house key."

"I don't understand." She turned the key over in her palm. "We don't own this house, Ben. Why…what…?"

"We *do* own this house. Today, tomorrow, and for the next thirty years."

Her mind couldn't wrap around his words. She'd talked to the bank and the lawyer. She had seen the sign on the front lawn. "What about the auction? They're going to be here in three days, Ben."

"It's not going to happen. I forgot to take the sign down, but I'll do that tonight. I have to tell you, I was sweating it. I didn't know if I could pull this off in time, but everything came together at the last minute and"—he put out his arms—"the house is ours again."

Take the sign down. Pull this off. Everything came together. The house is ours again. She tried to put the pieces in order, but his words and the facts she knew jumbled in her mind. "But…the bank refused to work with us. I called. I even had a lawyer call the bank, and they wouldn't talk to him, either."

"I found another bank, Nora. And I got another mortgage." Ben kept on talking, and Nora stared at him, hearing the words but not understanding how they could be true. "I had to put down some money, but with the added equity from finishing the kitchen and bathroom, I had just enough."

"Money? What money?" She gasped and put a hand over her mouth. "Oh God, please don't tell me you gambled with the kids' college fund." It was the only sizeable pile of cash they had left. The one thing she had refused to touch.

"I didn't gamble with or on anything," Ben said. "Except the chance that you could fall in love with me again and we could keep our family together."

She wanted to step into this fantasy with him and believe it would all be different going forward. But Nora had history with Ben. A history that said he was just making another grand gesture, and in a week or a month, she'd find out that it was all based on a wing and a prayer, and her life would tumble down another rabbit hole. And they both still wanted different things—Ben with the big family, Nora with the urge to figure out who she was when she wasn't a wife and a mother. "It's too late, Ben. I'm sorry. I can't do this again. I just...can't."

She started to turn away, and he stopped her. His hand on her arm was warm and tender, and a part of her wanted to lean into that touch.

"I have never known you to quit anything, Nora O'Bannon." He paused a beat. Downstairs, the radio shifted into Bryan Adams's "(Everything I Do) I Do It for You," another song she loved. "Why are you quitting us?"

"I'm not. You did." Now the tears did come, rushing forward like a waterfall held back too long. She let them fall, no longer caring if he saw that she was upset. She was tired of arguing, tired of fighting, tired of feeling like this entire thing was an uphill battle. She didn't want to fall for the balcony and the bathroom and the cake and the damned mix tape. She wanted to guard her heart, keep it from breaking again, so she threw up the familiar walls. "You quit us when you gambled. And you quit us when you started spending every Friday and Saturday night with someone else."

"That's where you think I've been every weekend? With someone else? Nora—"

"Ben, stop. Just stop." She put up her hands and started to back away. She couldn't look in his eyes and listen to his voice and believe him. Not again. "This is all going to go away next month or next year. I can't fall into that trap a second time. We don't even want the same future." She pivoted away from him.

Except maybe a part of her did. She had sat in that diner this afternoon, seeing Magpie's glow of anticipation and joy, heard her excitement about starting a family, and realized how much she wanted her family back. All four of them, together again. Sledding down the town hill in the winter, picking the ugliest pumpkin from the pumpkin patch, dashing in and out of the cold Atlantic Ocean. All the things they used to do and then stopped.

"I pulled away from you, from everyone," Nora said. "I shut you out."

"I know you did. You were hurt, and when you're hurt, Nora, you withdraw like a turtle into her shell." He brushed a lock of hair off her forehead and smiled down at her. "I should have tried harder."

"We both should have." She shook her head and backed up. "Maybe it's too late, Ben."

"Don't you want to know why I quit gambling?"

She was halfway across the bedroom, ready to leave, when Ben spoke. She paused, closed her eyes, and let out a long breath before turning back toward her husband. "Does it matter? Because the reason you *started* is still there. Your family was boring, and whatever you found in that casino was better than us. I have news for you, Ben. Raising a family sometimes is boring as hell. There's dishes and homework and soccer games. Times I wanted to scream if I had to do one more load of laundry. You escaped all that, and you went into those casinos, and you left me here alone."

"I know." His eyes were sad, his shoulders low. "And I'm sorry. I'm truly sorry."

"And so I filled in those gaps with work and lists and organizing," she went on, the words a waterfall tumbling out of her mouth. Admissions she had kept tucked in her heart for months. Years. "I kept telling myself I had it all under control, and it was all going to be fine. I didn't tell anyone about what we were going through and I didn't ask for help because . . . because I was ashamed."

He tried to reach for her, but she stepped out of range. "Nora, I never meant to make you feel that way."

"You didn't do it. *I* did. I failed, Ben. I failed..." And now her voice broke, and the truth that she had hidden from her husband, her children, her family, and herself came rushing forward to fill that space. It wasn't all Ben's fault, and it wasn't all because he'd bet on a hand of cards. "I failed all of you. I thought I was doing all the things a mom and a wife is supposed to do. The dishes and the laundry and the job. I kept this tight grip on schedules and sorting the frigging socks, instead of letting any of you know that it was too much and I was drowning every single, solitary day."

He took her hands and pulled her to him. "I knew you were, and I deserted you. I kept thinking if I could make more money, I could solve all our problems. Hire a maid or let you cut back at the bakery. Now I realize that we didn't need the money, Nora. Or the schedules. Or the lists. Or more kids or a bigger house." He rubbed his thumb over her lip, a tender gesture he'd done a thousand times before. "We needed each other."

She wanted to believe that he meant those words. That going forward would be about the two of them, raising their family, having room between them for their own selves. The future she had once dared to imagine, before that winter day when she lost everything.

"Where did the money come from, Ben?" she said. "The down payment for the new mortgage. The countertops and cabinets and tile." *Please don't say you won it in a casino.*

"Every Friday and Saturday night for the past year, I've

been working for Jim Harcourt on a house he wanted to sell. He was building it on his own, without the company backing. He and his brothers had a falling out, and Jim wanted to test the waters but also keep it on the down low. He didn't have much to finance the project, so I agreed to help, in exchange for a cut of the profits. Jim's always been good to me and brought me in on plenty of projects, so when he said he needed help, I was there. I didn't tell you because..."

"We had stopped talking." The day Nora moved into the guest bedroom had pretty much been the last time she and Ben had a conversation with any kind of substance. After that, they became two passing ships, exchanging the bare minimum of words. She'd never asked about those weekend nights, and he'd never volunteered the information.

"And I didn't want to let you down again. If the house didn't sell, I would have wasted all those hours for nothing. I would have screwed up yet again, and I couldn't bear to do that. I had already hurt this family so much. Too much."

"We both did," she said softly. "I hurt us as much as you did."

"You, Nora, were amazing. You did nothing wrong. You held us together when I was lost. All I wanted to do was make that up to you, to show you that I didn't want to lose you or our family or this house." He smiled at her, a wide, happy smile like the one he used to wear all the time. "So I kept on working with Jim, pouring hours and hours into that project. The house he and I built did sell, and my share was enough to pay for the supplies here and the down payment on the new mortgage. As for the bank, Jim called in a few favors and found a sympathetic loan officer willing to take a risk on us."

She stared at her husband as if he were a stranger. Ben, the one who had never been serious, the one who had ignored the bills, had kept his head down all this time, trying to save something that she had already given up on. "You really pulled this off?"

He nodded. "I'm sorry I didn't step in when I should have. I'm sorry I left you to deal with all this for far too long. I'm sorry I left that day and didn't know what you were going through. I should have been here, Nora. For all of it." He drew in a breath and paused a moment, dropping his gaze to the lazy circle his thumbs drew on the back of their joined hands. "After I went to rehab, I felt like such a failure. What kind of father gambles away his paycheck? The guilt crushed me. Paralyzed me. And so I let you shoulder a burden that should have been shared."

Failure. It was a feeling Nora knew well. The two of them, hiding the truth from each other, from themselves, so afraid that it would all fall apart if they were honest. In the end, it had anyway, and now, in this first real and true conversation she'd had with her husband in years, she could feel the beginnings of healing. The knitting of a new connection, one built out of the common experience of being battered and bruised by life and bad decisions.

"You mentioned that the reason you wanted to keep our family together was because you wanted somewhere to belong. That that was what you were looking for when you married me." She sighed. "I was looking for the same thing, Ben, when I married you."

"But you have a huge family, Nora."

"One I never felt I really belonged in. Because I was lying to them every single damned day of my life. I was the one who had it all together. Had the perfect life with the husband and the kids, and now even a dog. But then, one day, I told them all the truth, and I thought they would look at me differently the next day or tell me where I'd screwed up. But no one did. My sisters and my mother loved me and hugged me and kept on telling me stupid jokes. What kept me from belonging was all that work I did to keep up this image that was so far from the true picture, I couldn't seem to find my way home again." She looked at the key in her hand. It was heavy, solid. "I want to go home, Ben."

His face fell and he stepped back. "Okay. If you want to go over that list, I guess we can."

Home. It wasn't a place; it wasn't a set of countertops or a balcony off the bedroom. It was something she had already had and didn't see, like she was Dorothy in a black-and-white world. She looked at the man she had loved for most of her life, the man she had almost thrown aside, the man who had the same eyes as the children they had created, and realized she had nearly gambled away everything that mattered.

"Everything can stay here, Ben. It all fits where it is." She stepped into Ben's arms and nestled her head in the crook of his shoulder. He was solid and strong, and she had forgotten that about him. She had seen the man who let her down for so long that she'd missed seeing the man he had transformed into. The man who was strong enough to be her partner, and the only man who knew her just as she was, with her lists and her planning, and loved her all the same. She was home, and so was he. "And I fit right where I am too."

THIRTY

Getting around you is becoming impossible," Nora said as she moved to stir the beans sitting on top of the stove. "I think I'm going to have to tape a sign that says Wide Load on your back."

Magpie swatted at her older sister. "I'm only six months along, Nora. I'm not that big yet."

Magpie made a beautiful pregnant woman, Nora thought. Her sister had that earthy look to her, with her long hair and the maxi dresses that skimmed the floor. She had arrived early for the cookout at Nora's house, even offering to make a potato salad. She'd forgotten the salt and undercooked the potatoes, but overall, it was a decent first effort. Magpie's child might not starve after all.

Outside, Nora could see the kids playing in the yard with Chance. The silly dog even had his own doghouse, built by Ben and modeled after their regular house. Ben was putting the finishing touches on the new swing set he'd built while Jake kept calling out and asking if he was done.

"Is Ma on her way?" Magpie asked.

"Yep. Her and Roger. They just got back from Denver this morning."

"That's the third trip they've gone on since Christmas. Hasn't he proposed every single time?"

"Yup. And Ma refuses to make an honest man out of him. I'm telling you, I think it's early Alzheimer's because the Ma we know and love would have never traveled around in sin with a man." But it was nice to see her mother so happy and to see her finally enjoying a life outside of the bakery.

She and Roger had gone on some double dates with Bridget and Garrett and come over to play cards with Nora and Ben a couple times. She liked Roger. He had a way of tempering her mother that brought out a whole new side to her.

Magpie laughed. "I think it's love. Did you see how giggly she gets around him? It's almost embarrassing."

Nora tasted the beans, pronounced them done, and turned off the heat. "How about you? Any new prospects?"

"Sister, I have my hands full with the only male I want in my life." She ran a hand over her belly, just pronounced enough that it looked like she was wearing a small watermelon. "I don't need a man right now. Maybe ever."

Nora added a little salt and then stirred again. "When are you flying out next?"

"Tomorrow. I'm off to Peru, then Brazil. But I'll be home in time for Jake's birthday." Magpie put her back to the counter and fiddled with the dishtowel. "I was thinking that maybe I should settle in one place for a while. *Boston* magazine offered me a staff writer position, and I think I'm going to take it."

"You, stay still? You've never done that."

Magpie's gaze went to the backyard. Under the shade of an oak tree, Bridget, Garrett, Abby, Jessie, and Aunt Mary were sitting at a picnic table. Iris had gotten up to go play with the kids, the girl now as much a part of their family as the rest of the girls. "I don't want to regret being away from my child. Life is short, you know? And I want to spend as much time with him as I can."

"Are you scared about doing it on your own?"

Magpie laughed. "Absolutely freaking terrified. You know me. I can barely take care of myself. But I do have one ace in my pocket, if you'll forgive the gambling pun."

"Not all risky bets are bad," Nora said, thinking of how she had come back home to Ben and how everything in her life had transformed. She was taking a pottery class on Tuesday nights and had joined a running group that met three times a week. She had a life outside of her kids and her husband and work, and every day she woke up feeling more centered, more...herself. "So what's this ace?"

"The O'Bannon girls." Magpie draped an arm over Nora's shoulder. "We may be slightly dysfunctional, but we love each other, and when things get tough, we're there to hold each other up."

"And none of us would have it any other way," Nora said. Then the back door opened and the dog came charging in, followed by Jake and Sarah. A muddy trail of footprints snaked across the ceramic tile and down the hall and then back again as the trio dashed out to the yard. Nora let the mud stay, picked up the beans, and went out to join her family.

After years of pretending she had a happy marriage and denying that she missed the friends and family she'd left behind, Bridget O'Bannon is headed home to restart her life. But working alongside her sisters every day at their bakery isn't as easy as whipping up her favorite chocolate peanut butter cake.

Please turn the page for an excerpt from *The Perfect Recipe for Love and Friendship.*

I f there was one scent that described the O'Bannon girls, it was vanilla. Not the run-of-the-mill artificial flavoring, but the scent that could only be awakened by scraping the back of a teaspoon along the delicate spine of an espresso-colored vanilla bean.

Gramma had always kept a jar of vanilla beans on her kitchen counter because she said they reminded her of how much work God went to just to create a single beautiful note. So many miracles had to dance a complicated tango, all to create one vanilla bean. The orchid's flower only bloomed for twenty-four hours, and only the Melipona bee could pollinate the buds. Without that bee—or in later years, the intervention of painstaking human cross-pollination—the simple orchid would never become a delicate vanilla bean.

"No two vanilla beans are exactly the same," Gramma had said, "like you and your sisters. Each is unique and beautiful and handmade by God himself."

It had been Gramma who had taught Bridget the joy of baking. It had been Gramma who had coached her granddaughter through the intricacies of piecrusts and cake batters, guided her hand as she'd swirled buttercream and painted sugar cookies. It had been Gramma who had propped Bridget on a metal stool and woven magical tales about mischievous leprechauns and clever fairies, while the two of them mixed and kneaded and baked and decorated. And it was Gramma she'd been trying to hold on to when she'd worked at the shop. Or at least that was what Bridget had told herself for years.

Maybe she was trying to hold on to the magic her grandmother had seemed to embody.

Now Bridget stood on the sidewalk outside Charmed by Dessert and inhaled the familiar, sweet scent of vanilla. It seemed to fill the very air around the little shop, like some confectionary version of the cloud over the Addams Family's house.

She hadn't been here in three years, but everything looked just as it had before. Charmed by Dessert had sat in the same location in downtown Dorchester for three generations, a converted home on a tree-lined block. It was housed in a small, squat white building topped with a bright pink and yellow awning, flanked by a florist on the left and an ever-rotating selection of lawyers and accountants who rented the space on the right. The street was peppered with old-fashioned streetlamps and wrought-iron benches beside planters blooming with flowers.

Once upon a time, Bridget had thought she would work here until she died, side by side with her grandmother, her sisters, and her mother. Baking pies and frosting cakes and sifting flour into clouds. But then Gramma had died, and Bridget had met Jim and—

Everything had changed.

Bridget had taken a job writing a food column for a local paper, but it wasn't the same as working here. Not at all.

The small silver bell that had once sat on a shelf in Gramma's hutch tinkled as Bridget opened the door and stepped inside. Nora looked up from the tiered cupcake display she was refilling, and her brows lifted in surprise.

For a second, Bridget expected to see Abby behind the counter. But Abby had quit the family—and quit the bakery. She was working at a Williams-Sonoma at the mall, the last Bridget had heard. She used to think Abby was her best friend, but the scene on her wedding day and the ensuing three years of silence said differently.

All these years, she had kept Abby's secret from the rest of the family. And in doing so, she'd lost her sisters. Lost the bond she used to have.

For what? For a marriage that had been fractured for a long time. A marriage Bridget had once vowed to do anything to repair.

"Bridget? What are you doing here?" Nora asked.

"I...I don't know." It was one of the most honest things she'd said in days. All those hours of pretending she was okay, that she wasn't feeling lost and alone and scared. Hell, she'd been feeling that way for years, but she'd told herself that planting some flowers and getting pregnant would set her world to rights again. Would prove something. To herself, to her family.

"Uh, okay." Nora dusted off her hands and slid the empty tray onto the counter behind her. She looked unsure of what to say, how to act, without the buffer of a funeral and Netflix playing in the background. "Uh, can I get you anything?"

A giant rewind button for my life. "Coffee?"

Nora nodded, her face slackening with relief at having something to do, something to put off the awkward conversation for another moment. She disappeared into the back, returning a moment later with two steaming mugs of rich, dark coffee. "Here." She gestured toward one of the bistro tables at the front of the shop. "Let's...let's, uh, sit for a minute. If you want to."

Now that Bridget was here, she wanted to leave, forget she'd ever walked inside. But where was she going to go? Back to the church? Hell no (and that thought made her whip through a quick mental Hail Mary just in case). Back home? Her house was a mile away, walkable, even in these ugly, sensible shoes, but no. She couldn't walk back into that empty space again because if she did, she'd curl up in that bed and never leave again. As much as she'd hated going to church, she had to admit her mother was right—she needed to get out of that house.

Move forward. Focus on the future. Somehow.

"Why are you here?" Nora said.

Bridget didn't want to say the truth, because she wasn't quite sure what the truth was, so instead she said the first thing that popped into her head. "I was thinking I should get a cat."

Nora arched a brow and took a sip of coffee before she spoke. That was how Nora worked—she thought about her words before she said them. She was the least chatty of the three O'Bannon girls, and the most serious one. Ma called Nora the umbrella of the family, because she was practical and dependable and the calm one in the midst of any family storm. "A cat? Okay. Sounds...good."

"Should I get two?" Nonsense words poured out of Bridget like a leaky tap, filling the too-sweet air in the shop and the empty cavern in her heart and all those questions about *tomorrow* that she couldn't bring herself to answer. "You know, in case one of them gets...lonely? I don't think I could stand to hear one of them crying because it was all...a-alone." Then her voice broke and the river of words jerked to a stop.

Nora covered Bridget's hand and gave it a little squeeze. "Ma made you go to church, didn't she?"

Bridget nodded. She almost cried, thinking how good it was that Nora hadn't thrown her out, that she had reached out and comforted her, and for five seconds not mentioned Jim. Or said anything about Abby. "How...how can you tell?"

"You're wearing that dress you hate, topped with a nice little shawl of Catholic guilt." Nora smiled. "Two cats? Really?"

"I don't know what else to do. I mean, what am I going to do with all of Jim's clothes? And the house? Oh, God, Nora, what am I going to do about all that *stuff*? How am I possibly going to handle it all a-alone?"

Nora's hand tightened on hers. "First, you're going to ditch that dress. No, not just ditch it. Fucking burn it in the backyard. It is uglier than hell."

The curse cut through the air, unexpected from the normally perfect Nora. It seemed to break the tension between them somehow, a crack in the wall. All these years Bridget had spent away from her sisters, her mother, and for just this second, she couldn't remember why. Didn't want to remember why.

But in her head, she heard Jim's voice. *Remember how they hurt you, babe. That's why we were an island, just you and me. Don't let them get close again.*

She wanted to argue back, to tell Jim he wasn't here anymore and what was she supposed to do about that? That maybe he'd been wrong, and maybe if she hadn't shut her family out for all those years, this wall between them wouldn't exist.

Instead, she tugged her hand out of Nora's and put it in her lap. "I hate this dress. I forgot I even had it in my closet."

"I swear, Ma has her homing instinct for outfits that make you look like Doris Day on acid," Nora said. "Remember the polka-dot skirt debacle of 2003?"

That made Bridget laugh again. God, it felt so good to laugh. Just as quickly, a wave of guilt hit her. Jim had just died. His body was hardly cold in the grave. How could she be laughing?

Nora's hand lit on Bridget's arm. "It's okay to laugh and run out of church and eat dessert, Bridge."

"It doesn't feel okay."

"Yeah." Nora sighed. "Maybe it will. In time."

Time. Bridget wanted to slow down the hours as much as she wanted them to pass in a blur. She wanted a second to catch her breath, to absorb what had happened, to accept this new normal. At the same time, she wanted to skip ahead to the days when hearing Jim's name didn't feel like a knife serrating her lungs.

Until then, Bridget had to do something. For so long, her life had been wrapped around the world she had created with her marriage, and now she wasn't sure where to step next. This widow world felt like a minefield. "What am I going to do, Nora?"

"I don't know, Bridge. I honestly don't know." Nora drew in a breath and let it out, as steady as a slow leak in a tire. "What do you *want* to do?"

"Go to bed. And stay there for forty years," she scoffed. "But then I'll become like Aunt Esther, and I don't want to do that."

A little laugh escaped Nora. "Nobody wants to end up buried by the *Globe*."

"I'd at least like to go out under the *Herald*. Better headlines: 'Hoarder Hunched under Heap of *Herald*s.'" The joke made both of them laugh, and the sound lingered inside the shop for a long, sweet moment.

"You know," Nora began, while tracing a circle in the laminate, "you could try getting back to the life you left. You're going to need an income and…well, something to do."

"You mean come back to work here."

"The door is always open," Nora said. "And Lord knows I could use the help, with wedding season coming up."

A wave of guilt washed over Bridget. She'd abandoned the shop, shortly after Abby had quit, and left Nora to run things on her own. Their mother stepped in from time to time, but she was getting older and didn't have the energy to last all day on her feet in a busy bakery. Nora had taken the reins without complaint, relying on a couple of part-time helpers to get through busy seasons.

There'd been a day, when the sisters had started working at Charmed by Dessert, when Bridget had been the chief baker. She'd developed a line of pies that got noticed at a Best of Boston competition and, for a while, put Charmed by Dessert on Must-See lists. Bridget had left the recipes behind when she walked away from the shop, but the pies had never been the same, from what she'd heard and read. Business had dipped a little more each year, and there were times when Bridget could read the stress in her mother's shoulders.

"You had that special touch," Nora went on. "None of us have ever come close to replicating that."

Bridget fiddled with the coffee cup. "I think it was luck."

Nora didn't say anything. The chef-shaped clock on the wall *ticktock*ed the seconds with a busy wooden spoon. "Do you remember the day you made the chocolate pies?"

The three of them had been together in the kitchen,

slipping in and out of each other's spaces like deftly woven braids. It seemed like they'd always been like that, ever since they were little girls, and even as high schoolers working after school, they'd been a team. Magpie had been too young to do much more than wash dishes, which had left the other three in the kitchen. Abby the director, Nora the planner, Bridget the dreamer. "You know what we need on the menu?" Nora had said. "A really good chocolate pie."

"One that's so good, it's better than sex," Abby had added in a whisper.

The three of them burst into giggles, and Ma had admonished them from the front of the store to get to work and stop playing around. They'd blushed and giggled some more, their heads together like three peas in a pod.

"I have an idea," Bridget had said. A vague idea, one that mushroomed into a recipe as she bustled around the kitchen, gathering a little of this, a lot of that. The other girls had drifted away, leaving Bridget to create. Bridget had hardly noticed because the world dropped away when she baked. Her mind was filled with flour and sugar, butter and eggs, cocoa and vanilla. Tastes and scents and measurements and possibilities.

An hour later, she'd opened the oven, pulled out the chocolate base, and then drizzled a layer of salted caramel on top and dropped dollops of fresh marshmallow around the edge. A few seconds with the flambé torch and the marshmallow toasted into gold.

"Your grandmother would be proud," Ma had said

when she'd seen the finished pie, her highest level of praise, offered as rarely as comets. To mark the occasion, she'd flipped the sign to closed, gathered her girls around a table, and dished them each a hearty slice. They'd sat at the table and eaten and laughed until their bellies were full and the sun had disappeared behind the horizon.

"That was a great day," Nora said softly.

"It was a long time ago," Bridget said, thinking of all that had been said since then, words that couldn't be taken back, hurts that couldn't be bandaged. "I don't think we can get back there."

"Maybe not. But you need an income now, and we need the help and—"

"Protecting the bottom line as usual." Bridget shook her head and cursed. "Of course."

Nora's face pinched like a shriveled apple. "This isn't about money, Bridget. We're family; we take care of each other."

"You know why I'm not working here." Being here every day would mean being around her mother, and Bridget knew that was a war she wasn't strong enough to battle right now. It would mean dancing that tightrope of *I'm just fine.* "I just can't do it. It's too much on top of everything else."

"Stop thinking about yourself for five friggin' seconds, Bridget." Nora clapped a hand over her mouth and shook her head. Her eyes filled but, in typical Nora fashion, she blinked away the tears. "Damn it. I'm sorry. I shouldn't have—"

"No, you shouldn't have." Bridget shook her head. "You're still Miss Perfect Nora, judging the rest of us screwups. You never do a damned thing wrong. You have the husband and the kids and the perfect house and you run a bakery and probably manage to make dinner every night, too, while the rest of us are...less."

"I never said that, Bridget."

"You didn't have to. You're just this"—Bridget waved a hand—"impossible-to-live-up-to Stepford wife. Who seems genuinely surprised that the rest of us aren't as perfect. I stopped working here because I wanted to. Because I was sick and tired of you and Ma and everyone else in the world telling me what to do. And because—"

But no. Those were the words Bridget didn't speak aloud. The family secret that she left buried under a pile of lies. The one thing she ignored because she knew, if she said the words aloud, it would shatter what remaining bridge she had with her sisters.

"I can't do this," Bridget said. "I just can't."

Nora rose and reached for her. "Bridget, wait."

Bridget shook her head and headed out the door and back into the sunshine. She kicked off her shoes, flung them into the grass on the side of the road, and walked home. Barefoot and sweaty. And alone.

Dear reader,

Every time I write a book, it's hard. There's a little of me in every single character, and I go through a lot of the same emotions as they do while I'm telling their stories. Some books, however, are harder to write because they are closer to my real life.

A few years before I wrote *The Secret Ingredient for a Happy Marriage*, I went through a divorce. It's always difficult when a relationship you thought would last forever comes to an end. It was a rough period in my life but also one of those events that I drew from as I wrote Nora's story.

When I started writing the book, I honestly wasn't sure how Nora and Ben would end up. It wasn't until I got to the very end and wrote the scene with Ben in the house that I realized I still believed in love and happily-ever-after, and I wanted to give that to Nora and Ben too. I'm an optimist at heart and believe in the ultimate goodness of people and the power of forgiveness and love.

The O'Bannon sisters' books also let me go back home to Boston in my mind while I write. I miss my hometown in the fall and spring (not so much in winter!), and it's like being around my own family when I'm writing.

I hope you love them as much as I do and find hope in Nora and Ben's story. I don't actually have a secret ingredient for a happy marriage, but if you ask me, I'd say it is grace and compassion. So, be kind to one another, readers, and never give up on love.

DISCUSSION QUESTIONS

1. What do you think originally attracted Nora and Ben to one another? Nora explains how she and Ben met at a party and how she felt about him. How do you think he felt about her? How much of a relationship is set in the beginning and how are changes made as we grow?

2. Nora and Ben's marriage is described as nearly perfect before his gambling changed it dramatically. Do you think it's possible for one event to have such a strong influence? Or do you think their marriage would have had major problems without his gambling?

3. When Nora finds out that Sarah was in a playground fight, she doesn't push for answers, choosing instead to ignore the problem for now. Do you think Nora's tendency to put off reality contributed to the problems in her marriage?

4. Nora lies to her mother about her life, telling herself that it's to protect her mother, just as she did when she was young. Why do you think Nora has done this for so long? Has it helped or hurt her family?

5. How do Nora's weaknesses and vulnerabilities play into the story? How do her strengths? Do you see her as a likeable character? A good sister?

6. Do you understand Ben? Did your belief in his guilt or recovery change throughout the course of the novel? How much did he contribute to his own problems? How did Nora contribute to them?

7. How does this novel explore the power of love, the danger of dishonesty, and the possibility of redemption? What aspect were you most drawn to—the family drama, the exploration of sisterhood, or the love story?

8. Nora thinks that Ben would have been the one to adopt the dog and lavish it with gifts. Yet, in the end, Nora does keep Chance. Why do you think she does that?

9. The Nora-Ben-Will triangle is one of the most controversial developments in the novel. How does Will really feel about Nora? Do you think his interest was

genuine and potentially long lasting? Did you think Ben's jealousy was valid and normal?

10. How do you feel about Nora keeping the miscarriage a secret from Ben? Is there room for secrets in a marriage? Where do you draw the line?

11. Marriages can get comfortable with the status quo, with each person carrying out their assigned role. When one person changes, it can upset the relationship, and one spouse may subconsciously try to keep the other from changing. How does this concept come into play with Nora and Ben? Do you think a small part of Nora wanted Ben's gambling to continue to be the reason their marriage wasn't working? What did Ben have to gain by continuing to act irresponsibly and letting his children depend on Nora instead? If Ben has truly changed, how might that impact Nora's role in their family?

12. Magpie's decision about her baby takes time, since her true feelings seemed to slowly surface. She made some important decisions about her lifestyle when she was younger and doesn't seem to want to acknowledge the change in herself over the years. Can you relate to that? How and why do people hide their true desires from themselves?

13. What role did Nora's relationship with her mother play in her adult life? What about Magpie's relationship with her mother? What about Iris's relationship with her mother?

14. Roger is far more trusting of Iris than Colleen is, despite the fact that he has seen and dealt with a lot of people who lie because of their addictions or circumstances. Why do you think he is more trusting?

15. The word *ingredient* in the title is used literally at the bakery and figuratively about Nora and Ben's marriage. What do you think is a secret ingredient to a happy marriage? Do you think it is forgiveness or something else? Do you think Nora and Ben now have that ingredient in their marriage? Do you have that ingredient in your marriage?

16. What do you predict in the future for Nora and Ben? For Colleen and Roger? For Magpie and her baby? For Iris?

ABOUT THE AUTHOR

When she's not writing books, *New York Times* and *USA Today* bestselling author Shirley Jump competes in triathlons, mostly because all that training lets her justify midday naps and a second slice of chocolate cake. She's published more than sixty books in twenty-four languages, although she's too geographically challenged to find any of those countries on a map. Visit her website at www.ShirleyJump.com for author news and a booklist, and follow her on Facebook at www.Facebook.com /shirleyjump.author for giveaways and deep discussions about important things like chocolate and shoes.

Learn more at:

http://shirleyjump.com/
@shirleyjump
http://facebook.com/shirleyjump.author/